Jarulan
by the River

Lily Woodhouse

Jarulan
by the River

HarperCollins*Publishers*

HarperCollins*Publishers*

First published in Australia in 2017
by HarperCollins*Publishers* Australia Pty Limited
ABN 36 009 913 517
harpercollins.com.au

HarperCollins*Publishers*
Level 13, 201 Elizabeth Street, Sydney NSW 2000, Australia
Unit D1, 63 Apollo Drive, Rosedale, Auckland 0632, New Zealand
A 53, Sector 57, Noida, UP, India
1 London Bridge Street, London, SE1 9GF, United Kingdom
2 Bloor Street East, 20th floor, Toronto, Ontario M4W 1A8, Canada
195 Broadway, New York, NY 10007, USA

National Library of Australia Cataloguing-in-Publication entry:

Creator: Woodhouse, Lily, author.
Title: Jarulan by the river / Lily Woodhouse.
ISBN: 978 1 4607 5313 2 (paperback)
ISBN: 978 1 4607 0778 4 (ebook : epub)
Subjects: Families – Fiction.
New South Wales – Fiction.

Cover design by HarperCollins Design Studio
Cover images: House by Paul Earl; Lake by Aaron Irwin/ EyeEm/ Getty Images;
all other images by shutterstock.com
Typeset in Baskerville MT by Kirby Jones

PART I

1917

1.

The idea came to Matthew Fenchurch in the early hours of the day after the clergyman's visit, soon after he woke in the high narrow bed in the room directly off the second landing, not the wide room he had shared with his wife but the one he had moved to when she was ill and dying. Even now, after all these years, he would wake with Min lying beside him. So closely was she here that when his eyes opened it was to the dark feather of hair high in the nape of her white neck, to the warmth of her back curled against his stomach, his knees nestled into the back of hers. Then she was gone.

Min was gone, and so was Llew. Gone forever.

He searched around the room wildly, sitting bolt upright and struggling for the breath to hold off his grief, sharply anew all over again, casting himself away from himself, desperate for comfort, to hook onto something, anything, a snared memory, no matter how banal.

Yes. Those faded curtains with the red fleur de lis had hung downstairs in the breakfast room throughout his childhood, where they had concealed the bellpull to bring the maid, the sounding of which was a favourite task of the children. The chest of drawers had stood in the room belonging to a long-dead unmarried aunt, a cousin of his father's. And this narrow bed with a tall carved Karri headboard was bought new for his son from a furniture maker in Casino. It was Llew's bed – as much as anything belongs to a boy growing up in his father's house, a house built by his grandfather – other than his clothes, his toys, his horse, his dog and his certain inheritance. Llew's future in the only grand mansion for a radius of a hundred miles, set around by three thousand acres, the finest estate of the Byron Shire in northern New South Wales. Jarulan. It would have been Llew's.

Min and Llew gone now, and the other son, Eddie, good as. Banished.

He would build a memorial to the son lost in the war. He would go directly to Lismore, today, to the stonemason.

A splinter of grey light came in under the blind and fell across a bare arm. It belonged to him, Matthew realised, the arm. His own arm, with the muscles and cords showing hard and dry like an old codger's. Was he? Old? All these deaths had made him old and he wasn't sixty yet. People used to remark on it, how youthful he was. Still working long days on the farm, still strong. They wouldn't now.

He shifted on the pillow, his nose coming to rest in a patch of mildew foul enough to have him rear up in his bed. On the mat beside him lay a damp pyjama jacket cast off in the night, twisted like a tortured man.

Out in the yard a dog started barking. He deafened his ears to it, lay down, slept again like a drunk and woke at noon to a white crease of burning sky between blind and sill. It was bloody stupid to be lying in bed at this hour. The bloody dog was still barking, on and on. He knew which dog it was.

Drive you out of your mind.

Now. Get up.

He swung his legs out and stood. Nan and the hands would expect him to stay hidden away but he would not. He would go out and about, get on with it in the heat of the day. Nothing would change.

But his legs wobbled a bit as if he'd been days in bed – had he? – taking him to the window where he could look out to the acres that lay to the south, the paddocks and bush and curve of the brown, flat river, away to the southwest, more soothing than the nearer view of the home paddocks. Dusty clover cowered under masses of seeding paspalum. Just the conditions for staggers. Some of the herd would come down with it – the staggers. Another bloody inevitability, everything was. Llew going away, poor damned Eddie adrift in the world.

Below the window the kitchen roof and those of the outhouses: the storeroom, washhouse and mudroom, the last being one of Min's least extravagant additions to the already vast house. The rear border of the yard was formed by the servants' accommodation, a row of empty small rooms that shared a central wall with the stables on the other side. Matthew couldn't see anybody about and nor did he expect to. Long ago the hands would have been across to get the horses and, depending on what they were doing, to get the other dogs. He lifted his eyes towards the orchard, to the cluster of buildings behind which the stockmen, rabbito and groom had their accommodation. He couldn't see them from here. How many of them were hanging about doing nothing, taking advantage of his illness? He'd never been able to keep a good manager.

Nance would be up and about, the only house staff left. The last one.

Sometimes when he woke early he saw her out there in the yard, risen hours before him, filling a bucket at the pump or sweeping the back verandah, or beating rugs. Earning her keep.

The dog hadn't shut up for a second. He lifted his gaze again, searched for it on the other side of the squat, brick creamery. There was the row of concrete kennels set in a semi-circle in the long grass under the laden plum trees, the carved Roman numerals above the door, from this distance illegible. At the end of his chain the culprit howled. Matthew could see only a part of him, the quivering tail and hind legs, yelling his stupid arse off. Sun glistered the long grass; the low, brown river was bronze through the foliage.

If Min was alive she'd be sending for the priest. He would come from the town on his red horse; he would have them on their knees, they would pray. If Min was still alive she'd be at her little desk in the morning room writing the letters, one to each surviving sibling, whom fate and nature had spread far and wide never to live here again, where they'd grown up, in this echoing, empty house. Twenty-one rooms on two floors. And Llew dead. A gaping, burning, loneliness.

Now. Go down to the dog.

Still in his pyjama pants he went unsteadily down the two flights of stairs, the deep well swooping and reeling around him. He was still half asleep, he wasn't properly awake; it was the effect of the sleeping draught Nance had made him take. There was a pressing around him of voices, of bodies, the sound of a dry hand scuffing on the banister behind him, a thread of music echoing from Eddie's wing, a shred of Min's laughter from the kitchen. It was the moment of despair at the window that had drawn them in, brought them close. He didn't want them close. They were dead and gone.

The back door opened to the light and the dog barking still, like a lunatic.

Who's the bloody lunatic?

The mudroom, with one small dusty window and smelling of old oilcloth and leather. A row of cracked and mildewed boots below the hanging coats. A milk can with a hole in it, somehow migrated over from the creamery. A half-finished native cat, the skin stretched over a wooden skeleton, sat on a shelf, head lolling and eyeless. A beetle had made a nest in one of its ears. One of his first attempts, one of the many he'd given up on. A quoll. He'd go out and get another one. Do it better this time. Every animal was different and you had to learn it, like people. How to read the best way for them to stand. How to position them.

At the back of the room in a locked cupboard were the guns. His eye lit on the walnut stock of Llew's hunting rifle, which seemed the most logical one to use in the circumstances. His dog. His gun. The dog was no use. Never had been. Should have got rid of him already, but Llew had made a pet of it and promised to train him properly when he came back from France. It was cruel – too much time on the chain. The girl who came to work in the house sometimes let him off, petted and fed him treats. Matthew had seen her at it and forbore to say anything. It was an appealing dog, he supposed, especially to a woman, with its fluffy white ears and begging face. Australian shepherd, prettier than the heelers.

Cool and heavy across his shoulder, the rifle weighed his left foot over the ringing boards of the verandah and out across the carriageway where the river gravel was sharp under his bare feet, past the empty creamery and hay barn to the first of the kennels. He could smell the oils in the gun, the spirit used to clean the barrel. Llew would have done that. A flash of his hands, the dirty rag, the whistling he kept up – just as clever that way as Eddie, but with twice his common sense.

No point in wondering what had set the dog off all those hours ago. Could have been a wallaby. Or a rabbit, one of the hundred bloody thousand rabbits. Or maybe one of the plague of peacocks stalking by, a descendant of the fecund pair introduced by Min. Or maybe one of the hands going across from the accommodation out to work. Maybe Albert, the young whip-like Black who strangely looked a little like Llew from a distance, a long loping figure you'd see across the fields, and if the dust was lifting or mist off the river it was easy to mistake him, to let your heart rise.

The dogs, his dogs, had heard him coming and were watching him, knowing better than to bark or they'd feel the edge of his boot. Llew's dog barked on, but quieter, whimpering and whining.

At the first kennel was the puppy, a blue bitchie, the pick of a neighbour's litter. She cowered away into the dark of her house and he wondered if she should have the bullet, too. A good dog had more gumption. When he bent to look in, he could see the whites of her eyes. Some cockies thought it was a mark of intelligence; Matthew never had. Nervy breed, excitable. But nerves could plague any living creature, man or beast. Min, for example.

A fresh wind rustled the plum leaves and he straightened again to feel it on his skin. It had rained lightly during the night and there was still some residual sense of it in the air, but it promised as hot as it had been for months. The rains hadn't come. Late summer just south of the state line and winter in Europe. The last letter had talked of the cold, of icy mud, of how running blood would freeze in the snow. The censor had cut whole chunks with scissors.

Plums had dropped into the grass – and he remembered then his bare feet, and the long grass, and the likelihood of snakes. But the dogs would keep them away.

Yes. He needn't worry. He stooped for a plum and bit into it, the juice so prodigious it ran down his chin, the surprising beard he wiped it from. How had he grown a beard? Had he been in bed that long?

When Min was here, she and Nance and the maids would gather the fruit and spend days in the stifling kitchen, preserving. A memory of his wife broke – early in her pregnancy with the second child, or was it the third? – running from the kitchen where she had insisted on helping. 'I get so bored just sitting about, Mattie,' her refrain in those days, 'I get so lonely when I hear them laughing in the kitchen!' and she had run to the river, divesting herself of the shapeless frock she had worn then for her condition but retained later for the climate, and submerged herself in the brackish water. He had stood at the river's edge, imploring her to come out, to behave herself as he thought she should, the lady of the house, but she had splashed and laughed as if it was all just a game, or worse, as if she was losing her mind. Why else would she want the stifling kitchen? Why else would she throw off her clothes when there was a chance she could be seen? When finally she emerged, a long thin leech had attached itself to her buttock, which she only discovered when she went upstairs to dress, wrapped in the sheet that Nance had come running with, and so for the second time that day her shrieks had brought him from his work. This time he found her laughing hysterically, giggling even while he made her lie curled on her side around their unborn child so that he could hold a taper to the fattening, swelling leech. Immediately it had shrivelled and fallen off.

The year? Eighteen ninety-eight or -nine. Before the new century. What had happened then, that day? After he fixed the leech?

He couldn't remember. He knew what should have happened: the door closed on the comings and goings in the many-roomed house, his young excitable wife in his arms, the release of his concern and love for her, his entry into her wild pleasure brought on by her escapade to the river, by the heat, by her blooming pregnancy. Instead, as was his habit in those days, he gave way to rage, mute and cold and transporting, allowing it to bear him away down the stairs and out to the haymaking.

'Damn fool!' He said it aloud and laid the gun against the bitchie's kennel, muzzle pointing to the sky. Better to lead the shepherd away, around the side of the disused creamery, where the others wouldn't hear. But of course they'd hear. And smell. The dogs would have smelt even his murderous intention.

Had they, though? Standing square and pensive outside their houses, dark ears pricked, the painted dingo faces were turned towards him.

Llew's dog was a different breed. Good dog, so the story went. But it's not what we're used to, Matthew had told him; stick with what you know, lad, your grandfather's heeler bloodline down through the sixty years they'd worked the farm. But Llew had not wanted the familiar. He wanted the new and different, the unknown dog, the unknown war. He'd talked his father into seeding the farm with paspalum and kikuyu; he'd got rid of the separator and sent the milk to the factory at Byron Bay. The largest in the world! – so they bragged. After the miles it was forced to travel in the heat it was good only for cheese. Llew, Llew, Llew. What else did you want? The river frontage, where you extended the jetty, built sheds and stables and bought a small coaster, going into trade as the Lismore population grew. And the new tractor to replace the one they already had, which Matthew preferred, with its spark arrester on the chimney and woodbox at the rear. An unfriendly, temperamental machine more stupid than a bullock. Llew's was a high red monster that terrified dog and beast with its roaring engine and cost a fortune to bring all the way from Ballarat. Cat's pyjamas, high in the steel saddle, towing the harvester last summer. A year ago, nearly. Almost exactly. The lad had been starting to take over the farm.

A bolt of fury rose without warning from his stomach into his throat, half-choking him. New dog, new tractor, new war. Any fool could see what would have happened if Llew had come back from France, how he and his son would have battled it out over every innovation. Farming was in his blood all right, but the boy took too many risks. Anything new he wanted to try. He followed a neighbour's lead in planting out a paddock with pineapples, and did it again after the first crop failed. Talked about wanting to try arrowroot, jute, have a go at bringing back coffee. He went visiting the Chinks up river to glean information on the growing of tobacco. Talking loudly at the saleyard or dances or anywhere they could be overheard, he and the other youngsters around and about would announce that dairy farming could never be long term, how the soil would be soon exhausted.

How they would have argued and the son would have won in the end, eventually. The young always do have their own way, even if it is only by outliving their fathers.

And what was the father's way? He would go on the same as he'd always done. Nothing needed to change. Not now. Not unless he wanted it to.

The shepherd had her pointed face turned towards him too, quiet now, one black patch over her left eye, the rest of her face white as clean bone. She lay across the threshold of her house, the morning breeze ruffling the fine floating hairs of her coat. Too pretty to be a hard worker, too pretty by half. Ugly old Jingo, next along, stood at attention. Daylight showed through one ear, battered and torn, the tail with a permanent kink from where a steel-rimmed cartwheel had run over it, his eyes going milky in the sun. Blue muzzle more white than roan, starting to slow down.

There's an idea. Line the jingbang lot up, young and old, and shoot them to buggery.

'Mr Fenchurch?'

One of them had learned to talk. The pup. If she had a voice it'd be like that, wispy, whiney, insubordinate.

Irish.

'Mr Fenchurch?'

There it was again and there was a light touch on his shoulder.

'Shall I start your washing? You haven't put your things out. Nan sent me to find you.'

This girl was favoured by Nan then, if she used the pet name, what the children had called her when they were growing up. The laundry girl, one of the Tyrells. The girl who let the dog off.

Such blue, blue eyes, almost violet, and wild black hair. Irish face as white and bony and all-seeing as the shepherd's.

'It's Saturday.'

'It never is. It's Monday. Washday.'

She had seen the gun. 'Llew's.'

Observant girl, then. Why would a scrubber like her notice a gun, unless she'd seen it at close quarters? Had they gone out, she and Llew, rubbing stirrups? Surely not. Wasn't like that, Llew. Not like some of us. The Fenchurch men, taking their pick.

He watched her look along the line of dogs.

'Which one? Which one is it you were going to shoot then, Mr Fenchurch?'

She was talking to him as if she was his equal or his nursemaid. He supposed she hadn't seen him in his pyjamas before. She said 'were', as if he'd changed his mind. Had he? He didn't answer, ashamed suddenly of his naked chest and crossing his arms.

When had the clergyman come? If the girl was right, then yesterday was Sunday, the one full day of the week the parasite had to work, his busiest day. He wouldn't have made the trip from Clunes then, unless he'd received the telegram on Friday and held on to it. Ludicrous. Mudguts Dog-collar visiting the families of the district laden with doom, intent on plumbing the faith of the newly bereaved.

He tried to remember. There had been a knock on the door and he'd opened it to a fat man he hadn't seen since after Min's funeral.

No, that's not it.

He had been sitting alone on the verandah, the summer evening in full flow, a fiery sunset in the distant west. A long green and blue dragonfly had come to rest on the post, its wings spinning and flashing like blades, and he was about to get up to look at it more closely – damselfly? – and to decide whether or not to kill it when he saw a horse and rider come along the path beside the river. A big man in a black hat. The white horse red with dust. The Anglican vicar.

Then he was on his feet, looking for escape, standing by the heavy grapes hanging purple and lush on the trellis above the steps with the engines of hidden wasps near and far among them, and the boards at his feet suddenly leading away to nowhere. He remembered this as if he had stood a distance off, watching the horse bear Death up to the house, watching two men shake hands, watching one lean in and whisper, rummaging in his coat pocket for the proof.

And then? He drew a blank.

'Should you not be getting back to your bed, Mr Fenchurch?' She was offering her arm as if he was an invalid and here was old Nance steaming along towards him, face like a fried egg, and the women were one on either side, one big, one small, both persuasive – 'Come on, dear, let's find your clothes.' But somehow they didn't, they were hauling him up the stairs and here he was, the sheets tucked so tight around him he could barely breathe, staring at the ceiling rose and trying to think what he'd done the last two days.

*

Early evening he woke to Nance coming in with soup. He watched her place it on the bedside table, light the lamp and pull the blind on the deepening sky, and quelled a desire to empty the bowl over her head. But it was tomato soup, sweet and thick, the way he liked it and he suspected she'd made it specially to tempt him. The spoon had left a round entry mark in the surface on its way to rest at the bottom of the bowl. Little flecks of melted butter floated, yellow flowers on the grave. Had they buried him? Did they know where he fell?

'Nance?'

She was on her way out. He didn't want her to leave him alone just yet. She looked old. Older than him.

'How old are you now, Nance?' Rude to ask a woman even if she was a servant, but weren't they about the same, and he was feeling old and she might commiserate.

'Forty-six,' she said resentfully, as if he should know the answer, as if he'd kept tally of the decades she'd been at the family's disposal.

Younger then, ten years. He had never liked the way her arms hung heavily at her sides when she was idle, the muddy shadows in her damper dough face, how her knuckles were red and swollen enough to notice. To be waited on by the pretty Irish girl would be more cheering, but he supposed she had gone home, back to the Tyrells' hovel.

'I told you about Llew,' he said now, absently, in the same tone he might tell her the farrier was coming for the horses, or that a tourist boat on the river might call in for refreshment, yet another enterprise of his son's finished for good.

'Yes. You came into the kitchen to tell me.'

'Did I?' He didn't remember.

'You have to tell the girls. And write to him in New Zealand.'

'You write to Eddie, Nance, if you must.' A look crossed her face then and he knew she already had, or was about to, and that she had possibly written to him before. Perhaps she made a habit of it, keeping up with Min's favourite.

He couldn't care less. He closed his eyes and turned towards the wall, willing her to go away.

2.

Nancy Elizabeth Dean went down the stairs full of resolve, Nan to the four little Fenchurches now grown up, gone or passed on. She and Min had brought the children up together in accord, so that Nance grew to love Min and Min to love Nance, more than either loved another living adult. The love Min gave Nance – quiet, unspoken, not demonstrated in any open way – had begun like a bruising, a result of her husband's anger and neglect. It was like that at first, Nance would sometimes let herself remember. She had begun by offering comfort, before the love grew to be its own self, with its own nature and rules.

At the bottom of the stairs Nance closed her eyes for a moment, partly from exhaustion – twenty-one rooms and none of them closed off! – and the rest from a moment of doubt.

Am I right to do this, Min?

In answer, her footsteps led her down the hall towards the morning room, exactly as it was when Min died, nothing shifted except for the dusting. There was a carved emu egg that showed the colours in the layers of shell, a pair of china dogs on the mantle linked with a gold chain, a pink Dresden clock and an American eagle under a dome, who shared its house with a moth-eaten platypus, its tail fashioned from mottled wax. There was a browned parlour palm, silver-webbed by spiders, scarcely more alive than the ill-paired taxidermied creatures, who could never have met in real life, much as Matthew and Min should never have, if it wasn't for rich people's liking for travelling and gawping at other people's countries, which is what Eddie had done with possibly disastrous consequences.

Thrown over the back of the green velvet settee was an Indian silk shawl, which Nance had tried to rearrange as carefully as Min had thrown it carelessly in the week before she died six years ago, the exact drape and folds, but it was artless, the spirit flown. She snatched it up again, held it to her face, but the scent was almost gone, more imagined than real.

At the small bureau by the French window she took the tiny silver key from its hiding place under the blotter, and after a brief struggle – longer than the last time, which was years ago now – the roll-top retreated. But then Nance was good with keys; she had a feel for them after so many years in the big house. There was the compartment that held pen and inkpot, and the little stoppered bottle of water to mix with the ink; there were paper and envelopes and, best of all, the soft suede-covered notebook which held the addresses of the children, as well as those of many mysterious Californians.

Nance lit the lamp and put her glasses on the end of her nose. She'd thought she would write to them all more regularly after Min died, but she hadn't. It was not for wanting to – she did – but because she could think of nothing that would interest them. The girls would not have been curious about Llew's changes to the farm because they'd married – one to a Queensland cropper, the other to a wealthy Sydneysider. And neither would Edmond, dear Eddie, Min's favourite, who after her death had taken himself off to New Zealand. He was the oldest son and the one most like his mother – impulsive, trusting, high-spirited, intoxicating to everyone other than his father. If only she could rest her eyes once again on his lovely liar's face.

Before Min died she had shown Nance the money, hundreds of American dollars, stored in a locked chest in the belvedere. Give it all to him, she had said, and let him get away.

From one of the cubbyholes Nance pulled out the last letter from him. Four years ago, the first and only communication since Min's death. She knew it almost by heart – that he had bought a farm on the North Island and had married a Maori lady, the daughter of a chief! She didn't know whether to believe him, all of it or some of it. A farm or a wife, the daughter of a chief, or an ordinary woman, Maori or not. There could even be a child now, or children. She had never breathed a word of it to her employer and he never went near Min's desk. Did he know anything about his son? Bad enough Eddie had lost so much money in the first place, bad enough he'd had to leave, worse that he'd gone to New Zealand, and who knew what old Fenchurch would make of a Maori daughter-in-law, if she really did exist. Once or twice she'd thought she might bring it up with him, but not now, not after this tragedy.

'Dear Eddie,' she began and went no further. She could not write the same as other letters she'd heard of: 'It is my solemn duty to inform you ...' though she could see why people did write that. It meant you didn't have to think. She couldn't remember what she'd written after Min died but then Min had been sick for a long time. Released from suffering. At peace at last. That's what she wrote.

Do not think of Min, Nance told herself sternly, and tried instead to remember the exact wording of the telegram. The fat Proddy priest had showed it to her, after Mr Fenchurch had fallen wailing to his knees on the verandah, after the priest had half-carried him through the house to the kitchen, where they'd propped him in a chair and fed him brandy, which had done him no good. After they'd lugged him up the stairs to bed – the vicar was a big man, twice the size of Father O'Donnell, overfed by his wife but strong even so – and after that, back in the kitchen she had given him the boss's brandy while she read the telegram, now crushed. They'd had to prise Mr Fenchurch's fingers apart to retrieve it. What were the exact words? She couldn't recall.

'Dear Eddie', the words stood alone for another few moments until she took a deep breath, dipped her pen and went on, 'I have verry sad news. Your brother Llew has been killed in the war in France. Your farther is not himself otherwise he would have writen himself. I know you wood be verry sad to read these sad words. I hope your life in New Zeland is all you hope.

'I am always, as ever, your loving,

'Nan.'

She read it over and thought perhaps having 'sad' three times was not ideal composition, and neither was 'himself' twice, or 'hope', and that if she was back in her brief years at St Margaret's, Sister Horatio would likely give her a rap over the knuckles, which pained her now even more than they did then, especially when, unaccustomed, they were forced to grasp a pen.

Determined, she wrote two more letters, one to each of Eddie's sisters, word-for-word the same but substituting Sydney and Queensland for New Zealand in her hopes for their happiness.

Sealed and addressed, Nan pocketed the envelopes deep in her apron and went upstairs to collect her patient's bowl.

3.

The rains came as suddenly as always but in April, two months later than usual. There was an idea, a long way south in the Government, that the north was wet and didn't suffer the drought. Not a real drought. A real drought wasn't made of low rivers and putrid dams, of stock not yet starving but fast losing condition, of fruit only days off withering on the vine. No proper wet for two years. That wasn't a real drought. Oh no. The fools.

So finally, when the rain came, all of the Big Scrub relished it and would do so until newly nourished fungi flew to afflict man and beast, until mould flecked clothes and bed linen and set them reeking, until food spoiled quickly enough to be able to watch spores settle and form pustules, until the ongoing deluge forced cockies rich and poor to move stock away from the rising river.

Yesterday afternoon, from high in the belvedere, Matthew had watched the squalls coming down in lines, enjoyed seeing steam rise in great veils off hard-baked land. The she-oaks on the riverbanks were shaking off their dusty coats and the vicar's horse was returned to her grey-white. Matthew had watched her come along the river road and her rider pause outside the gates, not game enough to come in to see how Matthew was faring, before he had gone on up the hill to gauge the progress of the memorial.

Now Matthew was set on the same business, which was more his business than the vicar's, riding out to the site chosen for its peace and beauty at the westernmost corner of his estate. The sun was shining fitfully between clouds and the country was glittery, washed clean. It would rain again soon, you could feel it.

He was in no hurry, this new slow mood of optimism allowing him to breathe the fresh moist air and think hopefully for the first time since February – of the future, of what it could bring, how the war must end soon, of the imminent visit from his married daughters. As he let his horse take her own pace, a familiar figure came dawdling in and out of the foreshortened shadows of the ghost gums that lined the long carriageway.

The Irish girl. Their paths had not crossed since February when he'd had a slate loose. Taking her time – his old horse progressed at the same rate as she did, which gave him plenty of opportunity to watch her, slight and bony, hair hanging rainsoaked around her face, wet dress clinging to her small high breasts and skinny legs. Her eyes, when he got around to them, were black lashed, challenging, lifted up to him, the only blue in the near world.

'Good morning.'

'Good morning, Mister.' She said it to the horse, stroking the mane.

'Late, aren't you?' There must have been an edge to his voice because the girl looked up at him then.

'Keep your wool on.'

'Watch it, lass—' and he gave out a sudden, astonished laugh, a single bark that rang out in the still morning like gunshot. The horse weaved a little, but the girl took hold of its head and soothed it, talking softly.

'When I'm late Nan goes butchers,' she whispered to the horse. 'He don't need to as well.'

'That's enough,' he said shortly, it being no concern of his. He would have moved on then but the horse was taken by her, head lowered and mumbling the bit. A flock of white cockatoos shrieked overhead, the pink undersides of their wings flashing, and settled in the nearest gum. Girl and horse took no notice, the rhythmic hand went on stroking Flora's lowered head. The wind was coming up – it stirred the mane of the horse and the top of the glossy black head.

'Where do you sleep?' he asked her.

She looked at him directly now, but said nothing.

'When you stay on Monday nights, where do you sleep?'

'In the kitchen. Nan puts a shakedown by the range. She says the servants' quarters have been turned over to storage.'

'Oh.'

There was a hint of belligerence in her upturned face, lips pressed together so hard they showed white. 'Do you remember my mother, Mr Fenchurch?'

'What was her name?'

He was trying to please her, he realised. How about that? Matthew Fenchurch trying to please the little Tyrell who rubbed her fingers raw washing his clothes. He nudged the horse.

'Do you know my name?'

'Kathleen?'

'No.'

'Bridget?'

'No.' She giggled like a child.

'Donah? Cheeky Moll?'

She stepped back then, abruptly, eyes wide, letting go of the horse – he'd offended her, not meaning to, so he went on until he reached the gate with its twin stone lions, where he turned for a moment in the saddle. In the dappled light the girl stood stock still, waiting, as if she knew he would want to turn back to her.

'Evie Tyrell!' she called, with a kind of unappealing shrillness. 'That's my blinkin' name!'

He would give no indication he'd heard her. A Tyrell. Black Irish, multitudinous, two of her brothers slammed in the Lismore lockup. None of them volunteering, when the army could be the making of them, if it took them on. In the Catholic way, the father had inherited an unviable run, a scrap of steep land that was his share after division among a second generation of half a dozen sons. He'd been dead a year and the family were still scrabbling for a living off it, with only two sons moved away, and that at His Majesty's Pleasure.

You had to pity them, poor devils. Min had taken an interest in them, since they were the same colour of church, and she would make him turn a blind eye whenever they stole a beast as long as it was only once a year. Years ago, she'd even paid for a doctor when one of the children was badly burned in a fire. He'd kept his distance since Min died, tried not to employ them on the farm, sent the hands round to rough them up after the last stolen steer. But there it was: a Tyrell laundry maid.

The horse, accustomed now to these early morning jaunts to the crossroads, turned towards the memorial site without any prompting. As they went along, the clouds began to thicken and blow in from the northeast, bringing more rain. As expected.

*

The mason was there, with his boy. Horse and dray waited in the lee of some spindly she-oaks. The rain sounded heavier than it really was because they were close to the falls and you could hear the river, swollen in the wet. River and rain beyond the eucalypts, almost indistinguishable one from the other. A family of kookaburras huddled sullen in the upper branches, quiet now it was raining. He'd heard them calling for it as he rode up the hill, yelling like larrikins, and now they'd got what they wanted they didn't seem to enjoy it, sitting still and hunched.

The memorial had made little progress since yesterday. From the vantage point of his horse, Matthew could see the pegs and string marking out the square for the plinth, the large slab of glistening grey aggregate dug from a nearby hill. Quarry-faced ashlar, the old mason had called it. It stood still in the dray, though the mason had his pulleys and ropes ready to move it to its resting place. Until a week ago he'd had a grown son working with him, but the lad had signed up for the colours and overseas adventure. The new boy, squatting up there beside the stone, looked like a half-wit, a mouth-breather, flat-footed.

These are the ones we should be sending to the slaughter, not strong, clever boys like Llew.

'You going to be all right? Can you work in this weather?' he asked. They were never going to be able to do it alone. 'You want me to send someone to help?'

The mason shook his head. He had been looking at the drawings – he held them still, drooping from his hand.

Matthew wouldn't blame him for the slow progress. He'd been slow himself, with the design. For two months he had dreamed and sketched, having always a pencil and a notebook in his pocket. Tall and narrow black granite with a spire. Or short and squat Sydney sandstone capped with a brass plaque. Or in Italian marble an Australian digger in boots and puttees, the rising sun etched into his hat. Or an obelisk of Victorian bluestone, unadorned and severe. Which? The stonemason had wanted it left up to himself to decide.

'But I'm paying,' Matthew had said. 'I decide.'

Nearly every day, it seemed, there was news of another casualty to add to the list, another lost boy from the district, so many he began to fear he would be overwhelmed by the numbers, and that one edifice should be built for his son and another for everybody else's. Why not? He could afford to build a hundred of them. Still plenty in the bank, a little more gained from Llew's successful projects, a large remnant of the fortune his wife had brought with her to the marriage, and some of what he'd inherited from his own father. No – he would build one grand cenotaph fit for a hero, for all the heroes, fit for all the lost boys born within a day's ride in any direction.

When it was finished, the ashlar would sit on the base, and mounted on that, four pillars to represent the corners of the world. They would be of fluted stone with olive branches carved in at their upper edges – *crockets*, the mason had said. All four of the faces would bear legends: Llewellyn would have his own, leaving two sides for the other names, and one empty, reserved for 'The Unknown'. Topping the pillars a cupola of wrought iron would culminate in a cross, at the centre of which he would place a piece of Venetian glass, red for the bloodshed, positioned to catch the first light of each day rising above Jarulan.

From here there was a perfect view of the house, the platoon of chimneys and tent camp of gables advancing through the rain. The highest point was the ornamental turret of red brick on the western wing, and below that the long wooden and glass belvedere that ran atop the full extent of the stone house. As a boy he had played up there, as his sons had after him, summer and winter, a many-windowed eyrie that gave the true extent of the family lands, the thousands of acres that awaited them, the cattle, the sheep, the crops, the timber, the river. He found himself up there a lot these days, dreaming and remembering, living in the past. If he were up there now he could be looking this way, seeing himself standing by the emerging memorial, locked in history.

When it was finished, all that would stop. He would look forward to the rest of his life. He would even think about marrying again, a wife young enough to bear a son or two, boys who could one day take it all over. He would change his attitude. He would, once his beloved Llew was here on the hill, in stone. As much of a homecoming as he would ever get.

4.

Evie had no way of telling the time except to know it was later than it should be by the column of grey smoke rising into the pearly sky from the washhouse chimney. She had ridden over seated behind her brother Jimmy on the swayback horse, Jimmy being on his way to pick fruit at the next orchard, but this morning he had a bad head from drinking all Sunday and they were late. Even the horse had dragged its feet, as if it had a blinder as well. The smoke was a signal that Nan had made a start, and Evie wished she wouldn't – it usually meant a clip around the ears. Past the rose gardens, a wild sodden mass of pink and cream and yellow, she felt a wind of exhilaration blow through her, as though her whole body had burst into bloom, as if her brain had switched on like an electric light. Mr Fenchurch paying her court! No one would believe it, but he had, he had, he had! He had liked the look of her. She had no need to convince herself but she did so anyway – he did, he did, he did! – in time with her quick bare feet clipping along the gravel path beside the old creamery and into the yard. There was no time to detour this morning to the poor lonely puppy dog whose life she had saved. All those months ago Mr Fenchurch had been demented with grief and gone out to shoot it, but he couldn't with her standing there, he couldn't do it.

If Mr Fenchurch sought her out again – and she knew he would, there was a light in his eyes, a longing she'd seen once or twice in other men – she would ask him if she could have the dog. She would see if he'd make a present of it to her, since he didn't want it anyway, and she would take it home for the brats, where it may not have a long life but at least it would learn what it is to be off a chain.

It was a shame that the afternoon they first met properly ended so badly, but it was only because she'd noticed the rifle leaning up against the kennel when she'd gone out to the lines after they'd got Mr Fenchurch back into bed. How was she to know it was loaded and sprung? The accidental death was regrettable and Nan had shed a surprising tear over the peacock before she helped her bury it. Afterwards she comforted a terrified Evie that Mr Fenchurch would never find out, that part of his madness since his wife died was to give orders to the gardener that the only beds he was to attend were the vegetables and let the rest go to wilderness. It was another detail to add to what Evie knew from local gossip – how mean he was, how solitary, said the people of Clunes and round about; how he was letting the fine house run down, though he kept up the farm. No one would ever find the peacock in what used to be a fuchsia bed now overgrown with weeds.

All through the morning's work, the soaking and scrubbing and stoking of the fire, the grating of the soap and dollop of Rickett's Blue, the boiling and the suds, the rinsing and the drudge, she thought only of Mr Fenchurch and how happy she had made him just by stroking his horse, how the corners of his old (but handsome!) mouth had turned up the moment he'd seen who it was coming along the road, and how he had asked her questions as if he'd cared for her comfort. Nan came in once or twice to check her progress, and helped her put the bed sheets through the wringer, heavy linen from the land of her forefathers that she could not have managed on her own.

The third time Nance came in to check on her she found the girl as she had before, dreaming over the copper, holding her hands out over the steam to warm them.

'What's wrong with you? What's that gormless grin? Hurry up.'

But Evie didn't hurry up because even though Mr Fenchurch was expecting guests it wasn't until next week – for a fortnight his two daughters and their children all visiting at once. There was much to prepare. The everyday tablecloth was discovered to be too badly stained for further use but still had to be washed and dried today, starched, ironed and put away tomorrow, and now Nan was saying the next best was also in need of freshening before it took the other's place.

'How many children will there be, Nan?' asked Evie to change the subject.

'Three apiece,' Nance said, 'and each with another on the way.'

'And what about the husbands? Are they bringing them?'

'No. Just Jean and Louisa.'

'Why not? Don't they all get on with Mr Fenchurch?'

'Nothing like that,' Nance said shortly. All the Tyrells were too nosy.

'Why then?'

'Because Jean's can't leave the plantation and Louisa's can't leave his city job. They're coming to see their brother's memorial.'

'Will the memorial be finished then?'

'Who knows? Stop dillydallying, girl!'

'Maybe take on another maid for the time they're here,' suggested Evie as they carried the heavy basket of tablecloths and napkins out to the lines that ran across the yard from the back verandah. 'Me, I mean. I could stay in the house. Like a proper maid.'

'You'd have to work harder than you are now,' Nance told her. 'None of this mucking about.' She had pegged a whole row in the time it took Evie to do three pillowcases. 'We'll send word to your mother, so she doesn't worry.'

'Oh, she never worries, Nan. I'm sixteen now and Ma only worries when I don't show her the shillings, if you want the honest truth.'

Nance didn't but she got it anyway. Evie rattled on with the full gospel of Da dead drunk, of her brothers setting another unwanted bushfire, of another brother stealing a horse from the Blacks, of her mother suffering a miscarriage with what would have been the eleventh child – Nance knew much of it already since the Tyrells were a gabby family who broadcast their misfortunes and adventures. And Ma was her friend. In a way.

'Be careful who you tell these stories to.'

'No one cares,' was Evie's response. 'Not even Father O'Donnell. He came to see why young Jimmy wasn't christened and there's three more babies since and none of them dunked.'

This was gospel too, the priest knocked off his horse with a well-aimed bottle, which may or may not have been thrown by Ma Tyrell, depending on who was telling the story. Halfway back to Clunes he'd come to, lying across the saddle, flung there by unseen hands while still unconscious. He only made it home because his horse knew the way. The story was legend and happened five years ago now, though Evie told it with as much excitement as if it had happened yesterday.

'Did he come to see Mr Fenchurch?'

'No,' said Nance.

'The enemy was it, then?'

Nance nodded. The basket was half-emptied now – the girl could do the rest.

'Did the fat git show him the telegram? Or did he tell him straight out – Llew's dead? How did he take it, the poor cove? Handsome enough for an old fellow, don't you think so, Nan? Good teeth.'

Two small hands appeared now above the washing line, smoothing the damp damask cloth along, and though these hands were chipped and work-worn they brought to Nance's mind another pair, white and pure. The little voice chattered on while the cool, damp expanse hung between them.

'Do you think he misses her still? And now he's got his lad to mourn as well. He let me stroke the horse. She's called Flora, isn't she, Nan? And he asked me where I slept, when I stay over. It's as if he's suddenly noticed me, Nan, though it's been two years now since I've been coming, since Llew went to the war. It's because in that time I grew up, didn't I, Nan?'

Although Evie had an Irish lilt learned at her mother's knee, there was the Australian note to it too, which combined to sing in Nance's ears in another cadence altogether. Almost American. Once a man got a taste for a certain look of woman, then that was the type they would always prefer, like a favourite cake or biscuit or breed of dog; it became instinctive. She'd seen it happen again and again. Her own father had married one big-boned, red-headed woman, and after her death replaced her with another the same, a stepmother frequently taken for Nance's real mother, since they were so alike. The Chinese grocer in Clunes had brought a third wife from Peking who bore no discernible difference to his first two wives, except for her relative youth. And Edmond had always had a taste for the dusky maidens. Now he'd gone so far as to marry one.

Evie looked like Min, didn't she? A little? A passing resemblance?

'Don't you be a silly girl, now,' she said, going around the lines to take hold of Evie's arm. The girl's head barely reached her shoulder. 'Next time you see Mr Fenchurch you smile and say hello but you keep walking, you keep busy, you keep back.'

But Evie laughed and wrenched her skinny arm away, barely giving Nance a backward glance as she hurried back to the tub.

5.

THE MARRIED DAUGHTERS ARRIVED BY COASTERS, ONE FROM Brisbane and the other from Sydney, within a few hours of one another. Neither small ship had an easy crossing at the river bar south of Byron Bay, two of the Arkenstall children sick and having to be attended to by their nanny who was poorly herself. Neither Louisa nor Jean was ill – childhoods on riverbank and horseback had given them strong stomachs, even in these early months of pregnancy.

Eight of the clan united in the rusting, listing, roasting-hot wharf house at Lismore. Cousin discovered cousin, some not met before and none remembered from meeting at their grandmother's funeral, since the oldest were now only eight and the youngest barely walking. Tom and Cedric shook hands and five-year-olds Lorna and Clara kissed one another gravely and promised to be friends. The nanny stood by morosely, her black dress spattered.

'And who is this?' asked Jean, meaning the tall, fair woman who stood at her sister's elbow.

'My maid, of course. Rufina,' said Louisa. 'Did you not think to bring yours?'

Jean hadn't because she had none, not a lady's maid; there were none to be had and no money to pay for one. Neither did she have her own nanny – though Louisa had promised to share hers, since there would be little help while they were at Jarulan.

Louisa's maid smiled at Jean and with a deferential glance at her employer murmured in heavily accented English, 'Perhaps, if Mrs Arkenstall can spare me, I can help you with your hair or – I mean, if there is to be a party or . . .'

Where was the maid from, surely not Germany? She had sounded German! What was Louisa thinking? She'd made no mention of this in her letters.

'Are you . . .' Jean began, and Louisa gave her a warning glance. 'Yes. She is. What of it?'

There was a bench set against the wall and Louisa went determinedly towards it, taking a book from her carpetbag. The maid, after meeting Jean's eye and Jean knowing that she saw her fear and unease, followed her. She sat at the other end of the bench, her hands folded in her lap and looked out over the river.

There was a long wait before the oil launch would arrive at its arranged time – almost four hours. Through most of it high spirits bubbled among the children. Tom and Cedric ran up and down the pier and along the river track, disappearing at one alarming stage for a full hour to explore. The little girls compared babies, taking their young siblings from the nanny and Jean and closely examining each hand and foot, drawing Jean into a comparison of eyes and hair. Louisa's Lorna sang to her little brother in a high-pitched, true voice, angelic – and her mother never lifted her eyes once from her book to listen or praise her, so Jean did, and the child came to sit on her lap, almost dropping her damp burden. Jean told them stories to pass the time as they sat in the warm gloom. There were no windows, but shafts and pins of light showed through the rusted iron walls, which leaked a little when a shower of rain came over.

A riverboat came in and some of the passengers recognised them, nodded and said hello. One old lady, possibly gone into her second childhood, came right up to Louisa and fingered the fine stuff of her dress as if she was a dressmaker's dummy! Neither did Louisa like it when a young Aboriginal woman came along the narrow river track, leading two small boys by the hand, and the city cousins had run to meet them. So fascinated was Cedric that he had stood eye to eye with one of the little Black boys touching his hair, until Louisa called him away, and Jean had had to tell her there was no harm in it. A little later a group of watersiders came to unload a barge of timber, and Jean walked her fractious one-year-old down to see if the activity would distract him. One of the men openly stared at her, and at their piled quantity of luggage, and she was sure she heard the whispered name. Fenchurch. The Fenchurches. *The Fenchurch girls.* She wondered if they knew about the memorial her father was building, so far out of town.

The thud of an engine drew her attention along the river, which was rain swollen enough to sit only a foot or two below the wharf. Llew's launch, without Llew at the helm. The sisters remembered it from the last visit in 1911, for their mother's funeral. In the six years since, the boat had lost its shine. Green mould streaked the once-white hull, the brass fittings were dull, the smoke stack blackened. A letter from Nan had mentioned how hard it was proving to keep up the house since Min's death and their father's melancholy set in – were they to find everything as ill kempt?

If the sisters recognised the launch, they did not recognise the pilot, as he brought the boat neatly to the jetty, wash slapping up to their feet. One of the Blacks from the farm.

'The boss is busy,' was his greeting, with no apology forthcoming for their long wait, but the sisters were happy to be removed from their surrounds.

*

It was better on the launch heading up river, away from the steamy town. The rushing air dislodged some of the mosquitoes that had discovered them on the wharf. One had bitten the German maid on the chin. Her pale European skin mounded in a red flair, a rising core. She took from her purse a bottle of strongly scented cologne and dabbed it on – wincing – and Jean shook her head at her, called out over the thudding engine, 'Won't help!'

Sighing, the girl sat down heavily between the two sisters in the stern, so that Jean was balanced almost on the very edge. She braced herself against the rails and gazed at the familiar much-missed scenery, the last of the little wooden houses strung out along the banks of the high river, the white river gums, then the dripping, thickening bush that extended from the surrounding hills to the water's edge. There were dense groves of she-oaks, gums and candlenut trees, alive with squawking parrots. Tall thickset eucalypts had boughs that almost met overhead.

Nan had sent a basket – a thermos of tea and corned beef sandwiches. The children were scolded and made to sit still and eat, which possibly was a mistake, since shortly after lumps of meat and shreds of bread made a reappearance, mostly over the side. Louisa's baby, another pointy-faced, dark-haired one to match her other two, set up a clamour mostly drowned out by the engines. It wasn't long before Jean's plump fair baby – he looks just like the Pears baby, was little Lorna's assessment – went out in sympathy and yowled louder and longer.

It was a full, slow, bawling hour before they saw, on a bend in the distance, the sentinel stand of Bangalow palms. When they were children, their mother Min would tell them it was a family of mopheaded creatures that came alive after dusk and went about the estate putting the day's wrongs to rights. She'd told them the story to quieten them on long rides home from Clunes, or Lismore, where she would go in search of company.

Jean glanced at her other children, intent on the river, saw the delight on their faces. How lush and wet it all was, after the Queensland plantation. There were the Chinese gardens and tobacco fields, the lower beds shored up against the river.

The riverbank was lowest here, with flooded paddocks spreading beyond. On the next rise was the small stand of remaining red cedar, then the cherry orchards, gardens, and on the next curve Jarulan, the grandest house for hundreds of miles, vast and incongruous as always, home for three generations of Fenchurches and the last generation flown.

'What a pity,' said Louisa quietly beside her, 'that Grandfather Fenchurch didn't decide on Sydney. How much more fun we would all have had, how much better it would have been for Mother.'

*

The painter was thrown over the post and the Aboriginal man leapt as nimbly as Llew would have done to the warped boards of Jarulan's jetty. It was Jean who noticed this small likeness, the long legs and narrow frame, and it was bewildering, unsettling. Since they'd had the news she'd seen Llew everywhere, once sure she had seen him pass her best room window, when it was her own husband, who bore no similarity. Never would she have thought a Black could resemble him but there it was, the same grace, the same light in his eyes, the gentle way he gave her his narrow hand and helped her from the boat. If it wasn't for the presence of the children she would have sobbed.

Instead she and the older boys helped the nanny unload the luggage onto the pier, while Louisa and the German maid stood indolently to one side staring up at the house.

'Who will come to help us up?' Louisa asked plaintively and the maid shrugged, though Jean thought the question was directed more at herself. The place looked abandoned. The Aborigine set off with some of the luggage and the women waited.

Before them was a wide sweep of long, probably snake-infested grass, which the sisters had only ever seen close-clipped, with trimmed hedges and flowerbeds. Now the hedges were high and impenetrable, waving long tendrils of orange-flowered honeysuckle at the thundery sky. Roses, lilies, strelitzia and geraniums shoved against one another like hooligans, woven through with tall unknown weeds and bright lantana – the refuge and stalking ground of their mother's menacing peacocks. Only the upper treads of the stone stairs beyond were visible, fringed by classical statuary garlanded by creeper.

The short dusk was coming on, earlier for the weather and approaching season. Before darkness enclosed them completely someone had to take charge – *someone really did* – so Louisa barked orders. Her maid and the nanny set off with two of her children, Jean leading the way with the little girls and Tom and Cedric, who very quickly overtook her.

Watching them disappear into the undergrowth, Louisa realised it was her Sydney conditioning that made her wait. As if someone would steal the luggage! There was no one around. The river was deserted, the nearest houses miles away. Still, it was likely that if a servant came to carry up the luggage – who knew who that would be, since her father had let most of them go – she would need instruction, so wait Louisa would.

Consternation rose into the still air, a woman's shriek – a peacock darting out, perhaps, or an echidna or even a water dragon, startling the maid and the nanny. Flying down the steps above the enclosing wilderness, passing between the statues, a young dark-haired woman raced to the bottom and vanished into the greenery. She had on a white apron and an old-fashioned dress to her ankles, but was too far away for Louisa to make out her face. Jean must have sent her on quickly, because the girl was at the jetty in a moment, assuring Louisa that the luggage was to be moved as soon as possible out of the weather – it was starting to rain again – and that they should follow her up to the house to Nan. She had a proprietorial air about her, as if she had come to give Louisa orders, pointing towards the kitchen end of the house. And she called Nance Nan, which was the family name for her. What liberties.

'I know the way, Missie, you don't need to tell me.' Exhaustion weighed on her suddenly, the two-day journey from Sydney catching up. Louisa hoped it was going to be worth it, this monument her father had built, her decision to come to see it – despite her early pregnancy – brought about from the infectious excitement in his letter. It was his first invitation since their mother's death. And then he couldn't even organise himself to be at the jetty to welcome them! Typical.

The Irish girl – doubtless one of the Tyrells – led the way through the bush and along a track worn to the bottom of the stairs, where the statue of Aphrodite, with her one exposed breast and proffered apple, was green streaked. Louisa's mother had chosen her to stand across from Hera, goddess of love and marriage, her stone drapery growing moss and lichen. The next pairings at the fourth step were Hebe on the left, goddess of youth, and Athena, goddess of wisdom. Above them stood armless Venus de Milo, sharing her latitude with Fortuna. Louisa remembered all their names, remembered even the arrival of many of them in their packing cases, shipped all the way from Europe, and greeted by her mother when they rose from their wood shavings as if they were long-lost friends rising from the dead. There were no male identities, only goddesses, all of them, all the way up to the top, where supreme above the Greeks and Romans stood the Virgin Mary, demure in her blue veil, her eyes cast down and hands clasped in prayer. She was Mother's one act of open rebellion, the effigy sailing from Rome but only after the death of Grandfather Fenchurch.

'You will find your da in good health,' the servant girl was saying, 'in case you're wondering if this is any indication he's not.' She waved her hand at the overgrown garden, the paint peeling from the verandah ahead – at Fenchurch's absence.

Louisa was not in the habit of engaging in conversation with servants. It was more and more the fashion to treat them as equals, which would likely end in cheek and insubordination. This girl was waiting for her at the top of the stairs. It was only now that Louisa saw that she carried Jean's weighty carpetbag and a duffel over one shoulder, and that her free hand clasped Cedric, who had fallen far behind the others and was grizzling now from the haul up a steep, slimy ascent and a scrape on his knee. Was the girl possessed of some superhuman strength? In the dying light her cheeks were flushed with blood, her teeth very white, she was scowling – and she had bare feet.

'I see you've lost your manners!' the girl said, as haughtily as if she was one of Louisa's loftier Sydney friends, a Rose Bay matron chastising a sullen delivery boy.

Impossible hobble skirt rucked to her knees, jacket buttoned too tightly over her already swollen two-months-pregnant stomach, Louisa climbed the last steps in silence, looking up for an instant into that pale face and experiencing a moment of discomfort, a frisson of fear. It was a face capable of anything. The feeling dissipated as soon as she reached the top, where she handed over little Gordon to the girl, glaring at her, and pressed on, struggling to disguise how out of breath she was. *You don't frighten me, Missy!* Across the carriageway she took a fast clip, past the long dry fountain, smoothing her skirt down as she went, around to the front of the house and up the steps to the verandah, where she paused to issue a directive over her shoulder for Cedric and Gordon and the luggage to be taken around to the kitchen to Nan.

The girl certainly had the look of a Tyrell, peasants gone bad with drink, the neighbouring family of brothers that had waged violent war in the bush on Eddie and Llew. The Fenchurch brothers were usually seriously outnumbered. She would deal with the girl later, explain the formalities required.

Resting her hand on the heavy knocker of the front door and giving it a gentle shove – it was always unlocked – Louisa squared her shoulders and felt herself very much the new breed of independent woman who would travel despite her condition, who would exercise her worldliness in understanding the workings of her father's grieving mind. Jean had taken some convincing to undertake the voyage, to be persuaded that their father's invitation should be accepted, despite their pregnancies. 'We are healthy and strong,' Louisa had written to her, several times. 'There's no earthly reason why we shouldn't travel now. We will be gone and back within three weeks – it's nothing.'

The high-vaulted hall beyond was gloomy, the plaster arches throwing deeper shadows against the varnished walls, curtains pulled, the lamps unlit. At the far end, one of her father's resurrections flew in the shadowy ceiling, facing the freedom beyond the front door – a wedge-tailed eagle suspended on wires, the span of its wings the width of the hall, eight feet at least. Dusty cobwebs hung in spirals from his claws, and more from his hooked beak, as if he carried them to soften his nest. As a child Jean had been terrified of the bird, avoiding completely that part of the house, but Louisa had always rather liked it. After their father died and the farm was sold and the house broken up, she would make sure it came to her in Sydney. She had just the place for it, in the billiard room.

Soft lamplight glowed from the open library door. Her father would be there, bent over his accounts, or reading in his leather chair, and she would forgive him his oblivion to their arrival. She would not even mention it, but concentrate on getting a sense of how he was. He had adored Llewellyn. More than any of them. Poor Dad. He would be heartbroken.

Light step cushioned by thick Turkish carpet, she advanced on his back view, as he sat at his desk. His hair had grown thinner, he had got bonier around his shoulders; his neck seemed vulnerable in an old-man kind of way she hadn't expected. Nor had she expected the rush of tenderness for him, which so took her by surprise that she laid a gentle hand on his shoulder.

'Evie,' he said, in an odd, hoarse voice – she was sure he said that, 'Evie' – and he turned her palm to fill it with kisses.

6.

Nance, frantic in the kitchen, had given Jean instructions as to which rooms the family would occupy, though both wondered if they should wait for Louisa who would doubtless have her own ideas. In the end, as the Sydney nanny had her hands full of infants growing fractious and having to be fed and quietened, or with older children running excited in and or out of doors to see the dogs or peacocks or fountain or anything at all in the paradise they found themselves in, it was Louisa's German maid and Jean who went upstairs to the pile of luggage left on the landing. It was strange to be going step by step up the long flights of stairs with a German, and Jean was anxious that the maid might say something in defence of her country, or even mention the war at all, and that she wouldn't know what to say in response.

Silently, they lugged portmanteaux and cases down the long dark passageway, which lightened progressively with the opening of doors onto windowed, dusk-filled rooms. The maid seemed to know which bags belonged to whom and worked quickly and neatly, taking the heavier loads.

Doubtless Louisa would emerge when it was all done. She hadn't even come yet to say hello to their darling Nan, being huggermugger with their father, who was in his library and hadn't come out to greet his other daughter, or his grandchildren.

'I've always been Pa's favourite,' Louisa was fond of announcing when they all still lived at Jarulan, whenever there had been the slightest evidence that she could be – a few gentle words, a pat on the head, a new pony. It was her way of making herself important to him, a fantasy, since Llew had his heart more than either of them, especially since their mother had died and Eddie sent away.

At the far end of the west wing, the nursery had been freshened and made ready for the two youngest and the nanny. The other four children were to share the two rooms on either side. Her own children would likely get lost if they got up in the night since they had never before experienced a house of such proportions. She would remind Louisa's nanny to tell them to stay in their beds.

When at last it was done, Jean felt dizzy with exhaustion. Perhaps Nan would have a cup of tea ready; she longed to return to the kitchen, to sit with her and have a moment of her company before supper, to hear news of the neighbourhood and the farm, everything that had been going on in the river district. When they reached the top of the stairs the dark-haired kitchen maid in the dirty pinny was coming slowly up with a long, glowing taper to light the gas lamps in their brackets. As soon as the girl noticed them above her she came over all queenly, holding the taper as if it was a sceptre and curtseying deeply, back foot extended into midair above the stairwell. When she rose from her moment of theatre, she smiled so winningly at them and gave a great shout of hoarse laughter, like a kookaburra.

At the bottom of the stairs the German remarked quietly, 'Someone's putting on the dog,' and the Australian expression sounded so funny in her accent that Jean laughed out loud herself then, and so did Rufina.

'How did you come to this country?' Jean asked.

'I came out with a lady whose fortunes changed when the war came. She couldn't keep me. I am very lucky to have found this position. Not many people would have employed me.'

Did the people who spoke like her look like her too? The people who killed Llew? Was it a particularly German look she had? Jean took in the hair, almost as fair as her father's had been before the silver came, and the eyes an odd clear grey-blue, like marble; they reminded her for an instant of the blind carved eyes of her mother's statues. Her mouth was pale and mobile, her profile in the glare of the lamps regal – an odd observation to make about a servant. But there was something strong and calm about her. If she wasn't Louisa's maid and German, perhaps Jean would have asked more questions. She was interesting, exotic.

The library door opened at the far end of the hall and Louisa emerged, trailing their father in her wake. Even at this distance she looked pursy-lipped, as tightly enraged as she would be when they were children and the boys teased her, or if Jean failed to follow her childish orders to the last letter. Why is it we are always angriest with those closest to us, wondered Jean. And did that particular rage belong more to first-borns? Her own husband, hundreds of miles north on the drought-bound plantation, was prone to bitter rage against his long dead father and younger brother who had made his own way in the world and prospered. There had been a fearful row about the expedition to Jarulan, about the cost of taking the children.

She kissed her father and stepped back to look at him properly. He had a lightness to him that had been quite extinguished after their mother's death but was perhaps returned. How thin and bent with grief he had been then; now he seemed returned to his full height. What of Llew? How could he seem so recovered when it had only been three months?

'I believe I must congratulate you, as I congratulated your sister,' her father said, formally.

How peculiar to have mentioned that first. Jean felt herself blushing with discomfort, felt the world shift sideways into something she didn't recognise. What about Llew, the clever, busy boy he had been, the sunny spirit, why didn't they talk about him?

Their father took the lead, guiding them both – Rufina had vanished quietly away – through to the dining room where Nan, and Jean supposed the Tyrell girl, had laid out a cold supper.

*

Throughout the meal Jean had the impression that Louisa was trying to convey a vital piece of information by odd potent looks and cryptic remarks, but just as often it seemed she was trying to hold something back, as if she had a secret that could burst from her at any second. She was uneasy with their father, not at all as festive and high-spirited as Jean had predicted when the visit was first suggested: Louisa would have expected to be the centre of attention. For his part, their father was even more bereft of conversation than she remembered. Without Min to chatter about whatever entered her agile mind, to ask questions about the children's development – what a wonderful grandmother she was in her good times – his silence seemed more in evidence.

Jean volunteered some information about the plantation, how bad the drought had been, how they were struggling, and she could feel Louisa staring, even suppressing a laugh.

'Oh, Jean!' she said. 'I know it's not funny at all – but it is funny, seeing you as a farmer's wife when all we ever wanted as girls was to live in a city! I had no idea you took such an interest in it all.'

'You should come and see us,' Jean responded, though it was the last thing she wanted at all really – Louisa dipping her finery in the dust and complaining about the heat and flies.

'Still coming down?' Their father narrowed his eyes at the row of tall windows behind them, the heavy drapes still open. Jean got up to close them, noticing for the first time a band of river mud clinging to the hem of her skirt and saw that it was still raining, heavier now. The rainy season. Of course it was.

Her father seemed to be off his food, taking only a mouthful of ham and a bit of salad before he swigged back the last of his scotch and got up to replenish it.

The girl came through to clear. She scraped the plates at the table, dumping them loudly onto a perilously laden tray.

'Coffee all round then?' There was a note of impatience as if she had more pressing duties.

'I've never heard the like!' said Louisa, after she'd gone, and their father shrugged as if the girl's ill manners were no concern.

'I'll talk to Nan about her,' Louisa offered, touching him lightly on the hand. 'We'll see if we can do any better. She's a Tyrell, isn't she? We'll see if there's someone else.'

Jean sat back in her chair and fiddled with her napkin. The meal nearly over and still Llew had not been mentioned. Would she be the brave one, risk raising tears from her sister and ire from her father, since rage was often his way of expressing sadness? After Min died he was furious enough to cut contact with all his children except Llew. Countless letters had flown back and forth between the sisters for the first couple of years, with the same plaintive refrain: 'Have you heard from our father?'

'Can you hear the rain now?' Jean asked him. It had grown heavier still, a silver fall from the verandah roof onto the overgrown flowerbeds.

He nodded, watching the servant girl who had returned with coffeepot and cups and was passing behind the sisters. She set the coffeepot directly on the polished chiffonier behind them.

'Use a trivet,' said Louisa sharply, twisted in her chair, 'or you'll mark the varnish.'

'No varnish where I'm from.' The girl had her back to them.

'We're not in the slightest interested in where you're from,' Louisa said, shooting to her feet. 'You're here to do a job, not talk back.'

The maid spun, coffeepot raised, and for a moment Jean thought she was going to throw it at Louisa. She was perhaps a little crazy, this girl, not right in the head. You heard stories about the Tyrells, how for generations they had intermarried, first cousin to first cousin, how they were mad and stupid.

This one was eerily beautiful though. The eyes were perhaps too large for her thin face, the nose too small, her colour too high. The silver coffeepot in her hand steamed gently, a faint plume rising from its narrow spout.

'Put it down, Evie, there's a good girl,' said Matthew mildly. There was a pause before she did as she was told, gently enough, putting everything back on the tray and setting it on the table at his elbow.

'We'll do it as usual, then. When it's just you.'

There was a loving tone in her voice. It chimed in the room like a bell, and Jean saw that Louisa had heard it too, slowly regaining her chair and staring at their father, who was lighting a cigarette.

There was an ashtray set among the coffee things. He never used to smoke at the table. She would say something. Or not. They should be comforting one another.

'Dad,' she began, 'have you heard anything more about how Llew—' but Louisa got in ahead of her.

'I am so disgusted.'

Their father pushed his chair back and stood. 'I'll leave you girls to enjoy the coffee. Then get an early night. You look dead beat, Jean. We'll ride out to see the memorial tomorrow, first thing.'

A clap of thunder sounded, not quite overhead, somewhere beyond the river, over the hills. In heavy rain like this when they were children, they would go up to the belvedere and pretend they were underwater, pretend they were Jules Verne a thousand leagues under the sea. It was Eddie's favourite game. In storms the hurling rain became white-capped waves; to climb out of the windows onto the narrow ledge was to swim with the fish and risk certain death.

'Sleep well,' her father murmured, but absently, patting her shoulder and pointedly ignoring Louisa's outstretched hand before he headed for the door.

7.

He came to her that night in the servants' quarters just as she knew he would. Even with his daughters here he wouldn't be able to stay away.

Her room was at the end of the line, the farthest away from the house and closest to the dogs. Sometimes they set up a clamour when they sensed him coming, but tonight they were quiet, staying out of the rain, the same rain that muffled his tread on the broken step, that muffled the squeak of the rusted hasp as he pushed open her door and came to her narrow bed. He was ready for her the moment she got his trousers off and she knew that he must have been thinking of her for a while before he came out of the house.

Early on what was to be their first night together she had slipped outside to watch him through the dining-room windows, Matthew Fenchurch alone at the long mahogany table, smoking his Capstans, the tin beside his unfinished meal. Nan had sent her to clear away but first she'd wanted to gauge his mood. It seemed you could tell a lot about him just by staring at him through a pane of glass. You could see how a thought came to him and then went away, how he shifted and sighed with their ebb and flow. She'd seen how vulnerable he was, how his eyes rested now and again on his wife's portrait over the mantle, how mostly he gazed at nothing, blowing smoke, his bony elbows on the table.

Evie resolved to tell her sister Bridgie the whole story just as soon as she could. She would tell her how she had come inside, how she had gone down the hall to the dining room and closed the door after her, how she had sat on his knee and how he'd wired into her like she was a lamb chop put in front of a starving man. She would tell them how, close up, you could see that Mr Fenchurch's strange, pale gold skin was made up of freckles all joined up, how the wrinkles were not so deep as to worry you, how even though he was old he was up to doing what you expect any man to do. Her sisters would know what she meant, although until that day all three were virgins and two still were. They'd learned from watching their own father, who had always been after giving Ma a poke – thirteen children took some bally effort and you couldn't always be private about it. How many times must he have looked up to see the sisters standing there, but his eyes were always so weirdly blank as he banged away, it was as if he was blind.

She would tell her sisters about Matthew Fenchurch as soon as she saw them, but she hadn't yet, and she'd had him every night since.

He thrust the side of his hand between her legs and she could smell the cigarettes and whisky on him before he kissed her, before he came up open-mouthed at her like one of her brothers coming up for air at the waterhole on the river. After the kiss he let her look into his pale marble eyes in the candlelight and it was her time to dive then, a high dive off the top rock to the river in flood. There were submerged trees, whole acres of long-lost pasture waving green blades three feet below the surface. Her brothers knew their branch of the river; they ruled it better than she ever could this one.

But this was their eighth time – she was keeping a tally – and she was getting to know him.

She could make him love her, if he didn't already. She knew enough about life to understand what she gave to him. It wasn't nothing. It was what men wanted. And it was a way of getting on – such a way! It was more than what her old goat of a father had made of it; it was surely sparkling and precious. It was elating, mysterious, more sacred than church, which she saw now as existing only to stop people having more of this other thing. Poor Father O'Donnell for never having a woman. Why didn't people talk about it more? Polite society was so against human nature that it was a miracle dreary, pursy old Proddy dogs like Miss Louisa could get pregnant. Maybe she liked it as much as her father did.

Yes, she would give Mr Fenchurch not only poke but tenderness, such tenderness as he'd never known. When she was with him, this kindly, sad, rich man, his gentleness made her think of feather beds and rich food, even though the bunk they lay on was rough-hewn planks and a lumpy pallet, covered over with a tartan blanket. It made her picture him with his men, the way he sat his horse, the way he ate, the way he talked, the memorial he was building for the district, his house, his money. She loved his complete absorption in the sensations she gave him.

And it seemed he felt it then, felt her open up, because she hadn't before, not really. One moment he was poking her for all he was worth, the next he was washed away from her, and it felt like she'd done it, by wanting him too much. It was too dark to see his face, but she reached for him to kiss him, to bring him back, but he was fading, so she brought him on with her hand as she'd seen her brothers do – or one brother, Jerky, the others called him, the dingbat always with his hands in his pants unless her mother tied them together behind his back.

It didn't work. She wanted to ask him, 'What's wrong?' but she knew he wouldn't like it. One night while they were doing it he'd clamped his hand over her mouth. She made room for him now on the bed, lying on the point of her hip while he lay against her.

Evie lay as still as she could, listening to him breathing. She listened as his breath grew more even and quietened, until she could have sworn she heard a gentle snore. Would he stay the whole night? Nan had wanted her up by five to help in the kitchen in case the children were early risers, or if either of the daughters needed something.

Not that Louisa or Jean liked her much, Evie could tell. They seemed almost frightened of her, which made her giggle, though she shouldn't have, because it woke him up.

*

He wasn't asleep now, though perhaps he'd dropped off for a minute or two. The girl had her arms around him and she was murmuring endearments, calling him her dotie, her sweetie dotie, stroking his flank with her rough little hands. Should he reprimand her now for her behaviour in the dining room, ask her to treat his daughters with respect, to keep their secret? The words formed on his tongue and died away, and in their place he felt his need for her rise again. In the uncomfortable bed he turned, held her close, gave her what she wanted until she cried out loudly at the finish, rather overstating her case, he thought, remembering how quiet Min was despite her otherwise excitable nature. What was she trying to prove? Not his skills as a lover, since he had none.

She was sitting astride him now, dreamily stroking his cheek; he could feel her gazing at him in the dark while the candle guttered. The sky must be clearing – moonlight filmed the single smeary window, but not enough to be able to see her face. From the stable on the other side of the wall one of the horses stamped and whinnied – Flora. It sounded like her. He thought he'd heard her on some of the other nights. She sensed him nearby.

'I want to do it in your bed,' Evie was saying, 'tomorrow night. I'll come upstairs. No one will hear me.'

'None of that.'

'Who's to say?'

When he didn't answer immediately, she slapped him once, hard, on the chest. It stung enough to have him grab her by the waist, shove her away so that she fell backwards against his legs. He pulled away from her, stood up, and for a second couldn't make her out in the gloom, among the tangled bedclothes. He stood staring at the bed until a tap on his shoulder from behind startled him out of his wits. When she laughed he heard how she knew she'd frightened him and how she found it amusing.

He felt old again, old and defeated, and wanted nothing more than to get his clothes on and get away from her. Wooden crates of old china and crocks and jars were stacked against one wall and he stumbled against them, searching for his clothes. There was the smell of the stables rising off the floor from the other side of the partition, as strong as the smell that rose from Evie herself, of fucking and washing soda and grated soap, slopwater and sweat. She had her arms woven tight around him from behind and she was singing softly. He supposed she imagined it was soothing to him. It wasn't, it was irksome, high and tuneless, and it occurred to him suddenly that she was dangerous. She could do anything, say anything. He pulled her arms away, groped again for his trousers and shirt. Evie's shadow retreated against the wall and he heard a tinkle as she brushed against the china and half-thought, just for a second, that she might lift a jar or cracked plate and smash it on the ground, or over his head.

But she was there again when he sat to pull on his boots in the gloom, sliding singsong onto his knee, her arms around his neck.

'Do you care for me at all, Mr Fenchurch? Would you cry if I died and left you all alone?'

She was a child, just a child, light on his knee, the smell of their sex stronger now, her paw weaving between the buttons of his shirt.

'Give me a kiss, why don't you?' She offered her cheek and waited for him to oblige. When he didn't, she climbed off his knee and went to stand before the door.

Fenchurch got his boots on.

'Come on, girlie, this is silly. Let me by.'

'Stay the night here with me.'

'No.'

'Let me come up to your bed, then. I'll be gone before the dawn comes.'

'Not far from that now. Get out of the way, Evie.'

'No, I won't.'

He let it go on in this vein for a moment or two, but in the end he had to push her and she fell against a crate of china, which made a hellish noise behind him, halfway across the yard. He heard her call out, a curse word, one he'd never before heard from a woman's lips and he heard something whistle past him and smash into the flagstones around the tank-stand. From the shelter of the back porch he risked a backward glance – Evie stood naked at the door of her room, her little white body gleaming with anger and defiance through the dark rain.

The door to the room next to Evie's opened and a tall blonde woman emerged, a knitted jacket pulled on over her nightgown. Tucked out of her view, Evie stood there in the doorway, as God made her. He would not wait to see the outcome, even though he had no idea who the other woman was and why she was in the servants' quarters. If he hadn't been so intent on escape it would have alarmed him, a strange woman emerging from the long-disused accommodation, long-jawed as a white horse gorping over the stable door. A ghost.

To bed, to bed, to bed. Too old for this lark.

'By your age your father was dead,' Min had remarked on the day he outlived the old man. He remembered how they'd laughed at her turn of phrase. They were in the library in the days when there were still books – all Min's. After she died they'd shouted at him from the walls, gloating over the time she'd wasted with them and their maddening fancies, time that could have been spent with him instead of losing her senses, envious, unsatisfied, longing for change.

He could feel his desire for Evie slipping away. He wouldn't go to her again; the girl was trouble, like all the Tyrells. There was a servant girl from Jarulan, years ago, who had married into the Tyrell family. Matthew remembered his mother sending a wedding gift, the bride a girl who had let his old man have the best of her, just like Evie was now with him.

He'd cut it out. Too much whisky, too many cigarettes, and now the Irish doxie. He needed to rein himself in.

*

Nance hadn't had a chance to get up to his room. His bed was unmade, chamberpot unemptied, dirty linen on the floor and a scatter of shit by the wardrobe, bat or mouse, too small for a possum. Besides, there were bugger all of them left, too-easy targets for three generations of Fenchurch boys. And the Tyrells, who weren't above eating them.

A red wasp was trapped against the window, so he went and flung it up; it could take its chances in the rain, which was falling again in earnest. The insect lumbered out, stunned from its afternoon spent head-butting the pane, and flew jaggedly down into the dark yard. He risked a glance at the servants' quarters. As far as he could see all five doors were shut fast.

No more. Too old, too past it, not that enchanted. It was a relief. He drew the curtains over his open window and felt himself take a step away from the last few days, as if they'd happened not to him but to a brother or mate, and that it had fallen to Matthew to chastise him.

Bloody idiot for banging the girl in the first place, then for letting her yabber on and get ideas she was lifting your burden of grief and loneliness, that she was reminding you of love. Have Nan send her away tomorrow.

Here's the pillow. Boots off.

8.

Rufina went back to her bed. When first she heard the rutting in the next room, the man and woman crying out, she had put her hands over her ears. An icy heat had burned at the back of her throat, her heart had leapt and pounded, and she'd asked herself sternly did she have any idea what went on on Australian farms, on any farm for that matter? Even in Europe she had never spent a single night among beasts and peasants. She supposed her English boarding school had been in the countryside, but she had never heard anything like the noise in the room next door, the banging of bed against the wall, the awful zoo noises.

If only the authorities had taken her away with Herr Schneider and locked her up with the other Germans then she wouldn't have had to put up with all this – but so far the authorities had taken only the men. She prayed they would come for her too, save her from this and let her be among her own kind. Anything would be better.

Before sunset she had worked to make the horse-smelling room habitable, sweeping out the corpses of strange alarming creatures – bugs, beetles, a cricket longer than her hand, a horny lizard, a tiny bat with flies crawling around its eyes. She had bribed young Tommy with a penny to check under the bed for snakes, which any eight-year-old boy in this country always seemed game to do. She couldn't have borne it if there'd been a snake. She would have gone down on her knees in front of Louisa and begged her to let her sleep in the house.

Against one wall was a stack of some half dozen trunks, and on top of them several roughly made crates, full of books thrown in any old how, some open and bent, some of them perhaps valuable with gold-tooled leather covers. There were names she recognised from the Schneiders' new English library – Mark Twain, Oscar Wilde, Jane Austen, Rudyard Kipling, Robert Louis Stevenson. Tommy had wildly thrust a stick into the gaps, and they had unpacked a few from the top, but there were so many that to check properly would have taken hours.

'Hoy there, snakie,' Tommy had shouted, 'get away!' and assured her snakes were as scared of people as people are of them. They'd had plenty of chance to escape.

After he'd gone, Rufina extracted a book by a woman, Edith Wharton, an American who lived in France, and set it by the abominable bed. Possibly the mattress was stuffed with stones or gumnuts, but prettier for the white quilt spread on it, a farewell present from her mother. Together the drawn-thread quilt and finely knitted bedjacket had resembled a spartan trousseau, as if Rufina had been going to Australia to be married, which she was not. Never. She was to be paid companion, as briefly as possible, then adventuress. So far the plan had not successfully played out. She could write to her mother – and tell her what? That she longed to come home? She hadn't heard from her for so long, she thought perhaps the mails weren't getting through. It was such a very long way from wherever Rufina was to Berlin.

Sleepless, she wondered who it was that had crossed the yard from the maid's bedroom. He had turned into the shadows of the porch the moment she had seen him and it had been too dark to make out his form, let alone his features. She wished she was brave enough to cross the dark yard herself, to go into the house and ask the old woman in the kitchen to rouse Mr Fenchurch and tell him that one of the farmhands had … what? How could she describe it?

An hour or so dragged by. If she could light her candle she could perhaps read a little of *The House of Mirth*, but the big woman in the kitchen had been stingy with the matches, lighting the wick for her and telling her to cup her hand around it as she went along the verandah and across the yard to the servants' quarters. Rufina had wondered why she'd felt it necessary to tell her, because wasn't a candle flame vulnerable to the breeze the same way all over the world? Did she think Rufina was stupid?

The dark weighed on her like a tombstone.

It was because they'd found out she was German and so disliked her immediately. The same thing had happened with the staff in the house in Sydney, where the undermaid and chauffeur particularly would avoid her if they could, even though one of the half dozen motorcars the chauffeur drove for Mr Arkenstall was a Mercedes. Herr Schneider had brought it with him on the ship and sold it to her new employer before the former was taken away to camp.

'Make excellent motors, the Germans,' was about the only thing Mr Arkenstall had ever said to her. He treated her as a charity case, which she supposed she was. Frau Schneider had been a friend of his wife's – until the war. He didn't agree with taking a German maid into the house though he commended Louisa for her kindness. Kindness!

Rufina closed her eyes. The mean old servant was a general, as they said here, not meaning a military ranking but a woman worked to the bone. She had perhaps decided to condescend to her, to make sure Rufina understood she was less than them. One match for you.

If she had some more she could light a candle and write to her mother, tell her about the voyage and their arrival, the house, where she slept – but a romanticised description, so as not to worry her. Neither did her mother know about the snide remarks in Sydney, the staring on the street, the ill-behaviour of young Cedric, the petty snobberies of Louisa's friends, and never would she know about the carry-on in the next room.

Had the man hurt her? Some of the sounds could have been anguish. Could she tell Jean? When they had laboured together upstairs apportioning the luggage to the various rooms, Rufina saw what a good woman she was. None of her sister's airs and graces and, it seemed, nowhere near as much money, had married down perhaps, if such a thing was possible here. When Jean had bent to pick up one of the Arkenstall children's new leather suitcases, Rufina had noticed a finely worked mend in her old-fashioned dress where the skirt had snagged. There was an innate, unquestioning kindliness about her that was absent in Louisa. Jean's children too were like her, with their carefully patched clothes, their broad brows and freckled faces, straw hair and strong limbs.

Tomorrow, thought Rufina, I will likely meet Mr Fenchurch, who is a widower. As she had learned from eavesdropping on the sisters' conversation while they waited at the Lismore wharf, he had become a virtual hermit. There had been daughterly anxiety about the father's state of mind, and she gathered that they had worried similarly about their late mother. This Jarulan was a place to drive you mad, then, miles from anywhere, all dust and brown river and jungle. Perhaps that's what the name meant. Jarulan. Jungle.

Just before dawn, a cat began wailing from a tree behind the stables. It chilled her, the loneliness of the sound, the savagery of its longing. Perhaps the cat was trapped farther away, in one of the bony gums that grew as close as ribs around the river. She pictured the small pink mouth opening, the sharp white teeth, its throat dry as it called on and on, on and on, across the country, which she found she had no way of picturing in the night – how the moonlight lay on the trees, the direction from which the sun would rise. A horse shifted and snorted on the other side of the wall, stomping a foot.

How would it be to steal it and ride away across the land? She could look for gold, write a book, fall in love with a rich man. Adventure and prosper.

As she dreamed, the day grew lighter and a bird began a monotonous, alien single-note cry, as persistent as the cat's had been. Over and over, on and on. She lay very still with her fingers in her ears.

9.

As Nance had predicted, the children were up early running about the house. The Sydney children lived in a grand Vaucluse mansion above the harbour, full of valuable art and furniture. Most children couldn't tell the difference between what is worth a little and what is worth a lot, but the little Arkenstalls did have an inkling, as they tore about the corridors and rooms and stairs, that their grandfather's house was not quite as richly decorated or as new as their harbourside mansion. There were bangs and scrapes, marks on the walls, scuffs on the stairs and a chip out of a newel post that showed the cedar beneath, red like blood. There were fewer busts and paintings, and those there were, darker and dustier than at home. The library, when they found it, was empty of books.

For the Sewell children, Jarulan was a palace. Their father could often be heard shouting at their mother, 'Go back to Jarulan, then!' Now they could see why, and they wished she would, and bring them with her. Tommy was the most larrikin of them, leading a way past the room that they understood was Grandpa's now, and another huge room, which was where he had slept when poor dead Grandma was alive, whom none of them remembered. There were other doors, one opposite, which led into a musty, dark, strangely cold space that contained nothing but a medicine cabinet and a leather chair that had straps attached to it and the stuffing coming out. There were no lamps this far along the corridor – though there used to be. They had been pulled out of their brackets, leaving black scorch marks like pictures of strange, pointy-chinned faces with sticking-up hair.

At first Tommy didn't see the staircase at the far end, so camouflaged against the dark panelled wall that he was sure it was meant as a secret, or just a decoration. It wasn't until he had run past the last of the closed doors and come to the bottom step that he realised you could climb up, so he did, the others following him. It had no railing and wide gaps between the treads, like a ladder.

Set into a panel in the wall at mid-flight was a small cupboard, hanging ajar, and inside it a toy lead tractor, painted powdery red with yellow wooden wheels. It had a little black chimney and a box at the back, which, on investigation, proved full of little pieces of wood, perfect branches, as if they'd been cut off a tiny little tree. It was distracting enough to slow him a little and the other children ran past him. With a great effort of will he slammed the cupboard shut and ran up, up towards the opening, blue sky sectioned by myriad white-framed windows. On his way down from this attic right at the top of the enormous house he would fetch the tractor. He would fetch the tractor and it would be his. Cousin Cedric ran past him in his hard, shiny Sydney shoes that rang on the wooden treads loud as a volley of stones thrown at a tin fence, like bullets from a rifle, from guns in the war, and the battle sound urged Tommy on, light and quick on his bare feet to overpass him at the top and emerge triumphant into a long windowed room shining with light. It was where an attic should be, but it wasn't an attic. It was magic.

Patterns of red and blue from squares of stained glass set into the upper windows trembled on the long shellacked wooden floor that ran the extent of the huge house, bending a little at a midpoint to follow the line of one of the two wings below. The low roof was painted white, beamed and cambered like that of a pirate ship's cabin, and there was only one chair, set to face west at the far end. Immediately Tommy took off towards it, Cedric behind him skittering a little on the polished surface, glowing rectangles of warm sun falling away under their feet. Rabbit-sized balls of dust rolled against the walls and a spider's silver web covered a whole pane.

The far chair was exactly like the one in the dark room downstairs with wings and the stuffing coming out, old brown leather all cracked and crazed, though this one had fewer holes and a soft blue cushion. Set beside it, a sea chest used for a table offered a full ashtray, a pipe and an empty crystal tumbler, which, when Tommy sniffed it, gave off a smell of whisky, a smell he knew from his father. It made his stomach roil, worse for putting the pipe in his mouth, which, when he sucked it, filled his mouth with old tobacco spittle. He heaved, spat it into the glass, and had to sit woozily in the chair for a moment – Grandpa's, he supposed – while the other children ran around behind him, looking out of the windows and pointing at the river and the trees and the distant mountains. His cousin Lorna was counting the windows and was up to twenty. From the window Tommy could see along the carriageway up to the gate, and up the hill to a pile of stones at the crossroads. There was a horse and dray up there, and two labouring figures.

Grandpa sat here on his own in this chair and looked out, he thought, and a sad feeling rose up out of its stuffing suddenly, together with a bitter old brown smell from the pipe, which made him concentrate on making lots of spit in order to hoik into the glass again. Then a sudden inspiration had him up to swipe the thick crocheted antimacassar from the back of the chair and show the others how you could take a running jump onto it and skid for miles along the floor. Cedric took off his silvertail shoes and raced him in his stockinged feet.

*

From the room that was once her mother's, Louisa heard the noise directly overhead. She had registered the children come along the hall, open the door into the room opposite and her nephew – it was not her Cedric – say, 'There's only that old chair.' The baby in her womb had given a little kick, a fluttering, as Louisa lay there listening to the swarm going on, she supposed all four of them, up to the belvedere, which was an alarming prospect since it was dangerous, with the narrow staircase not railed and empty risers.

Reaching from her pillow, she tugged the tasselled bellpull for the maid, the convenience of the summons one of the reasons she had chosen this room. In the other wing there was only one bellpull, in the corridor outside the nursery, so one had to get out of bed to operate it. She'd gone against Nan's wishes, since a room had been prepared for her there, given Louisa's youngest was only two years old – but Min's daughter had made up her mind she would sleep in Min's old high bed. The night before, as she had climbed up using her mother's low step, though she was really tall enough to have no need of it, she had fancied her mother's perfume clung still to the sheets, that the pillow smelt of her favourite Worth and that the counterpane retained a filament of hair or an invisible print from her hand. It was ghoulish to think like that, frightening herself, but she did so miss her, her mama, who had burned so brightly, so intermittently.

She went to the foot of the stairs in her nightgown and called up. There was the sound of breaking glass and a whoop from a boy not Cedric.

'Ceddie? Ced?'

The high jinks continued and just as she thought she would have to climb up, since no staff was in a hurry to appear, her oldest son put his head over, looking down the narrow well.

'Is Lorna there? And Clara?'

Cedric turned his head away from her to search into the reaches of the belvedere, as if he hadn't noticed whether or not his four-year-old sister had followed him, or his young cousin.

'Come downstairs at once. And bring the others with you.'

10.

MATTHEW PATTED THE GIRLS' HEADS AND SHOOK THE BOYS' hands, all the children lined up with the Sydney nanny on the verandah, where he'd been quietly taking his morning coffee. His daughters stood behind them, beaming proudly, which contrasted with the chastened nanny and the tallest boy, who was churlish until Jean shushed him.

It seemed a number of them had earlier got away from the nursery and up into the belvedere before their mothers were properly awake. The children had perhaps been woken the same way he was, by a catbird shrieking from a casuarina behind the stable – though he trusted their innocent sleep was more peaceful than the two hours he'd had. If the bird were there again tomorrow he'd go down and shoot it. It might be a good enough specimen for taxidermy, a hobby left off since Min died.

In the front parlour a large vitrine filled a whole wall, with some twenty specimens of bird and marsupial arranged in lifelike positions, in movement and at rest. There were no green catbirds; they didn't often come out of the forest, and it was years since he'd gone into the heavy bush with a rifle. He hoped it would stick about. The catbird would be a welcome addition, hopefully sleek and fully grown; he'd sit it near the crow to show off its emerald feathers.

'Did you hear the catbird, then?' he asked the children.

They shook their heads, gazing at him. The years had passed so slowly since Min's death he'd thought they'd be older by now. The eldest boys – what were their names? Tommy and Cyril.

'Are you going to tell Grandpa what happened, Cedric?' Louisa asked, pushing the boys forward gently.

Not Cyril, then. Cedric. The other one, a true Fenchurch with his freckled skin and straight mouth turning down now at the corners, looked stricken. Cedric, smaller, narrower, resplendent in a kind of sailor outfit, crossed his arms and looked impassive. What a city boy he was. He knew how to conduct himself, with his sharp little pointy face and flinty eyes, flicking from his mother's face to his grandfather's.

'Cedric?' he prompted, and the child flashed him a sudden, intense smile, delighted that his grandfather had addressed him by name. Poor Tommy had started to tremble as if he feared the belt, and the grandfather wondered if the father was too free with it.

He drew the boy to him, kept his arm around him. The nanny and children were dispersing and he nodded at his daughters to follow. Women were always too intent on drawing close, wanting to be part of things that were none of their business.

'Off you go.'

Over her shoulder, Louisa gave him a look, which he failed to interpret.

'What's the matter, lad?'

'The little tractor.'

'What tractor?'

'In the cupboard there was a new tractor. I seen it.'

'In the nursery?'

Perhaps some of the old things were stored there, he didn't know. Llew and Eddie had had regular parcels from Min's mother in San Francisco, train sets and tin soldiers, a lead horse with articulated joints. He didn't recall a tractor, but they hadn't been properly invented then, had they? There had been a little steam car with working parts that ran on kerosene. Maybe that's what he'd seen. But a new tractor, he'd said. Perhaps he was a story-spinning child.

'What my mother wants us to tell you,' announced Cedric softly but ruthlessly, leaning into Matthew's legs beside his cousin, 'is that we broke a whisky glass because we knocked a table over doing what Tommy said up there,' he pointed into the verandah roof, 'in the attic.'

To no small degree the child resembled his father, the banker son-in-law recently elected to the Legislative Council. The child had his father's easeful, oily upperhand, and the same thick dark eyebrows, incongruous in his young face.

Did Louisa want him to chastise the boys, Matthew wondered. He had only just met them.

'You chaps took the others up to the belvedere?' he asked casually now.

'We skidded on a cloth. He did it.'

'Don't dob your mate in, Cedric,' Matthew said sharply. Damn fool of a name. 'Did anybody cut themselves?'

'No,' said Tommy. 'I took care of it, Grandpa. I picked up the big bits of glass and Ma did the rest.'

Good old Jean. From what he'd heard she'd got used to shifting for herself. Now that the boys were gone, he would adjust his will, make sure she got more than Louisa, help her a bit.

'Good boy.'

The child lifted his sombre face to meet and hold his grandfather's eye. He took a step back and shook his grandfather's hand. Honest, direct, a true Australian.

'Off you go now. Don't worry about the glass.'

Matthew gestured widely at the farm rolling away to the north, the river glinting along its western boundary.

'You've got a lot to explore. Don't get in anyone's way.'

Llewellyn's dog came around the corner and lolloped along the verandah. It nudged up against Tommy, who turned to it with glad cries, and Matthew remembered then what else he'd seen early that morning, when he'd gone to the window to see the catbird. Its cries had set the dog barking, straining on its chain, and after a moment or two Evie had come out of her room and disappeared around the stables, across the carriageway and along to the kennels. When she next came into sight she'd had it bounding along beside her. He'd watched her disappear under the verandah roof, his head thumping.

Bloody stupid. No more.

Both boys were running away now, the dog going with them, and Matthew wondered idly where it had been in the interim. He remembered his resolve of the previous night to send Evie on her way, but he supposed the women wouldn't thank him for it.

On his feet now, he set off for the stables to see if the sulky was ready to take his daughters up to the memorial. There could be tears, since it was the closest they'd ever get to a funeral. He had prepared a little speech.

11.

It was a long time since breakfast had been formally
served at Jarulan. Packed away in the sideboard were the silver
chafing dishes and their paraffin lamps, the English bone china
breakfast service with its pattern of violets, and the honey jar
in the shape of a beehive. Gone were the silver samovar, the
starched napkins and pearl handled bread-fork. Nance would
cook Matthew whatever he wanted, but most often he took no
breakfast at all except for an early cup of tea before he went out to
give orders and to work among the men. Midmorning he'd return
for another cup, with scones or bread, or boiled eggs, cold meat
and tomatoes, whatever she had on hand, eaten at the scrubbed
and blackened wooden table in the kitchen.

Nothing had been said about how they would proceed with
the family here, and Nance felt it wise not to wait for orders from
Louisa, who seemed slow to catch on to the fact that it was just
Nance and Evie to do the cooking and waiting, and Evie not
trained or natural to it. There was something wrong with Evie
this morning, arriving in the kitchen with swollen eyes and Llew's
dog at her heels, which Nance had sent outside immediately.

'Dogs in the kitchen!' she'd scolded.

Evie seeped tears. 'But she's my only friend in the world,' for
which Nance could only scold her further.

'There'll be none of that round here, my girl. Feeling sorry for yourself!'

She'd lifted the teapot from the hob and poured the girl a cup, which Evie drank sinking to a chair as if her legs were weak, as if she was going to be no use at all.

Nance bided her time, let her finish her tea, before she got her up to get the milk from the safe. She could hear the children now, coming along the hall from where they'd been taken to see Mr Fenchurch on the verandah.

By the time they came in at her back she was slinging out the porridge. Jean appeared to set them around the table. Gently, she lifted the little ones to the bench seat and cautioned them to be careful, that breakfast was hot, and Nance saw how her yellow and white dress was as worn and old-fashioned as yesterday's pink one. Life was much harder for this sister, then, than it was for Louisa, who appeared at the kitchen door now with an impatient expression on her wide, healthy, sun-burnished face. Louisa had always been a woman for outdoor pursuits. In the long-ago days when there was a full staff, Nance would be recruited as umpire on the tennis court – the young Fenchurches were mad for the game. Louisa had worn a pair of her brother's short trousers and played always to win, and usually did, game after game, even against her brothers, until they grew taller than her.

And here she was, winning again, while the nanny sat the babies on her lap and Jean waited on them, bringing the infants a shared bowl. A mistake, since one of them had a nose streaming with a cold, but Nance forbore to say anything. At least the children's breakfasts hadn't had to be carried upstairs, as the bossy Sydney nanny had suggested. Perhaps Miss Louisa had been the source of that idea and that was why she seemed as though she was on the lookout for a shindy. If the girl was once again ten years old, Nance would have given her a smack.

'Has anyone seen Rufina?' Louisa asked, scowling.

The little girl Lorna called loudly for sugar and the nanny burned one of the babies' mouths or pinched its leg or something, because there was a sudden unholy wailing taken up by first one baby and then the other, in sympathy. If Jean answered her sister, Nance did not hear it. She certainly did not answer, and neither did Evie, returning from the safe, drooping at the door with a jug of milk warming in her lazy hands. She gazed disconsolately at the screaming babies.

'Hop to it.' Nance gave her a poke with the wooden spoon. 'Go and get some more coal for the range.'

'Nan,' Louisa shouted above the racket, 'have you seen Rufina this morning?'

Rufina must be the German maid. Jean had told her there was a German and that Louisa had also had a German friend who had been locked away and that Rufina came from her.

It wasn't right. She shouldn't be here. It would be the talk of the district.

Nance rubbed butter into flour, the biggest of the Delft basins set up on the bench to make the scones, and wondered why on earth Louisa would have chosen to have a German maid when a German killed her brother and Sydney must be full of Australian girls looking for work. When she next looked up she saw that Louisa had gone and registered also that the infernal noise had stopped. It had persisted in her head somehow, even though the infants were quiet. Jean had taken her baby from the nanny and was sitting with him at her breast, having turned a chair into the window for privacy. Peace.

Thank you, Lord.

This was the nicest time of the day in the kitchen, when the sun glided briefly by the high south-facing window and disappeared before it got too hot. The brass of the stove gleamed like gold; there was the sweet smell of hot milk and the day's bread cooling on the wide stone sill, the window open onto the garden. It was to be a soft day, damp and grey, gentle and misty, the sky blooming grey and white with coming rain, puffy and slow.

Late May and roses blooming still in the overgrown garden beyond, so as to be against the kitchen windows. For Nan. Pink and yellow. Tea roses and climbers.

My Min.

Beside her, Evie came to lean against the bench and dreamily watched the rise and fall, rise and fall of flour in the bowl, the soft butter drawing it together, the soft white hills and valleys growing steadily yellower and crumblier. How her hands ached. The girl could do it, and Nance could sit with a cup of tea and perhaps get hold of a baby. She could nurse the little fella, get him to smile, forget his cold.

'Like this, see? Fingertips only – rub rub rubbity rub. Try not to let the flour reach your palms. Quick and firm, like this.'

She took hold of Evie's hands and lowered them to the flour, noticing too late how black the nails were, though the skin was clean enough from the sink.

Nance sat down and took Louisa's baby from the Sydney nanny, who was in any case intent on eating her own porridge, spooning it fast into a wide mouth. She was plump, a bigger woman than Nance, though she was the same height.

Worked too hard my whole darned life to be fat like you.

It was as peaceful as it could be, the soft whisper of Evie's industry behind her, the scraping of spoons in bowls. Jean's child – too old to be still at the breast – had gone to sleep, cradled in her mother's arms.

The little boy gazed at Nance for a moment and she saw that his eyes were bright and healthy, that he was not so sick after all. She took a clean napkin from the drawer set into the table and wiped his nose and thought this one was more like Min, darker, small boned. Or was that the father, the rich banker?

The child wriggled to be put down, and hit the ground running, taking off through the kitchen door and down the hall, the two four-year-old girls going after him, motherly, concerned, at speed – 'Gordon, Gordon, come back, Gordon!'

Nan found that she was grinning. How lovely it was to have them here, to have children in the house again, to be close to the life they brought.

12.

THE STABLE WAS THE OLDEST BUILDING ON THE LAND, OLDER than the house, and the staff quarters had been built against its northern wall. In all her life Louisa had never been inside the tiny rooms: their father had forbidden them for the servants' sake and their own. True, on rainy days in the years before her marriage she had sometimes cut along towards the stables under the narrow overhang past the washhouse and boiler and on past the quarters. Only one of the five doors was fully closed. Rufina's, she supposed. A slump had formed in the shallow step up to the verandah and almost sent her flying, but the skills honed from years of sneaking up on her younger siblings stayed with her and she landed as quietly as she could outside the closed door. There was a crack in the uncurtained panel of glass set into it, so covered with soot and grime from the boiler and Jarulan's chimneys that she could see nothing until she licked a finger and formed an eyehole.

In the small gloomy room a tuft of brown grass grew high in a corner, a flimsy, stained wall subsided against a pile of wooden crates. Surely Rufina wouldn't have slept here? Why hadn't she come to ask to sleep in the house? Louisa had no idea the accommodation was this poor. Nan had given no indication, just said the maids were out here.

And one must not forget that Rufina is only a maid.

And there she was, barely visible, on a narrow pit-sawn bunk against the back wall. She had a book angled to the light from the pane in the door, the only window, and after a moment seemed to perceive it inhabited. The book lowered and she peered above it, which filled Louisa with fury at the injustice of a maid lying in bed, when her employer's day felt half-over already. She flung open the door and Rufina leapt up to stand by the bed. An attempt had been made to hide the book under what appeared to be a very fine white coverlet of drawn threadwork and French embroidery.

'Where did you get that?'

'My mother made it for me when—'

'I mean the book.' *Edith*, read Louisa. *Mirth*.

'There.'

The crates against the walls were full of books, her mother's, she supposed. This was where he'd put them. What on earth for?

But Rufina was more arresting than the exiled library, and Louisa's eyes were drawn back. What a nightgown! Nainsook. She took a pinch of the fabric between forefinger and thumb, palest blue fine cotton, with pink satin ribbons woven into the collar and white broderie anglaise trimming the wide sleeves. There were pintucks and a bodice of delicate smocking, white and cream. It was more exquisite than any nightgown Louisa possessed, despite intensive perusal of Sydney's finest drapers, salons and outfitters.

'And this too? A gift from your mother?' Louisa gave it a little tug and felt a satisfying pop, a tiny stitch coming away further up, at the yoke.

'What of it?' Rufina asked, her voice hard. Any shame she'd felt at Louisa's entry appeared to have flown. 'Do you think I have stolen it?'

'Perhaps you helped yourself after poor Irma Schneider was taken away.'

Rufina said nothing though her gaze did not waver from Louisa's, and Louisa had the surprising thought that her maid was resenting her intrusion.

'After all, you took the book without asking.'

Rufina was silent. It seemed she was not going to enter into an argument, much less defend herself, and quite suddenly Louisa found herself also struck dumb. Two can play at that game, she thought, though it seemed like cheating. Life should always be exposed to bright daylight; there should be no dark corners or unnecessary shadows. It was best to have everything out. Otherwise one ended up like Min, tied to a chair in a darkened room when the layers of untruths became too difficult to bear.

'Upstairs. In half an hour.' She nodded curtly, turned and went out across the yard, quickly but careful of the slippery bricks, holding up her skirts.

It was beginning to rain again, wispy, gentle, so softly she barely felt it.

13.

EVIE HAD BEEN SET TO DIGGING THE POTATOES AND THEN TO peeling them for the baked dinner at noon, but the potatoes with their shrouds of clinging soil, and the pumpkins with their cargoes of miscarried seeds, only made her think further of death. The subject had occupied her since Fenchurch had left her in the early hours of the morning and she had thrown the plate. What if her aim had been true and she had killed him? Then what? She had a vision of herself in Clunes pokey, or maybe taken further afield to Lismore or Casino, or even to Sydney to the gallows. Evie Tyrell swinging by the neck. Plenty of Tyrells had done the same in the old country and she could do it here to keep up the family tradition.

'Hurry up there!' Nan put her head in at the scullery door. 'Nice and clean. Pick out the eyes.'

The potatoes were to be first rolled in flour before they were set around the joint. Evie's stomach rumbled. No one had thought to give her any porridge and she hadn't seen fit to take some, even after she saw the kind sister waiting on the nanny. Worse than a dog. Even the dogs got fed. She felt like breaking something. Another plate. She'd knock about like this for a little while, just for the extra shillings, but not for long, not forever. Forever like the gallows were forever, like the penury her mother endured on the Tyrell run was forever, with barely enough to eat and never a new dress.

When did she last taste legal mutton, wondered Evie. Not since years ago, before the wool had rotted on her father's sheep and the animals had sickened and died, the ones that hadn't already succumbed to flystrike or heatstroke in high summer. The Fenchurches were more scientific and kept a small flock among their thousands of cattle. The dead son had been famous for keeping them healthy with dips and doses. She wished the whole family of Fenchurches would go to blazes.

The little scullery window was open for the breeze and voices carried from out by the stables, Matthew's among them, and the stamping of horses. There were the high excited tones of the young boys and the barking of Llewellyn's dog, but joyous now, not the strained despairing howl come from days on the chain. She listened for Matthew's voice again, heard him tell the boys not to drag on the reins, and thought that she should leave tonight, but that she could give him one more chance and if he was just as cold-hearted she'd leave him in the lurch. She'd take the dog with her. Da had been bad with dogs, indulged them, entered a battle of wills. Her brothers needed a good one and they'd like the shepherd. They'd like it more than what would arrive later, in January. About then. If she was gone it was only a couple of weeks, nothing, a seed, but she felt it, a dread that lay flexing under her ribs like a new muscle. The smells of the kitchen and scullery were more intense. The world was brighter, harder, as if it had grown suddenly into a louder, more determined version of itself, one that she had always known was there but hadn't entered. Did every girl know this early? This fast, so soon, so early in the moon?

Ma had. She used to let it be known that another little Tyrell was on its way so early on that the baby came slower than Christmas. And when they did come, how Ma had lavished her tenderness on them. The older ones would catch the longing eye of the third one up, or fourth, the child still hopeful for her loving on her lap. Ma would know Evie was gone the moment she set eyes on her.

When she carried the potatoes through to the kitchen it felt as though the heat leapt away from the range like an evil witch, slap up against her in a single bound, fierce and sharp as teeth, turning her guts with fear and hunger. Red-faced and sweating, Nan was hefting the joint out of the open door and the rich sister, Miss Snot Louisa, was striding past back to the stairs. But a thought must have occurred to her before she got there, because she doubled back to call out from the hall, 'When Rufina comes in, could you ask her to bring my coffee up?'

And Nan, poor cow, owned by the Fenchurches body and soul, nodded. A slavvy, that's what Ma said she was. Worked to the bone. Dumb as a donkey. Nan didn't mutter or roll her eyes at the extra demand. After a moment she left the joint steaming on the table and went after Louisa, wiping her hands on her apron and calling, 'Aren't you going out to the memorial? They're leaving soon.'

'I've asked them to wait.' Louisa's voice floated from the landing. 'Send Rufina to Mother's room as soon as possible.'

When Nan returned to the kitchen she was shaking her head. 'He'll be champing at the bit.'

She said it so quietly that Evie barely heard her, but she felt a sudden lulling, a comfort, Nan talking about him in that soft, intimate voice. She remembered him as he was the day she met him on the drive, kind and stern, rich and old, high on a beautiful horse with more silver on her than a queen.

And then again as he was last night, eager for her, his heart open. The feel of him in the dark.

The new tendon under her rib softened and melted away and she thought perhaps she'd be staying after all. If only the day would hurry through, the mountain of food prepared for the family cooked and served, the afternoon of drudge and tedium passed and night falling, then she could wait in her bed listening for him, for the click of the screen door on the back porch, for his hollow step along the verandah, his quick strides across the yard.

And she would try again. Did he think it was just calf love? It was for real. She would marry him if he asked her.

The German was at the kitchen door and Evie wondered for the first time if she had heard anything of last night. Yesterday she'd seen young Tommy showing the other children a new penny got from her for checking her quarters for snakes, and it was then that Evie had realised she'd been put in with her, hopefully not in one of the thin-walled adjoining rooms, but one further along. The next room had old books in it anyway, trunks and crates and boxes. Hers had cracked china but less of it, and she'd only chosen that room because Nan had told her it was the most watertight, though what would Nan know as she'd slept inside the house ever since Mrs Fenchurch was ailing?

Nan gave the directions to the sitting room, and told her also that Evie would bring the coffee up. The German looked hard at Evie, almost curling her upper lip with disgust, and Evie saw that she did know, that she had heard them, perhaps even seen something. What did it matter? She couldn't care less. But even as she felt herself rally, as she put down the basin of potatoes and straightened her back, she had a vision of her mother coming to tell Fenchurch of the situation. To ask for money.

Nan went back to the roast while Evie made the coffee the way she'd been taught only a fortnight ago – it felt like years! – pouring the hot water on the grounds in the tall, earthenware coffeepot and setting the tray with sugar and cream. Up the two flights of stairs she went and along the corridor to Mrs Fenchurch's big old room, which she entered without knocking, her hands being full, and in any case the door was ajar. Flowered curtains hung at the windows, the bed was draped in a mosquito net of the purest white. Clothes were scattered everywhere; a string of pearls lay in the centre of the Turkish rug, as if laid there as part of the design.

At the dressing table, Rufina was helping her employer out of her day dress and into a divided skirt, while Louisa's own fingers flew at the buttons of a white riding blouse with a black bow at the neck. The only sign that she had noticed Evie come in was the tiniest of nods, reflected in the mirror, to direct her to the small table set by the fireplace, where Evie found herself stranded. Her feet refused to turn around and carry her out of the room. A silk chemise lay across the back of one of the fireside chairs, rippling in the light like a river stone under water. She could hear Louisa's voice running on behind her, quiet enough for only Rufina to hear the words, and it sounded haranguing, as if Louisa was scolding her. And there was a slightly bored tone to it, as if Louisa could barely be bothered but felt she must.

The bedroom fireplace was of unadorned pale stone, and the iron grille clean, used perhaps for a month or two of the year. On those nights cold enough for fires Matthew would have joined his wife here, sometimes, on the little settee drawn up beside it. And on chilly mornings when the fire was lit for him to dress by, he would have stood here warm from his bed before he went out to give the orders to the hands and stockmen. Evie stroked the marble of the mantelpiece, white and veined like a woman's breast, indeed, very like her own breast, she couldn't help thinking, but cold, cold to the touch, which hers wasn't. Surreptitiously, she took stolen glances to examine the bed her lover would have lain in with his wife.

When she was mistress it would be hers, with its carved posts and little steps, pretty linen and embroidered net, its view over the river to the forested hills, perhaps even a glimpse of the distant roofs of Clunes. What were you to see if you lay down against the pillows – could you see as far as that?

'Poor it,' said Louisa shortly, taking a seat at the dressing table while the German knelt before her to lace up her riding boots. It took Evie a moment or two to realise that Louisa was not offering sympathy to any living animal – Llewellyn's dog, perhaps – but speaking directly to her. Pour it. The eggshell cup threatened to tip with the first stream; the coffee splashed a little.

Louisa drank it down in two or three gulps like a man, while Rufina opened the hatbox and took out a fine lady's straw, which had to be pinned through the shining chignon and then a veil arranged around the brim.

Quick, light footsteps were heard along the corridor and Mr Fenchurch appeared at the bedroom door.

'Hurry up for Pete's sake, Louisa. We're all wai—' He halted midstream, and Evie hoped it was because he had noticed her standing with the tray, waiting for Louisa's empty cup. She could see herself reflected in the tall Cheval mirror, her old dress, tatty shoes and untidy curly hair – and she saw how her lover's eye swept over and past her and arrested on the smooth profile of Rufina, who was carefully fastening the white muslin to protect Louisa's snooty face from sun and insects. She saw how Rufina bobbed in his direction, a curtsey, how she lowered her shining head.

Mr Fenchurch laughed, that same single loud astonished crack of a laugh as he had that day she'd held his horse's head on the driveway. Only weeks ago. It felt like years. Years and years.

He was hers.

'A curtsey! We don't stand on ceremony here.' He took off his hat and came into the room properly. He had bathed, put on new moleskins and a clean, faded blue shirt. Even with the expanse of rug between them she could smell his clean skin, smell the sunshine on him from the yard.

'My maid, Rufina,' Louisa said and there was a pause, as if her father had thought she would go on, as if Louisa was introducing a woman who was his equal.

'Matthew Fenchurch,' he said. 'Louisa's father.'

'A pleasure to meet you.'

Rufina's voice was just above a whisper but her accent sounded stronger and her dress, Evie saw now, was plain but beautifully made, expensive, a close-fitting dark blue that made her elegant, like one of the toffs, but old-fashioned. Leather boots showed beneath her too-low hem, a small gold locket dipped at her white throat. She was a Cinderella. She was a nob fallen on hard times and she was looking right into Mr Fenchurch's eyes and she was smiling, smiling and smiling.

The bitch.

Louisa didn't appear to have noticed, since she was rummaging among her things in an enormous trunk – it was the biggest of the luggage Evie had seen on the wharf – and coming up with a small leather case, which might contain a flute, or a very small violin, but it was a riding whip, a pretty red lady's crop, with a forked tongue.

'Come on then.' She took her father's arm.

'You're never going to ride astride in your condition! Sulky's all rigged and ready to go. You can sit up with Jean.'

'*This is the twentieth century,*' she said to him, and she said it like a quote, as if she was imitating someone with an American accent – Mrs Fenchurch, of course. Mr Fenchurch laughed, fondly, and they went out and along the corridor towards the stairs, leaving Evie and the German maid alone.

Now would be the time to warn her off. Evie watched as Rufina went around the room, tidying and straightening, returning the day dress to a peg in the closet. She was pretending Evie wasn't there, as if she didn't approve of her, as if Evie was somehow beneath her, less than her, when it was the German who was the intruder, the woman on the make, and it was people like her that had killed Llewellyn and thousands of other Australians.

She put down the tray and was across the wide room in a single bound, her fingers weaving themselves into that thick blonde hair, her lips close to the ear. 'Keep away from him.'

Rufina reared back, her bun scattering iron, glaring at Evie, at once scornful and pitying. She was taller by a head, her shoulders broader. Stronger, better fed. Better. Better. Better.

Thinks she is.

Evie lifted her fist to job her one but the German maid was pushing past her, rapidly crossing the room and picking up the tray.

'Put it down,' said Evie. It was her tray.

Halfway across the rug with everything jingling, the heavy coffeepot sliding on the tray cloth, Rufina said something in German, which sounded dismissive, superior, so Evie ran after her and yanked at the back of her dress, not as hard as she could have. She could have pulled her over. She could have kicked her head. She should have. Why hadn't she? Hardly altering her stride Rufina was disappearing, her fast clip sounding along the bare wooden floor of the corridor. She would go downstairs and nark on her to Nan. Of course. It was inevitable. Evie'd have to come up with a good story between now and whenever she was next looking at Nan.

Louisa's hairbrush lay at the foot of the bed, an ivory-backed hand mirror beside it. The bed was unmade, undergarments strewn around. The silk chemise, soft and creamy, folded away to nothing, an inch square, easily concealed in Evie's pocket. On the dressing table was jewellery in a pink quilted box, a string of jet beads hanging half out, a diamond watch, a silver bracelet set with blue stones, a gold ring with flashing green – an emerald, thought Evie. There was a cameo brooch and gold filigree earrings with red gem drops that sparkled and caught the light. Rubies. She would take something. Something that wouldn't be noticed straight away. The earrings.

No, not both. Just one. Louisa would think she'd dropped it. Evie would give it to Bridgie to tie around her neck or pin to her dress.

Just as she dipped for it she saw a movement in the mirror and felt herself observed. Behind her at the door, low down, a child was watching her, one of the grandchildren perhaps, or was it Rufina crouching and spying, not gone downstairs at all but waiting in the corridor, tricking her, biding her time, knowing that Evie would be tempted?

Clasping the earring she slipped to the door and looked out. No one. Nothing. There hadn't been time for a spy to vanish down the long corridor and around the corner to the stairs, and she'd heard none of the heavy wooden doors into the bedrooms open or close. The house was quiet. She must have imagined it.

At the other end of the corridor against the far wall there was a flight of narrow steep stairs, more like a ladder, leading to an upper floor. Evie had never been up there. The belvedere, they called it, where the children had played early this morning. A week ago, before all the horrible family had arrived, she had asked Nan, 'Where is Mr Fenchurch today?' She'd seen them setting up a tick gate for cattle coming through from the wet river pasture to be checked, and she thought he'd be there working, but Nan had answered, 'The belvedere. He's always up there these days.'

Carrying her shoes now to lighten her tread Evie hurried along to the foot of the stairs and looked up into the well of light, the rounded roof and high panes showing speeding clouds. There was a curious soft scraping sound from the floor above, more like a rolling of small wheels, like a tea trolley or a carpet-sweeper. The sound came in short bursts, as though whoever was operating it was checking now and again that the wheels were working properly. Matthew, was it, fixing an old toy for the grandsons?

She went up quickly to the top, stepping into the long bright room. The sound came insistently, quietly, from the far end where an old wing chair stood at the westernmost window, a small table set beside it. There was a wet mopped patch on the floor and a sparkle of broken glass. They'd missed a bit. Nan wouldn't go butcher's hook at her if she went downstairs carrying the shard – she could say she'd found it on her way downstairs, that one of the children must have dropped it. As she hurried to pick it up, running lightly down the long empty, echoing place, the noise stopped or passed out of her hearing. Perhaps it had been more of a rasping noise, something to do with one of the farm machines, a blade being sharpened outside the barn, the sound lifting. Or an insect trapped in the room, banging against the glass.

She was alone. She felt a wave of disappointment; she had hoped the wing chair concealed him from her view as she hurried along – it didn't. But in consolation was the view he favoured, over the long carriageway with his fields on either side, up to the road, the river running beside it for miles and the bush-covered hills on the other side. It was beautiful, peaceful, but she felt sorry for him that his favourite place to sit was here, all alone, sad and lonely. He was lucky he had her to keep him company as much as she did. She had more to give if he wanted it. Did he ever move the chair to the far end to look east, she wondered, over the top of the dry fountain with its strange naked writhing figures that made Evie uneasy whenever she looked at it? Did he ever look over the first fence to the farmhands' quarters, then the paddocks, the dam, the field of lucerne, and beyond that a sagging collection of roofs and ruins that were the Tyrells'?

Likely as not.

There were flashes of colour below the canopies of the gums on the carriageway, moving along until the last bend, where the family emerged at the end of the avenue, almost at the stone lion gates. Mr Fenchurch and Louisa were at the head; he was riding Flora and Louisa the tall gelding that had been Llew's, which obviously didn't get ridden enough. Skittering and shying, it refused to take Louisa's direction to turn out onto the road. Louisa gave it a larruping with the crop. The little whip flashed.

Behind them came the sulky, driven by Jean, with a small girl sitting either side and the older boys standing up at the back, waving and jumping, joshing one another. They looked as though they were going on a picnic, or a visit, not to look at a gloomy memorial, which Evie could see rising at the crossroads, peak and thrust like a small steeple, with its cross and eye of red glass. The stonemason and his boy were low to the ground, laying paving. It looked as though trees had been felled to improve the view of it from the house. They had! They'd cut down a ghost gum. And some others too. The hill looked bare.

She laid the shard on the narrow sill and yawned. It was warm, still, and she felt as though she could go to sleep in an instant.

One of the children had left a toy on the chair, a little tractor. It was red with yellow wooden wheels and levers that responded when you pushed or pulled them. Pulling the silk chemise and ruby earring from her pocket, Evie sat down with the tractor on her lap. Imagine if she could go home with all of it. The tractor would belong to the rich children, to the pointy-faced boy. Cedric. He would have a hundred of them and wouldn't miss it. Imagine if she could go running the two miles across the fields and give it to Malachy, her youngest brother. Imagine his face, his delight in it. Imagine if she could give the chemise to her mother and what she would say. She held it up now to the light. Lace trimmed the square neck and arms. The silk was so fine that you could see through it. Ma would treasure it always. Evie could tell her it was a castoff. 'Miss Louisa gave it me,' she'd say. 'We're more friends than anything else, you know.'

And the earring. The precious wisp of gold, the ruby of the exact same red as the glass brought all the way from Venice for the memorial. She wanted to relish the jewel now, let the drop of frozen blood spin in the sunlight and cast its glow around the room and imagine her sister's surprise and pleasure.

It had disappeared. She stood up, searched the old leather chair, the floor around it, shook out the chemise, shook the tractor upside down. She shunted the chair, so that the old wooden legs squealed on the polish.

There – a glint – but it was another piece of glass, smaller than the shard she'd laid on the sill. She felt into the seams of her dress, her pocket. She tore the dress off, shook out her hair – had it caught there somehow when she pulled the things from her pocket?

Lost.

She must have dropped it coming up the stairs. Yanking her dress back on, she tucked the chemise into her bloomers as the best hiding place and retraced her steps, keeping her gaze close on the floor. Halfway down the stairs a small cupboard was set into the wall; it was probably used to store a lamp or candles should a Fenchurch decide to come up here after dark. The hasps and lock were rusted stiff. It looked as though it hadn't been opened in years. She prised it ajar, slid in the tractor and shut it tight. She would come back for it if she could.

At the bottom of the steps she dropped to her hands and knees and searched the narrow space beneath the open treads, where an earring could have landed, kicked aside on her rapid ascent. Dust had collected in shanks, an old bedhead leaned against the wall, a rolled carpet gave off a smell of must and old wool. There was the desiccated corpse of a small bird, dull green and yellow, a poor honeyeater who had got stuck inside one day when a window was open.

But no earring. When she stood up her knees were brown. She remembered the piece of glass then and would have run up to fetch it if the sound hadn't started again, directly overhead, the rolling and scraping.

Even as she told herself it was an insect burring or a kookaburra banging and rolling a lizard or a snake on the upstairs verandah to kill it, the hairs rose on her arms. It was sounding faster than before, more insistent, and there was a patter of small feet running, even though the older children had gone on the expedition to the memorial and the babies were with the nanny.

Or rain. Was it just the rain beginning? She went back to the lower step and peered up towards the light – the windows at the top of the stairs were clear, unspeckled. Her foot on the stair coincided with the belvedere falling silent for a second or two until another sound started, a kind of tuneless humming, which didn't sound human since whatever was making the noise didn't need to stop for a breath.

As soon as the thought occurred to her, Evie ran as fast as she ever had in her life, down the corridor, down the stairs, across the kitchen yard and out into the paddocks, until she could find a perspective on the house that would allow her to see the kookaburra on the roof murdering its prey. The problem was that whenever one part of the roof became clear another was obscured, and in the end she whistled to her dog and set off towards the river to try to put it out of her mind.

14.

THE OLD BLACK MARE PULLING THE SULKY WAS STEADY AND could mostly be relied on to get on with the job, for which Jean was grateful. She had been a favourite of their mother's for the same reason – her strength and phlegmatic nature. Watching Louisa struggle to control Llewellyn's Boss – aptly named, she saw now – she wondered why Louisa had insisted on riding him, or at all, unless it was to show off her new habit, bought specially for the holiday, now spattered with rain. When Jean had admired it, Louisa had told her it was from France and how much it had cost. Jean had felt the oxygen drain out of the air at the amount, and hadn't been able to help fingering the delicate wool of the divided skirt, the polished silk of the blouse, before her sister led Boss to the mounting post.

On the sulky seat her niece, Lorna, snuggled in on one side of her and her daughter on the other.

'He's a naughty horsie,' pronounced Lorna clearly, as Boss swerved for the fence-line and dropped his nose to the long grass.

'He is,' Jean agreed, bringing Blackie to a stop. Her father was waiting further up the road, looking back, his face shadowed by his hat. The rain would pass. There was a lot of blue in the sky.

'Come on, Jean,' he called, 'come up. Louisa can follow.'

But Blackie didn't want to pass Boss, who was cropping enthusiastically at roadside grass. She stood firm and wouldn't budge until Matthew rode back down the hill and took hold of her bridle.

'Come on then,' he said gently, 'come on, girl.'

The sulky's wheels spun on. Boss lifted his head as it passed and Jean fancied that she could read his expression – he did not want to be left behind. He leapt immediately back to the road, cantering past them in the narrow gap and rose to a gallop as he disappeared over the crest of the hill, with Louisa clinging on and shouting. Matthew went on after her in a flash and Jean found herself left behind with the four children, the little Arkenstalls bellowing with alarm and Tom leaping with excitement on the back of the sulky. Her own Clara was silent, thumb in mouth, watching events unfold while clamped to Jean's side. She was used to calamities, perhaps. At three she had seen a man slice his arm to the bone one day when Jean took her along with the billy and midday sandwiches to the cane fields. Tom had helped carry everything out then vanished to find one of the cutters who was always ready for a yarn with him, and so had been spared the sight. How much Clara had seen or understood Jean wasn't sure, but adults shouting and running made her so quiet now she barely breathed. Jean gave her a little joggle and the thumb popped free.

'Naughty horse.' It was pronounced in the same tones as Lorna had a moment before, Lorna now wailing loudly.

'Ma-ma!'

Blackie hung her head.

'Up, Blackie.' Jean flicked the reins and felt at her back the sulky rise a little as Tom leapt down.

He came around and took hold of the old horse and spoke to her in the same tones his grandfather had, warm and gentle.

With the resumed movement, Louisa's children quietened and went the rest of the way attentive to the road ahead for a possible glimpse of their mother. There was none, though when they reached the crest of the hill they could see that dust hung above it and Louisa's shouts could still be heard a distance away. Boss would be able to outrun old Flora easily. Catastrophic scenes unfolded in Jean's mind, one after the other like concertinaed postcards of the Capuchin crypt that Louisa had sent from Rome on her last European holiday. Instead of the catacomb of arranged dried-out monks, Jean saw images of her sister broken. Or miscarrying. And the same mildewy brown.

The visions felt suddenly wicked, like an indulgence remembered from her childhood, or even the years before her marriage. Louisa had been the most overbearing sister imaginable, quick to snatch, scratch and pinch, and always behind their mother's back. Even in those days there had been a terrible, guilty pleasure in imagining her suddenly taken ill and confined to bed, or breaking a leg or arm so as not to be able to run about with the rest of them, with Jean and Edmond and Llew and the older Tyrells. It never happened. Louisa maintained rude health until she went away to boarding school in Armidale. Of course, now they were grown, she wanted no harm to come to her sister. It was just that the disastrous pictures flooded into her mind, a habit she'd got into up north on the plantation.

Floods and fires, fires and floods.

You won't do it now. There's no point to it. Or end to it, once you start.

The shower petered out and the sun was suddenly hot. As soon as they reached the site, Cedric leapt from the back of the sulky and he and Tom began running around and around the memorial, leaping over the puddles that lay in the road after yesterday's deluge, especially where it was churned up around the monument. Jean clambered down from the sulky with the little girls. The stonemason and his boy nodded in greeting and laboured on, and Jean took her time to walk about, to quietly look at what was left of Llew. Australia could one day be covered in memorials not so different from this, one in every town, at every crossroad. Monuments to the youthful dead, never to be forgotten.

Her father had certainly chosen a beautiful spot – there was the elevated view of Jarulan, the fields and bush, the river on the other side and distant hills to the north, so that the memorial surveyed all of which Llew would have been lord. Beyond the house and the Tyrells' small run the valley opened out to the east. From the globe at the top of the memorial, if you were to somehow climb up, there might be a distant glimmer of the sea in the east. How wonderful her father had done this, she thought now, how unlike him, really, to even think of it. She loved him for it.

Still holding Lorna and Clara's hands, she approached the first stone face. 'The Fallen', it read, with a list below: a Pidcock, a Williams, two Smiths, two Braes, a Lidcomb, three Robinsons, with rank and battalion. There was room left to add more names, a cold stony space waiting for the worst. Where would they come from? How could there have already been so many from so few families?

And where was Llew? Where was his name?

Tears welled. Something of her grief must have passed through her and into the two small clasped hands, because the girls were both looking up at her with melancholic faces.

'Is Uncle Llew's dead body under there?' asked Lorna.

Jean shook her head, swallowed, and tried to get hold of herself.

'Is that really his grave?'

'No. It's to help us all remember him. A memorial to him.'

'Where is his deaded body?' Lorna's upturned face was a small version of Louisa's, but kinder, more curious.

'In France.'

'France.' The child repeated the word, wonderingly. France. Where the war was. 'Have you been in France?'

'No, but your mother has. And so had your grandmother.'

Min had travelled there from San Francisco at the end of last century, a wealthy young American absorbing it all, the art, the literature, language, the cuisine. It was where she had met Matthew, on his only tour. Once upon a time France had been stories at Min's knee, stories of a country Jean had imagined she might one day visit. Now it was the resting place of her favourite brother.

On the next face he stood alone, named for both his grandfathers.

Pte Llewellyn Mungo Dominic Fenchurch.
41ˢᵗ Battalion of 11ᵗʰ Infantry Brigade
Died of wounds. Aged 20
Fell December   1916

There was a gap left to fill in the date, another detail the War Office had still not provided. The empty space was awful; it was the mass grave, the unknown place. Or had they buried him properly? Who knew?

Western Front, Armentieres, France

This side of the memorial the ground was as yet unpaved. Picking her way between the puddles, Lorna went up close and reached as high as she could to touch the bottom of the *F* of *Front.* 'Does that say France?'

'No, darling. But it is an *F.* Clever girl.'

Clara was lifting her arms to be picked up, so Jean put her daughter on her hip and went around to the third tablet set into the column.

The Unknown

It was terrible, more than the listed names, more than seeing Llew's, because it was unexpected, because of the deaths hidden behind the dumb, blank face, the women and children left behind, the aching, deadening loss. How could the world ever be the same again? A heavy stone dropped from her heart into her belly, and she felt the baby shift, low down, a flickering above her groin.

'Mumma?'

Clara rode higher on her arm and pushed her face into her mother's, the blur of her blue eyes up close before she kissed her, wetly, on the cheek.

'In France they eat frogs' legs,' Jean told them, 'and speak a language called French.'

There was still no sign of her father or Louisa, so she took the children closer to the trees, getting them to listen for the waterfall concealed below the cliff. She pointed out birds and flowers and a candlenut tree, telling them how the pioneers would cut the tops off the hard, brown nuts, float a wick in the oil and use them for candles.

'Can we do that, Mumma?'

She pointed how they could see the belvedere from here, the lovely room they'd climbed to that morning. Half an hour passed and she was thinking of perhaps finding a sandwich for all of them from the picnic when she heard a horse approaching, a single set of hooves, and Matthew, hatless, was riding up in the same direction they had come from, up the hill from the gates. The boys ran to see him as he crested the hill, waving and shouting, but he ignored them, rounding the monument to pull up close to Jean. Too close. Clara was used to horses but Lorna startled and clung.

'Louisa fell. I took her back to the house along the low road, through Tyrells'.'

Lorna set up a wailing then, louder than before, and Cedric, white-faced, ran away towards the sulky before changing his mind and hieing away down the hill.

It was affecting, their display, since Jean suspected they were mostly left in the care of the nanny. It seemed they genuinely loved their mother, and so she did her sister too, of course, despite her worst imaginings. Why then did she feel nothing? Only a numbness. Trust Louisa. On this morning of all mornings. If she had not insisted on wearing her finery and riding rather than driving, then it would have passed very differently. Their father would have said a few words. Perhaps they would have prayed together, not that they were a family for praying, since the opposing religions had cancelled each other out and left them with nothing. Jean had the sensation of falling, dropping fast down a long, shining tunnel with no hand holds, no comforting words on the slide to despair.

The stonemason was standing, arching his back, and when he saw her haste he helped her, handing the children up to the sulky. Matthew waited for Jean to set off, following along behind.

'Mumma will be all right,' she whispered to Lorna, pulling her close. And she would be, she knew. Of course she would be.

Halfway down the hill was a clear view between the trees of the carriageway – and there, riding for all she was worth, was Rufina, her skirt blowing back to show her strong, white legs gripping the sides of the horse, small clouds of the dampened dust lifting in her wake. As she drew closer and then away to take the curve of the drive, Jean saw that she rode Boss, who seemed at this distance no worse for his escapade. Horse and rider emerged between the stone lions and turned right, taking the road to Clunes.

She was riding for the doctor, Jean realised, since there were no telephones in the district. Ahead the road widened for a few feet and Matthew took the chance to slip past.

'I'll see you there,' he said, giving Flora a nudge and going quickly down the slope, not turning in at the gate as Jean expected but going on, at a gallop now, to catch up to Louisa's maid, whose hair had come loose and was streaming behind her, licking at the air like a pale flame, or the petals of a flower.

It stood to reason Matthew would go in her stead and send the maid back, thought Jean. There was little he could do – Nan would need help and that Evie girl seemed pretty hopeless. Jean thought she remembered her from before she went away to begin her married life – one of the smallest ones, only six or seven years old then.

'Hurry up, Blackie.'

The old horse was dawdling, watching Flora and Boss disappear, and Jean could have sworn she heard her sigh.

'Home, Blackie,' Jean said, to reassure her that they wouldn't be going after them, flicking the reins again.

From behind her there came a soft chuckle.

'Funny old horse.'

Tom. Dear Tommy, who in the hurry to get the sulky turned around and the little girls either side on the bench seat, and Cedric running off on his own in his slippery city shoes, she had almost forgotten. Solid, dependable, honest. How lucky she was to have a son like him. She had not got to the bottom of the business about the toy tractor. Perhaps Cedric had made him a promise he didn't keep to let him play with it and Tom had been suffering the betrayal. He wasn't a child given to stories and invention. 'Balm to my soul,' she'd said of him from the time he was born, or a few weeks old, when his clear, pragmatic, intelligent eyes showed her who he was. 'Balm to my soul,' she would say as a kind of refrain when she nursed him, until one evening her husband had snapped, 'Oh all right!' being, as she had learned, a man who allowed the many difficulties of his life to overwhelm the pleasures.

Tom was down again, pulling on the horse, and then trotting along beside her, else she should stall again.

'You drive,' Jean said to him, and he climbed nimbly up to take the reins while she lifted Lorna to her lap.

'Nan will be looking after Mumma and she has Evie to help,' she told the child, who was still whimpering and calling for her mother. From the other side of Tom came Clara's arm, hooking firmly around her brother's slender waist.

'Up up, Blackie,' he said, and Blackie finally got the message and hurried herself along.

15.

He came to ride beside her. She knew without turning to see, as soon as she heard the flying hooves, that it was Matthew Fenchurch.

'I'll go,' he told her, passing now. 'You go back to the house.'

'I'll come with you,' she answered and saw that he was pleased, or at least he didn't suggest otherwise, and she felt Boss surge under her to overtake the older, slower horse.

'*Verlangsamen!*'

Matthew heard the German word and noticed how easily she controlled the horse. There was skill and learning there, an innate understanding of the animal, but he was reluctant to ask any of the questions that rose in his mind. Her nationality made him uneasy; it would be wise not to allow her to talk about her past.

But admiration had gilded his eye and Rufina saw it, just as she had in Mrs Arkenstall's room, and saw too how quickly he closed it off. She supposed he was preoccupied by the condition of his daughter, who had been carried in and laid across the settee in the morning room. Nance had looked into Louisa's eyes and pronounced that she was concussed but that there were no bones broken, and Matthew had taken that as a signal he could go and fetch the other daughter and the grandchildren from the memorial. It was only after he'd gone that they'd noticed the blood.

'Go for Doctor Becker,' Nance had said to the Irish maid, who had responded tardily to Nance's call and received a scolding, though she would have had worse if Rufina had told Nance the full story, how her hair had been pulled and her dress torn. She had felt abased by the girl, who had sulked by the morning-room door, her high colour faded. Pointedly, Rufina had turned away from her to the window, through which she had seen Boss, unchastened, tethered in the yard.

'I'll go,' she'd said. 'I can ride.'

And couldn't she? It was a long time since she had ridden her father's premier horses, and even though her previous employers had stabled more inferior steeds in Centennial Park for the purposes of fresh air and exercise, Rufina had never been invited to ride them. Boss chafed now against galloping behind Flora, just as he must have done on the ride out.

The road straightened to run towards Clunes across the plain so Rufina brought him to ride two abreast. Where the road ran closest to the river the way lay under water and Boss delighted in thundering through the ponds, sending up great surges of water. Mr Fenchurch was intent on the road, not glancing at her, and they went at such a pace and noise there was no chance of talk. She could have told him her mother's name was Flora, the same as his horse, and that she hadn't heard from her for months – almost a year – but why would that interest him? She would rather ask about the strange trees they passed, the palms and broad-leafed shrubs that broke the monotony of the gums, to ask about the bright birds sheltering high in the boughs. The surrounding country was as much the same as the hinterlands of Sydney perhaps, as much the same as it was different, in the way a field in Schleswig-Holstein might differ from one in France. There was less evidence of drought, the hills green from the recent rain. On a flat rock at the river's edge a bearded lizard separated itself from its dripping surroundings, a comical jointed leg and toes held out towards them as they thundered past. It was an ancient creature, from before the Bible, from before Adam and Eve.

At the outskirts of Clunes the rain started in earnest, straight down in the warm, windless air, dampening even the fires of the blacksmith, which smoked and blackened. Here was Saint Peter's, the wooden Anglican church, the general store with its sagging verandah, the little butcher, the two-storey hotel and finally the doctor's house, with its brass plaque and night-bell. Lightly, fluidly, Matthew dismounted with the ease of a man who'd spent his whole life around horses, like Rufina's own father, who had refused for too long to see the changes coming, an eccentric crank who kept up his once-successful Berlin horse and cartage business in the face of irrevocable change, who spent too long and too much at the gaming tables.

The doctor was not to be roused. The house had no fence or gate to prevent people rounding it to what must be the doctor's living quarters, so Matthew was free to go and investigate, rainwater falling with a sudden gush from the back of his hat as he pushed it higher on his brow.

Boss trembled a little and whined at Matthew's disappearance and Rufina soothed him. The doctor's house had an overgrown garden of white flowers, daisies and others, taller, coarser, more primitive, that Rufina had no name for. It was one of the most frustrating things about this country, how plants, animals, valleys and mountains would hold on to a savage anonymity, even with two languages to apply. It was at once primeval and brand new, unformed. Hadn't some of the earlier explorers been German? What name would they have given these flowers? The petals were as thick as flannel.

Doctor Becker, read the plaque. A woman came from the house next door and called from the shelter of the porch, 'He's gone away!'

Rufina nodded, unwilling to reply or ask where he had gone, for fear that the woman would hear her accent. Becker was a German name. He had more likely been taken away.

Matthew reappeared and mounted Flora, shaking his head.

'Is that you, Mr Fenchurch?' asked the doctor's neighbour, and she explained to him what had happened, and Rufina's suspicions were confirmed. Poor Doctor Becker, whoever he was, taken to Trial Bay Gaol.

'I didn't know him,' Matthew told her as they rode out of town. 'He's new. He's not the doctor that attended my wife. Old Doctor Mahoney died a year or so ago.'

'I would have thought doctors were in short supply,' Rufina said. 'How could it matter if the doctor is German? We have the best doctors in the world. You were lucky to have him in such a backwater.'

Matthew gave her a funny look, a tight little smile, before he rode ahead for a while. The warm rain was starting again, but what did it matter, since she was soaked to the skin. Rufina revelled in it. What a strange pleasure. She felt it slip through her hair, thick on her scalp, like oil. Further along, Matthew was waiting for her.

'It could be dangerous for you to go back to Sydney,' he said as soon as she drew level, not looking at her.

'Dangerous? How? The war is dangerous. The war is not here.'

'There is a lot of anti-German feeling.'

'Do you think I am unaware of that?' She thought of her employer alone in Sydney, frightened to go out, of how the women clung together with their men taken from them.

'If Louisa can spare you then you should stay at Jarulan, hidden away.'

He met her eyes again and Rufina saw his intent suddenly and it alarmed her. It hadn't been there before. His expression was kind, though; she could see by the way his mouth had set that he had been a man given to laughter, though not so much in recent times, perhaps since his wife died. The sun-bleached blue of his eyes was strange – though you did see men with eyes like that here. Penetrating, lucent and somehow ruthless. He could be thirty years her senior, in his fifties, or not; the men here often looked older than they were.

Rufina kicked Boss on, though he hardly needed the encouragement, and rode ahead of Fenchurch all the way back to his house. The rain was sleeking, delicious, and as she rode she tipped her head back to let it trickle down her throat. She could feel his eyes on her all the way home, even when a bend in the road would have obscured her.

16.

Even from this distance Evie could see that Matthew had eyes only for the German bitch, the back view of her riding before him and turning in at his lion gates so that he didn't notice the black and white dog bounding away towards the Tyrells' place, and neither did he see Evie, passing through the long grass behind it. Evie saw them though, riding back separately and without the doctor.

'The doctor was taken away last Wednesday,' she could have told them if they'd bothered to ask, since one of her brothers had told her when they'd met on the lower field. She hadn't asked Donny what he was doing there and neither had he asked why she wasn't at work up in the house; instead he'd told her the latest news. She'd wanted to tell someone of her own developments, but Donny wasn't the one. If it had been either of her closest sisters, Bridget or Teresa, she would have told her, told her everything. Everything!

The Fenchurches wouldn't miss her. Besides, she couldn't stay another moment in a house where she wasn't appreciated, and that was in any case haunted. On her return from the river Nan had taken her roughly by the shoulder and given her a shake. The German had tittle-tattled on her after Evie pulled her hair and yanked her dress, sitting at the kitchen table with her eyes swollen from crying and her nose red.

She should toughen up. Evie had been on the brink of telling her so and giving her a slap, biding her time until Nan went off to perform a task elsewhere when they had heard Matthew calling from the yard. He'd sounded panic-stricken, and Evie had flown to him, Nan and the German following. Between them they'd carried Louisa inside, Nan going ahead and giving directions to one of the musty downstairs rooms. It was pink and gilt, with a roll-top desk and a glass dome that contained a poor platypus and a cruel bird. Who would want to look at such an ugly thing, full of mouldering death?

When I am mistress I will have it carried outside and tossed on the rubbish heap, Evie had thought, and risked laying her open hand on Matthew's back as he bent over his prone daughter. Either he didn't feel Evie's touch or he ignored it – Louisa's mouth was open at a peculiar angle, as if she'd dislocated her jaw when she fell, and she was breathing loudly, while the German was untying the black ribbon at Louisa's throat and Nan shaping the pillow under her head to keep her airways open. Then Nan was opening one of Louisa's sightless eyes, and then the other, until Louisa opened them for herself and looked up at them all.

She was like a dead person coming back to life. When her father felt the hinges of her jaw and clicked them in place, Louisa cried out. Then they asked her to move her limbs and she did, with Nan gently squeezing along them, checking for breaks.

'Just stunned, I reckon,' Nan said, 'from the fall.'

Evie retreated to the door and suffered a wave of nausea, which she tried to lessen by taking hold of Matthew as he passed a moment or so later from the room but he pulled sharply away, hissing at her, which so destroyed her that she was unable to reply when Nan asked her to go for the doctor. Then, after the German rode off instead of Evie, Nan had said, 'She's losing the child,' and sent Evie to boil water and fetch towels, and Louisa was crying and screaming and clinging on to Nan, so as soon as Evie had fetched the things that were needed she went out to the yard and whistled again for Llew's dog.

She came straight away, as she always did, happy to leave forever a life of imprisonment and neglect. She would be happy at her new home, where the younger children would love her, though Evie considered that they may not get that far, this particular field being alive with snakes. One day, only a couple of years ago, when Llew was here, he and Donny found a whip snake, a young one, not yet grown to full venom. And they'd seen others, bigger, with yellow faces, more poisonous. Evie hoped they were still here, in their hundreds: death adders and tiger snakes, hurrying now to her bare legs and feet, looking for life to feed off and choosing her. Mr Fenchurch could find her body bitten all over; he could weep and wail, he would regret treating her so shabbily.

But she reached the sagging fence that marked the boundary safely, without incident, and climbed over. There was the yard, turned to skilly mud by the rain; there were the rusting low roofs of the house and the outbuildings, the bulging wattle-and-daub walls of the rooms her father and brothers had added to the original small house. Out by the dunny the house cow nosed through a slew of brown cabbage leaves and it seemed she was the only one home until Evie saw that the door to the chicken shed stood open. Ma's rear view was only just discernible in the gloom of the fowl house – the raggy bow at the back of her pinny, the trodden-down backs of her boots. The white chickens showed as luminous as Ma's pale legs and Evie felt a slight pang. She thought perhaps she had missed her mother, missed home. People were supposed to, weren't they? Even if home was just over the fence.

'Ma?'

Ma spun round, astonished. 'You're back?'

'Standing in front of you, ain't I?'

Her mother came out into the light, a chipped enamel basin of five eggs in her hand and looked closely at her. 'So you are. With a face like rent day. They treating you well up there?'

Evie nodded but the tears welled. 'Look what I brought you.' She turned away from her mother for a moment to pull the chemise from the leg of her bloomers, the puff of silk and lace. As she spun to face her again it caught the light and shimmered, and she saw now that it was smaller than she'd thought, that it would not fit her mother. She was a bigger, bonier woman than the rightful owner. How out of place it seemed here in the rank fowl house. It would seem less so when they went inside. She would smooth it out on the bright crocheted quilt of her mother's bed.

'Your brothers have gone to the Eltham pub,' Ma said. Not a word of thanks for the gift but a hard look. Evie saw that she knew it was stolen and that she was not grateful for it.

'And the children?'

'Bridget and Teresa are in the house with the babies. In you go.'

Ma held the chemise away from her, as if it would burn her.

'If you don't want it, Ma, I'll—' and she put her hand out for it but Ma shook her head.

'Did they pay you all right?'

'I'll go back for it,' Evie said, realising as she said so that she would have to, that if she was quick they may not even have noticed that she'd gone. Nan would have, of course. There would be Nan to deal with. She'd be on the warpath.

No, she couldn't possibly go back. Nan would be the least of it. Evie had slipped for a moment into that alternate world where there was no child to be thinking of. She'd ask Tessa to go up to collect her wages. Tessa would be avid for it, to be going up to the big house that rose like a fairy tale on the tongue of the land, to see them all there and hang around as long as Nan would let her. All the Tyrell children, the ones old enough to remember, had loved to go to Jarulan when Min was alive, to see the beautiful lady who gave a children's Christmas party, who had sent for the kindly old doctor when Bridgie had fallen into the fire.

There was a flash of marbled black and brown and white, a dash from behind Evie to the shed, a joyful bark and explosion of feathers. Llewellyn's dog. She had forgotten all about it and now it was killing one of Ma's best layers, the chook's open beak jagging back and forth with the dog's vigorous shake, the other fowls flying in all directions until Ma waded in, shouting, drawing back her heavy boot and kicking the dog in the guts. It reeled back, teeth bared, barking, bloody mouthed.

'What the dickens is going on?' Youngest sibling on her hip, Bridgie had come out onto the porch to see what all the commotion was and Evie wanted right away to go up to her and tell her what had been burning in her heart these past few weeks, but the chicken killer had come to weave itself through her legs, still barking, and Ma was yelling something about her being a dingbat and a fool, and to go back and get the money, and the only thing to do was to run.

It wasn't until she was halfway across the snake field that she remembered seeing the chemise leave Ma's grasp to land in the mud, and how Ma had trodden it in as she'd lunged towards Llewellyn's dog, and how the last word ringing in her ears that exploded from Ma as Evie put a safe distance between them was 'Thief!'

'You or me?' she asked the dog.

She slowed a little, decided to take her time. When Bridgie had come out, it had seemed for an instant that they had swapped places, and that she was looking up at herself, she and that particular sister being so alike, or so Ma said they were until Bridgie got burned. It had seemed, just for a second, that Evie's life was going on at home regardless, with Bridgie wearing a pink and white striped dress that Evie had once favoured, now too small for her and stained and faded. And then, just before Ma began yelling, she'd seen the rest of it too – what would come. The desolate yard, the stink of shit and wood smoke, the baby on the hip her own baby, and the inevitability of her brothers' drunken return. Da had brought them up to it and since his death last year they adhered to the family tradition. Some nights if you weren't careful with your mouth or where you put yourself, it was easy to clock a blow going spare.

She wouldn't come back here. Or go to Jarulan. Neither place. Ever. Her feet led her on, aimlessly, to where the track branched, the sandier way leading back to the big house, the other muddier one down to the river. The poor dog was limping from where Ma had kicked it, looking up at Evie now and again as if to ask her what its future was, more so when they reached the river and took the track along the banks that was used more by the Blacks than anyone else. It was slippery-going, thick mud full of broken timber and stumps left from when the river gums were felled for fuel during Llew's short-lived riverboat enterprise. Since then, boats rarely came this far up.

Swollen and slate-grey, the river's surface wrinkled and smoothed in patterns set by the currents and pocked with new rain. At the far bank, which was not so far – they could swim the distance as children – the bush was smoky, the ranges behind veiled in a skirl of wet and wind blowing in from the north. Evie found herself talking to the dog, crooning to it, soothing herself as much as it, asking why it never killed the Jarulan chickens, which would peck around it in the yard and not a whisker would stir.

'What's your name, girlie?' she asked it. 'I wish you could tell me.'

One night in bed she'd asked Fenchurch the dog's name and he'd drawn breath to tell her then slammed his mouth shut. It was perhaps their second time together, or their third. There was his face in the candlelight, wide and pale, and a wall coming up in those unearthly eyes. It had reminded her of the cats when they got sick, the white third eyelid that would pass across, only this time cloaking a bleary heart, and the thought of him as a sick cat had made her giggle. A sick old tom, battle worn, ears chewed, a kink in his tail. She'd tickled him in the ribs, kissed him, licked the sweat doglike from his neck. 'Tell me.' She'd wheedled and played. 'What is its name, then, your dotie best doggie?' And then she'd rattled on with nervous nonsense about how it followed her around, that it loved her, even though she could see he was closed to her now, that, somewhere a long way off, was growing angry.

'Tell me its name, go on. What harm could it do?'

Eventually, wearily, he'd roused himself enough to say, 'There were tears when he said goodbye to that dog. I won't hear another voice say the name, least of all yours.'

She'd lain down beside him then, quiet, to let him sleep since that was what he wanted, and entertained herself with notions of how different they were but how much the same. You heard of men who took Aboriginal women in to live with them. There was one in Casino, and a farmer out on the heads. They were not as different as that, she and he; at least they were almost the same colour, though some of the Proddies called the Tyrells black. She wasn't black, not like the Abbos were black. Love bloomed. It could bloom. If he let it.

There was a stump up ahead, a little higher, where you could sit and look back at the river side of the house. The jetty and the launch were clearly visible, the boat tugging at its moorings. Just there the river was always swift. When the Fenchurch children had wanted to swim they would come up river to the same waterhole as the Tyrells, the safe one below the falls. In those days, before the river gums were felled, you could run along the track through the dappled shade, barely having to watch where you put your feet, passing the small Aboriginal settlement – really only a handful of houses and even poorer than the Tyrells – before the bush grew more dense and closed overhead. People came and went from those huts and houses and very often there was no one there at all, but Evie remembered long-ago days at the waterhole when a group of shy, slender children might appear and swim, their dark narrow limbs flashing in the clear sunlit depths. Llew and Edmond, who were the youngest of the Fenchurches and so closest in age to the oldest Tyrell girls, didn't mind the Blacks coming to swim, but if Louisa was there she would send them away. Evie had only vague, indistinct memories of her from those years, being ten years younger: Louisa with her nose in the air, passing the washhouse on the days Evie had gone to help her mother; Louisa asking Jimmy Tyrell, who had worked as a groom, to saddle up one of the prime horses then leave it standing waiting for hours, drooping in the heat while she attended to some other matter more pressing, like sitting on the shady verandah with her book, or gossiping with her mother or sister. Even at five or six years of age, Evie had wished she had been born a Fenchurch and not a Tyrell, wished for pretty dresses and handsome horses, for a gentle mother with soft hands and kind eyes.

Once, she had earned a slap from Ma for asking if she could go and live in the big house, asking if she could be given to them as a present. Thinking back on it now, it seemed the slap had been administered not from wounded motherly love, but more as if Evie had said something indecent.

'You're not a puppy,' her mother had hissed at her. 'And don't call Nance Nan. You're not family.'

She tried now very hard to remember Matthew from those days. Perhaps little girls don't notice grown men as much as they do women and other more grown-up girls. Matthew from those days had somehow merged among the other men of the farm, the white moleskins and faded blue shirts, the leather boots and straw hats worn by all of them.

Evie drew her knees up against her stomach and propped her chin, letting the new rain slake her head and face. She was not born a Fenchurch, but her baby would be. She would make sure the world knew it was Matthew's. She would lie if she had to, play a dirty trick and say he had forced her, when it had been the other way around. Not that she had forced him, really – how could she? It was an impossible thing for a girl to force a man, but that first night when she had gone into the dining room and sat on his knee, his pale eyes had lit more with surprise than anything else. Lust came later. No, she wouldn't call it that. It *was* love. Love of a kind.

She could have strung him along a little, not slept with him that very first night, but what would have been the point? It wasn't as if she had anything else to give him other than herself. Rich people played all kinds of games before they banged; Evie supposed that was because of money. Why else? They had to make sure the other person was worth the price and then you only gave it over on the wedding night.

Well. She wasn't like that. She didn't have that quality to sell, not like the first Mrs Fenchurch, the class and elegance, though she had the same religion. Neither did she know how you got hold of that quality unless you had been born with it; and it struck her with a warm, delicious flush that ran the length and centre of her bones that this child could have it. Quality. Matthew would know it was his. It would grow up at Jarulan even if Matthew wouldn't marry her. No chance of raising it at home, overcrowded, unwelcoming and full of fleas. She could never do that.

If they were to live in the same house they would have to be man and wife. She could see no other way. Other women had made clever marriages. An old man in Mullumbimby had married his young housekeeper, only sixteen. Because of the war there would be lots of marriages that would never have happened if so many young men hadn't gone away to fight. Old men were all that were left and they were hitching up with the pretty girls.

The rain had lessened but fell still. Once again the river dimpled and swirled with watery patterns and so much reflected the soft grey of the sky that it was almost white. It was like a length of satin or silk, thought Evie, the same silken cloth as the stolen chemise, but laid out for cutting into a wedding dress. Here is where you would cut the long sleeves, with a ruffle of bronzed river grass. Here is the stuff for the bodice, pure and undisturbed, the surface smooth as a pearl. And over there, where the rushing water pleated around the rocks in the shallows, that would make a skirt to fall gracefully from the waistband. The river was her wedding dress.

She wriggled happily, sitting on the wet stump, and lifted her feet to examine them. Her wet frock clung to her legs and her feet weighed with great clods of mud. Less her trousseau, more her grave. Life was so exciting she didn't know if she was delighted or terrified, if she wanted to live or die. She could throw herself in the west-running river right now and travel down past the house without anybody noticing, past Jarulan and the Chinese tobacco farm, past the orchards and fields and bush to Lismore, where perhaps somebody could fish her out, and then there would be a funeral and Ma and her sisters would weep at the graveside. Matthew would feel compelled to attend and would weep too, in spite of himself, and then everyone would know the secret of how he loved her. If God was merciful He would let her spirit fly around the church for long enough to see Fenchurch's grief, before she was condemned to the Fires of Hell. She could see her dotie weeping, walking behind the coffin.

In the meantime no one would have any clue where she'd gone. She would only try to swim a little bit; she would trick God into thinking it was an accident. It would take a while for the mud to melt away from her shoes, it would hold her down but maybe not for long enough to drown and then what?

The adventure palled. She put her arm around the dog, her mind swimming with the terrible vision of herself not dead but damaged, miscarrying, losing the next heir to Jarulan, being sent away to a hospital or a madhouse.

What then?

17.

Matthew himself piloted the launch to Lismore so that his son-in-law and grandson could take the coach to Tenterfield to join the Great Northern Railway back to Sydney. Luxury. An alternative to the rigours of a sea voyage. Surely the nanny and the little ones and Louisa could have gone too. All Louisa wanted to do was to languish in her bed and eat for two or more.

On his way back to Jarulan he reflected that he felt more than a little bruised by their company, especially Arkenstall's. His son-in-law had tried to broach the subject of the increasing dereliction of the house. On the morning of the day Matthew confronted his grandson about the lost earring – a mistake if there ever was one – he and Arkenstall had gone out riding to see the memorial and from there they had looked east over the farm. Matthew had explained some of Llew's innovations – the herd of banded Galloways, the first in the district, the north-facing slopes he'd given over to Queensland nuts, the attempt to grow cotton on the flats, how Matthew was keeping it all up.

'The roof could do with a paint,' was Arkenstall's only response, gesturing towards Jarulan itself. 'You're letting the place go.'

A farmer will always invest in his land before his dwelling, Matthew could have explained, but couldn't be bothered. It seemed disingenuous considering that he didn't lack for funds. A city man could not possibly understand.

He could have explained that through the dry winter he was having an irrigation channel dug from the river to a new dam, because even though at certain times of the year many acres were inundated, there were parts where the soil stayed as dry and sterile as dust. Fifty, sixty years ago, after the great cedar forests were first felled, cattle grew fat and crops flourished from the moment the seed hit the ground. Already the land was exhausted. Already farmers were searching for alternatives and solutions. If Jean had been with them she might have contributed to the discussion, but she and her children had gone back to the struggling plantation in the north.

Matthew breathed in the first real cool dry evening of winter, the rich clean smell of the river, heard the satisfying chug of the oil launch. The citified son-in-law could never be a replacement or even a salve for the loss of his own sons, one dead and the other as good as. The conversation, such as it was, had faltered.

No point in even thinking about him now. He drew the oil launch close to the jetty and tethered her to the post. How much longer would Louisa be with them at Jarulan?

Up the stone steps he went, between his wife's lesser stone goddesses. Some of their names were slipping from his memory now that Min wasn't here to remind him, but Diana he remembered, with her bow and arrow, golden apple and regal profile, which reminded him now of Rufina, a likeness he enjoyed, even though she had been cool towards him, actively avoiding him since the day they rode for the doctor. Yet she'd stayed at Jarulan after he had made himself plain. She hadn't run away.

On the top step a paver had come loose and almost tripped him. He paused long enough then to see how green the statues had become, how they had begun to merge into the shrubbery around them as if they were in final retreat, a return to their original material. He would send Evie down with sugar soap and a scrubbing brush to clean them up or ask Nance to send her.

No, he corrected himself as he crossed the carriageway and went along the verandah, he would tell her himself, boss to girl. There would be another maid to assist Nance, more capable, and then he would send Evie away. It's too much for Nan, his daughters had told him again and again, as if Nance was an old woman, which she wasn't. She was younger than him. 'She's got Evie,' he'd replied, and in response Louisa had given him a direct denuding glance. None of her business if she'd worked it out.

Her room was abandoned. Or seemed to be. He had a look around. He'd known all along who it was who had taken the earring. He had suspected it earlier, while Arkenstall was still here, but he'd used his son-in-law's presence as added incentive to stay away from her. For the life of him he couldn't remember what Evie had lying about in here before. He supposed the usual things women had, brushes, petticoats, face cream. Not that he could picture her making use of any of it. Now there was just the bed, a rough-sawn wooden frame with sagging wirewove and kapok mattress, the boxes of old china, a dry smell. He sniffed the air. Perhaps there was a whiff of Evie herself, that coltish smell she had with a hint of yellow soap and soda. He hadn't been her first, though she'd told him he was. He didn't believe it. She'd responded too eagerly, too readily. He hadn't had to teach her anything.

The bedclothes were gone from the bed, such as they were. A thin old sheet and blanket. It was as well she'd done a flit because he had a sudden need of her and might not have been able to stop himself. Where had she gone? He hadn't missed her presence in the house. Sullen, distant and slow to please; a less able servant than she was mistress.

Mistress! Listen to yourself!

A rather lofty term for what had been going on between them. Men who had mistresses were grander than he was. Arkenstall, for instance. He was a prime candidate. Rich, powerful, with an ailing wife domiciled in the countryside. He'd doubtless have one or two. Evie was never a mistress.

Matthew came out onto the narrow verandah and squinted up at the house. The rear south-facing windows reflected the evening sky, a deep clear blue lit by a streaming sunset, a sheeny obscuring of any face that might be looking down at him. High gold-flecked clouds were skimming swiftly behind the belvedere, so fast it made the house seem to lean towards him, the whole weighty edifice, as if it could at any moment topple and crush him.

A memory broke from his childhood, of lying on the paving by the fountain. In those days it was a modest affair, a simple fluted column that culminated in a wide dish, with one point of egress for the water. Embossed on the column was an attempt at a coat of arms: on the shield a saddle, a gun, a red cedar and axe, a bull's head, and in the centre a gold nugget and pick. The family's history condensed; a pictograph of how Jarulan had been bought and farmed by his grandfather on his return from the Northern Territory, which was where he had learned the word he gave to his estate as its name. The crest above the shield was in the form of a crudely carved wedge-tailed eagle carrying a burning twig. Jarulan: a fire started by raptors. He remembered his father telling him the story when he was a boy, how birds of prey were smart enough to know how to drive small prey out of grasslands by dropping a fiery brand, how they waited, hovering in the smoke before diving to catch their dinner. Natural strategists and opportunists, he supposed they were, and so were the Fenchurches.

Min had got rid of that earlier fountain, replacing it with a much grander, very expensive construction shipped all the way from Italy. Naked writhing figures, male and female, had scandalised the district. Min had explained it to him when the first drawings arrived, the satyrs and sirens, nymphs and naiads, and Matthew had done nothing to curb her enthusiasm for fear of a tantrum, and also for the delight he took in her brazen disregard of the old man.

But the crass extravagance fled now from his memory, replaced by the earlier, modest creation, and himself as a small boy lying on the hot stones, feeling his skin frizzling through the thin fabric of his shirt, looking up at the wide spreading roofs of the house and listening to the playing water. He remembered how it sounded to him like one particular she-oak, a favourite tree close to the river. Every she-oak made its own individual song as the wind rubbed against the whorls of its bark and small scales of its leaves. That tree – as long gone now as the fountain – made music as watery as the river itself. He remembered how that boy had had these fanciful thoughts and how also he had quailed at the enormity of his inheritance, that the farm would fail, that he would make mistakes, that the grandest house of the north would fall under his watch, his father's only son.

Never.

He went around now to the fountain, remembering how the grandchildren had asked him to make it play again. His response had been that it was broken, though he suspected that all that was wrong with it was silt stopping the flow from the upper dam, or fallen leaves plugging the mechanism. The figures were less green than the statues flanking the stairs, but verdigris-coloured growth filled the crevices and cracks, and flocked bowed heads and uplifted faces. Weeds flourished in windblown soil caught in the folds of scanty robes; the undersides of breasts were cupped with moss.

Someone was sitting on the low wall of the surrounding empty pool. He could see a dark skirt pulled up to expose a familiar slender leg in the early winter evening sun, stockings rolled down to the tops of two brown boots. The last time Matthew had seen that leg it was clamped to Boss's sweaty flank.

Rufina was reading a book, perched between two broad-chested mermen, whose tails had been fashioned to flop over the rim of the pool and made a kind of chair, though he had never seen anyone sit there before. When she heard his footsteps on the loose river stones of the carriageway she flung her skirt down and stood up, blushing violently, her gaze lowered. A true lady, thought Matthew, the most ladylike woman he'd ever met, more so even than Min because she was quieter.

He waited for her to look at him, and she did eventually. Grey eyes, paler than his own. Clear, clever, dignified. Something else from Evie's chatter snagged in his brain, though he always did his best not to listen to her – *the Hun is a nob fallen on hard times. Her da was a gambler, did ya know?* Had Rufina told her something of her past? He would find out himself, who her people were.

He offered her his arm, inviting her to walk with him, and couldn't help noticing that she glanced up at the eastern face of the house, as if to check that nobody was watching. Who would be, considering the house was virtually empty? Louisa would have to have got out of bed and come down the corridor to the stained-glass window under the belvedere stairs to see them. And the servants would be occupied with their duties and Lorna and Gordon, the remaining children.

'Bring your book,' he said, wondering why he found women who read so fascinating, considering he couldn't be bothered with it himself.

Waste of time.

The last few sunrays to reach the fountain caught a frond of weed growing behind Neptune's ear, setting it gleaming like a plume on a Roman soldier's cap. He wished he had the lip to comment on it, a way of putting it in words to impress her. Rufina followed his gaze.

'It's a shame it no longer plays,' she said, turning to look at the fountain, the riot of breasts and legs.

Matthew supposed European girls were more used to that kind of thing than Australian girls. Some of Llew's lady visitors to the house had giggled and gasped. Rufina did not seem to be at all embarrassed, smiling at him, giving him not only her arm but her book to carry. They began a turn around the fountain.

'What a confusion!' she went on. 'Neptune, Pan, Hercules, Aphrodite … I think. Romans, Greeks and pagans all mixed up together.'

Matthew didn't remember who they were and didn't much care.

'It is very … ersatz!'

It was a word he didn't know, though he was sure Min would have. Rufina's arm was light on his, their steps in time. He asked her the question he'd planned and she told him the story, of her early life in a fine house in Berlin, the boarding school in England, how her father died in the same year as Min did, with hidden debt, and how her mother's friend Frau Schneider had taken her in, bringing her with them to Sydney, where they had lived for two years until Herr Schneider was arrested by the military police.

'And Frau Schneider? What happened to her?'

'I had a letter to say that she has taken a house in South West Rocks with another German woman, to be near the Trial Bay Gaol. I was lucky to get another appointment so quickly and easily. Many Germans are without work now. But Mr Arkenstall had taken quite a shine to me, even before I came to live with them. In a fatherly way.'

Matthew had detected none of this – but then during Arkenstall's stay he'd rarely been in the company of them both at once. Since Louisa's fall, Rufina had taken her meals upstairs. 'Company improves the appetite!' Louisa had announced, in that way she had of imitating Min. It unnerved him how many of Min's little sayings Louisa remembered, and also how adept was her mimicry. Occasionally Arkenstall had dined there too, at the little table by the fireplace, and on those nights Rufina had perhaps gone to the kitchen to eat with Nance. And Evie, he supposed. He had stayed away from her since the night she biffed the plate.

Rufina should have had her meals with him. He would suggest it.

'Sometimes I wish …'

Rufina trailed off. They had come around the fountain and down the wide marble step to the carriageway, and Matthew supposed he could take her around to the rose garden, such as it was at this time of year for the season and the lack of care. At least the sun would be on it still, the few last blooms, coming over the garden wall before it began its rapid slide below the western hills.

He didn't prompt her. He didn't have to say anything.

'Sometimes I wish I had gone with them, anyway. Even though I would have no money of my own.'

'You must be out of sorts, then, to wish that. You think loafing about in a country town would be better than looking after Louisa in Sydney?'

Rufina blushed again. 'But I am not in Sydney, am I? And … And I think that to be among other Germans, to not be constantly on my guard, it would be …'

He patted her hand. 'You don't have to be on your guard here. Even though I have lost my son.'

The hand stiffened but did not pull away. They passed under the arch of roses, the old canes wound around one another, the blackened leaves. The path was narrow, overgrown; Matthew was compelled to walk in the long grass.

'How old are you, Rufina?'

'Eighteen. I was just fifteen when I left Germany. I have not had the adventures I would have liked to have had. Not yet.

Or at least, not as many of them. We saw a lot of Australia, the Schneiders and I. We went by ship to Melbourne, took the train to Adelaide. They have relatives in the Barossa Valley. But I have never before been this far north.'

'Do you like it here?'

'I do. But I want to be either on the move, having adventures, or ...'

'Or what?'

They had paused beside a straggling foxglove, the weather not yet cold enough for it to have died away. Sometimes they lasted the whole of winter, he'd observed, since the gardener was sent off. A whole season of hanging on, rotting and half alive, of waiting for real cold to bite into its marrow, to send it back to the earth. It never came. Browning trumpets were webbed by spiders; one hollowed stalk a home for a large brown beetle, its antennae waving. If he was on his own he'd shake it out onto the ground, have a close look at it before squashing it under his heel.

'Or having my freedom. Being able to please myself. I understand Frau Schneider pleases herself pretty much – though life is dull, and even though they are not in the camp with the men they feel constantly observed. But here am I on the outside and having always to do another's bidding.'

'Your English is very good,' he told her, his first compliment.

'I went to school in England. And I had an English grandmother who lived with us, so ...'

'And you can ride like the devil!'

She laughed then, the first time he had ever seen her laugh properly, her head thrown back, her white teeth and full lips.

'So. You would have adventures. Or you would ... what?'

She shrugged, not looking at him but bending to sniff at a coiled bud.

'You mean you would be mistress of your own destiny,' he said. A phrase of Min's. 'Authoress of your own fate.' Min again.

'I would!' She was smiling at him, delighted with his words. It inspired him to go on.

'Mistress of your own domain. Householder.'

'Yes. Yes, I suppose so.'

'Marry me.'

He was as astonished as she was. Had he really asked her? She was staring at him with those cool grey eyes and he could see that she was thinking about it, that she wasn't horrified by the idea, that it didn't disgust her. Perhaps she was an old hand at this, perhaps in the two years in Sydney she had fielded proposal after proposal from men more youthful and cultured than he was. Knocked them back, one after the other. Waiting for a better offer.

She might also have been thinking of how she was eighteen to his fifty-whatever, that he would most likely pre-decease her by decades, that she would be a wealthy young widow. Did she think that far, he wondered, to a time when she would have this longed-for freedom? Why wouldn't she, though, since the word 'love' had not once been mentioned by either of them? Min and he had fallen in love the first time they'd met, at a hotel in the south of France – the charming, wealthy American and the callow grazier, the first of his family to make the trip back to Europe, to take a Grand Tour. He'd spent a lot of time bemoaning his paltry education; he knew so little about the countries he passed through. Min had been holidaying on the Riviera for the fifth or sixth time with her mother.

But now was not the time to be thinking about Min, about a day from thirty years ago, when he was as hopeless at courting as he was now, but younger and, he supposed, better looking.

This is the twentieth century!

There was a rustle at their feet and a small green carpet snake emerged from the fallen leaves and slid along the brick edging of the flowerbed, still visible through the long grass. Rufina did not scream or have the vapours, which pleased him.

'We have snakes in Germany, too, you know,' she told him calmly, 'not that I have ever seen one.'

But she was stepping away from it, rapidly, and he found that he had caught her up in his arms, that he was kissing her sweetly on that smooth white cheek.

'The answer is yes,' she said simply, 'and as soon as it can be arranged.'

He kissed her again, less demurely than before, her blonde lashes flicking for an instant like insect wings against his lowering mouth. She wore the same dull blue dress as always; he supposed it was a kind of uniform. The bones of a corset ridged under his hand. After they were married, even before, she wouldn't dress like this. He wanted her in soft colours; he'd buy her a riding outfit of her own, better than Louisa's.

'We'll tell everyone in good time. But there are a few things I have to sort out first.'

He tried to kiss her a third time but she was nodding, giggling suddenly, girlish. 'A snake! Who would have thought a snake would come? It is like something in a story.' She bent away to pick up the book he'd dropped a moment before, and patted it. 'We could read about it in here.'

Matthew read the name, D.H. Lawrence, and he thought he remembered it from Min's library, but couldn't be sure. *Sons and Lovers.* He looked from the book to his future wife and felt out of his depth. She seemed to be amused by something that excluded him.

'How? What are you talking about?'

'Symbolism. The snake. If one were to appear in a book, then it would be an omen, would it not? A sign of something to come for us, something already on its way, good or bad.'

'There are snakes by the hundred here. There's no getting away from them.' He didn't like this turn, this superstition. That's what had got Min in the end. Only just tolerable that she wouldn't give up her religion, riding most Sundays all the way to Saint Kevin's in Bangalow, that she'd won on that one; much worse that she periodically surrounded herself with ghosts and terrors, a cycle that tightened and sped as she got older. He regarded Rufina now, who was looking at him challengingly, but with a soft smile on her young mouth.

'I'm not afraid of anything.'

He pointed behind her then, into the long grass, pretending he could see the snake again, or a different, more deadly one; he couldn't resist the tease. She was instantly alarmed, clinging to him and looking earnestly around, which made him laugh, and she as well, that lovely big laugh, and they kissed again, properly this time, lip to lip, before they walked out of the garden. All the way she held tight to his arm, back to the wider path to the front of the house, facing the river. In silence they crossed the white carriageway and stood at the top of the stairs, looking down between the avenue of statues to the water running at the bottom, fast and silvery. He could sense her looking at it all with a new understanding, that it would be hers.

A gaggle of children emerged from the trees on the bank, mid-flight, dropping down between two of the statues and going on down the stairs. Thin, black-haired, scruffy, knobbly-kneed – some of the Tyrells. They had with them a small koala bear, a rope tied around its neck, and a girl much too small was half-dragging, half-carrying it, another child, older, holding the rope and tugging on it.

'Oh, the poor thing!' Rufina had left his side, hurrying down the stairs calling out, 'Children! Children, please stop!'

By the time Matthew joined them – she could run like the dickens in that heavy old dress! – she was holding her arms out for the bear, bracing herself on the flight of steps to take its weight.

'No!' he said. 'It'll scratch you.'

People were stupid about koala bears; they'd even stopped the Abbos eating them. He had a display in the parlour vitrine – a whole family, a baby on its mother's back. Rufina would not have seen it yet. It was a treat in store, to show her all that. She might like him to add this one to the collection.

'Do they have *very* small brains? Look – see how he's looking at me, how he turns his head. He is staring all around! Can we keep it, Mr Fenchurch?'

Her first request. He wouldn't dream of denying it.

'Matthew,' he said, gently.

'It's our bear,' said the boy with the rope. 'We caught 'im!'

'On my land. Go on. Get.'

He took the bear off the girl, who immediately began weeping and wailing, streaming snot and tears. The Tyrells. What a trial they were generally.

'You don't mind us shootin' the rabbits now, do ya?' the boy tried.

One of the sisters came to put her arm around the weeping girl. They stared at him with hatred while the bear clung to him, its claws sharp through his shirt. Rufina was murmuring to it in German, endearments he supposed, while she stroked its ears.

'We already got one tied to a tree at home. It's got a rope so it can climb up and down,' said one of the older boys. 'It's lonely. It's dying of loneliness so we got it a mate. Give it back, Mister.'

'It hardly knows what is going on!' Rufina said. 'Look at the poor thing. Its slow, trusting eyes. *Liebling.*'

'Off you go,' he said sternly to the Tyrells. 'And don't be cutting through here. You're trespassing.'

'What have you done with our Evie?' dared the girl doing the comforting. 'Ma wants to see her.'

Matthew pretended he hadn't heard. He turned, the bear clinging, the particular smell of eucalyptus and piss and clean dry dirt coming off it, and the fur of its ears tickling the underside of his chin as he bent over it for the climb. Rufina was following him, asking him where the koala would live and what they would feed it and how long he expected it to survive. He felt the Tyrell children melt away at his back, his misgivings with them.

'I'll take care of it,' Rufina said when they reached the top of the stairs, slipping her hand around his upper arm. 'I would love to have the care of it, Mr Fenchurch.'

'Matthew,' he said again. He would have liked to kiss her again but his arms were full of koala.

'There's a few tricks. Its food and so on. Otherwise they die pretty quick.'

'But nothing to be afraid of?' She gave his arm a little playful squeeze as they turned towards the kitchen, the yard.

'We'll tie it to a gum round the back. Like the kids said – it has to be able to climb a tree for the leaves. That's all it eats.'

'I'm not afraid of anything, you know.' She had an arch tone he'd never heard before. 'Not even Evie.'

His step faltered a little, but he went on, rounding the fountain to the path that led to the yard gate. The bear was heavier than he'd anticipated. Rufina kept pace with him, not saying anything more, and he knew she wouldn't. It seemed that she had let him know that she knew, and that she wasn't afraid of the situation, that she could deal with it. He glanced at her profile, hoping that he was right, that her old-fashioned sensibility would forbid her from discussing it with him.

'Ask Nance for an old kero tin,' he said. 'We'll stick him in there overnight.'

18.

It was encouraging how easy it was to stay hidden. The room she had chosen was tucked away in a dark corner under the little-used west-wing staircase, with an upside-down staircase ceiling and door set almost invisibly into the dark panelling. Evie couldn't guess what the strange little room had been used for, or when. It was sparsely furnished with an ottoman, a tall, narrow chest of drawers and a spindly wooden chair. There was evidence it had once held a heavy piece of furniture, because there were scrapes on the polished floor from when it had been moved away. A pale square on the streaky wall showed where a painting had once hung, and another larger shape cast by something Evie fancied might have been an upright piano.

It seemed that her midnight thefts of food and candles from the kitchen had gone unnoticed. She was very careful in what she took, even though Nan was probably harried enough to not keep a close eye on all the supplies. On Evie's return from the river, nearly two months ago now, she had hurried down a twisting corridor until her hand came to rest on the tarnished handle of a door she didn't recall ever seeing before. She took her ignorance of the room as a good sign. There was a single window, which retained shabby green curtains printed over with ducks on the wing, and gave out onto a small yard once occupied by the gardener – a potting shed, a brick wall studded with hooks which held his clobber – rakes, shovels and spades, and a giant pair of hedge clippers, the blades rusted to the colour of the bricks. A ragged tarpaulin extended from the shed roof, meant to protect the gardener from the rain. He had been an old man, Evie remembered, a pensioner who had worked as hard as any of the stockmen or rabbitos half his age.

There was also a water butt, the contents of which, as far as she could tell, were untainted and pure. On rough shelves were sacks of fertiliser, tins of thallium to poison rats, wooden seedling trays, and a high bench was set beside the shed. She kept the curtains closed but the window onto the yard open, just a crack, so that, should anyone come looking for her, or into the room for any reason at all, she could fling it open, run and hide. One day she'd hefted sacks of old mulch and grass seed to conceal a place under the bench.

The door had no lock, so she'd pushed the ottoman against it, to give her warning if someone should try to come in, though what she would do really, she didn't know. Already she was bigger, less agile, boredom and loneliness combining to make her more clumsy and leaden than she really was. On one of her nocturnal excursions she went out to Rufina's old room in the servants' quarters and collected an armful of books, but reading was a struggle, since she had never really gone to school, only for a few days here and there after the teacher from the Clunes Public School came to find out why the Tyrell children weren't attending. She liked the title of one, *The House of Mirth*. Mirth meant laughter, she was sure, though it wasn't a word you heard often.

She wondered about the lady that wrote the long story, Edith someone, and whether she sat in a room like this, all alone and thinking too much, and in the end had to escape into a world that wasn't real. Did she struggle to come back from it? You could go mad thinking of so many words and then writing them down.

Evie resolved to stay in the real world while she read, and she persisted with her attempts for a full week, but the story eluded her. No sooner did she feel she had caught hold of it, sounding out word after word in a laborious, headachy chain, than it drifted away again. It was like being underwater and struggling to breathe, the only relief afforded by closing the book firmly and going to the window to stare at the triangle of sky left uncovered by the tarpaulin.

Eventually the books formed themselves into a kind of stool underneath the window, where she could sit to watch the crack of light between the drapes play itself across the floor and far wall throughout the day.

The dog she'd tied up on her return, but someone had been letting it off because it had found her and would come into the gardener's yard to snuffle at the window. It seemed to know not to bark and Evie would fling the window up, lean out and cuddle it while it stood on its hind legs, whimpering and licking. She wished it was a magic dog from a tale, a sentient creature able to see that she was half-starved and so run to fetch a loaf of bread and some hard-boiled eggs. She wished it could tell her if anyone wondered where she was, if Ma had come up to the house for the wages, if she'd talked to Nan and raised an alarm. She wished the dog could tell her if Fenchurch had run around searching for her, that he was distraught when he heard that the last place she was seen was the river. Face pressed into the ruff of white and black fur, she breathed in the sweet smell of liberty, of grass and cool winter winds, envying the dog and forgetting for a moment that she was kept prisoner by her own design and could walk free at any moment.

Let them all think she had drowned!

She would stay hidden for as long as she had to. 'Twenty-one rooms and none of them closed off!' Nan liked to say, over and over, though this end of the house as good as. No one went farther than the morning room at the mouth of the corridor, and that was mostly and rarely only Nan to sit and mope with one of Min's shawls pressed to her mouth. It was the room she had led them to after Louisa's fall, as if she thought her employer was still there to comfort and advise her, sad old goose.

This wing had once been Edmond's domain. Evie remembered guests staying for weeks on end, cronies from neighbouring estates and further afield, toff layabouts like himself. They had mucked about in boats, played tennis and croquet, gone hunting dingoes and possums and wallabies and anything else that moved, leaving them where they'd shot them, or in quivering mounds of feather and fur, and talked and laughed in loud voices. Young men and sometimes a handful of women, stuffed to the craw with wealth and freedom.

More than once she and her sister Teresa had snuck away across the snake field and along the riverbank to spy on them drinking and boasting while they lay about in the shade above the jetty. One afternoon they had been spotted, and Evie worked out that she must have been about nine or ten at the time, because Mrs Fenchurch had been there, the only woman among the young men. She and Teresa had watched her accept a chair and a glass of something light green poured from a tall jug; something that Teresa said had grog in it. They'd watched old Min mag and sing along with the best of them, before going up to the house to get out of the heat. While she was alive, Eddie could do no wrong.

On that day Teresa was only thirteen, long skinny legs out the bottom of her outgrown dress, little titties pushing at the too-small bodice. After Min went inside, the young men had called them over to tell them they were the most beautiful girls in the land and that one day they'd return to have the best of them, and they'd all laughed. Evie had not understood what they meant, but Teresa had blushed and taken fright, grabbing Evie's hand and dragging her away, running as fast as they could. They'd gone around the house to look at the fountain, which played in those days, until a long-gone maid had opened a bedroom window and sent them home.

Evie had always remembered those young men. Some of them had been quite handsome, with expensive clothes and good teeth. And she had believed they would come back and one of them would fall in love with her and take her away from here, though he never did, because they never came back after Edmond went away to New Zealand.

While she lay on the ottoman, fighting hunger and enduring bouts of despair, she would think about how Fenchurch didn't like Eddie, how it was no secret he was happy to see the back of him. He didn't like his son gallivanting about, taking more than one Grand Tour of Europe, twice visiting Min's family in America, and making an extravagant voyage to the South Sea Islands. One spring Evie's brother Jimmy was helping with the bobby calves, and he told Evie he'd seen Fenchurch grab Eddie by the collar and give him a shake, that he'd heard him shout at him to do some work, to involve himself in the farm goings-on, to mend his ways and make use of himself.

Eddie never did, just blithely came and went from the house, always with an entourage. On washdays she and Ma would hear him playing the piano and singing, all the latest tunes. Sometimes his mother joined him in a duet, and they were perfect together on the close harmonies, as if they were one creature singing with two mouths, male and female. The mother kept close to him even after she died, sending him away with a fortune from beyond the grave and Nan said was right to, because if he had stayed he and Matthew would have destroyed each other. She and her husband had made their choice, one son each, and Llew would inherit the farm. But now Llew was dead and Evie would rescue the situation with a new son. A better son, properly of the country, since both parents were born here, with the river in their blood.

Edmond had too much American in him and Llew too much of the adventurer. It was fated. The farm would go to her son.

Her son!

Hours would pass in daydreaming, in picturing this son as a handsome young man, striding about the farm and issuing orders, riding a tall shining horse, and Evie meanwhile kept like a queen by Fenchurch, because she'd given him the perfect heir. She dreamed how it would be to hold the little lad in her arms after he was born and how Fenchurch would fall in love with her properly because of him. She would have horses and jewels and cakes and sweets, she would have pretty clothes and a maid and a gold ring on her finger. The fantasies kept her content, especially the ones that involved food – she was so hungry, so hungry – and helped to fight down any rising panic.

Carefully she listened for approaching footsteps amid the sounds of the day, and often through the night, her young body restive from lack of exercise and the new, gnawing hunger that came with the baby. 'They take what they need,' Ma would always say, when there wasn't enough in the pot for her and she gave it to the children, even though they could see she was out at the front of her dress. Ma said in Ireland she had seen babies born from women who were skin and bone, babies that lived.

Don't worry, kiddies, it'll take what it needs.

She tried not to worry now, concentrating instead on every sound, every bird and insect, the lowing of cattle in the home paddock, the chug of Llew's tractor driven by one of the farmhands, the ringing axe from the woodpile, footsteps above her in the nursery. There was another sound that seemed to come from within the room itself, a beat like a pulse. It wasn't there all the time, but sometimes when it was, Evie wondered if it was her own heart beating loud enough for her to hear it. Hand on heart she timed its rhythm with the sound; it would slip in and out of keeping, and the independent beat felt strangely companionable.

One day she went around the walls, pressing her ear to them, convinced a large animal had come into the abandoned part of the house and taken up residence in one of the adjoining rooms. The sound grew louder at the empty chest of drawers, the top drawer of which was locked. Out the window she went to fetch one of the gardener's tools, the hammer he used for building his seedling trays. She tapped and banged, stopping to listen for any approaching footsteps, dreaming of a few coins, a few pounds even. A gold pin. Something of worth, worth keeping. Or a tin of biscuits, still edible. A sweet.

But it steadfastly refused to open.

Some days the confinement of the small room grew unbearable and it was as much as she could do to wait until the night came and with it the chance of momentary escape, of food, of flitting in the shadows. She was like a bat, she thought, all folded up on herself and upside down.

At least it was winter now. The days were shorter, if only by a little, and the household kept to its routine – Matthew giving his orders in the yard, sometimes his voice carrying to her ears if she was sitting at the window, before he rode out on Flora for the day's work. There was the smell of smoke as the kitchen fires were brought to life, the first task of Nan's day. The old mare rose with the sun, just as she had always done. On Mondays when the laundry chimney puffed into the sky, the smoke lifting above the washhouse roof in the lowest corner of the triangle of sky, Evie couldn't help feeling guilty, but for all she knew Nan had another girl to help her, possibly even Bridgie or Tess. There was certainly a younger, snappier set of footsteps around the house, as well as the ones she eventually identified as belonging to the German. Sometimes she confused them with the Sydney nanny, but not often, since the nanny's steps were heavier and most often accompanied by the running, stumbling steps of the little children.

One still, fine night the house took hours to settle and Evie waited impatiently until she could slip away down to the kitchen. It was perhaps eleven, or even midnight, when she heard a man coughing, just on the other side of the potting shed. Fear gripped her so suddenly she felt the bile rise in her throat. Had he seen her candle, which she had only just extinguished? The cough came again, less a cough than a deep cry, and she realised it was a koala come close to the house. She and her brothers and sisters had had a progression of them, one after another, kept tied to the same tree near the house, but they had all died.

Cough, cough. And then a short, sharp scream, as if it was under attack. It was silent then, it seemed for several minutes, before the coughing began again and this time with more despair, a kind of hooting and bellowing, and Evie began to feel sorry for it. Chill in her tight grubby dress she climbed out the window, and went around by the light of the moon until she saw the glint of the chain on the ground. Collared and sad, the bear slumped by the trunk of its tree, easy prey to Llew's dog or any other free to roam. It faced into the darkest part of the garden, a low, grunting noise lifting from its chest.

'Quiet, little fella. Easy now.'

It turned its head in her direction, fluffy white ears catching the moonlight, the gleam of its eyes and inverted-spoon nose. They could move quickly on the ground, when the mood took them, much more themselves slow and high in the branches, their rightful place. Smallish, not fully grown, it had very long black claws, the points of which could match the long scar on one arm that she bore from one of her girlhood captives.

She came as close as she dared, reaching forward to undo the buckle of the collar. A smell of piss rose from its fur, thick and soft around her scrabbling hands, finally managing the rusted pin, and giving the animal a little push to prove its liberty. If the koala was game enough to cross the carriageway, and scamper round behind the creamery, then it could make its way to the first trees of the last forests this side of the river, the big bush that covered the gentle, wide incline all the way up to the memorial. It would be safe there.

At first the koala didn't move, just sat there blinking its big button eyes, face still set in her direction but she felt as though it wasn't really looking at her, but around and behind her, looking at what she wasn't, rather than the tiny piece of the night that actually was Evie Tyrell, flesh and blood, the rescuer. It was unnerving. It made her feel as though she didn't exist.

'Off you go,' she whispered, pushing it again, and the koala did then, tentatively, dropping forward to lope along on its funny bendy legs and she went along behind it, chivvying it towards the trees, still a hundred yards away. When she reached the creamery she glanced back at the house, thinking of what she hoped to find in the kitchen – cold meat in the safe, a heel of bread, a carrot, a piece of cheese. Her stomach rumbled.

A plate set specially by Nan. A pear. A jar of jam. One night soon she'd find Nan waiting up for her in the kitchen, sitting in the dark, an ambush.

From the south side, Jarulan's windows were black, except for one lamp still burning on the second landing, the tall stained-glass window set in the arched frame. There was a bird in the pattern she'd never noticed before, a bird flying among the Fenchurch crest – the rifle, an axe, a bull's head, a tree, a saddle, a gold nugget and pick, all of it out of proportion. The bull's head was smaller than the nugget. Was it a bird, or a crack in the glass? Evie peered – it was a bird, a black eagle, with a stick in its beak. Or a candle? At one end of the stick a flame burned.

There was a change in the light behind the red cedar, a half form of a young woman moving in the clear part beside it, looking out into the night. The blue dress was gone and replaced with a fashionable skirt and white puff-sleeved blouse, her hair arranged more softly on top of her head, instead of her usual tight prissy knot. Had Rufina seen her? She was looking above the shadowy trees, her head level – perhaps even tipped back. She can't have seen her. Evie stepped quickly into the shadows, among the trees, and the next time she looked up at the window the light had been extinguished and it seemed as though the figure was looking directly at her. There was no way she could run back to her hiding place now, Rufina would see her. Evie froze, thought desperately of what she should do and remembered how, in the face of the enemy, a mother wombat will throw her joey from her pouch and act as a decoy in order to save the infant's life.

Rufina hadn't moved. Her gaze had shifted elsewhere, over to Evie's left somewhere, she was sure of it. Or had it?

Once, out hunting with her brothers, Jimmy had fired his airgun at a wombat's bony arse and the old fat sow had grunted and growled as she'd run, throwing out her baby near enough for Evie to see it, and so take it home for a pet. It was a hairy-nosed wombat, she remembered. She'd let it go after a few days.

She would lead Rufina away from her hiding place so that she could return safely to it later. Hands cupped under her swelling belly, Evie ran towards the dense bush below the memorial, round behind the creamery and the row of kennels. A mistake. Llew's dog started – Evie recognised the bark – and the others followed. On the other side of the fence there was a lamp still alight in the old rabbito's hut, set apart from the rest of the accommodation and closest to her route. Surely even if the old man came outside it was too dark for him to see her.

She veered away, taking the more open, dangerous path down the slope towards the river. There were stones here, sharp in the dirt, which hurt her feet. Had she pulled the window closed after her? Had she left them any clues?

If Rufina was running to Matthew to tell him what she'd seen – if she had seen anything – would he come after her? He might even saddle up Flora and let the dogs off to hunt her down. Her lungs burned, her thin, weak legs felt wobbly, her rounding stomach a band of pain that extended into her kidneys and lower back. The further she climbed the hill, the more dense the bush, the louder with insects and nightbirds, the more paralysing her rising terror of snakes, until she could go no further. She was above the river; she could hear it rushing through the trees. There was an open space at the top of the low cliff, enough moonlight to see anything shifting in the bush, and she found a place she could hunch – heaving for breath, dizzy and sick – and wait. She would wait a few hours and then set off towards the room before dawn. No one would see her.

Her breath steadied and she felt the night wrap her round. An open patch of sky showed a flock of tiny birds – no, they were bats, catching moths, moonlit specks lifting like ash from a fire. Night insects buzzed and sawed, a roosting bird shifted somewhere far above her head. A soft, hazy moon slung low above the western hills, and the rhythmic call of an owl came from nearer the river, on and on, like a heartbeat.

A pulse, a heartbeat. She half wanted them to come after her because then there would be a chance of food. She was so hungry she sucked her fingers. An hour or two, here on this flat rock where she could keep watch for snakes or insects crawling towards her, where a patch of moonlight shone, that's all she could bear. An hour or two before she had to eat something. What if an Aborigine came along, one of the few left in the district, and found her food right here under her nose? Food that was here all the time. She lifted a stone, put it down again, yanked a paspalum stem and stuck it in the corner of her mouth, dreamed of stew and potatoes.

19.

No food had been taken. The things Nan had left before she took herself to bed, the plate of cold beef in the meat safe with the jar of relish she'd put near, were untouched. She suspected Evie had not been near the kitchen, which surprised her; the night had been windy, wild and banging, the perfect weather for thieves. A dropped cup, the clatter of a knife, a too-urgent spoon – all would have been concealed by the clamour and howl of the spring winds blowing in from the coast, great cool gusts bringing the smell of the sea from twenty miles away. One night soon she would wait up to lay eyes on her.

No one had seen Evie for weeks, not since the night she set the koala bear free and run away into the bush, and that was only Rufina. Fenchurch had decided not to believe it – Rufina was mistaken, it would have been one of the younger Tyrells come to claim the animal they had caught and wanted for their own. They could have it. Stupid, smelly animals, he said.

Had she been too obvious in her provisions, Nance worried. Surely Evie would expect that she would notice the disappearances and could tell Matthew. It had been going on for so long now that it felt almost normal to come soon after dawn each day into the empty kitchen and look for evidence before she did anything else. The first few nights she'd prepared the plate it had been ignored, with the thief continuing as she had since early in the winter, raiding the dry stores, the bread bin, and God help the poor deluded girl, the pig bucket, where she might find a cooked potato, or a bone from Matthew's plate with meat still clinging to it, or a half-eaten serving of rice pudding. Lately there would have been slim pickings – Fenchurch seemed to have his appetite returned, which may or may not have been encouraged by the German, who took most of her meals with him now, leaving Nan to collect Louisa's tray before she cleared the plates from the dining room.

Should she cook extra portions for Evie? Proper meals? The plates she left for her were usually scraped bare. By this time, mid-September, Nance was convinced it *was* Evie, not midnight raids by the Sydney nanny, who grew daily more creamy and plump. Or one of the younger hands stealing over from the accommodation, a lad still growing, seized by hunger pains in the small hours of the morning and knowing better than to steal from old Arthur, the stockmen's cook, who was a martinet and wouldn't have them helping themselves.

Today, Nance resolved, she would find her. The hideaway must be near the house – possibly even *in* the house. She knew every nook and cranny. She would find her.

Breakfast was prepared for the dining room and stacked on the trolley, Fenchurch never having returned to his kitchen habits since his daughters' visit, and breakfasts for the nursery and for Miss Louisa were laid out on two trays. Nance got the new Tyrell girl to carry up the trays, one by one. It was the sister who had fallen into the fire when she was a child, the poor unfortunate with the badly scarred face. Bridget.

'Where's the other one?' Louisa had asked on Bridgie's first day. Bridgie had shrugged her narrow shoulders and looked to Nance, since she didn't know and neither did anyone else. Louisa had sent Evie's sister from the room and informed Nance that she preferred the crazy one, that looking at the new face upset her, with its ridges and puckers and strange croaking voice from the fleshless slit of a mouth.

'She's the girl we've got now,' Nance had replied, thinking that it was high time that Louisa got out of bed, that too much time had gone by without a muscle in her body working, other than the tongue, and that indolence wouldn't encourage an easy time of it later.

Setting out now with the creaking trolley, Nance went down the hall towards the dining room. The German preferred a more elaborate early breakfast than Fenchurch would ever have – coffee, fresh fruit, finely sliced ham – and had requested more than once fresh rolls. Rolls!

I ask you!

When she shunted open the door with the trolley, she surprised them, their hands clasped on the table between their plates, though surely they must have heard her approach, the racket the little wheels made on the thin carpet of the hall. She parked the trolley beside Rufina and turned to leave the room – but Fenchurch stood to detain her.

'Nan? Wait a moment.'

She met his eye, thinking of her lost Min and how she must be spinning in her grave. First Evie and now this one, and from him who never before displayed this kind of behaviour, though it was common enough. Hadn't his own father taken his pick from the Irish and the Blacks, some even younger than these two? Rufina was the older, perhaps nineteen or twenty – Evie was still a child.

'Not a word about this to anyone, Nan?' Fenchurch was saying.

'About what?' She knew she sounded abrupt.

The German was blushing, like blood spilling on white stone. Yes, Nance thought, staring at her, doesn't she remind me of Min's statues the day they were lifted from their crates, frightening, strange.

'Rufina and I are getting married in November. We will tell Louisa this morning, and write to Jean.'

And him in New Zealand, thought Nance automatically but didn't say. The news hadn't sunk in. 'Married?'

Fenchurch nodded and took his seat, Rufina never taking her eyes from him. Her shining, loving eyes. Or was she only pretending?

He had no idea what he was doing. Why would he want another wife and one so young, and a German? She would be mistress of the house. Everything would change. A seismic wave roared across the sinking plain of Nance's years of service and drudge, reared over her head and froze there. The horrifying pause before it broke. And break it would.

Oh, Min.

'You can go now, Nan,' Fenchurch said gently, because she was staring at them. Man and wife. A German younger than his daughters. The enemy. A murderess.

She went out of the room and found her feet leading her up the stairs to the second floor and down the corridor, past Louisa's door. A glimpse of the swollen patient showed her spooning up porridge, a book wedged open under the edge of her plate. Nan hurried on towards the steep belvedere staircase and began to climb – the aching knees, the shortness of breath – but find Evie she would. She would think only of that, and not the lovebirds downstairs, who made her stomach churn; she could throw up it was so sickening, but her stomach was empty, there being no time yet for her own breakfast.

Where could the girl be? Not here, of course, since it was a favourite roost of Fenchurch's, less so in the last few weeks. And it was empty of furniture but for Matthew's chair, so there was nowhere to hide.

But oh wasn't the floor in need of a sweep, the panes a wipe with vinegar, the rolling dust bunnies set free to fly from the windows? It was too much to bear looking at. Too much to keep.

From the eastern windows she looked out towards the Tyrells' run, where two thin black-haired sons were bent over in the weedy back field, one of them pulling the plough in lieu of the horse, since their old horse had died and there was no money to buy another one. When Min was on the Bangalow church welfare committee the Tyrells were often recipients of some little available charity, and no good it did them. At least there would be no more babies now that the old man had turned up his toes – until the oldest boys brought their own wives home for a baby a year. The land couldn't be divided up any more than it already was. It was how the Proddies held onto their land, leaving it to only one son – more greed and inequity, second nature to them.

Evie was, of course, pregnant with Fenchurch's child. It was obvious early on, when the morning sickness took hold and the girl was more gormless and dreamy than ever. After the fourth morning in a row, a knowing look had passed between Nance and the Sydney nanny across the breakfast table, when Evie's porridge was abandoned, the girl suddenly pale and heaving and running for the back door.

Then she had gone to earth, like an animal. Where would she have gone? If Nance were Evie, where would she choose to hide, dark and warm and out of the weather?

Already, over the past few weeks, Nance had gone out to check some of the outbuildings, the abandoned creamery, the barn, the quarters. The stockmen's cook hadn't seen her, neither had the rabbito. Ma Tyrell had been up to the house three times since the vanishing – once for the wages, once to bring the burnt girl, Bridgie, and once to see if there was any news of her other daughter, since she'd had none herself. Like Nance, she didn't believe the story of the river taking her – they agreed that the wicked, spirited girl burned too brightly to have any notion of doing herself in. She wasn't the type. They agreed also that she wouldn't have slipped and fallen in by accident, since the girl had grown up on the river and was as sure-footed on its banks as a goat. By the time Ma left, she had a gallon of tea and half a dozen scones inside her, weighing down the swayback horse on what was to be its last day on earth, a slow amble across the fields.

Nance began a traverse of the length of the room, taking her time at each window, each frame a bird's eye view – sublime, high, green and blue, made you want to sing. No wonder all the children had loved it up here, a place for soaring spirits and high jinks and make-believe. At the northern side was the view over the top of the fountain, which played again now since Fenchurch fixed it. From this height it looked like a group of visitors caught in heavy rain on their approach to the house, with the stone steps leading down beyond them into the overgrown lush bush, and then the river, silver under the high grey sky.

At the far end of the room was Matthew's wing chair, with its sea chest for a table, whisky glass and ashtray. The window before it gave a perfect distant aspect of the memorial on the near west horizon, the groves of candlenut trees and gums and she-oaks on either side of it, and in the northwest the bush running down the slope towards the house, a glint from the bend in the river.

Once when Nan had come up to the belvedere to clean and dust, to collect away the smeary glass and empty the ashtray, she hadn't been aware that Fenchurch was sitting there, gazing out. It had given her a fright, coming upon him motionless in his chair, silent as stone, his pipe grown cold.

The chair was again occupied. There was a long exhalation, a sigh, the shadowy crown of a dark head. A familiar, thin white hand came to lie on the armrest.

'Evie?'

There was no answer and perhaps that was because Evie was not the first name to come to her mind, but another, an impossibility. Heart in her mouth, she hurried the rest of the distance to the chair – it was empty. Of course it was empty, the cushion dented for Fenchurch's head, the translucent, chalky print of his lips on the glass.

She gazed for a moment at the view of the monument, the glinting red jewel in its crown, the woven wrought iron of the cupola, but it offered no comfort. She could only remind herself that she had never been one for wild imaginings, which had been Min's one failing, her sickness. Nance had never been persuaded of any of her feys and stories, which disappointed and enraged Min. There was always a stage of Min's recovery when she had regarded Nan as a travelling companion who had abandoned her before the journey's end. Who had betrayed her.

Really? You really won't come with me?

The whiff of French perfume. A soft hand in the small of her back.

She was wasting time – to hell with the clearing away and the breakfast dishes! Down the belvedere stairs she went and along the corridor, opening every door on the wing and tip-toeing past Louisa's, glancing in to see her asleep now in the high soft bed, her breakfast digesting, book cast aside.

The door immediately opposite led to the room they had kept Min safe in when the furies took her. There was nothing in there to damage herself on, no high point to invite a hanging, and the window nailed shut, barred over.

Nance had not been in there for six years, not once, and she remembered, as she turned the key in the lock, that she had once confided that piece of information to Evie before she sent the girl up to give it a sweep out. Is this where she was hiding? But surely she wouldn't choose this room, since it was a long way from the kitchen and the outside dunny, and Rufina was up and down to Louisa and might hear something and surprise her. Evie would have chosen a place with an escape route.

The door was locked, rather than unlocked – someone had been here since Evie, then. She turned the key again and went in. There was the tattered chair and the brown blind over the window, showing twinkles of daylight where the fabric had perished. There were the streaked walls, the thin mattress on the floor. And here was the face pressed close to hers, distorted with laughter and now with tears. The arms locked so tight Nance could hardly breathe, the close smell, the sweet perfume overwhelmed through long, stinking hours waiting in the hot airless room, while the poor love ranted and raved, threatened suicide, made wild schemes to leave Jarulan for a life worth living in Paris, Rome, New York. Even Sydney! A life worth living, Nan!

It was those fancies more than any other that drove Fenchurch into bringing her here, into having the dulling medicine administered in spoonfuls from the brown bottle, chlorodine and ether, into tying her to the chair. Once she'd got as far as Lismore before he caught up with her, obliging Eddie into taking her down in his boyhood sailboat and going the rest of the way by road. Fenchurch brought her back with enormous difficulty, after a violent scene at the wharf that kept tongues wagging for months.

And it wasn't as if she hadn't had long months – years sometimes – with none of those episodes puncturing her usual calm and kindness. And it wasn't as if Fenchurch kept her prisoner at any other time. Once a year she would go alone to Sydney to visit Louisa, to Queensland to Jean, and each time Nance would pray that the sickness didn't come upon her while she was on ship or train, away from those who would care for her.

She sank down on the battered chair for a minute. Just for a minute, then she'd go on. If Min was here, the real, true Min, the loving heart, she would want Evie cared for. Years ago there was another girl, one of the milkers, who'd got into trouble with a farmhand who took off the moment the girl's condition was known. Min had given her money to get away after him, to try her luck. The milker had been an older girl, older than Evie, of a more pragmatic nature and may have prospered from Min's generosity, who knew?

Evie must not on any account be sent away.

There was a softening in the room then, a change in the light, Min smiling, because Nance had finally found the right solution.

Locking the door after her, she went down the corridor to the top landing, crossing the wide carpet to the door that led to the nursery wing. There was scarcely any point searching those rooms, since they were so fully occupied by the Sydney nanny and children. The door stood open – and here was the nanny herself herding Lorna and Gordon ahead of her, sunbonnets tied firmly under their chins. Under Gordon's arm was a red toy tractor with yellow wheels, and the driver was a tiny wooden koala bear made perfectly to scale. Proprietarily as they passed, Lorna reached to stroke the walnut-sized head and looked up at Nance with a proud little smile.

'Out we go!' said the nanny to the children. 'Before it gets too hot!' She had a little smear of cream and sugar crystals at the corner of her whiskery mouth. 'Down to the garden!'

And the children scooted off at her bidding, across the landing and down the stairs, Lorna having now plucked the koala free to wave him above her head. Gordon raced ahead, whooping, the tractor riding the banister beside him, the wheels perfectly fitting the carved grooves all the way down to the bottom. The back door banged and they were gone. Gordon was just nearly three years old and the Sydney nanny hadn't shifted.

'It's all right,' she said. 'They know not to go further than the fountain – can't get enough of it now.'

The fountain. That had been a carry-on the afternoon Fenchurch and Rufina spent scrubbing the stone figures. The German had come to ask for scrubbing brushes and buckets, sugar soap and a blunt knife, and then Fenchurch had got into the act as well, both of them splattered and filthy by the end of it. Their laughter had rung out, there were splashings and unnerving shrieks, and later Rufina's voice droning on, not quite audible from the front parlour, where Nan had been dusting. She had been explaining something about the figures, whom they were supposed to represent. At the curtains, drawn to protect the furniture from the sun, Nan had peeked through and seen how they stood easily together, with his arm draped over her shoulders. Then the children came clamouring down the stairs having seen them from an upstairs window. One of them was shouting gleefully, 'Grandpa's playing with 'Fina in the fountain!'

'He got the thing going from the dam,' said the Sydney nanny. 'Waste of water if you ask me, even if it does go round and round.'

She was off a farm west of Mudgee, and you wouldn't do it there. A fountain!

'He did it for the German. Are they courting?'

Courting! Nance's heart skipped a beat, which brought on a rush of heat and a wave of nausea, which had been happening more and more since … Since when? Since around the time that Evie had come to live at Jarulan and upset the natural balance.

Sydney Nanny, for all her airs, was a dull lump of clay with squinty brown eyes and freckles, a big bosom and wide bottom. Solid. Presbyterian. If he'd had to take his pick from the staff then he might have been better to choose her, instead of dallying with one and settling for another.

'The children. They're getting away from you.' Nance gestured towards the stairs.

The nanny departed and Nance went on to collect cups and plates from the nursery where everything was in disarray – clothes, books and toys. The nanny did not tidy; she did not think it part of her duties. Nance made a few piles of things, though it made no difference, then picked up the carelessly stacked tray and went down the corridor, jangling. At the top of the stairs she stopped to rearrange the sliding china, balancing the tray on the railing.

Someone was standing at the foot of the belvedere stairs, looking down the long extent of the east wing. A dark-haired woman in white – Evie, in her nightgown? – but by the time Nan had arrested the sliding china and looked properly, the figure had vanished. The sun was slanting in from one of the high belvedere windows, angling down the open stairwell to light up a cupboard set almost invisibly into the dark panelling.

Tray set on the floor with a clatter – oh that uncomfortable bend! – Nan flew as quickly as her legs would carry her to the end of the corridor and yanked the cupboard open.

It was empty. Or at first glance it was. And smaller than she remembered. It could not possibly have concealed Evie, or if so, at great discomfort. A five-year-old child would be cramped. Tucked against one side there was a rolled-up length of cartridge paper: on investigation a yellowed map of the night sky. That's right – old man Fenchurch had been an amateur astronomer, as much as his son was taxidermist, and the cupboard was once used to store his telescopes and charts, to keep them away from dust and insects.

Nan's knees felt weak, the joints gone stewy; she perched on the stairs, the cupboard open beside her.

In the farthest corner, just out of reach, was a shimmering gleam of cream silk, an oblong fuzzed with blue-grey mildew. A beetle scuttered dry-legged as she reached in, angling her body for the stretch; she grasped it and pulled it out. A silk chemise, finely worked, with pintucks and Belgian lace, and very old, thought Nan, a relic of the first Mrs Fenchurch and used to dust the stargazing equipment. Or perhaps was intended for that and never used. Despite the mildew, Nan could tell that the chemise had been carefully laundered and folded, and attempts had been made to shift a mud stain that resembled the imprint of shoe or boot.

She slipped it into her apron pocket; she'd give it a go, try to shift the mould. It would fit Evie, after the baby came. She would be showing by now.

'I will find you, missy. You know that.' She'd said it aloud, her voice startling in the still, quiet air, as alarming almost as the vision had been. Ladies in white nightgowns! When Min was sick it was musicians. She saw them everywhere, and sometimes surrounded by people with Saint Vitus Dance, all wildly convulsing to a drumbeat.

Can't you see them, Nan?

Hauling herself to her feet, she clunked down the belvedere steps and along the corridor to the landing, where she collected the tray and went downstairs, resolutely not thinking of the vision. Musicians. She wouldn't go straight to the kitchen. On the chiffonier outside the morning room she deposited the tray and turned back towards Eddie's wing.

Eddie's wing. She still thought of the ground floor west wing as that. It was where he had taken up a suite of rooms when he came home from boarding school so that the two of them could sit in private and enjoy one another's company. Not only did they like to sing and play the piano, they were both yarn spinners of the first water, never letting the truth get in the way of a good story, competing with one another for the most arresting metaphor, the least expected and most surprising ending. Nance had sat with them many an evening, mending or sewing, as a willing captive audience. If the muse wasn't with either of them, then one would read aloud from a favourite book. Eddie had wanted to be a writer, and no wonder, with a mother like Min who indulged all his fantasies. Perhaps, right now in New Zealand he was bent over a growing pile of papers that would one day become a book to be read all over the world.

Imagine that, Min!

The door to Eddie's wing stood ajar and, beyond, all was in deep gloom, every door onto the corridor firmly closed. Dimly, at the far end, was a wide room with ceiling-to-floor windows heavily curtained. In Eddie's day they had always stood open. Sofas and ottomans were arranged as they were then, with low tables. There was the sprung dance floor, surrounded by a forest of long dead, spider-webbed parlour palms, inhabited by a smaller version of Venus than the one that stood outside. Or was it Aphrodite? Nan had no idea. The figure was bare-breasted and blind-eyed, dusty hair piled on top of her head in stone curls that looked like the open ends of pastry horns. It looked ridiculous, though not as much as the other figure, a round rolling man, fat bellied and laughing, a bunch of grapes carved from the stone to cover his private parts. The God of Wine. Bacchus. Another gift from Min.

It had never come easily to Nance to criticise her beloved, but could it be that she had wanted Eddie to turn out bad? One indulgence after another, and most of them foolish. The day the boy left he had streamed tears of farewell to his mother and dread of his furious father, driving wet-faced away in a newly purchased Buick, the first in the district. Nance's heart ached. How would it be to see him again? They said New Zealand was not that far away, though it seemed so to Nance, who had never been as far as Sydney to the south or Brisbane to the north. If life from now on really was going to be at Rufina's beck and call, then perhaps she should go and seek Eddie out. Across an ocean wider than the thick rug, more sparkling than this smeary dance floor, which had a piano in one corner and room for a band. Coils of dust hung in plumes from the heavy red curtains, pillows of it filled Aphrodite's upturned breasts.

Sneezing, Nance groped for the rope pull and opened them. There was a skittering of bugs and blind flying moths, a tearing of spider webs and rotten cloth far above her head.

Five years since the room had been lit up, and five years in this climate was a long time. The room had got away on her. It should have been cleared out, closed up. A white foamy fungus attacked a velvet settee; heavy rain had sneaked through a leadlight high up, streaking the wall and floor with green. Aphrodite's pastry horns hoarded a colony of beetles, Bacchus was patched with mildew.

'Evie?' tried Nance, then louder, 'E-vie?'

The upright piano was wonky, one leg rotten and partially collapsed, the lid standing open. She let a finger rest on one of the laden, swollen yellow keys and a soft note sounded deep in the box; a gecko ran out from a hole in the side.

Eddie had wanted a grand piano; it was one of the few things Min had denied him. At sixteen, on his return from school, he had brought a man from Brisbane to teach him how to play jazz. The man was Italian, a dandy, a little older than Nance. She had caught him looking at her with something not far off pity – but it hadn't stopped him trying to lure her into his small sloping-roofed room under the western-wing stairs, where he would lie on the ottoman playing his piano accordion. Against her better judgement Nance had gone there once to find the Italian less interested in her than in trading jovial insults with the old gardener through the open window.

What a long time ago that was now. Almost ten years. The Italian had asked her, 'And where are you from, Nancy?' and he had seemed so exotic and handsome she could not bear to answer, 'Bangalow.' She had said nothing at all, and so he had kissed her for her innocence – at thirty-six! – and tried to undo her stays, but she had stopped him. It had been a very hot day, she remembered, perhaps ninety degrees and he had been perspiring heavily, his sweat slicking her arms and the front of her dress. When he saw her revulsion – and she was repulsed by it – he had done a strange thing.

'You see here, Nancy!' – and he'd mimed taking his heart from his chest, before unlocking the top drawer of a Karri tallboy and dropping the heart inside. 'There it will stay until you decide to love me!' and he had swallowed the little key. Nan had wondered what it could do to his insides. It was only a tiny key, but pointy enough to puncture his guts.

He seemed to suffer no ill effects. Soon after, he and Eddie had had a drunken row and the Italian departed for who knew where, leaving his heart locked in the drawer.

Eddie's wing was past saving. The German might have ideas of what to do. A small hope flared that the German might be modern enough to want to see the whole house demolished and a new one put in its place, with fewer rooms, easier to clean. Brick or wood, single storey. Nan was not sentimental. In fact, she almost hated Jarulan, despite having spent most of her life here. Most mornings she woke desolate to the work ahead. She left the party room, closing the door firmly after her.

The door to the Italian's room under the stairs was locked, or so it seemed at first, until Nan bent her eye to the handle to see the door had no lock at all, so she pushed again, harder, and this time there was the squeak and scrape of a piece of furniture laid across the other side, and with it the sound of a window being thrown up, of a panicked scrabble and then a cry of pain as if the escapee had injured herself.

20.

Evie wanted to get out, to run away from the thudding drawer, away from the footsteps real or imagined that passed up and down the stairs above her head and round about, the tuneless whistling from the corridor outside that had started up after her return from the bush, and now she would run away from Nan who was inside the room, her arms closing around her chest and half-lifting, half-dragging her back to the ottoman, skewed now across the floor with the door open behind it.

'Skin and bone, skin and bone,' Nan was saying, and Evie saw that the old girl's eyes had filled with tears, that Nan was sympathetic to her predicament, that everything would be all right.

'What did you think you were doing?' she asked. Evie drew breath to tell her the piece of lore learned from her mother, 'Babies take what they need,' but Nan was telling her to hush, stroking her forehead and asking if she was well enough to walk down to the kitchen where there would be some left-over breakfast waiting, or if not, she would cook some just for her and that she needn't worry, that Fenchurch wouldn't send her away because his attention was taken now by the German, his future wife. After the long months of waiting, the solitary incubation of his child, Evie felt nothing at this news. She'd known the night

"

she set the koala free and looked up to see Rufina framed like the Holy Virgin with the light behind her. The new clothes and softened hair spoke of the attention of a man, who could only have been Fenchurch. Who else was there?

Tears threatened but they were not for lost love or any bally claptrap like that. They were for the tenderness shown by Nan, for the melting away of the deadening loneliness that had frozen her heart solid. She wanted to ask Nan, 'Will the baby be all right since I have no love left in me?' but how could Nan know the answer to that, and besides, was it even true? Nan was examining her skinny arms and legs, exclaiming softly and shaking her head, then asking about the baby and whether Evie had felt it move.

'Of course I have. He kicks all the time,' replied Evie, and would have gone on to describe how she could see him, a strong young man on horseback, the dead spit of Fenchurch for the structure of his face and build, with none of the Irish taint. Master of Jarulan, gentleman farmer.

'Can you see him too, Nan?' she wanted to ask. 'All this will be his.' But Nan was urging her to stand and to lean on her and go quietly down the long echoing corridors to the kitchen.

'I'll look after you, dear,' the old girl was saying, and Evie knew it was true, that she could trust her. 'We'll keep you secret till it comes.'

'Not even Ma,' Evie said. 'No one.'

She sat at the table and Nan made her eggs and bacon, a cup of tea, and sliced up an apple. The German and Fenchurch had planned to go out riding, she told her, and Nanny had taken the children down to the river.

'Hurry up now, Evie. Eat up and back to your room. I'll be down to see you later.'

The food made her sleepy and she dreamed all afternoon of Fenchurch, of herself and Fenchurch rubbing stirrups, the two of them out riding over the rolling green hills. She felt the sun on her skin and the shift of muscles of the horse beneath her, smelt the crushed grass underfoot and the haze of oil lifting from the baking eucalypts. She could feel her belly resting on the tops of her legs and her heart swelling with happiness. Most of all she was aware of the great, abiding love from the man who rode beside her, the man she had won back from the German.

21.

Armful of clean towels from the linen press on the landing, Rufina began to retrace her footsteps towards the corridor that led inexorably to Louisa's childbed. She would not hurry. She would take her time, have a break.

'God in heaven, if I had wanted to be a nurse or midwife then I would have trained for it. A girl from Woldingham School less able than I went on to train as a doctor!'

She said it aloud, like a character in a play, like an *aside*. It was because she was lying to herself, a solitary lie speaking to the crowded truth. There had never been enough time to fully consider a career after that terrible day some weeks after the funeral when her mother had come to fetch her from her boarding school in England. Not yet realising the extent of their penury, Mutti had brought their private train carriage, leaving it in Paris for the return trip. Together they'd cried all the way home, dampening one another's shoulders, tears gathering and falling from the edge of her mother's veil to spot her black mourning. It was perhaps the only time Rufina cried purely for her father and not for herself and her uncertain future.

The Berlin house was sold, together with their goods and chattels, and still there were debts, more and more, bleeding dry the small reserve. Then, within a month, her mother conceived of a plan to live quietly and frugally with her sister. Rufina would rather have been buried alive. That's why Frau Schneider's offer of employment was a gift from heaven, or so her mother termed it.

And it certainly was, even though once or twice since they had come to Australia Frau Schneider had seen fit to remind her that she was a servant, not a daughter, and to respond more quickly to commands. The memory of the scoldings made Rufina flush with fury and she was glad no one was there to see it. She knew how the colour rose in her face, and how often, for the widest variety of reasons. Any intense feeling would draw it up, a prickling in her flesh and sudden heat – and she would be blushing again. Frau Schneider used to tease her for the violence of it. She called her *Feuerlilie, Laterne Gesicht.*

Orange Lily. Lantern face. She turned into the hot, stifling bedroom, her face burning at the memory.

If fate had kept her with the Schneiders, this horrifying situation would never have arisen. That employer, so her mother had confided in her, was unable to bear children. This one certainly could and was in the very act of doing so, frightening and hideous.

Nance was with Louisa, as she had been since yesterday. Even though this was Louisa's fourth confinement, she seemed to suffer as though she had never before endured it, falling asleep between pains and waking with shock and terror to each fresh spasm. Her eyes would fly wide open, those dark blue eyes, which were not like Matthew's, but those Rufina had taken the time to study in the portrait on the dining-room wall downstairs. Deep blue, they flashed above the glittering gown and picked up points of green light from an emerald tiara. A tiara! Ludicrous! Americans gave themselves such airs. The eyes were a sparkling match to the New York dress and sumptuous surrounding room, the soft dark winter light with snow piling on the sill visible between velvet curtains.

It was painted just before the first Mrs Fenchurch was married, but the subject could have been Louisa, so closely did she resemble her mother, the Irish heritage prime. Fine bones, fair skin, the hair sleek and black, though this hair not prettily dressed but thrashing on the sweaty pillow.

Bog Irish, an Australian friend of the Schneiders had described Louisa before the war, and Frau Schneider had replied that she did believe the mother was American. Such an expression. Surely it was Evie that was bog Irish if ever anyone was, with her angry white face and greedy red lips. You could see it also, still, in the poor burnt sister that had replaced her in the house, sent down an hour ago to boil water on the stove despite Ma Tyrell's plea not to give her tasks with stove or copper or boiler. It had been Evie's job, but she would be miles away, hunting down the man that had put her in pup.

Gluck! Good luck to her.

Once or twice Rufina had thought to tell Matthew about it, to describe the night she heard the girl mating, and perhaps she would one night after they were married. After they'd done it themselves, which she supposed they would.

Soon.

Or was he too old? So far he had only kissed her, and last night his warm, dry-mottled hands had risen to lie alongside her corseted breasts but no farther. A deep disarming shiver had run through her and did again now, making her blush furiously and turn away to sort a clean nightgown for Louisa. Soon she would find out what it would be like to know him completely. Head bowed at the drawer she relived the moment of the kiss, remembering how she had kissed him urgently, with no thought to what she was doing, until he gently pushed her away; he could wait until their wedding night, even if she would not.

She loved him. How could she not? Look at what he offered her! Already she had a horse of her own – the lovely wild boy once Llewellyn's – three new complete outfits and a new hat, and some German novels coming in a case from a bookshop in Adelaide. And she found herself so at peace in his company, saw how he would sit and admire her beauty, how he was curious about her opinions, the world she came from. Sometimes his questions had a sad, dutiful air to them, as if he was making up for some past omission or crime. Or was it only that he wished that he had seen more of the world before he found himself as he was now, bound to the farm, to this extraordinary primeval place, in his fifties?

They would share this world now. She would learn all there was to know about it, his world, since she found herself loving it, riding out with him during the day on Boss, talking long and leisurely in the evenings, bidding a chaste goodnight. She loved seeing the gentle wallabies come around in the early morning and at dusk, learning about the birds, the catbird that had cried on the first morning here, the whip bird that sounded just like his name, the bower bird with its passion for blue – Matthew had told her that one had stolen Min's sapphire ring! When the first koala was set free, Rufina's heart had broken in two – but mended, even toughened, since two more captives had died and a third responded to more attentive care. She loved the ugly red lizard-headed brush turkeys, how the male built and cared for a mound of leaves for his family to live in.

And she would learn everything she could from Matthew about the management of the farm, the less interesting side of it, because who knew how his health really was, and how long he would live? This sort of climate was not good for white men; they were not made for it. That was why they had brought the Kanakas in up north, because they didn't mind the heat and damp. She would demand more than he did of the Aborigines. On the few occasions she had sighted some they didn't appear to be doing much, the small number that were left.

Where had they all gone? she asked Matthew. He hadn't answered her, not really. 'You don't want to know about that.' But she did. She wanted to know about everything. As soon as the war was over she would suggest a trip to Europe to see her mother and she would tell her all about the farm. As soon as the war was over.

Louisa was hooting and panting again, and Nance was trying to calm her, so Rufina returned to the bedside, the nightgown over her arm. In the portrait, the small painted hands were frozen in the caress of a lap dog. These fleshly ones scrabbled animatedly at the air, one of them tangling with the mosquito net and inadvertently pulling it across Nance's face. Exactly the same, with narrow tapered nails that grew naturally to a point. Sheeted invisible legs, possibly also belonging to Matthew's dead wife, thrashed about in the bed. If she resembled her mother, then perhaps he had given her his nature – that will to be obeyed. Rufina had seen him with the men, heard him speak sharply to everyone but her. Perhaps childbirth was easier if you were weak willed, if you just gave yourself up to it.

Murmuring and hushing, Nance wiped Louisa's dripping brow.

'Where's the doctor? Where's the bloody doctor, you stupid old bitch?'

It was the hundredth time she'd said it, the abuse unchanging, no longer shocking. Nance and Rufina had given up telling her that the German had been sent away and a new one had not come.

'You will be all right,' said Nance again, and Rufina believed her, even if Louisa didn't. She was screaming again, on and on, so loudly that it seemed impossible that Matthew could not hear from where he'd taken refuge in the empty library.

'I was there to see all of you arrive,' Nance said again, as she'd said several times in Rufina's hearing. 'Stop fighting it. Let the baby come.'

Rearing up in the bed, Louisa pushed her red, wet face close to Nance's. 'Do you think I'm stopping it? Do you think I have any bloody control? Bitch!' She waved a clenched fist at Nance.

Please God, never let me fall pregnant. The silent prayer was as fervent as any Rufina had ever made. Why would any woman go through with this – or, if it happened once accidentally, why would she ever let it happen again? What an alarming notion it was: every person walking this Earth, every single last one of them since the beginning of time, only did so because a woman had suffered just like this. Because of her *travail*. Horrendous. So much pain in the world. Too much. And for what? So we can kill them scarcely grown in wars, or work them half to death in factories, or half starve them on farms and plantations.

Nance had taken hold of the savage fist and was patting it, unfolding it, telling Louisa that she had to check now to see if the baby was coming, and Louisa was shaking her head, embarrassed suddenly. A movement at the door and Bridgie appeared with a steaming basin of water, which she placed beside the towels on the dresser.

Then the three of them stood around the bed, watching Louisa writhe as another pain took hold, and she cried out again, but with a different tone and pitch than she'd had during the eleven hours already passed. Before she had a chance to recover, at least enough to be able to push her away, Nance had flicked the covers back. She took hold of Louisa's knees, lifting them firmly, so that the soles of her feet skimmed along the damp, rumpled bottom sheet, and peered between the thighs. Moaning, Louisa threw a humiliated arm over her eyes.

The thighs were softer than Rufina remembered, having observed before how muscly they were from protracted bouts of tennis with lady friends on Vaucluse courts, from sea-bathing at Watson's Bay and twice weekly rounds at the Royal Sydney Golf Club. From the long bed rest they had grown lax, delicate, white and waxen, one of them retaining for a moment the print of Nance's hand.

'Not long now. I can see the top of his head.'

She made a small gesture, as if to invite Rufina to look too, and the same blue heat of mortification burned at the back of her throat, the same as it had the night she'd heard the lovers.

'I wouldn't know what I was looking for,' she said, a remark that Nance seemed to find amusing. She snorted, chuckled, wiped her cheeks of perspiration.

'We're all made the same way, girlie.' She replaced the sheet and sat heavily on the bed beside Louisa, who was sleeping again, between pains, as suddenly as if she had fallen unconscious.

'But I have never ...'

Intent on the patient, Nance made no response. Perhaps she hadn't heard her. Just as well. If she had, then she would wonder why Rufina had said it. Of course she was a virgin; there should be no reason to suspect otherwise. It went without saying.

'Help me to lever her up a bit. She'll find it easier.'

'And then I will go out of the room,' Rufina said firmly, because she really did not want to see the mess and the blood or so she imagined it would be, or to hear any more of Louisa's keening and wailing. And it was likely Louisa didn't want her there either, since the last time she had spoken directly to Rufina it was to accuse her of bringing the labour on, so startling was the news of the engagement. She had even screeched at her beloved father, whom she seemed better able to love at a distance than at close quarters. Her so often declared concern and homesickness six hundred miles to the south in Sydney had ebbed away in the heat.

On either side of the bed, Rufina and Nance helped Louisa to lie against the bank of pillows. Bridgie had opened the windows to their fullest extent and was replacing the flyscreens, clipping them into place; not a breath of air penetrated the mesh. Late October and the thermometer on the verandah this morning read eighty degrees. Rufina had gone with Matthew to look at it after breakfast.

Her blouse stuck to her back. She wished she could go outside, find a place in the shade, sit with him.

'It's time to start pushing,' Nance said gently, holding a glass of water to Louisa's lips. 'Come on, dear. You must see that – you've been through this enough times, haven't you?'

Louisa glared at her. 'I had twilight for the others. I was utterly out to it.'

'Well, you're not now. Hurry up. Get pushing.'

Nance stood up, as if she was threatening to go out of the room as a means of persuading Louisa to push, whatever that meant, so Rufina out-stepped her, clipping briskly towards the door. At her back she heard a bestial strain, a primitive groan, a sound that made her blush so violently she felt her hair follicles contract and the hair stand up on her head.

She wouldn't turn around, she wouldn't, even though Nance called to make her stay, even though the little servant girl was there to help. Bridget seemed hardly affected, her awful face turning contemplatively towards Louisa as Rufina passed her. No doubt she had seen it all before; it was second nature.

Rufina went downstairs to Matthew, who was anxious for news of his daughter, and Rufina found she had none other than that the baby had not come. How could the words 'Nance can see the crown' form easily on her tongue, without the blood rushing painfully to her head when it had only just gone back to where it was supposed to be?

They took a turn of the garden, at Rufina's urging, even though it was the hottest part of the day, the sun blazing in the empty blue. For a moment or two they stood in the deep irregular shadow cast by the fountain and it was then she saw the first saint.

She was hidden between a Roman centaur and one of the mermen. St Agnes. Her ankle-length hair covered her nakedness, her gaze was brave, direct; a lamb lay at her feet and she held a palm leaf. The water fell from the fountain in such a way as to rush across the penitent mouth, to make it wet and alive. An impulse rose to show Matthew, to point her out and search for more, an impulse that died away even as Sebastian made himself known to her, a blade-bristling figure set into the frieze on the fountain wall. If she was to point them out, then he would know she was raised Catholic, and she would keep it from him at least until they were married, though she scarcely understood why, since Matthew was not interested in religion. He'd told her he didn't believe in God, that he never wasted time thinking about any church and she'd replied that she was the same. Exactly the same.

It was of the greatest importance to set herself apart from the first Mrs Fenchurch. She would be everything Min was not. It was the dreariest fact that they had shared the same faith, though the Americans had in no way suffered like the German Catholics had. It was like a different church, one free, the other oppressed and persecuted. Rufina pondered. Other than her religion and vague hints about her bouts of madness, what else did she know about her predecessor really? Very little. But she resolved that the second Mrs Fenchurch would be different. Prudent. Irreligious. Practical. Infertile. Most definitely the latter. Let the dead wife lie deep in her grave; let her seep away from the widower's heart.

Turning away from the fountain, Matthew was suddenly intent on the open window above their heads. So deep in thought had she been that she'd not at first heard the sound until it came again. The thin wail of a newborn. Such an expression washed over the grandfather's face – pride, amazement, love – that Rufina was struck by furious jealousy. Perhaps she would bear a child then. Just one. Then he would look at her with that same naked intensity. The expression vanished, to be replaced by his usual laconic half-smile, one corner of his pale mouth lifting higher than the other.

The temperature of the day had leapt again. Rufina laid a hand on the fountain rim and pulled it away immediately, her palm scorched. Heat and exhaustion had addled her brains. The water offered no relief; it felt warm enough to bathe in – and she almost suggested that they do so, a swift fantasy of frolicking in the wet sprays and plumes, herself modestly cloaked by freakish long hair.

'Let's go inside.' Matthew drew her to him, an arm around her waist, and they fell into step around the back of the house, past the stables and servants' quarters to the yard. As they went he explained that now the child had come he would set off on the business waiting since yesterday morning. Since it was midday already he would camp the night with the stockmen he had sent to round up cattle out on the far northern boundary.

'Don't you want to see the baby?' Rufina asked.

'Nan'll bring it down if it's fit to be looked at.'

'Why wouldn't it be?'

'Why? Well ... because of the fall.' He had led her inside and they were momentarily blinded by the sudden dark. Until their eyes adjusted he stayed close, the occluded shapes around them forming into the rising banisters of the main staircase, the pedestal table, the dresser outside the dining room.

'What do you think the fall could have done to the baby?' she persisted, but Matthew shrugged and wouldn't speculate, taking his leave of her to fetch his swag from upstairs. Rufina followed him and he made a joke of it, suddenly goofy, running ahead to hide in the doorway and jump out at her, then trying to keep her from entering his bedroom, the only one to open off the first landing.

'Who is there to see us?' she asked.

'You'd be surprised. Some of Min's antics were the talk of Clunes before I knew myself—' He broke off, as if he'd said more than he'd meant to or was it her too-avid curiosity? He glanced at her, and away, and she saw for the first time the room that he slept in.

It was a boy's room – the narrow bed, the tall chest of drawers, the mess of clothes discarded on the floor. There were no paintings, no books, no ornaments of any kind; an ill-fitting flyscreen lifted and banged with the hot wind. A campsite inside his own house. It was endearing, perhaps a little eccentric since he was so rich. Rufina caressed his cheek as she went past him on her way to the window. Below was the sloping roof of the verandah, the kitchen roof, the yard and servants' quarters, beyond the stables and accommodation. The overseer's view.

'Have you always slept here?' she asked but knew immediately that he had heard her inquisitorial tone – oh, she did not mean it! – and that he would not answer her.

He shook his head and she thought perhaps he was growing impatient, that he wanted to set about gathering his few things to roll into the blue blanket tossed on the bed, so she passed out onto the landing again and waited until he emerged, wondering if he would kiss her goodbye.

The smile he bestowed on her was as good as a kiss, as sweet.

'See you tomorrow,' he said and the dark well at the foot of the stairs swallowed him up.

The baby was crying again, this time more strongly, and Rufina was tempted to climb the last flight of stairs and go along the corridor to Louisa's room – she would shortly be thinking of it as her own room. But she was not curious enough. It was the cry itself, summoning, insistent. It was the remote chance the child could resemble its grandfather and therefore any child she might bear herself.

No. She would stay away. Louisa could take it into her head to order her to brush her tangled hair, or worse, to give her a sponge-bath. The sooner Louisa returned to Sydney the better; then the memory of Rufina as servant would fade. She was not that, never was, and never would be again. She would be ... what? Stepmother! How amusing! Ha! It would be as well, once Louisa had recovered from the birth, to have a discussion about how to proceed. For the most part they had got along, provided Rufina stayed within the boundaries. Now the boundaries had shifted; they waited to be redefined. There had been a letter from Jean to Matthew and herself, conveying good wishes, but anxious and strained. One paragraph, Matthew was certain, was dictated by Jean's husband, something about how they were counting on their inheritance to get them out of a hole. How dare he even think about Matthew dying? She would write back to them assuring them of his excellent health.

Downstairs to the kitchen where Bridget had left a pan of water boiling on the stove. There was more than enough to make a pot of coffee before she went along to the morning room. The sun had moved away from that side of the house; it was marginally cooler, though airless, the heavy drapes drawn. She opened them and the light poured through, illuminating the dust on the mantle, setting the dome around the platypus gleaming so that it almost looked alive. Sipping her coffee – she would have been better to have chosen a cool drink, her face dripped in the steam – she stood at the writing desk. There was a small dust-free square, reflecting a piece of light from the window, as if an object had sat there once but had now been removed. A clock, perhaps, an ornament, pinched by one of the servants.

A piece of paper protruded between the roll-top and the edge and tore a little as she pulled it free. It was a letter, unfinished, full of mis-spellings.

'Dear Eddie,' it began, 'I do not want to be the berer of bad news but your farther has decided to marray again to a german yonger than your sisters.'

There was a line crossed out and the paper held to the window did not give up the deletion, but was doubtless a version of some of what followed.

'I am verry worried. You shoud write to him and give him advise. It is not wise. She is almost thirty years yonger. Think of your mother and what she would say. The german has no mony. She is murrying him for his—'

And then the letter broke off as if the writer had been called away midword, or had been surprised by someone and so had pulled the roller down and hidden the letter away.

22.

Evie and Nan ate louise cake with Bridgie, the only one apart from Nan to know Evie's whereabouts. When Evie had first stood before her, weeks ago now, thin but big-bellied in an old dress of Min's found by Nan in the attic, a tiny smile had formed on the mobile side of Bridgie's mouth. She hadn't exclaimed, or run to embrace her, but then she was never one for cuddles or affection. Ma would say, 'Her poor skin hurts her. Don't you be pulling her around.'

Now, staring blankly at Nan, though with a surrounding air of gratitude, Bridgie picked off bits of the jammy shortbread and crumbly coconut and inserted them into the pocket at the side of her mouth, concentrating, chewing sideways. Bridgie's pouch, Ma called it, who held also that the long-ago accident had affected Bridgie's mind as much as it had her body; that the terror of the fire had burned away any stores of astonishment or alarm for the rest of her natural life.

Evie ate five pieces of louise cake, one after the other, her heart thudding. Only an hour before she had nearly been caught by Matthew as she came carefully down the corridor towards the kitchen. There had been a clattering of feet on the stairs above, and she had only enough time to lumber with her big belly to a hiding place behind the library door. She wished she hadn't bothered. She wished she'd carried on her merry way and met him at the bottom of the stairs, stood in front of him and made him face facts. He wasn't alone, he was with Rufina, and they were dressed for riding – Evie had caught a back view of the German in a white full-sleeved blouse trimmed with lace, men's moleskins and leather boots. It was an incongruous outfit, but had something modern and brave about it.

How Evie hated her. After Nan had told her about their engagement, Evie had cried for hours and hours and she'd felt like crying again at the sight of the hussy showing off her tall, slender body, with Matthew's arm around her narrow waist. It wasn't until after she watched them from the window riding out – Rufina on Llew's horse with Llew's traitorous dog following behind – that she deemed it safe to hurry across the entrance hall, past the dining room and out to the kitchen. Fury burned in her stomach, all around the poor baby; she could feel the poor thing boiling inside her like a spud in a pot. Nan's sweet cake and tea helped the anger melt away, though now, back in the dark close room, she wondered if she'd eaten too much of it. She felt sick.

'It's nobody's business but your own,' Nan kept saying. 'You keep as quiet as a mouse.'

And so she did, creeping down to her room at the mouth of Eddie's wing soon after the noise started, once they'd worked out it wasn't a crow screeching from the garden, or a bellowing distant cow going down with the staggers, and Nan had flown up the stairs on her vein-popping legs, as fast as Evie had ever seen her. Miss Louisa was having her baby.

Nan had put some things around Evie's room. A little clock she called a traveller, which Min had apparently taken with her on her holidays away from Jarulan to Sydney and America. A clock that had seen the world. A folded old towel, raggy enough to have been in use when Matthew was a baby. A soft white shawl for the baby when he came, as old as the towel but in better order.

A cream enamel water jug with a chipped rim, and a scratched old glass. A tin of shortbread. A couple of bananas going black. A pretty chemise, all pintucks and embroidery, like the one she had stolen for her mother but in better order.

It wasn't a drum at all. It was a heart. Boom-boom. Boom-boom. She got heavily to her feet and took the two or three steps to the chest of drawers to lay her ear against it, though she knew already that it came from the top drawer, which was locked. She had told Nan about it, finally, that morning, how she'd searched for an insect, an animal trapped in the wall, how she was frightened that she was beginning to imagine things.

'I think you are!' Nan had said, but Evie had registered the alarm in her green eyes and how she looked towards the chest with something like fear and hurried off to look after Louisa, leaving Evie all on her own.

It was when she finally succeeded in wrenching it open that the first pain came and with it the urge to bear down, though from what she remembered of Ma that was supposed to come later. Her waters broke with it and Evie found herself squatting in the puddle, the drawer flung open above her head. It was too early; she'd worked out the weeks with Nan. Not yet, little one, not yet.

But the pains came quickly, one after another with only two minutes or so between them, so that any attempts to reach the narrow bed and the comfort she hoped it would offer her were stymied. She stayed where she was, determined not to cry out. The traveller showed her it was half past one in the afternoon, an observation she made with the clear untrammelled part of her brain, as intently as if she had walked away from her body to where the clock sat beside the ottoman on the dusty floor.

But she was brought back to herself with another pain, so intense it felt as though she would be rendered in two by it, and she couldn't help this time but cry out, lifting her arms to embrace the warm wood of the chest of drawers, as if it was a friend and attendant.

How could Ma have borne this so many times? She always said she forgot how much it hurt, but how could she? Ma said that she prayed to Saint Margaret and that the saint helped her every time. Festooned in pearls and murmuring encouragement, Saint Margaret would appear nearby. Inevitably, she had the dragon at her feet, dead of having a cross shoved down his scaly throat. But Evie did not believe, not like Ma did. You had to have been born in Ireland for the saints, not in this place where a saint had never been born or was likely to be. In any case, Evie would not cry out for a woman who'd ended her life with her head off. Was that why she wore the pearls – to hide the ghastly cut in her neck?

It was animals she felt gathered around now, the animals that surrounded the grand house, creatures wild and farmed, the warm-blooded females and even the red-bellied black snakes, all the live young they must labour to spawn, and in her turn Evie felt herself spread out to meet them. The pigs labouring in their sty. The mother kangaroo giving birth to a twiglet so tiny she must barely feel it emerge, or at least only enough to stop her jumping about. How many joeys fall off and die? Maybe they only get born while the females are at rest during the heat of the day. And she had a sudden vision of herself among a golden-hued, gentle-eyed assembly under the shadowy river gums, the eternal rush of water, the spicy smell of crushed tussock and grass around them, the wail of a solitary black cockatoo from above – but it was herself crying out, the vision vanished and the well-travelled clock proving only a minute or two had passed.

There was something wrong. It was going too fast. Was it because it was too early? Even Ma had warning enough with Malachy, the tenth of thirteen, when she got caught short in Lismore. A kind passer-by had taken her to the hospital when she would have preferred the convent. Oh, if only Ma were here right now ...

Evie would go to her. Perhaps the pains would stop for long enough to climb out the window and run the two miles across the farm. So clearly did she imagine herself running away, away from the pain and fear, that she could feel the long grass of the snake field flicking against her bare legs. She saw a jacky lizard motionless on a rock with his orange mouth wide open, and a little further on a yellow honey-eater sitting on the fence post at the boundary, calling chickup chickup chickup ...

And then there was nothing but the closed lids of her eyes, a desperate hanging on in the darkness, all her attention on getting the hot air into her lungs, until there was a final pain that braced her, a slither and fall, an emptiness. The infant lay on the floor between her feet, the same bloodless hue as the pulsing blue cord, but pinkening as she picked her up – a girl! A girl when she'd wanted a boy. The surge of disappointment was short-lived – she had all her limbs, skinny but perfectly formed. Evie held her close, licking at the tiny nostrils and fretting for a moment that the mouth wasn't opening properly, that she'd somehow come out like Bridgie, even though Bridgie was born perfectly normal. But look, the mouth was opening in a perfect oval, a comical yawn, as if life was already proving wearying. Wriggling away from the wet part of the floor, Evie rested against the tallboy with the drawer hanging open over her head like an awning.

The eyes that never left hers were his: the same shape, promising the same lack of colour, the strands of slick downy hair on her head almost transparent. The tiny, sticky hand, unfurling and closing again, had the fan shape of his nails, the broad dimension of his palm. No one could ever doubt who the father was. No one would question it. She would give her an English name to go with the Fenchurch. A glamorous name. After the precious stone in the earring she lost. The sparkling light, the drop of blood. Rubies are valuable and precious. This is the ruby returned a hundredfold. Ruby is a grand name. Grand enough to inherit a fortune, even though she's a girl.

Or Helen. It was a name she'd heard. An English name. Nothing Irish or Catholic or anything to get in the way. Ethel. Or Helena? One afternoon, snooping through the house when everyone was out, she'd found herself standing before Louisa's dressing table. There was a beautiful jar, cut glass, with a white perfumed cream inside it. She'd dabbed some on and breathed in the essences that masked the lanolin. *Helena* said the label and another name beginning with R that she struggled with and now couldn't remember. Rubi something. Almost Ruby. Ruby as a middle name then, Helena Ruby Fenchurch, who would grow up here beloved of her father, who would not be able to resist her. She would be tall and creamy like Louisa, rich, well fed, go to school.

In the meantime Rufina would get bored and go away, or have a fatal accident.

Enveloped in pleasant dreams of Rufina thrown by Boss headfirst into a termite mound, or slipping from the bank to be submerged in a ravening flood, or bitten to death by a brown snake, or drained lifeless by colonies of leeches, Evie spent her first hours as a mother. When Helena cried she put her to her breast, and the visions of Rufina fled for a moment, to be replaced by musings on what Ma would say when she saw the little one, and Nan. They wouldn't be able to help but love her, for her daintiness, her pale fragility, her pale skin, her likeness to Matthew. She had his flat mouth, his chin, his wide brow. Evie would stay at the big house, with a proper room, and bring the baby up. It was inevitable that Matthew would not be able to resist the child since the loss of his own son. Here was his Helena, his natural daughter, who would drive Rufina away, if nothing else did.

When Bridgie snuck in around five o'clock, having been sent downstairs to boil water for Louisa, she showed no surprise at finding her sister calm and collected and the room in disarray, with puddles and the top drawer hanging open at a dangerous angle over her head, Evie's baby already born while Louisa still laboured on upstairs. She showed no surprise at all. Neither did she show any amazement at the drawer's content – a full layette, finely worked and spotlessly clean, that would perfectly fit her little niece.

'Where did it all come from?' she asked her sister, who only said quietly in reply, 'It's stopped now. The noise. It must have been my own heart beating.'

There was the business of the afterbirth, and they weren't sure all of it had come away, but they did the best they could, remembering from Ma how you had to put it back together, the shape it should take. Then Bridgie helped Evie back to bed, set the room in order, and fetched a basin of warm water from the kitchen to bathe the baby. Now the little one was tucked up safe on a pillow laid in the same beseeching drawer in the way Ma had taught her with the three babies that had come after Malachy, swaddled tight. Bridgie lay beside her sister, holding her hand – bother the rest of them upstairs – because she could sense Evie needed the comfort.

23.

High on the river road, rifle slung over her shoulder, Rufina paused to look down at the house, where very likely a baby was squalling. Even in a schloss the size of Jarulan the infant cry seemed to have a propensity for penetrating walls and carrying from floor to floor. It was a little like living in a nursing home, the two babies born only a day apart, almost exactly, one fat and round due to his mother's indolence, the other premature, tiny and frail, since for the entire gestation her mother had played at being a fugitive. Despite this disadvantage, or perhaps because of it, Evie's baby had a peasant determination lurking in its Irish eyes. Louisa's child, as Nance had it, might very well have been more affected by the accident than they'd thought. Its – his – eyes were certainly duller; it was slower to do the things people expected of babies. Rufina really couldn't care less.

Matthew was too lenient – bad enough he didn't encourage his daughter to return to her husband, worse that he carried on his first wife's habit of extending all sorts of largesse to the Tyrells. It would have to stop. The house would be divested of Evie and her bastard as soon as possible. And Louisa and her children would be encouraged to return to Sydney and Mr Arkenstall, to her rightful place. Christmas had come and gone, then all of January, while they waited for Louisa's baby to be strong enough to travel. Ridiculous. The child was robust, as far as Rufina could tell, wailing and crying far more than the other, though it surely had less call to.

A cuckoo – or at least, she thought it was a cuckoo – alighted on the low fence around the memorial, singing for all it was worth but plaintively, reflecting her mood. Only six weeks into her marriage and these morning rides were already a pattern, a way of filling in the lonely first hours of the day. After the wedding, Matthew had not altered his habit, still rising at dawn and going to the kitchen for an early cup of tea, then riding out onto the farm until midmorning when he returned for breakfast. At first Rufina went with him, but he seemed uncomfortable having his young wife hanging about while he gave his orders, and so did some of the men, shuffling about, not meeting her eye.

Not wanting to be left alone in the bed – and she did so enjoy their bed! – Rufina would rise at the same time. This morning they had been joined in the kitchen by mad Evie, who was helping Nance prepare Louisa's substantial breakfast, which she took upstairs, wallowing among her pillows. Evie had glowered at Rufina before sending Matthew a simpering little smile, of which he was oblivious, standing with his back to her while he drank his tea. The maid's baby lay in a box set on the end of the table – no, it had been a drawer, pulled from a chest. Rufina hadn't been able to help herself; she'd tweaked at the blanket to uncover a little of the face, wrinkled as an old man's, and scalded looking, as if its mother had left it out in the sun. It had looked up at Rufina with a challenging glint in its watery eye, an expression as unnerving as its mother's, so she had rejoined her husband, knocking back the scalding tea as quickly as he did before accompanying him out to the yard.

As she went she thought about how the men's clothes she wore had once been Llew's, as was the rifle she collected from the locked cupboard and the dog from the kennels to follow her.

Whatever it was that the dead son left behind came with her now, and even Matthew, bidding her farewell as she rode out high on Boss, had more of the father about him than the lover, an indulgent pride lighting his face. How lucky she was, given the situation. She would make the best of it.

The bird sat still on the memorial fence and a single, easy shot brought it down. The kill was hardly sporting, since the creature was motionless and so close that the bullet made rather a mess, though Matthew would mend it. Dismounting, she went to examine it more closely.

What a lovely bird it was, a wedge shape to its striped tail similar to the one that belonged to the giant eagle in the hallway. Of course, it was much smaller, only a couple of feet long, and in comparison to so many of the birds she was shooting and learning about, dull feathered. The trilling song, or what she'd heard of it, made up for it, being almost pretty. It seemed Creation had decided that in this place the gaudier the bird, the more alarming the cry; how many times had she been startled or set off into fits of laughter by the screams and chortles in the trees.

From her saddlebag she took the new field guide Matthew had given her – he had given her so much! – and confirmed from the coloured picture. A fan-tailed cuckoo, with his nutmeg breast and yellow ring around his eye. A perfect specimen for a vitrine in the front parlour. Or to be displayed on the white mantelpiece of their spacious bedroom, that room hard won from Louisa who had been moved, protesting, to a smaller one in the nursery wing.

Ha!

A dream broke – she had dreamed it last night – a kind of nightmare. She had walked down one of Jarulan's endless corridors, one she didn't recognise, and it seemed a baby cried from behind each of the closed doors. Doubtless one or two really did howl and her dreaming brain had drawn the sound in. Travelling ahead of her was a toy tractor, emitting tiny puffs of steam and the occasional trail of sparks, with yellow wheels that rumbled along the wooden floorboards just as Nance's tea trolley did. It disappeared into the gloom at the far end, where a soft light began to glow. Following along behind it, she had come into a vast decaying room, with tall ragged-curtained windows and a rotting piano. At the keys sat a young man in uniform, singing and playing, by his height and colouring a Fenchurch, bony hands spread on the yellow keys. He nodded once in a friendly manner at her entrance, before shifting his attention to a tall vitrine at Rufina's elbow. It contained no birds or koalas or snakes but a woman in a white nightgown, tied at her arms and legs with strips of silk to an old, patched leather chair. She was moving her shoulders and waggling her sweat-slicked head to the music and was obviously insane.

Evie, gagged, her eyes rolling furiously as Rufina drew near her glass cage. Or was it Evie? Her face shifted and changed to another woman's face, not as familiar, then back again, nightmarishly contorted.

Now, in the rapidly increasing heat of the early morning, Rufina shivered a little. What happened after that? She remembered no more but recalled that she hadn't been frightened, only curious about how Evie had got in there and whether she could get out again without breaking the glass. The soldier had been Llew, perhaps, but she had confused him with the remittance son gone native in New Zealand, who was the musician. She knew because the parlour piano stool was stuffed with sheet music. Eddie Fenchurch was inscribed in a florid hand in each right-hand corner.

She would not give the dream another thought. Frau Schneider was an avid aficionado of the new psychoanalyst Carl Jung, and put great store by dreams, even those best not remembered or talked about if one wanted to remain within the bounds of decency. If she was here, perhaps Rufina would tell her a little of it, and her old employer would tell her what it meant. Their nightly dreams had enlivened many of their dull days; life was certainly more eventful with Louisa, at least since they had come north.

Under her hand the cuckoo was soft and glossy, and although it was not a brightly painted creature – a rosella or parrot, the type of bird she preferred to shoot – it was a beauty, heavy and still warm. While she stood looking at its markings, listening to the river rush below the low cliff and the rowdy morning cries in the trees, Boss tossed his head wildly and before she could stop him cantered away down the hill towards home.

Something had *spooked* him, as they said here, though it was not a country for ghosts. The fatherland was full of them. If Australia was a country for birds, then Germany was a land of disappointed and vengeful spectres, otherworldly Prussian princes, landless kings and centuries of peasants worked to the bone. Not here. Here there was sunshine and prehistoric lizards, and an openhearted man who had offered her all he had. This was her chance and she had taken it.

'Boss!'

He was already out of sight between the trees.

'Come back, Boss!' louder this time and with a whistle to follow, but the hooves clattered on, heedless. Apparently he had obeyed Llew always, adoring him, fawning like a dog; in time she would win his heart just as she had won her husband's.

On the other side of the monument was a vantage point of the river road. After a few minutes she saw the horse appear, tail and mane streaming, and any irritation she had at his disappearance melted away. He was a fine animal, worth every penny Llew had paid for him – the price had broken some kind of record, Matthew had told her. Boss's beauty had her forgive him, love him all the more, even though she would now have to carry the bird home with the rifle heavy on her back and Llew's shirt sticking to her skin.

Halfway down the hill a group of wallabies gathered under some eucalypts, the dew-laden grass around them steaming in the sun. They looked up as she passed and she wondered at their fearlessness. One of them could have taken a bullet, one at least, and she would have lifted her rifle to her eye if Boss was here to help carry the quarry home. In imitation of a rifle shot she clapped her hands smartly together and the animals lolloped a short distance into denser bush. From among the trees they watched her, still, gentle, infinitely patient. She felt their eyes on her as she passed and had a sense of them keeping pace with her as the trees closed over her head, all the way to the bottom of the hill where she turned in at the lion gates. It was as if they were making sure she was leaving them.

As she went along she resolved again to write to her mother, even though it was by no means sure that a letter would get through. Her mother knew nothing of the marriage, and Rufina didn't know where to begin to describe it. Perhaps she could start by telling her how invitations were declined by several of the guests, most hurtfully by Jean and her husband: there was apparently neither the time nor the money to attend, an excuse that wore thin after Matthew offered the means. Jean had written privately, apologising.

It would be better to begin with the wedding itself, conducted in a dull little brick Anglican church in Lismore, since Matthew had taken against the Clunes priest who had informed him of Llew's death. She could describe in detail the wedding guests, because there were only five: Louisa, who had had to have a new dress hurriedly made for the occasion, now that she was too plump for the clothes they'd brought from Sydney; Nance, whose doleful demeanour would better have suited a funeral; the head stockman and his wife; and the scowling servant girl Evie, who was not invited but came anyway, bringing her baby, which caterwauled and grizzled through most of the service. A circus.

Not the wedding her mother would have imagined for her only daughter.

Rufina had a vision of her mother weeping with disappointment, unable to comprehend the depth of distrust and fear that surrounded the nuptials of her only child. She would understand that the occasion should have been an event, a celebration – the second marriage of a wealthy landowner – but perhaps it would have escaped her that because he was marrying a German it was not. People stayed away from the service, though they came to gawp afterwards, some of them with hate-filled eyes, others merely curious. A German bride half his age; look how she has two legs, look how she approximates a human being!

Rufina kicked a stone along the driveway, thinking bitterly that actually she had no idea what they thought, since none of them spoke directly to her, and if they had spoken to Matthew it was polite, deferential. He had never told her otherwise.

You would not weep if you could see this, Mutti! How would it be to show her the fields, the bush, the formal gardens being slowly restored, the playing fountain? Her fields, her gardens, her fountain! Flora would smile, she would announce that it was to be expected, that a rich husband was Rufina's due, and that after the war was over and Germany claimed Britain's colonies and dominions, and Germans came to Australia in their thousands, then Rufina's life would feel normal again. She would be one the same as many instead of a freak, a resented outsider. They would have German servants in the house – a house that, after all, was built with German labour and skill, a German overseer to make the farm more efficient.

It was a happy fantasy – and it was only a fantasy, even if it was unpatriotic to admit it. Any fool could see Germany was losing the war, despite the Australian propensity to exaggerate Britain's victories. It was as if no one at home had thought to look first at a map and count the number of countries painted red for the British Empire, as if no one had thought to count the potential soldiers in those countries, the combined armies of millions that Germany had no chance of vanquishing.

It was best not to think about any of it, but to look forward to Matthew coming in for breakfast and perhaps a kiss and a tender word from him. First she would check that Boss had returned himself to the stables.

Still carrying the cuckoo by its scaly feet, she came along the carriageway on the river side of the house, looking up at the gables and taking note of the host of small repairs the house needed – the rotten window sashes, the crumbling disused chimneys. It was Matthew who had told her the house was built by Germans before he was born, when his own father was a lad. Perhaps she could have guessed if he hadn't told her. It had an indefinable familiar quality, soothing, kind, accepting; a solid, pervasive German essence that overwhelmed the Australian stone and English design. All these years the house had been waiting for her, perhaps. They were a united force. There would be changes and all to the good. Eventually she would cease to betray her origins as much as the house had and become truly Australian. She would concentrate on erasing her accent, on forgetting she was German at all. What favours did it do her?

Nosebag on and one of the Aboriginal grooms rubbing him down, Boss was outside the stable and beside him stood Matthew's Flora. The groom glanced at Rufina once, his gaze travelling briefly to the dangling bird before returning to Boss, clicking at him, murmuring softly in his own language. It seemed that the groom didn't want Rufina to talk to him, that he was shutting her out, or as if he was obeying an order not to speak to her. Quietly, for a moment or two, she watched the long, steady brush strokes moving over her horse's gleaming, shivering flanks, and thought what an Australian picture it made – the graceful black servant in his faded, thin clothes and the piece of magnificent breeding that was Boss.

'Wonderful horse, isn't he, Albert?' she said. Albert looked at her then and nodded, his gaze shifting to the bird and his eyes filling with sadness.

As she made her way inside, Rufina considered that it was just as well Matthew had come back early because he'd know what to do with the cuckoo, which was beginning to smell, though it had been dead for less than an hour. As she went across the yard to the back door, flies followed in a steady stream, like bridesmaids after a bride, thought Rufina; and she wondered if she would have seen the analogy if her own wedding had been less of a disappointment, a wedding with no bridesmaids, though there may have been a fly or two.

In the cool of the hall, the flyscreen door slamming behind her, she lifted the bird to examine it again, the buzzing retinue only slightly diminished. She could see the tarnished eye and a clear liquor coming from the bullet hole, greasing the feathers. She supposed it had left behind no fledglings, that the Australian cuckoo behaved as any in Europe, laying its eggs in other birds' nests and compelling them to do all the work. A clever ancestral idea – how did it first evolve? Perhaps one mother bird did it by mistake and from thence forward her sisters realised it was a good way of having babies without having to tend them, but how did she pass the skill to her daughters?

The library door stood open and a snuffling, snivelling sound reached her as she came down the corridor. Underneath it ran a low urgent tone, which she recognised as Matthew's. She laid the dead bird on the hall table and leaned against the wall to listen.

In the years to come Rufina would sometimes pass an uncomfortable hour or two wondering how her life would have been if Boss hadn't run for home and so compelled her to return to the house early. Or if she had behaved with integrity and turned away, since she was eavesdropping, prying into a conversation that was not hers. If she had moved on, taken the bird to the trophy room or gone up to the belvedere, she would never have known the truth of Helena's paternity. Or what Evie believed to be the truth of it.

'This has got to stop,' Matthew was saying urgently, softly. 'If you keep trying to corner me like this I will send you away.'

'Away where?' came the wheedling tone, husky with crying. 'And what about your own Helena?'

'Not mine. Yours.'

'She's yours.'

'There's nothing to prove it. I don't believe you in any case, Evie. You can't stay here. Do you understand?'

The crying intensified, strangely as contagious as laughter, and Rufina struggled against it, though her tears were not for Evie but for herself. She had been monstrously tricked. Her mind raced through scenarios, flicking them over like picture cards in a pack: her husband in bed with his mistress – an Australian version of the European tradition, the *droigt du seigneur* – and surely not as tender as he was with her, surely not! She imagined Matthew hiding the girl away for the duration of her pregnancy and his pretence that he had no idea where she was.

One morning out riding they'd crossed at the top of the Tyrell run and met with one of the brothers who had rudely asked, without greeting, if there was news of his sister. He had directed the question at Rufina, though it was meant for her husband. Matthew had shaken his head and ridden on.

She would never forgive him. She would go directly upstairs and move her things to another room. She would leave the cuckoo stinking on the table outside the library – and if he didn't understand that *Metapher* then he was more of a peasant than she thought. What does a male cuckoo do? Take even less responsibility than his gadabout wife?

Just as she was about to step out of the shadows the thin, penetrating wail of a baby sounded from elsewhere in the house, and a moment or two later Evie appeared in the doorway, her face swollen, her hands rolled at her sides into fists. At first she didn't notice Rufina watching from the shadows, and she seemed reluctant to go to her crying baby. While she stood there a wet stain spread over the breast of her cotton frock, a sight so bestial and redolent of all the tragedy of her betrayal that Rufina cried out – and then Evie was upon her, scratching and biting, stinking of milk. Rufina barely fought back, lifting her arms only to her husband who was shouting with fury at her attacker, pulling Evie away. An expression of revulsion rent his face and Rufina felt herself offer up a prayer, despite her previous resolve to put herself apart from him – *Oh please, God, let him never look at me like that.*

Then Evie was running – not towards her crying baby, as you would expect, but along the corridor, across the entrance hall and out into the bright day, and Matthew was enfolding his wife in his arms, and Rufina knew he was praying just as fervently as she had done a moment before, but for her surdity or, failing that, the greater plea for her forgiveness.

PART II

1.

Auckland, 1916

IT HAD BEEN RAINING FOR WEEKS, LATE AUTUMN, THE UPPER North Island lashed with storms. The roads, sparse and poor as they were in 1916, were deep in mud and choked by boulders washed down from the hills. From Rotorua, Hohepa and the others travelled east, a day's walk to the coast, which involved perilous crossings of swollen rivers and a spectacular landslide which had to be navigated and so added another four miles at least to their journey. In the coastal village of Maketu they borrowed a schooner to sail north, a tub patched together from various ancient crafts and barely seaworthy, but the greatest girl there ever was. For the next three weeks the *Maori Queen* – her name inherited from a nineteenth-century coaster, along with some of her parts – gave them many adventures at sea and just as many landfalls, some which did not at all owe their occurrence to the poor weather but more a heartfelt desire to dally with friends and relatives along the coast.

The omnibus had been landed and left in its wooden crate on Queen Street Wharf. When a storm came over the Waitakere Ranges and scooped into the harbour like a giant spoon, waves broke high enough to come over the wharf and over the crate, breaking and surging, penetrating the gaps between the planks.

The morning after, some passing larrikins, curious about what the long tall box could conceal, had prised away the wood at one corner, a gap progressively enlarged over the following weeks by other curious lads, and also by a decommissioned sailor fallen on hard times who availed himself of several timbers for his fire.

Rain pooled in the driver's footwell, made ponds in the upstairs canvas seat covers and soaked into the seams of the leather upholstery. The brass rims of the headlamps lost their lustre. A fat wharf rat came with some of his cohort for a sniff around what could amount to luxury two-storey accommodation, and planned on moving in the very next day.

*

On the evening the lads finally limped into port, a low grey cap of clouds sealed the sky from horizon to horizon. Flashes of the sunset showed in the west as gentle glimmers, like half-hearted lightning, on torn sails, leaning mast and yardarm slumped. The crew of the *Maori Queen* were ill-provisioned and miserable with hunger while they tacked head-to-head with the persisting westerly and anchored at Mechanics Bay, an area the brothers knew well, either by experience or reputation, since it was where everybody stayed when they came to Auckland.

After a long and festive night at the Maori hostel in the company of many friends, old and new, they walked an early morning low tide along the mudflats to the Queen Street Wharf. Along the way they were astonished by some of the changes since Hohepa's last visit a few years before: the new land stolen from the sea along the Quay, the wooden houses built along the ridges, many of them grand. There was the occasional midden where those same Parnell denizens had dumped their rubbish, broken crocks and bottles, old rags, tin cans, human filth, logs and stone, and they had to be careful where they stepped. It was an indication of how crowded the town had become – and they agreed that none of them would stay there any longer than they had to. The ships, though – the ships! They saw some beauties – an old sharp-prowed iron-hulled wool trader cleaving through the Waitemata, her sails gloriously full in the cold westerly that was pushing her out to the Gulf, flying her away, sending her out to the Pacific, perhaps all the way to America. Who could blame them all for wishing for a moment that they were aboard, heading away, rather than embarking, as they were, on a tourist enterprise?

Steamers, barques and schooners lined up at rest, some of the bigger ships listing with the full tide. A floating crane had been hoisted to the dry up on the new concrete wharf that replaced the old warped planks of Queen Street Wharf. The square-rigger *Vindication* roosted on Calliope Dock, a castle and six masts, and was as old at least as the oldest parts of the *Maori Queen*. She would have sailed the seven seas, many times around the globe, and Hohepa wasn't the only one keen to go aboard for a look around. The wharf and tees were jammed with passengers for McGregor's Steamship, another for the Coastal company; ships were loading and unloading and, in addition, a grand liner sat sweet at anchor further out in the channel.

But where was the prize, the B-type omnibus with seats for sixteen inside and eighteen up top, brought all the way from London and paid for with money made from the sale of tribal land? It took time for the brothers to get through the crowds and past the many distractions – and then only to realise that they had gone too far and would have to turn back.

No wonder they'd missed it – it was hidden away in a crate of raw pine, swiftly constructed. A watersider sheltering from the rain in the doorway of the nearest shed gave them a claw hammer, but as soon as they had peeled away her shell, or what remained of it – it was as if she had tried to hatch herself – an argument ensued. Why hadn't Hohepa done what he was supposed to do, and that was to organise someone to get the omnibus off the wharf and into the dry sooner? It would be the first of many quarrels that concerned her, that damned bloody 1912 bus that had once driven the streets of London and had a mind of her own.

It was difficult to imagine the vehicle before the deluge and to gauge the damage. There was some wear and tear on the leather seats and rips in the sodden wet-weather covers upstairs. While he was upstairs, Hohepa had pushed on the sagging canvas and sent the pooled water over the sides, sending it gushing over the brothers watching him from below, and everyone laughed – including the tall, thin rich white man in expensive clothes, leaning up against a bollard and smoking a cigarette, who had watched them so avidly as they pulled the battered crate apart and argued that he knew something they didn't.

Some of the water from the omnibus roof had collected in the man's hat. He shook it off and introduced himself as Eddie Fenchurch.

'Where are you from?' they asked, and in reply he pointed at the liner *Niagara* bobbing in the channel and smiled, showing an even row of small teeth, yellow from smoking. He offered around his American cigarettes and they smoked companionably for a while, all standing around the bus and remarking now and again on some new feature – the tread of the running board seamed like plantain, the word GAS engraved into a pedal below the steering wheel, the rods the driver would manipulate for speed and braking. They imagined the many tourists that would be driven around in it to look at the buried village and the steaming pools at Whakarewarewa, the vistas of lake and mountain.

'Where are you from?' Eddie asked them, and when he was told, he looked blank because how would he know anything about this country, having only just stepped off a ship? They explained, pointing south, telling him the name of their village, their mountain, their lake and hot pools, but he knew nothing about anyone or anything. His eyes kept wandering back to the B-type and his hand strayed once or twice to her long shiny nose, patting and soothing.

'Not much wrong with this,' he said, their saviour. He opened the omnibus's mouth, closed it again, unscrewed the petrol cap and sniffed.

'Dead empty – all evaporated, I assume.'

Yesterday's glimmers of sunlight had likewise evaporated and the rain began to fall again, sparse heavy drops plinking and spreading on the smooth paint, streaking the few parts of the wooden frame that were still dry.

'We need to get it under cover,' Eddie said, and it wasn't long before he had organised to do exactly that with the help of a group of stevedores. As many as could lay their hands along the flanks pushed the omnibus along into the gloom of the nearest wharf shed, lit for the grey afternoon by a row of kerosene lamps slung high in the roof. Eddie opened the bonnet again and muttered something about a worm drive and a chain gearbox, and requested various tools which were fetched for him while the upholstery gently steamed and one of the brothers gave the headlights a polish with his coat tail and discovered to general relief that the rim was restored, more or less, to its previous lustre.

The Pakeha's facility with the engine was impressive. And when he rolled his sleeves up so was the quality of his shirt, the fine wool of his discarded jacket and the intricately tooled leather of his shoes. Early in the afternoon, when he suggested they adjourn to the Gladstone Coffee Palace – 'My shout' – there was a lilt in his voice different from that of the Pakehas who'd been here since last century.

All together they crossed Quay Street to the Gladstone, the proud corner building with its turrets and twiddles and tall windows, where groups of Maori were turned away at the door, but mixed groups were allowed. The youngest brother put a worried arm around Hohepa – only one Pakeha and six Maori; it might not be enough, it might not be allowed.

But the lady in the little lace cap let them sit down. She pointed to a big table in the window, where they were brought a giant silver pot of tea, plates of sandwiches, savouries, scones and cakes on tiered plates. While they ate, Eddie let them have his story.

He had been to California, for the third time, a place of which he was fond, for the parties, music, food and women. Before that he was in Australia, where he was born and grew up on his father's farm – a big farm of three thousand acres, more land than they ever heard of being in the possession of a single man. He told them he had come into a fortune, the details of which were hazy, and that his father had for all this time – three years at least – believed he was in New Zealand. And Eddie had come, eventually – here a distant look entered his eye – to make good his part of the bargain, the deal he had made.

'With your father?' asked Hohepa.

'My mother. My dearest lost mummy.'

And then he had fallen silent and shed a single tear that left a silvery track in his pale grimy cheek, and his new friends felt moved with pity and love. They watched the long white fingers move to wipe away the tear, saw the B-type-grazed knuckles and bruises from the unaccustomed work, the soft useless skin, and it was obvious that although he might know about motors it was a long time since he had done any real work. No one said anything until Eddie took a cigarette and lit it, before passing the tin around for everyone to join him, and they got fresh tea and another jug of milk.

When it came time to pay the bill, Eddie turned out his pockets. He was a whole pound short and the manager looked down his nose at them all, as if it was their fault that Eddie's pockets contained only crumbs of tobacco, a penknife, the stub of a pencil and a filthy handkerchief. There was also a narrow roll of soft felt and a small silver tool, which he said was a tuning hammer for pianos. In one jacket pocket was a scrap of paper with a recipe written on it for a rich pudding that involved cream, brandy and sugar. Between them they managed to find enough shillings and pence to cover the shortfall. Pakehas were usually very embarrassed over matters like this, but this one wasn't, not at all. As they retraced their steps to the wharf shed to see how the motor was faring, Eddie's wide straight grin was back in place and the spring bouncing in his step.

When he bent his head over the machine he said, 'Shame my brother Llew isn't here. He knows everything there is to know about engines.' He told them how his brother Llew had written a letter, just retrieved this very day Poste Restante from the Auckland Post Office, to say he was leaving on the Australian troop ship, heading for Europe. Perhaps because he was in the company of brothers and cousins he talked about his brother for a long time, leaning up against the front steel wheel, tools idle, stories about Llew's gift for horses, his kindness to strangers, his physical superiority, his innovations on the farm, the father's preference for that son over himself, and had to be encouraged to get back to work, to the tightening and loosening of bolts, the wiping of various parts with the filthy handkerchief.

At dusk Eddie straightened up, hands gripping the small of his back and pronounced that by morning the engine would be dry enough to crank it to life.

It was then that Hohepa had the idea that would change all their lives, Eddie Fenchurch's the most.

'Come home with us,' he said. 'We need someone to drive the 'bus for the tourists.' He remembered the scrap of paper with the recipe. 'And maybe help cooking food for them. In our tearooms.'

2.

Bay of Plenty, 1936

THE MARAE, BEING IN AN EXQUISITE LOCATION MUCH LIKE THE more famous Ohinemutu – which from some angles appeared to float between two lakes, Rotorua and Rotoiti – was not often compared to it except for its geographical similarities. The two lesser lakes that this marae stood between were little more than ponds teeming with sandflies, easily swum across and able to spread like spilt milk over the land after rain, testing their boundaries, running through the grass of the paddocks. Built for the most part on sodden ground, Eddie's marae was neither as old as the other, nor as prestigious, nor as successful in various tourism endeavours, and never before had it received such a guest as this one – at least as far as Eddie was concerned – in all the years he'd lived here.

The other more famous marae had welcomed various luminary Maori scholars and politicians from tribes all over the country, government ministers, including on several occasions the Prime Minister, and *twice* the Prince of Wales and his substantial retinue, all of whom were fed and entertained like kings. The only lofty Pakeha visitors to Eddie's marae were various interfering delegations from the Health and Education departments, much resented. Eddie had felt always a degree of separation, and had hung in the background as much as he could, except for when he was called upon to help with the entertainment.

This visitor was unfed and laughed least. His daughter had brought her along the road and up to the whare kai, having found her hovering nervously outside the marae, surrounded by curious dogs, her gaze averted from the staring eyes and carved genitalia on the tall red gates. The child knew better than to interrupt her father's piano playing and had whispered to the lady to stand quietly in the dining room and not say a word. Eddie carried on for another five minutes or so, enjoying their attention, humming to himself, cigarette at the corner of his mouth and the half-emptied hipflask – it was eleven o'clock in the morning – hidden in his pocket, while he played the new Cole Porter song 'All Through the Night', sent to him by a friend in California. Tonight he would play it with the band, let them hear it a couple of times this afternoon. They loved the new American songs as much as he did. Eddie, who had played and sung his way around the world until the money ran out, thought he had never heard anything like the band he was part of here, the effortless close harmonies, the easy reaching finger patterns on guitars, the weaving melodies of the horns. He'd died and gone to heaven. Who would have thought it? He wouldn't've bothered with all those other countries if he'd known this one was just next door.

The Scotch put its customary short-lived shine on his playing – he was sipping it slowly, making it last, more for economical reasons than for his health, and hadn't Hohepa started to voice his disapproval more often? Since Eddie loved Hohepa more than anybody else in the world, even his wife, he wanted to please him. It seemed sometimes that Hohepa would never forgive him for driving the bus into the lake, and why should he?

'Better at driving a piano, aren't you, mate?' he'd said, after the accident. He'd relieved him of all duties, mechanical and otherwise.

This morning, enjoying his unexpected audience – the well-dressed woman he'd only glimpsed out of the corner of his eye – Eddie found himself singing properly, letting the fag fall from his mouth to the sawdust floor and his heart fill with love and loneliness. It was a difficult melody, a descending chromatic scale and an octave leap, but so new and delicious that Eddie couldn't wait for the band to arrive and get started. As his voice swelled and fell he was aware of a snuffling, a shedding of moist tears, and a slow rhythmic shuffle in the sawdust, as if the listener was dancing a little in a restrained manner, as if she didn't want to but somehow found herself dancing anyway. Eddie had seen that happen before, to the posh wives of visiting officials. Once they had got over whatever aspect of the place that made them squeamish and anxious – the lack of toilets, the number of dogs, the hupe flowing unrestrained from some of the children's noses – they were sometimes seduced by a rhythmic song, Maori or American.

He reached the end, played the final liquid chord and turned to look at his solitary audience: an attractive woman, fair-skinned, tears flowing, and when she spoke – 'You are so like him!' – it was with a German accent. He stared at her, and she at him, and then he was up from his chair and standing to take her hands in his.

Rufina. Here. Only just remembered from the long-lost photograph Nan had sent, a copy of a portrait made in Lismore just before the marriage. The wide-spaced eyes as grey as they were in the monochrome picture, the knife-edge of the nose, the blade-like cheekbones. When he first saw her image all those years ago he had half-envied the old man – she was a beauty – but he had also felt afraid for him, a fear that had very quickly turned to a satisfying sense of revenge. She was so much younger than his mother – dear, mad Min – but with a stern old-world naivety in her face.

In his previous life Eddie had met the daughters of wealthy European families with the same look, a cultivated reserve that bordered on cruelty. The sharp intelligence in the photographed eyes had alarmed him, had chilled him to the bone, and there was the same face now, right in front of him, but tempered, dulled, softened, and why wouldn't it be? She was sixteen years older now. Sixteen years of putting up with the old man. In her thirties now, was she? There could only be one reason why she was here.

The old man had died.

She took a man's white handkerchief from the capacious pockets of her woollen suit, a jacket over a mid-calf-length skirt. Her walking costume, he supposed it was. While she wiped her face with the handkerchief, there was a flash of embroidered red in the corner – *M.F.* Just such a handkerchief was produced from his father's pocket to tenderly wipe his own tears at around eight years old. It had been out by the row of kennels behind the creamery, the Roman numeral carved above the door. *IV.* Ripper lying dead on his chain in the heat of summer, grey and white heeler snout in the dust, water bowl empty.

'But he was an old fella, Eddie,' his father had told him. 'He would have died soon anyway.'

It was the first of many crimes to do with his negligence, and the first when an animal on the farm had suffered because of him. The worst. What if his father had kicked his arse and yelled at him that first time, like he did every other? It might have shaped him better. Made him pull up his bootstraps.

Useless even then.

So he was dead now? An inheritance, then.

There was laughter from the dining-hall door – a group of girls was hanging about watching him and Rufina, laughing, talking in Maori, a language he had still not mastered after all these years of living here – but he heard his wife's name and shortly thereafter one of them scooted off to warn her that he was with a strange white lady, that he was embracing her.

His father's widow looked about for somewhere to sit, taking the end of one of the wooden bench seats at the long table. It seesawed a little; she slid along to balance it.

'Nance wrote to you,' she said, after a pause.

'To say you were coming? No. No, she didn't, did she?'

He shook his head. How curious that she should come all this way with no warning, no preamble, no seeking of an invitation. What sort of greeting did she think she'd get? Why come herself and not send an envoy? That loathsome husband of Louisa's, for instance.

Rufina's shoes were caked in mud; there were spatters on her stockings. But she looked a practical type, her unadorned cream blouse unsuccessfully spot-cleaned of travelling smirches. The brooch at her throat, clear yellow stone, old gold – had it been Min's? It looked familiar. Pale serrated hair escaped from the edges of her close hat, dry and ropey; her skin was lining up a little. She could be one of those women who lose their looks overnight, the climate catching up, her life harder than he might have imagined, even with all the old man's money to cushion her and send her to the dentist. What nice teeth she had, white and strong. And she carried a long black umbrella with a silver duck head for a handle. There were green gems set into it for eyes. Thoughtfully, he took a mouthful or two from his flask. What was he expected to do with her?

He should offer to take her to his house, where his second wife would have the fire going, but he saw only too well how this Mrs Fenchurch would perceive his whare with the small outdoor kitchen, the patched walls of slab and corrugated iron, the tilting rusted roof. A hovel. She would not see its bucolic charm – but then, neither did he, when he was honest with himself, which wasn't often. Life was too short for honesty, at least the kind of honesty that came from dwelling on one's misfortune. Or what others might see as misfortune.

He didn't feel misfortunate. Not at all. He was the luckiest man in the world, with rare momentary grief or guilt soothed by jovial company, and many gifted friends to make music and enough food to fill his belly, and plenty of grog if he played his cards right. He couldn't live this life, the life he had in New Zealand, this life on this marae with Hohepa and Mary and his children, anywhere else in the world. Even when the money came from his inheritance, he'd stay here.

'The letter from Nance,' Rufina repeated. 'Did you get it?'

Eddie sighed. 'The mails are irregular,' he said, airily, as a kind of joke. Rufina didn't smile.

'Not so irregular. We have not heard from you for many years. Nance wrote to you again. So did I.'

She had taken a maternal tone and Eddie had to remind himself that he was her senior, actually, by seven years. He had worked the difference out after learning of the marriage, thinking it would be an amusing tale to tell his companions, how his German stepmother was younger than he was. But his Maori friends didn't see anything amusing in it at all, since older men often took much younger wives.

'Nance says she wrote to you many times.'

Eddie nodded, though he didn't think there had been *many* letters. She had written, but only when she had what she considered momentous news. The death of Llew. His father's courtship and marriage. The unmarried Tyrell girl – Evie, was it? – who had run away to Sydney leaving Nance with a baby girl to care for.

'Did you get Nance's last letter?' The German was getting impatient, tapping the point of her umbrella so that sharp holes appeared in the yellow dust. Nearby, Hohepa's oldest girl wielded a broom, sweeping a patch near the table into a trapdoor in the boards. Another girl scattered fresh sawdust in her wake. The smaller girls gawping at them didn't seem to have any task to do.

They crept forward to stare from a closer vantage point, Eddie's six-year-old daughter among them.

'This is Gracie.' He hooked his arm around his six-year-old and Rufina looked from her face to his with a startled expression, which Eddie had no trouble in interpreting. The child looked like him, but also like her mother, and Rufina did not appear to enjoy seeing the Fenchurch traits translated this way. She would see, as he did, the shape of Matthew's chin in the small brown face, his flat Fenchurch mouth.

Why had she never had any children of her own? She was young enough, healthy enough.

'This is . . .' How to introduce her? Your grandmother?

'Mrs Fenchurch,' supplied Rufina.

'Are you my auntie?'

Firmly, Rufina shook her head. The child waited for the relationship to be explained. Eddie packed his pipe and struck a match.

Rufina told Gracie, 'I was married to your grandfather, Matthew. I am his widow.'

So he was dead then. He really was dead. The flaming match fell to the floor where it ignited enough of the sawdust to necessitate leaping from his chair to stamp it out, and while he did so he began to weep, though he scarcely knew why. His father was a brute. He was. Patient for only so long. He would have made Eddie into a dumb workhorse for his own benefit, for the eternal continuation of that ridiculous house and farm, of Jarulan.

His stepmother stood up too and watched him impassively. She didn't offer him any comfort and neither did he expect it. They were strangers to one another. His tears and nose coursed, and he had nothing to wipe himself up.

'Here.' She gave him the monogrammed handkerchief, slightly damp. 'Keep it.'

After a few minutes he was able to dry his face and blow his nose. He stuffed the thing into his pocket. Not looking at him, as if she was embarrassed by his show of emotion, Rufina asked, 'Is there anywhere I can get a cup of coffee?'

'Tea more likely.' He wanted to ask her how long ago it was that his father had died. He wanted to ask how, what from. But she was turning away from him towards the door, as if she would lead him, as if she was used to being in charge. He pushed ahead out into the brilliant winter sunshine, taking her arm and leading her towards the tearooms beyond the marae gate, of which he was the erstwhile manager. He could tell her about that, make it look as though it was only recently that he gave it away, rather than the eight years it actually was. He could lead her into believing that the success of his and Uncle Hohepa's dance band had precluded any chance of his continuing to run the successful business, which was why the tearooms were closed. The windows were smeary, dead flies lay along the sill, paint peeled from the front door where someone had drawn an arrow to point down the hill and the word 'HOTEL'.

A little of his whisky fog cleared and the ensuing clarity was sharp, hard-edged. She would think he was a failure, of course; everything his father and sisters would have told her about him vindicated. She would see him as a clown, a singing jester for the natives. But she had been kind enough to come and see him. He supposed she would have some of the money with her, or at least documents from the lawyer, a copy of the will.

'A casualty of the times,' she said pleasantly, and they walked away in the direction of the arrow, because the sign did give the impression that the hotel was nearby. It wasn't. It was a good half-hour walk away, up on the main road that took travellers towards the coast.

Reluctantly Eddie followed along behind her, puffing on his pipe. Cigarettes were a rare treat – but he'd grown to like the pipe better, the way you could just charge it up now and again, take a puff or two. With any luck the lady would realise in the next minute or two the distance, and give up on any hope of a cup of tea and decide to go back to her hotel. She must be on holiday, taking a tour, and seeking him out an addendum, a side trip. To make sure he got the news. She wouldn't have bothered coming all this way just for him. Surely.

The old man dead.

He trudged along beside her, smoking, trees meeting overhead over the road dripping now and then with the heavy rain of the morning. Little Gracie slipped her hand inside his, and some of the other children who had been hanging around the hall while he played the piano were following along behind them. One of them was leading the others in a song, singing in a high, true voice. They had been running around loose on the marae, which was not allowed, just like his clandestine whisky was not. Lucky none of the old ladies came along to tell them off.

'My mum will make you a cup of tea,' Gracie said clearly. 'Range'll be hot. Won't be no trouble.'

It would not have occurred to Gracie to be ashamed of their home, thought Eddie, and why should it? The kid had never seen Jarulan, and the cottage she was growing up in was only in slightly worse repair than some of the neighbouring houses, and perhaps she thought that difference was because she had the only Pakeha father and stepmother in the village. Who knew what she thought, really, except that she regarded Rufina Fenchurch in her tailored woollen costume and bird head umbrella as a prize to be proudly borne home to Mary.

Rain had turned the dirt road into a long, narrow creek of sucky mud, different to the mud at Jarulan. Why would he remember the mud? Oh the mud of Jarulan! Red silty skilly mud, which in places around the river would form thick enough to swallow a horse, not thick and brown and viscous like this, which threatened only to suck off their shoes, so that they had to go in single file along the driest part.

They came out into the open again, where green fields shimmered on either side and long blades of grass at the roadside glistened still, water-glazed. A fat old sow had got loose with two of her piglets and they rolled so happily in a puddle that Eddie fancied he could see them grinning. Why shouldn't all of them be grinning, her family and his? It was a beautiful morning, the mist cleared and the rain clouds skiving off towards the coast. At certain points, where the land wound around the lake, they could see it gleaming quiet and silver. He lifted his hipflask to his lips. There was promise all about them. Life going on.

There would be some money.

'Where are we going?' asked Rufina after a few minutes.

He pointed to the next bend in the road, where patches of roof and chimney smoke marked the location of the little village, columns rising in the still, cold air as proof of where Rufina could get her cup of tea, provided the stores were in. He hadn't been home for a few days – he'd spent several nights away with the band in Rotorua – and it occurred to him now as they took the narrow track up from the road that he might not be greeted warmly, or at least as warmly as did his neighbours from the doorways of their houses or at work in the gardens, waving and calling out as Eddie and Rufina and the children made their way to the last house in the village, the children singing again, the German walking strongly in country women's shoes. Lace-up brogues. She was fit, he'd give her that. Got out on the farm herself maybe. A worker.

And here was his estate. Not that he owned it. It was on loan from his first wife's people, this little house of lopsided slab, sagging under a roof of flattened kerosene tins, with no garden to speak of save for tussock, clumps of wilted silverbeet and frost-bitten rhubarb, and a wormy, leafless apple tree.

Mary was coming out of the cottage door, stooped over a chipped enamel basin of dirty dishes. She had the scarf tied around her face, the one that only made an appearance when someone had the toothache. It was tattered puce chiffon, the bow flopping tiredly on the top of her greying head. He gave her a kiss, high on her cheek – and she reared away. The swelling in her jaw had sent red tendrils of infection towards her ear, into the hollow of one eye, half closing it. She looked ancient, he thought, and generally sick, as if she could peg out at any moment.

What would Rufina make of her? What a shame she never met his first wife, his beautiful Roma. He went inside and came out again with a chair, which he put beside Rufina for her comfort, while Mary stared wordless. He knew what she would see at least – that whoever this was, the Depression hadn't hit her so hard she'd had to sell her jewellery. A gold band on her wedding finger, the brooch. The pockets from which Rufina was drawing a packet of Capstan cigarettes. The midlife vigour. Her health.

'I thought your wife was a Maori lady,' she said.

He watched Mary take it all in, the basin still in her hands. She would have been on her way to the spring near the house, where hot water bubbled out of the earth and the women gathered to work.

Gracie had picked up one of the new kittens and was pushing it at him, enjoining him to see how it had grown since he had 'gone away grogging'. It was a phrase she'd learned off Mary.

'See, Pa, see, Pa?'

He took it from her and petted it. Upended in a clump of muddy grass was a nail box, so he retrieved it and sat with the kitten on his knee with Rufina beside him, her bag on her lap, the chair wobbling a little on the uneven ground.

The old man's wife. Here. Who would have thought it? The hipflask was nearly empty.

Gracie took the kitten from him, jammed it under one arm and climbed up on his knee, showing him the place where a cut on her leg had nearly healed, and how the scab could be lifted to show pink skin underneath. The child felt bony, underfed, and the kitten squirmed to be released, digging its little claws through the thin fabric of his trousers.

'Where is your wife?'

'I'm his wife,' said Mary, 'pity for me,' the toothache making her more belligerent than usual.

'My first wife died,' Eddie said, 'in childbirth.' He made an oblique gesture towards Grace, hoping she wouldn't see.

'Mary Fenchurch. That's my name. And you are?'

'Rufina Fenchurch.'

'My father's widow,' Eddie said. 'He's dead, Mary.'

A look crossed Mary's face and he saw the avarice in it. Avarice or need? The wife knew there would be money. And there would be, wouldn't there? The old man would have left his only surviving son something.

'How long ago was it?' He'd like to know the date. When the old man breathed his last. What he died of. What killed him.

'Three years.'

'Three years?' She must have made a mistake. They wouldn't have kept it from him for that long.

'We wrote to you. Nance and I.'

'To what address?' A normal man would be angry about this. Three years.

'Here,' said Rufina, looking around herself, and he wondered if she was lying. He wanted to press her on it, get her to remember what she'd written on the envelope, but what was the point? If the will hadn't changed, it hadn't.

'What were the conditions of his—' he started, but she interrupted him.

'Must have got lost.'

'She keeps my mail for me.' He meant Mary. 'If anything comes for me, she keeps it.'

'Nothing came.' Mary put the basin down on the ground.

'Was it quick? When he went?'

'Quick enough.'

'An illness?'

'No it was …'

He saw her decision not to tell him, her thin lips clamp shut, the sharp line of her jaw turn away.

'The will,' he said. 'Is there anything for me?'

'Not directly.'

At the hut Mary was calling, 'Irving!' and Eddie's oldest son came to stand in the doorway, his dark hair ruffled and flat on one side, as if he'd been sleeping.

He'd come home while Eddie was away, then, home from the shearing gang. He was a worker; you had to give him that, his first-born. A good boy. Tall, strong limbed, more like his Uncle Hohepa than his father, and thank God for that.

'Not directly? Some cash?'

But Rufina was not going to answer him. She was gazing at Irving, as if she had seen the answer to her prayers.

*

She mustn't stare. He wasn't the first handsome young man she had seen and he wouldn't be the last. But what a combination of traits, of other faces that crossed his as she saw him for the first time. Matthew's, Louisa's, Min's from her portrait. Even a little of Evie's brat. All mixed in with his other side.

She mustn't gawp. Eddie had noticed her staring, the morning's drinking taking hold, narrowing his eyes, slackening the muscles in his jaw.

'You'll be taking the basin to Milly and Jess at the springs and coming straight back here to chop the wood,' the wizened Scotswoman was telling this Maori version of Matthew, her head at right angles in order to myopically focus on his face. He was six foot four or five, grinning at his odd little stepmother, patting her gently on the shoulder as if to reassure her. 'Aye, and you won't be patting me like some poor wounded animal either.' But she smiled at his attention, and shot her hand to the aching muscles of her jaw.

A doctor was needed, if there was such a thing. In Rotorua, surely. But then she would end by having to pay for it, since the circumstances were so very much worse than anything she could have imagined. What a creature she was! A pantomime witch, now at the range taking up a damp rag to open the fire door and stirring the flames with a blackened poker. The little girl with the kitten leapt from her father's knee to take her glorious brother's hand, jumping and skipping beside him as they went away down a track cut through green undergrowth, thick ferns and tussocks head-high among tall trees. Eddie balanced on his nail box, looking after them too, puffing on his pipe.

When they disappeared into the green Rufina said, 'Irving. After Irving Berlin, I suppose.'

Eddie seemed surprised that she knew about him. Of course she did. He was Matthew's favourite too. He had a record for the gramophone.

'"Bring Back My Lena To Me". Do you know that song? That's why your father called Helena Lena for short.' My God! She wouldn't talk about all that private business about which surely this far-flung outpost of the family had no idea.

'We called him Irving Matthew. Roma wanted him named after his Australian grandfather.'

There was such tenderness in his words. He missed that first wife, then, even though he had taken another. Not a love match –

Mary must be here only to raise the children and to keep the house, primitive as it was. How interesting it would be to look inside and see how they lived, and Rufina stood to do so – she was a tourist, after all – but the old woman could take exception. Was she an old woman? She might only be forty. She could be sixty. Rufina sat down again.

The range was set up away from the cottage, under a lopsided shelter of perforated iron, which would do little to protect the cook in inclement weather. If they had it inside and properly flued it would keep them warm in winter. Why did they not think of that themselves? Were they so cramped? Did they all sleep in there?

'Mary, would it be possible to trouble you for a cup of tea?' Eddie asked. 'Mrs Fenchurch has walked all the way from town and she's parched.'

At the range Mary shrugged, as if the five miles or so from town were nothing. Flames leapt at a crack in the iron flank, a battered black kettle hung above on a chain. She didn't move.

'Would you be so kind, Mary?' Eddie took his pipe and tobacco from his pocket.

An unfathomable look passed between husband and wife. Both had cause for resentment, Rufina supposed. She looked at him as a wife might, as if her thin nostrils scented his long night on the drink and pipe. Jacket and trousers were smeary with ash and spilt liquor, his teeth and once-white shirt in competing shades of yellow.

'Go on,' said Eddie, in a harder tone, and Mary did as he said, clumping away in her too-large boots, carrying a billycan, towards a water butt at the hovel door.

'Roma, now,' he went on quietly, 'shame you never met her. Roma was a beauty, body and spirit.'

'Nance has her picture.'

'Ah. That's right. I'd forgotten I'd sent it.' He puffed energetically on his pipe, reanimating. 'Did the old man see it?'

Rufina shrugged. 'Nance might have shown him. We never talked about you.'

'Never?'

'I tried a few times, but he wouldn't have it.' She took her cigarettes from her pocket again, offered him one. He put it behind his ear, shooting it through his lank, long hair – well, longer than most men wore it these days, falling wispy along the back of his neck.

When he spoke, it was wonderingly. Almost bewildered. 'I'm his only surviving son.'

'Yes.'

'You tried, did you?' He was sharper. 'He never forgave anyone anything, big or small. The old beggar.'

'Careful.' She would not have any of that, running him down. Not till the day she died.

Eddie drooped a little; for a second he was that sensitive, self-indulgent boy again, championed by his mother and scolded by his father. But the scoldings would have been deserved, and if the father ignored him at times it would only have been after many disappointments. Matthew was always scrupulously fair.

Too fair with some people.

At the range, Mary was wrangling a huge billy, tea and sugar. There was no teapot then. Not even a teapot! For most English families the absence would be proof of utter poverty and dissolution. Why had Eddie decided to live like this? She supposed he deserved some respect for never coming knocking at Jarulan's door, and Nance was adamant that he had never written for money. And his children – or at least the two she had so far seen – perhaps he had decided it was better for them to grow up here, among the people they most resembled.

The plan would have to be changed. The tempered, potentially grateful man she had hoped for, living and working among the natives, did not seem to exist. She had thought there would still be some of the first Mrs Fenchurch's money helping him along. She had imagined the Maori wife as gracious, kind, and helpful perhaps for speaking to the Aboriginal stockmen and their wives, since Rufina often found herself exasperated by them, at a loss and at a remove. A Maori wife could have been extremely useful.

No, this was not what she had expected. Neither Eddie nor his new wife would be of any use to her whatsoever. And how terrible it would have been if she had made the offer, because it was likely they would have accepted it, and then what? Camp set up in the wing long unoccupied, a new piano delivered since she had thrown away the rotten one, liaisons formed with unsuitable people, hard-drinking guests in the house, Mary fitted with false teeth and a blonde wig, and she and Eddie frittering away the money that was left.

It was too ludicrous. Rufina could be disappointed that she had wasted time and effort coming all this way to put the proposition, but thank God she had seen him before anything was arranged. If she had written to him unseen with the proposition and he had arrived, what then? A nightmare from which there would be no chance of awakening.

Mary brought her husband a grimy tin mug and Rufina a small fluted cup with faded violets at the rim, cracked and crazed. Was it her best china? She could be looking on Rufina as their saviour. Never. Not possible. Not with the Depression the way it was, not with any hope in sight that things would get better, the swags of travellers camping by the river, the men coming begging to the door.

The tea was hot and sweet and she sipped gratefully. Eddie sloshed some of the contents from his flask into his mug.

'So,' said Mary, who hadn't moved since she handed her the tea, 'you came all the way to tell us that the old man is dead?' She wore men's trousers underneath a coarse shift, a ragged knitted jacket, all filthy.

Rufina nodded and the drunkard beside her made a peculiar noise in his throat, a snort or laugh, derisive.

'Three years after the fact.'

'Why didn't you ever try to put it right?' What a spineless fool he was. Matthew was right to cut him off.

'Because I knew the old man would knock me back. Hated me.'

'He was capable of great forgiveness. He was. You never knew him as an adult. Not really. You left when you were not much older than a boy. You didn't see how it was for him. The farm, losing Min.'

Matthew on the front verandah holding Evie's baby. Matthew holding the child by the hand as she learned to totter. Matthew explaining the specimens in the glass cases in the front parlour. Matthew at the train station in Lismore waving her off on a holiday with Nance to Brisbane, a tear in his eye. Hadn't he acknowledged the baby stolen from him by a servant girl and then abandoned in his house? If he could forgive that, weather the social disapprobation, the Coventry, then he should have forgiven his legitimate son his lesser crimes.

I should have tried harder to unearth it all, she thought now, got him to talk about it, why it was he had put both his sons away in the darkest, least accessible part of his heart, and never looked for them again.

And she had not given him another one. How much simpler life would have been if she had done. Her own son. Their son. Old sharp pain. The years of longing and guilt. The foolish prayer she had made while attending Louisa's childbed had been heard, heeded by an intractable God. Or another mysterious, undiagnosed reason a baby wouldn't come. It happens sometimes, was all the doctors would say.

On the subject of his father's virtues, Eddie gave a studied silence.

'Have you heard from your sisters?'

He sighed, dug again in his greasy pocket for the battered hipflask and shook the last drops into his mouth. Immediately he held out his hand and inspected it, as if he expected it to start trembling the moment his supply was cut off.

Rufina had need of a lavatory. She had done for some time, she realised, but she'd suppressed it since the thought terrified her. Where would they have the facilities? Was there an outhouse behind the hovel?

'Eddie, love? The lady asked you a question,' prompted Mary.

'Jean sometimes. Louisa never. I never write to them, see, so I suppose it is discouraging for them.'

'I told him to, Missus, over and over. Write to your dear sisters, I'd say. You're lucky to have them. Mine are all dead and gone, Missus, dead and gone. Write to your sisters. Who have you got, if you haven't got your family?'

Rufina's bladder stung, her stomach ached.

The son called Irving was returning now, tall, brown Hansel to the witch's order. Fenchurch blood sang loudly in his veins, the height and long-legged gait. There was the grandfather in the smile he sent in her direction as he went into the hut, a smile to turn back the years. When he emerged a minute or so later he had combed his hair flat to his head, with a finger curl rising above his brow. How could he know his namesake wore his hair the same way if he was dressing for an evening in Sydney or Lismore? The wave in the pale hair duplicated in the black.

Mary was talking.

'I beg your pardon?'

'What's the will say?'

'Oh, it said ...' She would have to think of something.

'You came here to see if Eddie would be any good on the farm, didn't you?'

Rufina said nothing.

'He won't be. You can see that for yourself.'

Rufina turned to Eddie, who didn't seem to mind his wife pointing out the obvious. He nodded gently as if to concur.

At the woodpile at the far end of the hut, Matthew's grandson was swinging the axe, laying heavy branches across the listing block, his muscles moving under his shirt. His concentration was absolute and the job more difficult than it should have been, since the handle was foreshortened and the blade, even at this distance, looked rusted and dull. Now and again the wood did not split and the impact jarred his arms and shoulders, the blue fabric of his shirt jumping and shimmering.

If she did nothing else, Rufina would leave money to buy a new axe. And a dentist, if that's what Mary needed, to have the paining tooth pulled. The old woman had one hawk eye on her still.

'What's in your brooch? The jewel.'

'Only amber.'

'Only amber, is it?' Mary held out her hand. 'Let's have a look at it, pretty wee thing.'

At her words Eddie took sharply to his feet, the nail box keeling over in his wake. A peg doll was disgorged into the mud, scrap of red rag tied around it for a dress and pencilled crooked smile. The little girl's toy. Discomforted, Rufina leaned down and picked the peg doll up, turning it around in her hands. If Gracie only knew of the riches her Sydney cousins had, the toys, the books, the pretty dresses, the horses.

There was no way she would give Mary the brooch.

Eddie was bowing, walking backwards, waving his hat, Charlie Chaplin, a clown.

'Well, Mrs Fenchurch, a pleasure to meet you after all this time. I am going to take my leave – band practice, you know. Can't leave the chaps waiting.'

'But don't you go, lady, don't you.' A claw emerged from Mary's ragged sleeve and caught hold of Rufina's shoulder. 'Not yet. Stay and have another cup. After all, we're sisters-in-law, aren't we?'

She had got the relationship entirely wrong but there was no point in correcting her. She should never have come. She should leave as soon as possible.

'Cooee – Irving – come here,' called Mary.

The young man obliged, throwing down the axe and crossing the uneven ground in boots as old and cracked as his stepmother's. And Rufina had been wrong. His smile wasn't his grandfather's at all; it was wider, guileless, so engaging that her heart ached in fear for him. You can't go safely through the world as open to it as that, she thought. You will be grievously hurt. His youth shone, the hand that took hers was wiped first on his trousers warm and dry.

Impulse to depart subsided, Eddie had collected his nail box and resumed his seat, drooping again, as if he knew what Mary was about to suggest and it pained him.

'This one would suit you. He's young and strong and clean in his habits. He works around in the gangs. Shearing and that. Scrub cutting. He knows a thing or two about farming, eh, Irvie?'

The young man's eyes had not left Rufina's and she could detect no avarice there. His stepmother had that priority. Eddie could have told her stories of Jarulan as he would remember it before the devastation of the Depression – the prime prize-winning cattle, the varied crops, the majestic house. Had he shared all that with her? It was difficult to picture them exchanging confidences tender and true.

Mary's gaze wandered hungrily from the brooch, to the bulge of Rufina's pockets, to her good shoes.

'Is it sheep?' Irving asked.

'We don't go in for sheep,' Rufina said. 'They rot in the heat and damp.'

'Ah. I can turn my hand to anything, Missus.' His voice was light, even, respectful. 'Australia!' he said, wonderingly.

'How old are you?' she asked.

'Twenty-one,' supplied Mary. 'He's twenty-one.'

'All right. Come with me back to Jarulan, to the family farm.'

The grandson grinned with delight, and Eddie groaned, and Mary clapped her hands like a child.

'We can take the train to Wellington tomorrow or the day after,' Rufina told him, 'and a ship to Sydney just as soon as we can.'

'More than a jackaroo. He's the heir, not a jackaroo,' muttered Eddie.

'Australia?' Irving said slowly and wonderingly. 'To Australia!'

He laughed then, delighted, excited. The other siblings – there were six of them, mostly girls – returned from wherever they'd been and entered immediately into the spirit of things, congratulating their brother and even shedding ready tears at the notion of his departure. Rufina stood and went among them, drawing one aside to enquire for the lavatory – if she did not go soon she'd burst.

'You wouldn't want to go there,' the child told her. 'Better to find a spot.'

She pointed into the trees and Rufina headed in that direction – a nightmare! – and found a place quickly enough where the thick undergrowth would hide her. A thoroughly unpleasant place, as she discovered, that others had used before her and more prodigiously. There was movement in the branches above her head – a smallish grey-brown bird – it was an owl. Why was it awake during the day? It had its head bent towards her, watching. It was unnerving. She held her skirt clear.

On the way back to the house she wiped her shoes on some clean grass and walked on, resolving to give this young man a life that fate would never have intended. She would turn him into a gentleman wise to the ways of the world. She would see to it that he prospered. He would be the rightful heir, in place of

Eddie. What a stir it would create! Imagine what they'd say in Lismore – a Maori Fenchurch! Worse than a German! It would be a scandal. She would enjoy every moment of it. There were some liberal-minded people who ignored bigotry when they saw it or heard it; they refused to give it the dignity of a response – Rufina had seen it again and again. But she was different. She liked to go into battle. She liked to engage.

Eddie and his family were all waiting for her on her return and Mary was producing from the range, surprisingly, two high loaves of bread for their lunch, which she set to cool on the rack above. Rufina went to stand by Irving, and the questions that rose in her mind, such as 'Can you read and write?' 'Can you drive a car?' wouldn't articulate. She would never want to embarrass him, to make him feel less than he was. She could barely bring herself to look directly at him, never so curious about any human being as she was now about him. Matthew's grandson! What had he ever known but this life? He could offer her a future for Jarulan, while Jarulan would offer him a future.

He had a question for her, asking her directly as if he was discussing his luggage.

'There's a girl here I want to marry and bring with me. If it's all right with you I'll come later, not tomorrow, after the wedding.'

Rufina had to agree. Of course she did. She'd agreed before she even thought about it, nodding.

There was a kind of wide sloping shelf built out from the wall. It was their table. The family were gathering around it.

'We'll bring you some kai. You stay where you were, Missus.' Irving assisted her back to her chair as gently as if she was an old woman.

Which she was not! She would have liked to have been able to tell him she wasn't quite thirty – though that wasn't true, she was a few years older, just a few, and besides, what was going on in her head that she would even consider impressing her youth upon this young man?

But it was just his good manners, treating her like a lady.

On his nail box beside her, Eddie appeared to have fallen into a grogged reverie. Two of the children brought them slices of heavy bread, still warm, spread with dripping that was so on-the-turn that Rufina could barely bring it to her mouth. Politely, she bit a little from the least affected part of the crust, but there was nowhere to put it aside, no plates to speak of, though some of the children were provided with torn squares of newspaper. Around the makeshift table the family laughed and joshed as if they were attending a sumptuous feast. An older girl shushed them and had them bow their heads for grace, and Rufina saw that she had been preemptory in eating even the tiny amount she had. The prayer was given in Maori and it was the first time she had heard a number of voices gathered together in the language, the soft, fluid vowels and gentle consonants, the lilting tones. The wash of sounds made her think for a moment of French or Italian, of one of the Romance languages of Europe. It didn't for a moment remind her of the Blackfella languages she had heard at Jarulan. She had always supposed – the countries being the nearest neighbours possible in this part of the world – that the languages would be similar, the countries would be similar. But heard here, they couldn't be more different.

The family stood around the three edges of the table, hands clasped, eyes closed, and the prayer was as earnest as any Rufina had heard. Mary prayed with them in the same language. Eddie did not. His pipe was re-lit, his bread ignored.

Balancing her bread on her knee, Rufina dug in her pocket and pulled out her purse. At the bank in Wellington she had changed her money from Australian pounds to New Zealand, and she took three twenty-pound notes from her purse now, handing them to him. Quite a sum. There was a tremor in his fingers and his eyes, old-man rheumy with sudden tears.

'Don't spend it on grog,' Rufina wanted to say, as she knew Matthew would have. 'Don't waste it on women,' though surely his seducing days were over.

'Eddie,' as gently as she could, 'some of the money is to get Mary's tooth fixed, a little of it is to buy a new axe, and the rest is to improve the comforts of the house.'

He shook his head. 'I'll do with it as I like.'

He seemed to have taken a new lease of energy, the tears gone to be replaced with bitterness and irritation. How similar alcoholics were. Her father had been the same. While a baby will cry overfed and push away its bottle – Louisa's spawn, and Evie's, Rufina had observed it – the sot will rage to suck more of his, even though it makes him mad and sick.

He was muttering under his breath – she thought she heard the Anglo-Saxon swear word – and gazing at the money in his hand. He held still long enough for her to pluck free one twenty-pound note and stride across to the family. Mary was hooting with laughter, and the children close to her too, her mouth open, and Rufina could see a crust of bread inserted into the good side and left to dissolve there, since the infection would be too far advanced to allow easy chewing. One end curled under her chin like a preposterous tusk.

'Here. For the dentist and a new axe. Whatever else you could use it for. I've given Eddie forty pounds.'

At her back, Eddie took quickly to his feet and she saw him pass swiftly behind the range, heading for the road as fast as could, limping in his ill-fitting boots. Some of the children ran after him, the one called Gracie swinging on his hand.

'Missus?' Mary had removed the crust and taken hold of Rufina's arm. 'Give us another twenty. The same as Eddie. For clothes and that, for the bairns.'

Irving had come to stand beside his stepmother and the other children were looking for Rufina's response. The moment stretched out, all of them looking at the money in Mary's worn hand, until Rufina again dug in her pocket and pulled out her purse, which was now almost empty.

The grandson borrowed a horse and cart from a family next door, the cart of heavy pit-sawn timber and iron wheels, the horse scarcely broken in and jittery. Mary and the children came down to the road to say goodbye, Mary holding her cheek and jawing on. She had been talking for almost the whole time it took for the horse and cart to be secured – a full two hours. Rufina had heard the neighbouring men and women and Irving talking and laughing in their language at the back of the house. And the horse took a while to catch after that. Several times she had considered just walking off, not brave enough to call to them not to worry, she would make her own way back. But that would have been rude, and it wasn't raining, at least.

And now the means of transport was here, Irving holding the horse's head and gesturing for her to climb up; for the high step she had to ease the skirt of her costume. Mary was still talking, 'You see, Mrs Fenchurch, I've longed all these years to meet Eddie's Australian family. Such stories he tells the children, early in the drinking, mind you, not when he's far gone. He had one of them, what do you call 'ems, those little bears, for a pet.'

Rufina nodded and swung herself up to the seat, a memory stirring of the koala Evie had let free that long-ago night. She'd seen her doing it. She'd seen her under the trees and Matthew hadn't believed her. It still rankled.

'Such stories of the farm he tells, of the animals, his father and you.'

Does she not know that he and I had not met before today, Rufina wondered. She took her place on the bench seat and straightened her jacket. Back to the hotel. A stiff Scotch.

'If you're glad of him you could send for Eddie – and me. Give us a chance too.'

Rufina kept her eyes on the road ahead, Irving folding the reins back now and coming up to sit beside her.

'Which hotel is it, Missus?' Mary reached to take hold of Rufina's hem, fingering the tweed.

'I forget the name,' which of course she had not. There would be no reciprocal visit, though she supposed that there were not so many hotels that Mary could not go from one to the other without finding her.

*

As they drove away a skylark lifted from a furrowed cornfield adjoining the house and flew above their heads, then another and another, and their song brought an engulfing wave of nostalgia for Europe, more intense than Rufina had ever experienced in all the years of living in Australia. It was because the climate of this place, or at least now in the early winter, the lushness, the rain, reminded her of the years at boarding school in England. It was not different enough, even with the weirdness of the smell of sulphur, the white plumes rising from the ground, the crowds of Maori people she had passed through in the town, the different twang to the tongues of the British. She longed for Jarulan. It was like no other place on earth. It was home because it was like nowhere else.

'The little birds, the skylarks,' she said. 'What do you call them here?'

Irving shook his head. 'No idea. I think they came over in cages, got set free.'

At the bend in the road she turned to wave at the family on the roadside, but they had already gone, melted away up to the cottage and the forest, or wherever they spent their working hours.

'Do the children go to school?' She had the uncomfortable sense that he thought she was prying, her voice rising clear around them with the sanctimonious tones of the missionary's wife, the health official.

'Aye. The native school. Sometimes I help there when I'm not away shearing. But today is Saturday.'

He spoke so quietly she could barely hear him above the rumble of the wheels. Had he said 'aye' or something else? Curious if it was the old English word persisting here. It had gone from Australia.

As the bush closed over them, the sun slid out from behind a cloud and disappeared behind another so quickly that the shadows jumped towards them, three dimensional, clawing, before the gloom descended again. Then they were in a green tunnel, dripping and cool, a blaze of light showing at the end where the road separated, in one direction the marae, and the other along the lakefront towards Rotorua.

A small figure came out of the light towards them. Gracie, and she had been crying. Her brother spoke to her in Maori, soothingly, and she sprang up into the cart, slipping behind Rufina to stand holding the back of the seat.

'You can't be worrying about your father,' Rufina told her. 'He is addicted to the drink. Do you understand that?'

There was silence from the girl then and also from her brother, though he darted his eyes at her.

Reprimandedly, thought Rufina. At the corner they had some trouble with the horse, who would not at first take the turn. There was no whip, and Irving was compelled to climb down and take hold of her head again, and walk beside her a short distance.

'When will I meet your wife-to-be, Irving?' she asked him. 'Before we leave?'

There was a pause, long enough for her to believe he hadn't heard her, and she began again on the question, breaking off when he answered, 'No. We'll leave it.'

'He hasn't got a wife!' exclaimed the child behind her. 'He hasn't even got a girlfriend.'

'You don't know everything, Gracie,' came the mild careless tone.

*

When they drew up before the wide verandah of her hotel Rufina could see two gentlemen on the cane settees, the same men who were there this morning. One of them had no legs and the other a drongo, a patch in his skull. Great War veterans by the look of them, permanent residents in the hotel, in the corner shadows with their uniformed nurse. The man with no legs caught Gracie's eye and held out a brand new penny. The child leapt from the dray to the dirt road, up the steps and along the boards, all grins.

Rufina watching, felt uncomfortable. All over the world children are given pennies, but this was different. The man was talking to Grace, nodding, as if he was encouraging her to do something, paying her for a service, and a second or two later her voice broke into song. By its cadence and lilt, not a Maori song, something modern. 'Won't You Come Home, Bill Bailey'. As she sang she grew more confident, louder, the words reaching the dray. 'I'll do the cooking, darling, I'll pay the rent, I know I've done you wrong.'

The man was transported, grinning, the nurse too; the other man staring with his big blue eyes.

'Bring the girl too,' said Rufina. 'If she would like to come.'

He was startled. 'Gracie?'

'Yes, why not? Give her a chance in life. Better than this.' She had half a mind to call her back from her singing. 'Promise me you'll bring her.'

'Won't be that easy. Pa is fond of her. So is Mary. So are lots of people.'

'Bring her, or don't come yourself. Riches, Irving. Don't forget. You'll inherit it. The only direct male issue. The only Fenchurch.'

'No. I have a brother, away working.'

'You're the one I want.' She wrote the address of her hotel in Wellington on a page torn from a notebook, not waiting for an answer. 'I'll wait for you for a week from today. And if you haven't come I'll leave some money and instructions for you at the hotel. All right? You and Gracie and your wife.'

He nodded.

It was arranged, then. As arranged as it ever would be.

3.

THE BATH HOUSE WAS A SHORT WALK AWAY FROM THE HOTEL, through a formal garden with willows, scraggy daisies and Phoenix palms. After her long, stiffening tramp the day before, Rufina had not slept well; the room had been stuffy and cold and now she drooped a little as she went along. The vision of a Tudor house lifting from the sward startled her – enough to lift her attention from her shabby shoes traversing the muddy paving around the pond.

Or what the English called Tudor. Europe had old houses the same – plaster and wood framing. To see it in this country, gabled, gleaming in the grey morning light, was at least as bizarre as anything else she had seen on her holiday. The little towns that tried so hard to be English and failed. The geography squeezed together, typographies of volcanic plateaus and meadows and coast so closely aligned as not to seem real. The stronger presence of the indigenous.

It was her opinion that New Zealand would never be as white as Australia was, as easy. There was a sense of displacement in almost everything here, more acute, for the sake of trying so hard to mimic that older country and failing. And fancy introducing the rabbit. The English colonies were so stupid. Yesterday, from the train window, just out of somewhere with an unpronounceable name beginning with T, she'd seen an entire hillside lift brown and white flashing tufts, departing at the rumble of the rail. If she'd had her rifle she could have cut a swathe through them.

Sulphurous fumes rose undisturbed in long tendrils from the geyser beyond the rickety fence. A peacock and his hens strutted through, feathers motley, sparse in places – maybe the sulphur affected them, gave them the mange. The unhusbanded Jarulan peacocks were splendid specimens in comparison – if one must be made, although any comparison to Australia had not proved useful so far.

She passed a group of seven or eight children, mixed brown and white, two of the girls rosebuds with ribbons, a pale little fellow in a sailor suit, and a highly energetic laughing Maori boy with three just like him. They all played together on a long swing shaped like a wooden boat, set on poles above a square of asphalt. The older boys, two Maori and two white, stood at either end to power it, bending at the knees and leaning forwards and backwards in unison. On the bench seats the younger ones squealed and screamed, whooping, healthy, delighted. It was idyllic, she supposed, proof of the stories she had heard about how the races abided together – until she noticed the mothers looking on, the Europeans sparsely grouped and the Maori mothers all together. There was a distance between them, a mutual suspicion, as one would expect. Wouldn't one expect that?

Overhead rain clouds spread horizon to horizon, forming a solid pearly cap.

*

The private bathroom contained a perplexing array of hoses and ancient pipes, with peeling signs exhorting users not to touch or turn on, but to wait for the attendant. The concrete bath was ready for her, small and square, lapping at the rim, designed so that a person had only to go down a series of steps to be submerged up to her neck in cloudy, demonic, stinking water. As she undressed, her nerve failed her – did she really want to immerse herself? Greasy, like a pan of fat. A slick shifting on the surface, a gleam through the steam. 'Living waters' they called it. Alive with what? The place had certainly seen better days – it was not as clean as she would have liked. There were chipped tiles and an underlying smell of mould; in the corridor there had been a mound of dirty towels.

Do it. You're here. Get in.

She picked her way down the slimy steps and found the seat, barely visible, easing herself down onto its pocked surface. And yes, it was a gift from deep in the provisioning earth, a delight to lie back in the pungent, cushioning heat and let the ice melt from her bones and the smell lessen its assault on her nostrils, to empty her mind, or try to.

Rest. A few seconds of thinking of nothing but the water and the heat and the white tiles and red-lettered signs. Do NOT TURN. Do NOT TOUCH.

But the troubling fantasy returned, as she knew it would, just as she knew she must school herself out of it, this ridiculous childish game: her old darling lying beside her, shifting his legs in the water, relaxed, their fingers interlinked on the floor of the bath.

'I've seen Eddie. He's in a bad way,' she told him.

'Inevitable.'

'Why did he turn out that way?'

'Bad blood.'

'Whose? Yours?'

He shrugged and so did Rufina. Bad blood. She wondered again if there had been a convict. She'd never asked, since it would have been the height of rudeness. There were so few conversations about the past in Australia. No one harked back to anything; the future was all. The past was either too painful or had never happened.

'I've asked his son to come back to Jarulan.'

'The Maori?' He let go of her hand.

'Yes, he's Maori. What of it?'

'He'll find it difficult. How can he know how to run a farm that size? And he's Maori.'

'So you said. Only part.'

'Can you think of what people will say?'

'Variations on the theme of what they've said about me.'

'You think the men will accept him giving them orders?'

'How can they not? They're all sorts themselves, aren't they?'

'Not as a boss. Never as a boss. Why did you invite the girl?'

'She's necessary. She will displace Evie's brat. We need a daughter in the house. A granddaughter.'

'I see,' said Matthew after a pause, during which she made the observation that he looked just as he had done soon after they married. A little plumper and happier than he had been when they first met. Content, genially having it all his own way. A softness about him, all because she loved him. She had worked that change in him – how surprising that she could make a man feel like that. Happy, fulfilled. In charge. It was lucky that she had realised early in her marriage that she wasn't the adventuring type at all, that to have a kind husband and a home in this most beautiful place was enough. There was the work on the farm and all the beloved horses, and the few friends in the district that had accepted her. She had read the entirety of the first Mrs Fenchurch's library and added as many books of her own. She'd learned taxidermy until she could preserve her kills as well as, and sometimes better than, Matthew. And tennis. She had never played before she came to Jarulan. In Louisa there was a willing opponent, who as the years went by spent less and less time in Sydney until she had completely retired from her marriage to her childhood home, settled into the nursery wing as if it was her own private hotel, scarcely lifting a finger. But Rufina hadn't minded, not really, not until the last six months when she took her time about dying. The expense. The trips to the hospital in Lismore. The endless calls for the local doctor when there was nothing that could be done.

'Do you know,' she remarked to Matthew now, 'this is the first real holiday I've had in twenty-three years, apart from the visit made to my old employer when he came out of Trial Bay. And Sydney of course, to visit Louisa. That is, when she wasn't . imposing on us at Jarulan.'

It was the kind of needling statement, vaguely self-pitying, that he never responded to.

'I do think that's a bit stiff, old darling, don't you? Not a single proper holiday. We were always going to make a trip to Europe together, to Germany to see my mother. And to England, yes, why not? But we never did.'

'Oh yes, I see,' said Matthew, sinking deeper, letting the water touch his chin. 'You mean to rule by division.'

He had returned to their earlier topic, ignoring her in death as he did in life when she put the pressure on. He couldn't countenance it, that she would demand of him the same things that Min had done: freedom and travel and the money for it. It had come in waves, moments of discontent. To please him she had never acted on it. But she would soon, after the farm was settled, after Irving arrived.

'What else can I do? The Tyrells are circling. Lena spends all her free time with them.'

'They are her family, Rufe. You should have made her yours when you had the chance. Evie left you to it. You could have done, could have made her yours, from the time she was little.'

I could never.

She wanted to scream at him – if I could have had my own child she would have been nothing like Evie's. Lena is dull and slow and you know she is. But at least she isn't crazy like her mother was.

But she didn't scream, had never done in real life and so would not now in her fantasy. Or whatever it was. She was being childish.

From the north wing where the men were treated came the distant sound of a torrent impacting against a wall, or flesh, and a muted visceral male groaning – whether in ecstasy or agony Rufina couldn't tell – an almost sexual distant roar that broke into her daydreaming, so amusing, so ridiculously bestial, that it made her giggle. A bear, waking to the spring, to the Aix-douche. It was musical, lifting and falling, and she wanted to sing suddenly, hadn't sung for years. And so she did, an entire lieder she had learned at school in England. Goethe's 'Fruhzeitiger Fruhling', all nine interminable verses, searching for the words across the decades and finding to her astonishment that they were still there, mostly.

Then it was quiet and her breath was the only thing disturbing the wafting steam. A corrosion in a pipe snaking above her head dripped a little, hissed and popped.

A moment or two of peace, ending with the realisation that she would have to remain in charge of Jarulan for some time yet. The grandson might not come, and if he did he might not like it. She would have to make him like it.

Young blood from the male line. A true Fenchurch man. That was what was required. Not Jean's – her sons in line for the father's struggling plantation, should they want it. And not Louisa's – Cedric in any case not the least bit interested in farming, although both he and his father tediously and intrusively fascinated by the estate accounts. And certainly not Evie's daughter, abandoned by her mother to a life of servitude at Jarulan. Matthew's largesse – unreal expectations founded in his gentle manner with her, pretty dresses, few chores – had ended with his death. If only Evie could see her daughter now – and she hadn't for years. She hadn't come back, not even for the funeral. What would she think? Cinderella and the wicked stepmother, when in actual fact the girl was stupid, lumpen and lucky to have a place in the shifting, unsteady world. No one was keeping her at Jarulan. Nineteen and perfectly able to go elsewhere, to make her own way. Or to go to live with her mother in Sydney.

An attendant went along on squeaking rubber soles outside her door. Beyond the cracked frosted window set high in the tiled wall, a bird chuckered, a strangled cry like the whirring of a clockwork device, like that child's toy the grandchildren used to fight over which somehow had worked itself into her dreams, a recurring nightmare of it leading her through the house, sometimes to Eddie's wing, sometimes to the belvedere – and Matthew was beside her again in the water, just as pensive. He had come back again almost of his own accord.

Irritating. Surely now that he'd gone she didn't have to endure his company at his behest. The worst of marriage. The hours you spend together because there's no one else to take your attention. She would never be one of those widows that put a gloss on it, beatified the dearly departed. In all honesty there were long hours in his company spent agonised with boredom, wishing he'd read a book so that they could at least talk about that, anything other than the day-to-day running of the farm, the hands, the grandchildren, the family. To have a conversation about a painting or a piece of music.

Outside the bird in the tree started up again, this time with less whirrs and clocks and more melody, high and bell-like, a magic sound like a bird from a fairy tale, and she thought she recognised some of the lilt of the song she'd sung earlier, the whole nine verses. A mimic, then. What did the singer look like? She wished she could see more than its dark shape through the mottled window and wondered, if she happened to be travelling with her rifle, and if she happened to be standing outside within easy range, would she take him for the collection? Such exuberance silenced.

'It'll be all right, won't it, darling?' But he'd gone again, slipped away in the steam just as she'd needed him.

Don't think ill of the dead if you want to keep them close.

*

More than a week passed in Wellington. Rufina delayed her voyage once and was very lucky to get a ticket on the next ship, since sailings were less frequent – few people had the money for a ticket. Thirteen nights in the second-best hotel the city had to offer, which wasn't bad at all, but she found the location dull, exhausting the attractions in the first two days – the zoo, the sea, the hills, the birds, the hills, the wind, the sea. And unrelenting cold wind unless you stayed indoors. It was as if, after all the years at Jarulan, she couldn't bear to be cold anymore – predisposition refused to come to her aid. She wrestled with herself over the cost, but finally went to a department store in a windswept street near the quay and bought a coat and hat, reassuring herself that it wouldn't be such a waste of money to buy clothes completely unsuited to Jarulan because perhaps now she could make the trip to Europe after the grandson made his appearance – and he would, inevitably, wouldn't he? She could go back to Germany to see how it was now; she could look for relatives she hardly knew were dead or alive. She could make her first return since her departure as a girl.

The hat and coat were not protection enough against the Antarctic gales; she would have to buy gloves and a muffler and a spencer – far too much of an outlay, so she spent much of her time reading and chatting to other guests in the shabby hotel lounge, doing her best to strip her accent of any lingering Germanic lilt.

A man who was on government business, newly appointed to the Meat Board, thought she was a German.

'I'm Hungarian!' She conveyed effrontery. 'I left for Australia when I was a child.'

Virtually a child.

Another conversation with a manufacturer's wife seemed to be an attempt to enlighten her.

'Oh, he's Maori,' said the manufacturer's wife. 'You should have said. They have no idea of time. You could be here for weeks.'

A racial prejudice as dangerous as any about the Germans, but it had brought Rufina back to her epiphany in the Bath House – she would remember it many times in the years that followed – that she would remain in control of the farm for some time yet. She was only thirty-seven; there was ten years' hard work left in her at least. Twenty. More. She wasn't a woman exhausted by child-bearing or poor diet, she was unencumbered even by a husband, and a husband could drain a woman of her vital energy even if he didn't want to, even if he had no idea that that was what he was doing.

Irving would come to Jarulan, or he wouldn't.

'And they never go anywhere alone, the Maoris,' said the narrow lips. 'You'll find that out soon enough. Either none will come at all or a whole gang of them.'

4.

Jarulan, 1937

ON A PARTICULARLY HOT JANUARY NIGHT, SIX MONTHS AFTER HER return to Jarulan, Rufina found herself in the belvedere as she did most evenings, trudging up the long flights of stairs from the kitchen where these days she took her meals – so saving Nance the effort of dragging it all down the corridor on the squeaky trolley. It meant she had to sit briefly with Lena and Nance, of whom she would already have had quite enough through the day, but Nance was sixty-five last birthday and plagued by lumbago. And by her veins, purple and red, snaking up her white calves. And by her back from too much heaving and carrying. Rufina could have laid her off any time in the last few years and replaced her with one of the women coming begging to the door but all of them had a man in tow. Or men. She couldn't be trusting them – and besides, if Matthew had had any deathbed wishes, which his sudden demise had prevented, he would have said, 'Look after Nan. Look after Helena.'

And so she did, by keeping them on, even though all protocol had been broken since her trip to New Zealand. In her absence they had got into the tiresome habit of talking openly about Evie, a habit they hadn't left off since her return.

'I wonder what Evie's doing tonight,' Nance would say, sometimes as soon as she sat down.

'She'll be going home on the tram,' Lena would contribute, blood flushing her face because somewhere, deep down, she must have understood that it was poor form to surmise at all, let alone in front of her father's widow. 'She'll be finishing up in the shop, she'll be closing the shutters.' Pink-cheeked.

Ludicrous, because no one knew anything at all about where Evie worked other than that some years ago she was at a milliners in William Street not far from Kings Cross. Surely fripperies such as Sydney hat shops had been knocked out of existence by the Depression, and besides, there hadn't been a letter for nearly a year. They had talked more than once about how the only person who could possibly go and look for Evie was Louisa's widower, Mr Arkenstall. And in Rufina's presence they had decided – or rather Nance had – that it wouldn't be worth asking him. He wouldn't approve. He'd say no.

'A letter might come tomorrow,' Nance said often enough. 'Don't you worry about your mother, pet, she's a tough little nut. She knows how to look after herself.'

Once or twice the girl had announced that she'd go and look for her, take the train down to Sydney for the first time in her life and walk the streets. But the idea seemed to terrify her after only a few seconds' contemplation and died away almost as soon as it occurred to her.

More often than not, if Nance and the girl didn't talk about Evie while they ate their tea, they would try to quiz Rufina about Irving and his imminent arrival. She'd told them about him once since her return and regretted it ever since.

'When did you say he was coming?' 'How old is he?' 'Does he look like a Maori or does he look like Eddie?' 'Where will he live?' 'How old is he, again?' 'Does he know about farming?' 'Is it like Australia over there where he comes from?' 'Can he understand English?' 'Does he wear normal clothes?' 'Have you written to him to see if he's still coming?'

She hadn't, and neither had she said a word about the child, Gracie. Gracie! Daily she tried to bring herself to a state of grace about it all, the insane idea. What would she do with a child here? A whim she should never have acted upon. But she was beginning to think that Irving Fenchurch would never come, and that she was worrying needlessly. She would come up with another solution to the problem.

The belvedere offered sanctuary, with her Scotch and cigarettes and the two chairs side by side, his and hers, Matthew's old cracked leather armchair replaced by two comfortable armchairs soon after their marriage. She let herself take one or the other, usually his, without thinking too much about it, the cushioned seat still holding his shape, the clink of the glass on the old sea chest that served as table – and took in the same view through the same window of the bush rising to the road, the glint of the red glass in the point of the memorial, pretty much the same view they had taken in together on evenings without number.

Although they did have a number. They came to an end.

Smoke rose from a swagman's camp down by the water, the only thing moving. It was hot and still, birds noisy before sunset. A group of wallabies rested in a clearing not far from the camp, and further along again one of the Tyrell men fished for cod on the muddy bank, his dark head pushed forward from his shoulders. Once or twice, immediately after Matthew's death, she had gone all the way to St Kevin's in Bangalow to see if it made any difference, but she and Jesus had parted company too long ago to offer any comfort. He was as elusive to her as the cod would be to the Tyrell fisherman. The cod, it was apparent, was fished out. Gone forever. A victim of progress. Like God.

How modern I am, she thought, with my lack of religion and independent life. When Eddie's son is settled in here and running the farm I could be even more independent, move away, live on the coast. After my travels. A little house with enough land for a garden and a horse; bathe every day in the sea.

But how she would miss this. The turn of the seasons on the farm, the blooming after the summer rains, the frost of a dry winter. The beauty of the swamp as it is now in February, frothing with white flowering foxtails.

The Tyrell had caught a sprat – a flash of silver flying on the line above the water as he brought it to the bank. Malachy, was it? One of the youngest, the deprivations of his childhood not evident in his square shoulders, his strong brown arms. Watching his small figure from this distance, bending to unhook his fish, she had the idea again of doing a Lady Chatterley. She had read the book, the only person to have done so in a radius of thousands of miles, she could arrogantly assume, because no one would politely mention it even if they had, because it was banned. It came for her last year from the Berlin bookseller she had dealt with in the past: *Lady Chatterley's Liebhaber* in a plain wrapper, slipping into the country undetected. She was like the character Connie, just like her, only even more frustrating to have a dead husband than a paralysed one. How would it be to seduce the fisherman, who was throwing the little fish to his basket and baiting his hook? Far rather one of the hands, one of the younger ones. The new man with the red hair. Imagine it. If she were a farmer out here on her own she would have someone. A maid. An Aboriginal girl. Should she do that, pick one of the Blacks, make him take care of her needs?

A truck was coming down the hill road, passing the memorial and moving behind the trees. A dusty truck that was once red, faded pink by the unrelenting sun. A truck Rufina had seen before but never this far out of town. It belonged to the Lismore carter. The plume of dust billowing behind fell away when the road dropped to the river, which could only mean one thing – it had turned in. There was a delay before it was visible again, as if the truck had paused longer than necessary to open and close the gate, as if the occupants had wanted to look at something. The stone lions? Surely not. They were commonplace enough, though not around here. She opened the belvedere window wide to catch the sound of the approaching motor. Under the avenue of trees passed the truck, and emerging from under a tarpaulin rigged up in the back were several men carrying swags. Are the travellers so cheeky now they'll hire trucks and drive right up to the house?

She leaned out as far as she could to see over the double verandah awnings, and just as the pink snout of the truck snorted its way out of view recognised who it was standing on the flatbed at the back, with how many … seven or eight of his countrymen? Surely not that many – but she didn't give herself time to count them, whirling away from the window, along the belvedere, through the golden oblongs of western sun on the polished floor, down the narrow stairs and past her own bedroom door, along the hall to round the turn to the upper flight, taking them two at a time to the middle landing before the last stairs. She flew under the looming wedge-tailed eagle and fan-tailed cuckoo coasting in tandem, with their new companion perched inexpertly on a rod beneath him – her own gaudy paradise parrot, the last to be seen in the district for some ten years now – and passed the library and morning room and the sheen of a glass case in the trophy room to the front door.

It proved locked. The keys were kept somewhere by Nance – though she was hardly responsible these days. When was the last time it was opened onto the flagstone steps above the circular carriageway, which is where the truck had stopped, and from where she could hear voices and laughter? Years ago. Years and years ago.

Turning, she hastened for Min's morning room, rarely used by anyone except Nance when she was sulking, and the French windows were never locked, so she fought between the musty curtains and pushed out, running again, hot and breathless, and only slowing her steps when she reached the fountain.

Calm down. What will he think of you? His ancient step-grandmother flustered and girlish, when you are thirty-seven, a widow, a landowner. Composure.

Saint Agatha was the closest figure, carrying her breasts on a plate. The story of Saint Agatha – what was it, again? She forced herself to think about it, to sit for a moment on the low stone wall and catch her breath, to listen to the dribble of water from the clogged pipes.

Think of Saint Agatha of Sicily, whose breasts were tortured for her chastity, who was consoled by Saint Peter but died of her wounds in prison. Far more disgusting than anything D.H. Lawrence could come up with.

She stood now, gathering her dignity. She would find out who these other men were, explain that things being the way they were they couldn't possibly stay – she only wanted Irving and Grace. Had there been a sign of Gracie on the truck, the little girl she had asked for?

Or rather, wanted to rescue from her drunkard father?

At a steady pace she rounded the corner of the house to the truck. The carter had alighted too, and his boy. Long shadows were cast over the rose garden – scene of that long-ago first uncomfortable embrace with Matthew. Shadowy fingers cast by the hedgerow cypresses covered a group of men looking towards her. Not seven or eight. Only five looking towards her from the shadows. Five was bad enough. One man was much older than the others and the youngest barely out of boyhood. They hadn't brought the child.

'Hello, Missus.' Irving was walking towards her, the men following him. One, a little younger than Matthew's grandson, looked almost identical to him. For a second Rufina wondered if she was greeting the right one. He drew her in as if he would kiss her or do that odd nose-to-nose greeting she had seen in Rotorua, but stepped away at the last, self-conscious, and she saw that his shirt and trousers were thick with dust, the swag he carried smeary and patched.

All of them were travel-worn and dirty.

'Jim. Jellicoe. Bill. Joe.' He gestured at them one after another, without explaining their relationship. It occurred to her that other than Joe, the one who must be his brother, he might have collected these companions on the way. In Sydney or Brisbane or wherever he'd been in the intervening six months since she saw him last.

The older man, Bill, she wasn't sure of. There was a sadness in his eyes, a desperation. Was he on the make? He was forty perhaps, difficult to tell. Perhaps he'd struggled to keep up with this vagabond band.

Footsteps sounded behind them and Nance and Lena appeared, Nance shedding volumes of tears at the sight of Irving, though Rufina couldn't think why.

'You must all be parched,' she said, wiping at her eyes with a corner of her apron. 'Come round to the kitchen and have a cup of tea.'

'They will need more than that, for goodness sake!' Rufina led the way towards the open side of the house remembering the pebble under her tongue. There was no point in interrogating them now. Later, she would find out who they all were and deal with the situation.

5.

Helena, walking along behind the men, thought they reminded her of her Tyrell uncles. They did and they didn't, since they were darker skinned. But from behind – the black hair, lustrous like hers. The shortish legs and long backs. You are like your mother, Nan would tell her, your nose and lips. But your fair hair, height and broad shoulders are Fenchurch. Put your shoulders back. Stand up straight.

She did, right then, strode out and wished that the path at the corner of the house was wide enough for her to come abreast of them, of Jimmy, Jellicoe, Irving, Joe and Bill. The most handsome men she'd ever seen, even the old one. Some of them with the same names as her much plainer brothers.

A cry pulled her up short, turned her around – and there was a little girl standing by the carter's truck, almost hidden by the shadows of the fast-falling dusk. She called out again. Tally ho, was it? It sounded like it, almost, but she left out the 'l's. Tie ho.

'Wait for me,' she said, as Helena grew closer. A grin spread across her sticky dusty face. There were twin tear tracks clear through the smut. Her hair rose thick around her head and fell below the worn shoulders of her brown calico dress.

About five, thought Helena. Or four, even. Dark-eyed, smooth-skinned, thin and knobbly kneed – and below them, below those knees were two crooked feet, wrapped in strips of cloth as makeshift boots. As she drew closer she saw that one of the boots had come adrift and that the child had been trying to remedy the situation. Ragged bands lay in a heap beside her; there were haphazard knots in what sparse arrangement remained around the crescent of a foot. A clubfoot. Two of them. One more bent than the other. Now the little crippled girl had her arms raised to be picked up.

Fenchurch women – that is, Louisa and Jean, the only true Fenchurch women that Helena had ever known – had wide hips, and so did she. Good, childbearing hips, Nan had observed often; don't let them go to waste! She didn't want Helena to have the same life she'd had with no children or house of her own.

'Where did you come from, then? How old are you?'

The child looked thoughtful for a moment before turning her attention to the passing terrain under her dangling feet, the pebbles of the garden path.

They drew level with the morning room, the French window standing ajar and a curtain billowing with a draft from the reaches of the house.

'What does Bill call you?'

'He calls me—' and there was a flood of incomprehensible words, Maori perhaps, and then gales of laughter, the child falling across her front towards Helena's other arm as she carried her along. She had made a joke perhaps, or said something rude.

'Careful now,' said Helena, straightening her, and finding that the child did smell a little, of clean earth, not dirt so much. She smelt of her travelling. She needed a proper bath with soap, clean clothes, a sausage, bread. Treacle. A treat.

As they neared the fountain the little hand stretched out towards it – the beards and spouting sea creatures, the embarrassing bare breasts.

From the verandah at the back of the house came men's voices and raised above them Nan arguing with Rufina about taking the men through to the dining room and not the kitchen. No – it was the other way around. The Roof wanted the dirty men in the dining room!

'They will be hungry!' she was shouting. 'And they will eat in the dining room. Family, Nance. Don't forget it.'

Family, Nance.

She supposed they were. All of them were family? Her half-nephews, since Eddie was her half-brother. Her nephews – and she was the same age as some of them, probably. She circled the low wall of the fountain, holding the child.

'Lena!' Rufina was calling her from inside the house, from the corridor, her voice muffling as she moved further away. 'Lena!'

'Put me here,' the child said, rising on Helena's hip as if it were a saddle and her arm the reins. 'I want to watch the pretty water.'

'There is no water,' said Helena. 'It's broken.'

'Put me!'

Showing her little pointed teeth, the child let out a piercing wail, so sharp and chilling, as if she was being burned alive, not just cross and wilful. She was lurching around, flinging herself out so that Helena had to lower her to the low wall to save her from falling.

'Just for a moment. Then I will come out and get you to take you inside.'

The child made no response. The men had obviously spoiled her rotten, made a pet of her, indulged her, unlike the hard treatment meted out to her myriad Tyrell nieces and nephews, or what she had seen of it, which wasn't much. She wasn't a true Tyrell, was she? She was a Fenchurch, and some of the family – Teresa, Malachy, Mikie – didn't let her forget it. Still, she went across the fields whenever she could to visit her grandmother and Bridgie, who still lived in the old house, along with three of the uncles and their wives and brats.

Maybe one day all of Jarulan would be hers.

You did hear of it, thought Helena, as she went on her way towards the house, leaving the strange little girl at the fountain. Daughters, unmarried daughters, inheriting the lot. When Rufina – or Mrs Fenchurch, as she forced Helena to call her – when Rufe, as Dad had called her, which actually suited her better since she was like a roof, low and cold and keeping out the sunlight – went to New Zealand, Nan had written to Evie at the last address they had. They'd decided Evie should know what the Hun was up to, going in search of a drunken nigger-lover.

That's what some of the hands said Eddie was.

The men were gathered at the kitchen water butt, and Irving was taking a towel from Nan at the verandah lines to dry his face. He could be her brother, she saw suddenly, they looked so much alike. He was big boned, like her; he had the black version of the strong sleek Fenchurch hair, the same wide mouth, which was smiling at her approach.

Nan turned to see her and said straight away, 'Away you go inside. Rufina is looking for you to set the table.' And then she was taking her arm and not introducing her, not telling the handsome men who she was. They were watching curiously – she could feel all their big brown eyes on her as she was hustled away across the verandah and in the back door. It gave her an odd feeling; it made her feel as though there was a snake in her belly, writhing around – it made her wriggle. She felt her hips swing; it was because of the way the men were looking at her. She could feel it, even though she couldn't see them while Nan kept a grip on her and let the screen door slam behind them.

'Don't, Nan!'

She tried to pull away, but the old girl was determined, guiding her towards the first bend in the corridor and pushing her into the dining room, which was hot and dark and airless. The door closed between them.

Had she really done that, with all the men watching? She felt giggly all of a sudden, though she shouldn't, not in this gloomy long tomb.

At the end of the cedar wood table, polished and empty but for the three silver candlesticks reflected in its dark depths, was the back view of Rufina. She was holding the curtain aside to gaze out over the fountain to the dusky garden. Helena could see her stepmother's face reflected filmily in the glass and a gleam of white foxtails below, clasped in one hand.

No. Not foxies. A handful of knives, silver blades catching the last of the day's light. As Rufina turned to face her, a sliver of light danced across the polished table to play on the underside of Helena's wrist, like the buttercup game, the flower held to the whitest skin. On the underside of the wrist, or under the chin. Who likes butter?

Who was it that had played that game with her? Evie, before she went away? Why did she know it? Ma Tyrell wouldn't, she didn't think. It was a soft-faced lady, she seemed to remember, with a soft lap to curl on.

Do you like butter?

She remembered it with a soft Yankee accent, like you hear at the pictures, and thought perhaps she'd only seen the lady a few times in the room opposite Dad and Rufina's bedroom with the cracked leather chair, where she used to play sometimes. She remembered the lady from before she learned to talk, from such a long time ago.

Why were her thoughts running on about such a silly thing when she'd rather think about how exciting it was that this whole new family had arrived? Which were brothers and which weren't? Nephews who were more like cousins.

Rufina let the knives clatter to the table, not caring if she marked the polish, obviously. But then she didn't have to do it, did she? Thought she was working hard if she mixed the food for the pigs or the horses, what remained of them. If she tried to tell the hands the business they knew better than she did.

'You are not to tell Irving who your father was.' Rufina spoke so quickly it was as if the words all clumped together mid-air before they separated themselves and made sense.

The long white face hung at the far end of the polished table, the silvering blonde hair, the colourless eyes. When she was little and Rufina had taken the strap to her or denied her food, or instituted a regime designed to keep her away from her father, Helena would go crying to Nan, would who counsel sympathy, tell her to offer up her misery to Jesus and be kind because the poor woman had no children of her own and that's what made her cruel; that it must all be her fault because Mr Fenchurch had had no problems siring children, did he, with the first Mrs Fenchurch and Evie?

Well, Helena thought now, dropping her gaze, neither do I have any family of my own, with my dad dead and my mother disappeared. And now I have new nephews my own age from New Zealand.

'What are you gawping at? Get on with it.'

Rufina gestured at the second-best cutlery she had thrown on the table, which Helena saw now had marked the surface, but there were so many little marks already that with luck Rufina wouldn't make a fuss. The worst, more towards the centre, was a deep short gouge where the point of a carving knife had dived into the cedar and was left quavering there until Nan came to clear away. It was the night Helena's mother had gone forever, chucked out.

Her or me. He had to choose, and he chose the German. After he threw the knife into the table. Helena had grown up with the story, couldn't remember now who had told it to her first. Everyone knew, the older station hands, the ancient rabbito, all the Tyrells. She'd heard it many times.

'Lena, you dunce – get moving.'

'Shut up. If you want all those men fed up proper,' she lifted her chin, 'then I'm more use in the kitchen. Set the table yourself.'

She turned and walked out of the room, heart racing. What if a fork or spoon – or carving knife – came after her to clock the back of her head? Rufina had slapped her before. Thrown plates, the works.

But not since she'd come back from New Zealand, from a place beginning with R. Roatoa something. The Maori word wouldn't stick in Helena's head. Where Irving and them were from. After Mrs Fenchurch came back she was different, until tonight, more relaxed, as if she'd proven something to herself – that she could go away on her own. Before she left she was a bundle of nerves, barking at people worse than a dog, off her food. She wasn't as brave as she pretended to be, was she? More than once Helena had caught her weeping, more often than she had when her husband died. Helena wasn't afraid of her anymore, even though there had been no tears since her return.

Nothing struck her, except the Roof's dumbfounded silence. For good measure Helena slammed the door after her – and remembered then, in a flash, the child she had left sitting on the fountain wall. From her place at the dining-room window Rufina would have been able to see her. How odd it was that she had said nothing, hadn't pointed a finger and asked in imperious tones: Who is that? Helena picked up her pace and ran down the corridor, out the screen door and around the corner towards the fountain. The men were gone from the yard, all was quiet. The birds even, since the sun was almost gone.

The fountain was shadowy, the figures blurring. A little darting evening breeze rustled the leaves on its floor. Helena walked the circumference, her heart thumping, frightened. The child couldn't have drowned, since the fountain was dry, and if she'd wandered off it would have been so slowly on her crooked feet that she couldn't have got far. What a darned nuisance it was that the child wouldn't tell her her name. Tally, was it? Is that what she'd been saying? Not tally ho.

'Tally!' she called and listened hard before she stepped over the low wall and peered into the figures as far as the pipes, as far as she could see – but even a tiny child couldn't fit in. The men must have come to fetch her. They can't have been half bad at looking after her, if she'd managed to come this far in one piece from those islands, which were a long way from the Northern Rivers, a long way even from Sydney, which was hundreds of miles to the south. Did the islands lie in the south, too? From her brief education before the Roof put an end to it, and with the little attention she paid, she didn't remember the map of the world below Australia. What was there? Ice and snow and mountainous seas. Her mother's people were from Ireland and her father's from England – those were the islands that had drawn her childish attention. Way way up the top, and pink like Australia.

Was New Zealand pink too, and whereabouts was it, exactly? She wandered aimlessly around the side of the house, thinking that she would go down to the landing and watch the river flow by, see who was down at the camp.

Someone small and bent was standing at the top of the river steps between the statues, almost lost in the dusk. It was the Maori child beckoning her to follow. Helena ran towards her.

It wasn't. Of course it wasn't. It was just an old wallaby turning tail as she drew closer, lolloping down the dark pit of bushy stairs towards the water.

6.

Since he'd only met her that one time, he hadn't been sure he would recognise her when he saw her again but he had, as soon as she had come around the corner of the giant mansion. She wore a loose summer frock, shorter than the women wore at home, the fabric so fine you could see the shape of her legs. She looked younger than he remembered and he wondered for the first time how old she actually was. Much younger than his grandfather, his father had told him once. Too young.

Her hair, cut shorter now, seemed to reflect the yellow gold of the sun, sinking now behind the hills. There were streaks of paler hair, where it was greying. She was looking at him and smiling, and smiling also at his brother and friends around him.

There was an uncomfortable moment – how should he greet her? – but she had offered him a hand so he took that and answered her question about how he had passed the voyage out – *Very well thank you, Missus* – though it seemed such a long time ago he could barely recall it. Three months he'd stayed in Sydney, helping out sometimes at the fish markets or the wharves, sleeping rough or in boarding houses. He'd met all kinds. Commos in the Domain, sailors at the port, nasty white men who kicked him out of pubs for no other reason than he was brown. There were kind people too, mostly people who had some kind of connection with

New Zealand, had been there themselves, were from home, but he didn't tell her anything of it because he didn't know where to start.

There was an Aborigine holding back, watching with his head lowered, looking up now and again to alight on a different face and examine it, until Bill or Jellicoe or Joe met his eye and he looked away. His people were treated badly, worse than dogs. Irving had heard stories of hunts. Not wars. Actual hunts. If that was how they treated their natives, then what would they make of him and the men he'd brought along?

Irving had gone up to him to shake his hand.

'Irving Fenchurch,' said Irving. He needed him to know he was a Fenchurch. 'Albert,' the man said shyly.

Then his grandfather's widow had been at his elbow, as if she wanted to hurry him. Together they had walked around the corner of the vast stone mansion barely exchanging a word. She seemed less certain of herself, which was the opposite of what he'd expected. This was her place, after all, where she stayed.

At the water tank she'd left them to have a wash and gone inside and he hadn't spotted her again until now, in a dusty, dark dining hall. She was taking the seat across the wide table from him. A heavy unlit light hung from the ceiling above them festooned with crystals, and floor-length curtains at the windows. Stuffy, airless, a smell of pepper and stewed beef. From a gilt-edged bowl with a matching lid his grandfather's widow ladled a thin brown stew with a large silver spoon.

Silverspooners. They didn't call them that here. They called them silvertails. He'd heard it in the Domain, and from the men he'd met when he worked a few days at Circular Quay, unloading ships. They'd cursed the silvertails, like he'd heard people at home, Pakeha mostly, curse the silverspooners. A silvertail was a person who sat down to work and earned a lot of money. One of the old stevedores had told him about a little Maori girl he'd met once, brought from New Zealand by an English couple. She was a cripple, in poor health, and had died on the ship while it was in port. The story had given him the shivers then and gave him the shivers now. He turned his attention to the portrait above Rufina's head.

An ancestor. Hers or his? Bearded, sharp-eyed. There was a pale rectangle on the wall beside it, where another portrait must have hung and was now taken away. Steam lifted from the tureen – he remembered the name for it, from meals with the vicar during that long-ago time when he'd thought about taking orders. He was only a boy then, younger than Jellicoe.

The big blonde girl who had been hurried inside by the old lady carried the plates around the table. Joe and the rest were waiting, as if for grace – but there wouldn't be one, because his father had told him there would be none of that. No religion. In a rare moment of sobriety, not long before Irving left, Eddie had explained that his mother's Catholicism had overwhelmed his father's religion, which wasn't much to start with, and now there was none. 'But I am Church of England,' Irving had said, faithful enough to accompany his employers' families to worship, if they were churchgoers. It was dispiriting how few were. Sometimes when he was away shearing, the farmer's wife would come into the shearing shed of a Saturday and tell them – if anyone would like to come to church with us tomorrow, please do.

He would talk to his grandfather's widow, ask her where the closest church was. Rufina Fenchurch. Could be a Maori name. Ruwhena. Ruwhenua. Earth shaking.

Beautiful, in her way. She was his grandmother, wasn't she, though? Good as.

The girl was at his elbow laying down his plate and he understood that she'd served him last in keeping with good manners, because he's family. His bowl, unlike the others, was only half full. Meat, onions, sour cabbage. Pepper and salt.

'Please start,' said Rufina, as the girl handed around a plate of white bread and butter. He'd get that last, too.

Family hold back.

His stepmother said it, when there were guests. Not that she had to, since it was in their blood, from both sides. The last of the meat. The milk. The bread. The last of anything went to the visitor.

Look after the guest.

If this transaction was going to work, the return would be of such value that he would end by reversing roles. Eddie had said to make sure the farm was legally his. On paper. Godless Eddie, porangi with booze, a sinner and a wreck but with occasional words of wisdom that stuck in Irving's head. 'Make yourself the boss,' he'd said. 'Don't let her push you around. Make sure a time comes when the farm is yours. On paper.'

On paper. How is he to do that?

Rufina had served nothing for herself and was leaning back in her chair. She had already eaten, he supposed. By the squat brown clock on the mantelpiece it was after nine. The serving girl was standing there quietly, her rough hands reflected in a narrow band of bevelled mirrors set into the wood.

'So. Where have you been, young Irving? All these months. When exactly did you leave New Zealand? How long ago?' Rufina sounded annoyed. She shouldn't speak to him like that in front of the others, who were picking up their spoons and hoeing in. Brother Joe caught his eye while the others tried hard not to. If only they would talk the way they had on the road, all the long trip on the train, the joking and high spirits.

Shifting her weight from one foot to the other, the servant girl swayed a little from side to side. Was she waiting for orders?

Rufina followed his eye line and turned in her chair. 'Off you go then, Lena.'

As she walked away he saw something familiar in the set of her shoulders, the droop, the slump.

Eddie.

Rufina got up from the table to close the door after her and her momentary absence relaxed the men. Jellicoe and Bill nudged one another, Jell's spoon slopping on the tablemat. Joe took a mouthful and sent Irving mimed disgust, eyebrows raised to his hair.

He was right. The food was bad. A thin broth, a faint rancid taste. Maybe they had it on the boil the whole time; maybe they just added a few gallons of water to an old stew. Why had she made them sit in this posh room full of stern ancestors when all she was feeding them was nothing better than the poor kai Mary served up at home? At least his men had relaxed a bit, talking in low voices.

'Welcome.' Rufina stood behind the carver at the far end of the long table, her arms resting along the chair back. The men talked on, so she tried again, and he heard a soft 'v' at the beginning of the word that wasn't there before.

'It is a pleasure to welcome you all to Jarulan. I won't stand on ceremony but I need to know exactly who each of you are in relation to the family, and how you fit in.'

There are only six of us, thought Irving. What's her problem?

'Joe is my cousin.'

'And the others?' Uzzers. It's because she's nervous. Her German-ness.

'Met them in Sydney.'

She looked surprised. 'So many of you?'

'Eh?'

'I beg your pardon?' Now she was offended.

Joe came to his rescue. 'I was on the ship with Irving. We met these fellas in Sydney.'

'Are there lots of you, then, in Sydney?'

Bill nodded. 'Been there coming up six years.'

Irving would have corrected him but couldn't be bothered. Bill hadn't been in Sydney for six years – much of it he was out past Parramatta, shearing, and was black as an Abo from all the hard sun, which had aged him, lined his forehead and bleached his hair.

'No. I mean, do lots of Maoris live there?'

'People go back and forth,' Bill said, after a pause. 'Not many. Don't know really.'

'Do you like it in Australia?'

'Pretty good. I was born here.' Jellicoe that time, the youngest of them, his voice barely broken. Jimmy's brother. Jimmy, taciturn as ever, hadn't said a word.

'And why have you come up north? Where are you going now?'

They were looking at him for an answer to this one.

'There is no work for you here,' Rufina said. 'Don't think that you can stay. Joe maybe. Not the others.'

He felt sick to his guts. Plate pushed away, he put his head down for a moment. He'd have to talk her round.

'But I told them ...'

'What? That they could work here? You don't know the first thing about it. I turn people away every week. Scads of them, coming to the door.'

'Not us.' He let her meet his eye. 'We're family. You said.'

'Not all of you. Not all of you are family, surely.'

'We saw them, people on the road. Everywhere. There were camps in Glen Innes. Met a man yesterday on his way to Cairns, said he hadn't eaten for three days. But knew we'd be right. We'd be welcome.'

She was staring at him, her lips parted, and he understood that he would be able to bend her to his will. She was just a woman, wasn't she? A woman on her own, apart from the lumpy girl and old cook. The men who'd come to gawp at them when they'd arrived, the men who had taken the carter and his boy over to their quarters for a feed, some of them might have to go away if there wasn't room here – but from the little he'd seen this was a big farm.

'This is the boundary of the Fenchurch land,' the carter had told him at the first bend of the river road. It had gone on for miles. The Big Scrub. That's what they'd said it was called, people on the road, whenever they learned of their destination. Dry, gaunt mountains and green fields below, rolling away forever. Rivers and gullies, bush, long reaches of marsh. He had heard there was a cedar forest here years ago, so vast that it covered all the land from the hills down to the coast, ten miles away from where he sat now, at Jarulan. Fortunes were made cutting it all out. The Fenchurch fortune maybe, among others. His fortune.

'You and I have to have a private conversation.' Rufina rose from the table as if she would take him this instant into another closed room, more interior, more stuffed with death and the past. How could the small group of women fill a house this enormous?

'The morning will be soon enough,' he said, standing, his men following suit. He led them out the way they came, down the corridor and through the screen door, around the house to the carter's truck, where they took their pikaus and blanket rolls from the tray and set up a kind of camp on the front verandah. What had he thought – that he'd be given a featherbed, a four-poster, silken sheets? At least the night was warm and dry and the wooden boards smoother than most of the beds he'd made since he took to the road.

Eventually Bill and the others went to sleep and Irving lay among them, trying to recall the conversation he'd had with Rufina all those months ago at home. Did she say he was to come alone? He couldn't remember. In fact, she'd wanted him to bring his sister Gracie but Mary would have none of it. Not my best girl, she'd kept saying, not my baby. Gracie was the one Mary raised from infancy after the death of their mother.

A soft flickering caressed his shin, a tentative, spindly motion towards his knee – a creature larger than a mouse, many legged. He brushed it off. A spider, was it? He couldn't see in the gloom or hear it either, scuttling away. It might have been poisonous. He should stand up, make sure it hadn't transferred itself to Bill or Joe or any of the others. But how could he see without a candle? He listened hard – perhaps there was a faint tapping along the boards, going away from the men.

*

Just after dawn he woke to the memory of a pair of dusty women's boots planted squarely in front of him, a pair of shapely white calves rising above them. A pool of golden light had trembled on the boards; there had been a lamp clasped in a female hand and lowered towards his face. 'It's all right.' Spoken softly. 'Go back to sleep.' And he'd done as he was bidden, must have done, like an obedient boy.

7.

All night pacing. Pacing around Jarulan in the dark, from room to room, corridor to corridor, wing to wing, with her stomach roiling and mind blank to everything other than the arrival. What had she done to offend him? How could Irving have done this, appear with all those extra mouths? Where were his loyalties? It was a bad omen, the way he held those men around him.

Just after midnight she had tried to sleep, lain down in the small room she had taken after Matthew's death. It was the room he'd had when they first met, his boyhood room. A single bed. A chest of drawers, a view out over the yard and the low-roofed servants' quarters. South-facing, cooler in the summer. It had comforted her to be there. Sleep had evaded her in the months after he died, but she could sleep there. Close to him, but not too close, not lying in the deathbed. Forgiven.

The forgiven part was very important. She'd done everything wrong. That was what the doctor had told her. She had washed the wound, once they'd found it. Matthew couldn't tell them where it was, since he hadn't felt the bite, just as he hadn't seen the snake. She had encouraged him to walk from the paddock up to the house. She should have kept him still. She should have called for help from one of the hands, someone who knew what to do, how to find the site, make the cross-cut and draw away the poison.

Why was she here then, in the spacious matrimonial bedroom, with its buggy old bedstead and sooty fireplace? Matthew shivering with cold those last awful hours, the fire banked high. After the funeral Rufina had given instructions for the master bedroom to be closed. Locked.

The key weighed cold and heavy in her hand. She must have gone downstairs to fetch it from the cupboard in the washhouse, gone down the stairs and out the back door still half-asleep, barely conscious. Or had she already taken it on her earlier drifting about, raising the kerosene lamp to the board and slipping the key off its numbered hook? She couldn't remember. The tablets were mucking her up, two of them, taken soon after she climbed into the single bed. As good as strapping herself down, usually. Or not.

How many nights had she spent like this, pacing hot and restless? The day's heat was retained here, because the room was at the front of the house, facing west; the air damp and curled like a weighty, dusty cat, the curtains hung thick at the windows with moonlight showing as a pale fuzz at the join.

Rufina put the lantern on her old dressing table, crossed the room and flung the curtains open to the glistening tops of the trees, the shadowy fence-lines in the near paddocks, the driveway glowing white on its last meander before the gate. It would be refreshing to open the window, push open the screens and breathe in the night. But her lamp would bring insects of the nocturnal kind, which were even more alarming than those of the day, even after all these years – especially the ones that came at you from the dark, whirring, huge, banging at the lamp shades or incinerating themselves in candle flame. One night, in this very room, a moth the size of a small bird had flown above her head with its wings aflame, and she had shrieked in horror while

Matthew laughed from the bed, laughing more when she raced to join him and drew the sheet over her head. In the morning on her return from the lavatory, still outside in those days, she had found a small pile of ash by the bed, the flame so hot it had devoured even the moister parts of the body.

'It would have been a quick death, I suppose,' she had said. Matthew was dressing at his tallboy, pulling on work clothes, running a comb through his hair.

'Wouldn't've felt a thing,' he'd answered. 'Wouldn't've known it was alive in the first place.'

'Every animal knows it's alive.'

On the windowsill was a tiny lamp – a modesty lamp, they were called at her boarding school – set in the curtainless dormitory window to render the room inside invisible. Her mother had sent it to her in a box with some other things from her childhood, a favourite doll, a tattered book of Brothers Grimm stories. She lit it with a taper from the mantelpiece, then pulled away the flyscreen and opened the window, unhitching it on the casement and flinging it wide. The glow wouldn't be enough to draw the insects.

Fresh air, warm, smelling of the river and the eucalypts, of flowers and dust. Moonlight, a glint of water, the dark shape of the hills, the faint gloom of roses in the near garden. Behind her the dark of the room and the lantern guttering suddenly. She turned it up, just a whisker, to be on the safe side. But she wouldn't be here for long, would she? She'd be back to her narrow bed in a jiffy, not in this room alone in the dark. Since Matthew's death she had only come here in the daytime.

A figure passed from the ground floor verandah to the edge of the rose garden to relieve himself. It was the one with the odd name, the youngest of them. Jelly something. How lucky men are that they can do that, she thought, watching him. It was one of the first things she'd had to get used to, out working with Matthew on the farm when she was first married, the way the men didn't go far away enough to be decent. On his return the boy glanced up at the house, directly towards her.

But he would be able to see nothing from there. The glow of the lamp shielded her. For him to have seen her she would have to have opened the French windows and gone out onto the verandah, treading above the sleeping men.

*

Heartbreaking. Lying on the boards like vagrants. Earlier on her rambles she'd gone to look at them. Only one of them woke up – she thought it was Matthew's grandson; it was difficult to tell in the dark. And she had been looking for the Irving as he looked the only other time she had met him, she realised, in New Zealand, not as he was now, with the marks of experience and defeat on him. He had had a hard time of it on the road. Too thin, a sadness in his eyes.

She went to the bed, laying her hand on the dustsheet, then found that she had sunk to sit on the edge of the mattress – a puff of dust-laden air and a scurry of departing beetle on the floor.

What would Matthew say about all this if he was here?

This would never have happened if Matthew was here.

If he was here she would lie in his arms now, she would have him. She felt like it, she needed it, more than she ever did when she was younger. Her thirties had brought with them the full force of her appetite – frightening, swollen, gross, a weed grown out of control since the gardener died. A flash of them together – entwined, lustful, private. How good it was. How he had known how to please a woman. He had taught her that there was no shame in it.

Lying down now, her hand between her legs, above her the same moulded plaster cornices and ceiling roses that her eyes had opened to for fifteen years. Unchanged – though a spider had made her nest between two plaster roses, an elaborate, translucent column of criss-crossing filaments shifting gently in the breeze from the open window, beautiful if you want it to be beautiful. And she did. She wanted everything beautiful, and why not?

Afterwards she lay dreaming about how she could make this room hers again, and made a mental list of the things she would have to buy or fix. It was a state of mind familiar from her married life, how her thoughts could run along the most prosaic channels after those mysterious joyful waves of sensation that Matthew hadn't known the name for and so neither had she.

Irving hadn't liked her. He hadn't liked the dining room or the food. He had refused her invitation to a private conversation. He was wary of her when she'd given him no reason. Why hadn't she intuited when she met him how arrogant and unbiddable he could be? He had seemed a sweet naïve country boy, a poor relation whom she had imagined would enter a state of obedient gratitude.

Did he realise that she hadn't had to go and fetch him? She could have found someone on her own side – a distant cousin in Germany, if any had survived the war and remembered her. For exactly half her life she had been in this new country. For most of the time, since she left the Schneiders, she had barely spoken a word of her mother tongue.

I am Australian, she thought, with conviction. Not German. I am a Fenchurch, and so is he. He will forget he is a New Zealander. We will come to an agreement about how things will be managed between us. Mutually respectful. Close or not so close. Close enough to be able to greet one another with a kiss in the mornings. Those lips just like Matthew's, the gleaming planes of his beautiful face. Close enough to sit across the table for their evening meal. Close enough to sit together in the belvedere in the evenings, to hear how his voice was like Matthew's, only different. To hear his laugh. Close enough to take his hand as they came downstairs. To hold him. How it would be to lie with him like this.

Her hand had travelled across her belly, following the line of her groin. Yes, this close, Matthew. This shameful, to be thinking of that young man asleep on the verandah, to be imagining what he could be for me. Within bounds. A kind of contract. A secret arrangement.

She lay awake for hours until there was the merest softening of the dark as the sun began to rise. Here, on the western side of the house, the sky responded with a faint, demure blush.

8.

Helena woke in the small room under the stairs, the room that had been her mother's until she went away and her own ever since, kept clean and tidy, the way she liked it. She would never consent to sleep in the servants' quarters, even though Rufina had had the roof fixed before the Depression bit. The rooms were still poor and inconvenient and small, and the only reason Rufina wanted Helena to sleep there was so she could continue with this bloody rubbish swindle she was pulling, pretending that Helena wasn't family.

'Didn't you ever tell Eddie about me in your letters? Do they even know about me?' Helena had demanded of Nan, because Nan wrote to him now and again, she knew. Nan had feigned bewilderment – or maybe she really was losing her marbles. 'Did you see the little crippled girl who came with Irving and them?' Helena had asked, and Nan had told her off for making up unpleasant stories.

'Little crippled girls! Bats in your belfry. Get on with the spuds.'

When she'd asked Irving the same question he'd looked bewildered, even frightened. Lena had begun to describe the child – the matted hair and strange bandages, the tattered frock, her high lilting laughter – and Irving, who was busy with hammer and nails as he settled into Eddie's wing had said, rudely, 'Go away, Lena.' This morning, looking up at the warping inverse wooden staircase that formed the ceiling, Helena knew that by now Nan would be in the kitchen waiting for her. It was a new thing she did. Waited until Helena got there to start the work: why should I break my back with a big hulking girl like you around to help? You look like you're more use than you are. Where's your gumption? If you knew how my legs were killing me – on and on. Sometimes it panned out all right because Helena would persuade her to sit tight at the blackened old cedar table and have a cuppa before they started, and sometimes the old girl softened enough to tell stories of them all when they were growing up, Helena's half-brothers and sisters. Or there would be a fair or a dance to look forward to, though since Dad died they didn't go out and about so much.

Rufina did. Went all the way to New Zealand, for Pete's sake!

Nan could do breakfast herself. Who was there to cook for now, anyway? Jimmy and Joe had gone, ordered off the farm by Rufina because they knew nothing about farming. The older blacker man called Bill was living over at the accommodation with Jellicoe – the one who had wept so piteously until Nan said, 'He's only a lad. Have some mercy, Mrs Fenchurch.' So Jellicoe had stayed on for no wages, only board and keep over in the accommodation. Yesterday Helena had watched him ride out in the cool of the morning with Albert, grinning from ear to ear, and she thought, *My, you've landed on your feet, haven't you, little bottler!*

A new pimple had formed on her chin. She lay on her back, pushing at the sore with a fingertip as if to force it into retreat, level with her skin. From previous experience she knew it would only antagonise it, make it worse. A great welling rose in her chest enough to hurt – why wasn't she beautiful enough for Irving to notice her? And he would notice her if she told him that he was her nephew. He would. Or cousin. She could tell him a version of the truth – not that she was his aunt. He mightn't like her enough if he knew she was his aunt, and she wanted Irving to like her a lot.

And why had the crippled child disappeared before she'd had time to find out who she was? The day after the men had arrived she'd gone over to the Tyrells to see if she was there, a scenario running through her mind that the child had made some progress on her own, crawling or whatever, and that one of her uncles had cut through the Fenchurch property and found her.

But there was no sign of the little girl and she'd found her grandmother in bed with a stomach bug and lumbago together at the same time, and ordering poor Auntie Bridgie around with basins and towels. Helena hadn't stayed long. If ever, she thought as she made her way back to Jarulan, if ever I am a lady who gives orders I won't. I will ask politely. I will not be like Ma or the Roof. I will be kind.

The Roof was kind to Irving. She had bought him a piano to replace the one that had rotted away with damp and termites. She had taken down the decayed curtains, still with threads of gold in the creases, and enlisted Lena's help to hang new ones of chintz. The carter and his boy had returned with a dinghy-sized leather chesterfield, a clutch of padded armchairs and a roll of Turkish carpet, and Irving had set it all about in the biggest room of the wing. Min's statues stood there still – though scheduled for removal. 'Can't live with them,' Irving had said, hanging cloths over their heads. The fat man statue with the bunches of grapes he'd turned to face the tall windows that looked out over the raggy rose garden towards the river.

Later, she would go over to the accommodation and ask Bill and Jellicoe about the little girl. Maybe they were keeping her a secret – although there was a strictly no girls or women rule over there. No women, except in the married quarters. They still held to the old rule, so the little girl wouldn't be there.

And it was a little girl, Helena was sure. Wasn't it? In the days that had passed since she'd met her, Lena had begun to wonder if she'd imagined it. Her mind kept returning to the little girl, pressing on the memory as if it was a sore, like the one on her chin. There was something about the girl that frightened her.

The dinner bell. *Ding-dong.* She ignored it. Was she the only one who had noticed the child? How could that have been? Or did she belong to the carter perhaps, who had come back in the dark to fetch her?

Perhaps she wasn't real. A ghost. A real live ghost. One that lived outside, as opposed to the one that hung about inside. Not that anyone had seen the inside ghosts – just heard them. The scraping of little wheels. The whirring, spinning, whistling. The rocking of a chair in the little room across from the master bedroom, where the first Mrs Fenchurch had gone for her turns.

Ding-dong.

Ding.

Nan was ringing the dinner bell! At breakfast time! Helena sat bolt upright in bed. She had done it once before and Rufina had been furious; it had put her out of kilter for the whole day, she said; she had struggled to find her balance.

Dong.

The deeper bell again. An emergency, or did the old girl really have a slate loose and thought the evening had come before the morning?

Flying out of bed, Helena tugged down her nightdress and ran as fast as she could barefoot through the shadowy corridors towards the kitchen, the bell tolling all the way, uneven, urgent, offbeat.

9.

RUFINA, MIXING PIGSWILL IN AN OLD IRON BATH KEPT IN THE barn for the purpose, heard the tolling of the dinner bell but gave it no heed. Nance was losing her mind and that was that. The wrong bell at the wrong time of day was just another minor symptom in a growing list. There was nothing to be done about it. With any luck, the decline would be rapid. If only there was a real family to take her back, look after her now she was old. If she had been a real servant then she could have paid her off, but she wasn't, in Rufina's opinion, the genuine article. Matthew had treated her more like an elderly aunt, a member of the family. When he was alive he had allowed her to eat with them in the evenings, the four of them, Lena as well. She had asked once, when Nance was bedridden with one of her many ailments: have you got a brother or sisters? She knew there had been no children.

The old woman had got weepy, offended, and hands had to be patted and apologies approached.

Oats, windfall apples, kitchen scraps, maize meal, skim milk, slurred and slopping around with an old wooden scythe handle, perfect for the job. Two heavy bucketfuls balanced either side, she walked the full length of the piggery, emptying them into the central channel that acted as a trough. They'd always kept pigs at Jarulan, since before she came. In Matthew's father's day they'd kept them for their own use. But this was new, different, modern – intensive farming, a new initiative of her own since Matthew's death. They did it in Europe, had done for decades, kept pigs in large numbers indoors, but it was only just catching on here, in its own way, with long segmented barns built of corrugated iron with stone floors.

In this snowless climate, the building was open-ended, built east to northeast to take advantage of the prevailing winds.

Even so, you had to have a strong stomach for it. The stench, especially on still mornings like this one, could take the lining off your nostrils and burn your throat.

Rufina carried the bucket down the shed, flanked by the farrowing sows, separate from one another in pens, and on the other side the store pigs and porkers, fattening for the market and doing so nicely. Tamworths – sparse soft white hair, smooth ruddy skins, even-tempered. The best. This time of year you had to worry about flystrike and fungal infections – but so far so good. The pigs made back the money she had invested. Even with things as they were, the English still wanted Australian pork and lots of it.

Back she went to the outhouse to refill the buckets and saw Irving pass by on the stallion she had given him, son of long-dead Boss and a stubborn hefty Waler mare called Tick. An accident – bad boy, Boss – but a good one. You could see the graceful father in the son, and Tick in his broad chest and thick neck. He was weaving his head and lifting his feet, wanting to go out into the day, impatient.

'Going to check the fence-lines.' Irving tipped his hat. They had bought it together at the outfitter in Lismore – an Akubra, the latest thing. Felt with a broad brim. Dark green. It looked so well on him.

'Which ones?'

Irving made a game of it, twirling his finger in various directions until he pointed north.

'You were only out there last week.'

He winked at her, grinning. She was filled with urgency.

'Stay here and help me with the pigs. There is a lot for me to teach you about them.' He could help her with the pigs. They could do the pigs together.

He continued to regard her, the kind warming eyes in the shadow of his green hat, the gleam of his smooth cheek, but then he said, 'I'm out and about today, Rufina,' and passed on by. Knocking her knees against the heavy bucket she hurried out after him, calling 'Irving!', slopping the feed, just in time to see him jump the first gate, where he kicked the horse on – though it hardly needed any encouragement, rising strong to the gallop almost immediately. She watched him ride out of sight as they took the fences all the way across the fields north of Tyrells', his blue shirt filling like a sail. So beautiful, the pair of them riding out, the green of the land drawing them in. Above the McPherson Range thunderheads gathered again but they wouldn't break; no rain for weeks, just heavy, steaming clouds that sat above man and animal like a lid on a simmering pot.

If only he had asked her to ride out with him. But why would he? What had he seen when he'd looked at her – hair scragged back under her hat, sweating in moleskin trousers and man's shirt and boots, and reeking of the Schweines.

Did she? Her bare arm smelt of nothing, but then one of the shit-caked sows would think she smelt of nothing, if you asked her and she could answer. There was no point in worrying about Irving, about his responses to her. She had to take it all slowly.

Ravenously the sow, due to farrow in the next few days, chewed at the trough, working her big red jaw and slurping and crunching the way she had when she ate the last litter. And the one before that. The trick this time would be to get them away from her as soon as they were born – or put her in a crate so she couldn't turn around. Cruel but effective. Crates made sense.

She'd have some built. Stop them from eating their babies, but also prevent them from looking after them properly, cleaning them and so on, from expending whatever version of love a sow felt. If they felt love. She thought they might. She certainly did, looked forward to the piglets' arrival.

Leaning against the low gate of the last sow's stall, she watched three-day-old piglets as they fed in a frenzy, corkscrews whirling, scrambling over one another to change places, as if one teat were preferable to another. There was a rhythm to it, because the sow let down her milk only in short bursts and the infants strove for as much of it as they could swallow in the time allowed. One piglet lay away from the others on the straw, listless, his eyes opening and closing slowly, furrowed brow deepening and twitching, as if the little of the world that he had seen so far disappointed him. She opened the gate and went in, scooped him up and carried him out.

What was the fairy tale about a woman who took a little piglet to be her own child? The enchanted Firkel that turned out to be the lost son of a king? Holding him now, warm and sleepy – sick? – she could see how a childless woman might well fall in love with a piglet. He was not much more than the size of a newborn baby, and he smelt as inoffensive as her arm had done, and he was brightening with her attention, a light coming into his little piggy eyes.

She held him up between her hands – the way mothers do to look into their infants' faces – and his eyes were oddly boy-like; his whiffling shovel nose and dangling cloven feet less so. The piglet's expression changed – from one of curiosity and trust to one of fear and suspicion, although was it because he'd only just realised how high in the air she held him? He pooped a tiny dribble down her arm, slimy and brown. From nowhere came a violent, momentary urge to throw him away, as hard as she could, to dash his brains out against the far wall, not because he had shat on her, but because even a small pig looked at her the way everyone else did – Nance, Lena, the hands, the new arrivals. With suspicion. They would protect themselves from her. They were unable to predict what she would do next. A lone wolf. Heartless, sharp, determined, wilful. The widow. A killjoy. Miesmacher. She was not.

But not Irving. He didn't think that of her, and was that because the shower of gifts – the horse, the furniture for the wing, the piano, new saddlery, boots, spurs and clothes – had blinded him to her true nature? A brand-new rifle. A swag of dogs: a red heeler, two shepherds and a collie.

The piglet was anxious, his ears twitching back and forth and four neat feet working the air. She turned him around so that he could look down on his mother and littermates, and his efforts redoubled, screwy tail wiggling and pink balls bulging small between his legs, buttocks wobbling. His hams. Tamworths are the only pig with bum cheeks, she had been interested to learn. One truly could say pig's arse and mean it if you spent hours in their company. He was greasy in her hands, distasteful suddenly, so she opened the stall again and went in to lay him among his brothers and sisters, whom she saw now were considerably bigger. The runt then, and likely to miss out on sustenance altogether, unless someone looked after him. Lena?

Bending to the sow, who regarded her warily also, she pulled away the fattest piglet and put the runt in his place and waited until he got started on a meal. After he was well away, she left the pigs to stand for a moment at the open end of the corrugated-iron shed for the best of the view. All was peaceful. The heat was less punishing than it had been, maybe, but it was still enough for the day to burn like a furnace later. In the grey glare, the air was almost purple. Away in the distance, in the opposite direction to the one Irving had taken, the tractor was towing the new combine harvester in the lucerne. Two men sat side by side on the tractor, and several others followed on foot to gather and bind, since the sheathing function on the damned harvester was playing up again. She would have to take it to the mechanic in Lismore if her own man really proved incapable of fixing it, and if she were to go into town then she could take care of some outstanding bills and visit the bank manager to plead for clemency on the loan that had fixed the belvedere roof, bought the A Model Ford, the harvester, and the new tractor, and the oil generator, and many other expensive improvements made just before the crash.

She hadn't used to work so hard on the farm, didn't need to even now in this Depression. Some of it was show since Irving arrived. Wasn't it? Go on, be honest. But she had to show him she meant business – she wouldn't hand the farm over to him until she was sure he knew what he was doing with all of it. The barley, wheat, tobacco, beef, poultry, pigs.

So far, Irving had shown no interest in crops. Or the pigs. Anything that didn't involve riding out, or horses or dogs. But then she hadn't made herself clear and she could see that she would have to – and it was something she would have to plan to the last detail, in case he took fright.

Inside she washed perfunctorily – it was pointless trying to keep clean in this place really, if you were going to do anything at all but hang about inside bored out of your mind – and went to Matthew's old desk in the library to begin the accounts. He could have had any room in the house as his study, but it had been here. He had put his desk in Min's library. To be close to his first wife, Nance had told her, in the days when Rufina would ask her searching questions about the first Mrs Fenchurch.

When she was in her early twenties, she was fascinated, wanted to know as much as Nance would tell her. It was as if she had to imagine that first marriage – even at its most intimate – before she could settle into her own. Thank God that obsession had burned itself out early so that she could enjoy Matthew properly for all the time that he was hers. She'd grown up, grown out of it, and she and Matthew had shared this room too, spent hours here.

As she came in from the hall she imagined opening the panelled door and seeing him in his chair by the window, the light falling on an open ledger or record book or newspaper, the green glow of the lampshade, his loving smile – and felt choked with missing him.

She went in, pulled open the curtain so that the light danced on the dust, and started on making up the wages. There were so few men left. Even the rabbito had gone, a man who had seemed to have grown out of the ground here. Matthew had told her the man was the rabbito's son, born at Jarulan, been there for longer than he had. The rabbits had got out of control, of course, thousands of the beggars, even with the swaggies and their wives passing through and putting them in their pots.

Making up the slips took no time at all, entering each amount in the book. Lena, being family, was unpaid. Three hands, the cook, hired labour when she needed it. The two Aboriginal stockmen drawing half the pay of the whites but the same tobacco allowance. And Nance and Bill. They would come to her if they needed some cash, otherwise she kept it all for them on scrip. At the end of the heavy green ledger, four pages in, was Irving's page. He had his own entry, hidden, in case someone came snooping after she'd gone. Arkenstall might. He had taken an unhealthy interest in the farm's accounts when Louisa was alive. Less so since she'd died.

Small beer, the expenditure on Irving. More an investment in the future. Clothes, saddles, the new rifle. The furniture and piano, although strictly speaking those items were for the house, likewise the curtains and carpets. He received it all with ease and grace, with no anxiety about what he should give her in return. The day she gave him the stallion he hadn't stopped smiling, even while he ate. She could let herself think about him for hours, just think of his handsome face, the peace and kindness of him. Is that what it was? A kind of purity of spirit. Purity! She was reluctant to use that word about any man. He must have done bad things, said cruel words, but she couldn't imagine it.

A shadow fell across her arm and the columns of the ledger, without definition. A shoulder, an extended arm, the peak of a hat – she spun in her chair, knowing there would be no one there.

Matthew? But it wasn't. She hadn't been playing that silly game, bringing him close to talk to, playing imaginary friends like a child. Sometimes he would come unbidden, she would hear his voice, feel him close, but mostly he stayed firmly on the other side, gone like the gentleman he was. Uncomplicated, decent. Silent on many things in life, but not as silent as he was now, abandoning her to this new presence. There was a smell in the room of petrol fumes and the sea. Frangipani. The smell of a city to the south, of Sydney. She felt as though she was waiting for him to speak. A sudden beam of too-hot light found its way through the leaves of a close tree, slanting across the figures and melting the shadow away.

If it was there in the first place. The smell was gone. The room smelt as it had before, of paper and dust. Of old pipe smoke. Of Matthew.

'Am I missing you so much I'm inventing other men for company?'

He didn't answer.

Tucking the payslips into her pocket she stood to lift the heavy ledger back to a low shelf, ashamed of herself. Flowers and petrol fumes. Haunted houses had ghosts that were seen by more than one person. There was Nance's story about the woman in white on the belvedere stairs, the noises in the house. Had they become a tragically demented gaggle of lonely females, imagining it all – the distant laughter of a young man, the rolling of small hard wheels on the floorboards? Min had heard things here, voices and music, part of her madness.

Irving's presence in the house would dispel the ghosts, make them go away. How fanciful you are, Rufe. She opened a window, let in some light. The sun would move away from this side of the building soon and the room would cool down.

Ghost stories. She'd never really liked them. But didn't most ghost stories tell of spirits that were rooted in one place, that didn't follow you around? They stayed in their own houses and on their own ships. They came out of the walls, not the heart. The ghosts, if they were here, had nothing to do with her. When she was a child she heard the story of the hunting lodge near Grunewald lake, not far from her grandfather's house, where the ghost of a murdered nobleman ran eternally down a flight of stairs, fleeing for his life, even though the staircase had been bricked up for centuries. He only ran down the stairs, nowhere else. Or the story of die Weisse Frau, who slew her two children with a golden needle, pushing it deep into their skulls, so that she could have the man she lusted after, and now paced from one Hohenzollern castle to another, from Bisingen to Berlin and back again, forever racked with guilt.

Outside. She couldn't bear to draw the curtains. She hurried from the room and went outside to find the old peahen she'd noticed yesterday hanging around down by the river landing with a broken leg and a wounded side. A dog must have got to it, or a quoll. It was bloody buggered, as Matthew would say, if he was here. She'd get her rifle and shoot it.

10.

He hadn't expected the land to be so beautiful. It was like his own country and it wasn't – the green, the rolling hills, but everything brighter, bigger, louder, a giant's country. There was a wide stream, shallow and bubbling, that ran at the northern edge of the pastureland before the terrain changed to climb the foothills of the Nimbins. Somewhere towards the hazy west, the creek would connect with the river that turned back on itself to run past the house. It all looked so good, so rich, the land, until you realised there wasn't enough cattle to cover it, considering the acreage. Three thousand acres, didn't she say? And she'd told him that the soil was already finished, that the farm couldn't support any more than she ran, even with prices holding steady. It was because a century ago it had been covered in forest, and after the clearing the soil was fertile for a while, but would not revive even with lashings of phosphate.

She'd told him that the first evening he'd spent with her in that strange attic room. There had been a few evenings up there over the three weeks since he'd arrived. They'd sit up there together and she mostly listened, got him to talk, told him this and that about the farm – the new machines his grandfather had invested in just before the crash, the new crops and lucerne. Nothing about herself. Nothing about her life before the war, before she came here and married his grandfather. Maybe she hadn't had much of a life, before that. Often they sat in relative silence, like real families do, people who've known each other forever, just sitting and looking out over their land.

He got off the horse, pulled off his boots and walked into the streaming pebbles. The light running over his feet reminded him of that room, not really an attic at all. Weren't they usually dark? This one was bright and clear. Watery with all the glass. She had a fancy name for it – belvedere. Often after they'd thrown down whatever muck that got put in front of them, Rufina would pour two fingers of Scotch into two glasses and lead the way up the long flights of stairs, along the third floor corridor and up the rickety steps to the high room, rain or shine. They would sit in the two chairs at the far end. Usually, in his limited experience, women only sat in silence if they were unhappy. Rufina was more like a man in this instance, thoughtful, quiet, though usually in one of the soft cotton dresses she put on when she changed out of her trousers and shirt and boots, after she took off the smeary old hat she wore jammed over her hair when she was outside. There had been no sign of the woollen walking costume and posh umbrella she had in Rotorua. No need for them. No rain and too blimmin' hot.

Boots slung over his saddle, he followed the fence-line above the creek. It was in good shape, recently attended to, so he left the roll of wire and pliers in the saddlebag. Long grass as high as his shoulder hummed with loud insects and probably hid snakes; he knew enough to keep to the track. If he was at home with grass like this he might fling himself down to lie among the tall green spears and watch the shifting sky, sleep for an hour or so. Not here. Rufina had gone on about snakes, how careful you had to be, what to do if one got you. One got his grandfather; those eyes the colour of rain had misted up when she told him. It was almost as if she blamed herself, but she didn't go into details.

That's it. Tears. Her eyes were the colour of tears.

His breath caught in his throat. Why was he thinking about her in that way, as if he was sweet on her? The other night, when he'd finished up his Scotch, he'd told her he was going downstairs to fetch another one.

'Why don't you keep a bottle up here?' he'd asked her, even though he didn't particularly like it.

'Only one drink a night,' she said sharply, like an old woman stuck in her ways. He'd gone downstairs, found the bottle and taken it down to his quarters. Eddie's wing, they still called it. Where his father had first started drinking, in vast interconnected rooms and high ceilings festooned with roses, spider webs and bare-bum cherubs. Where lots of people had got drunk at the parties he held. When Bill and the others helped him get rid of the Bacchus statue, they'd found dozens of champagne corks that long-ago idle revellers had posted through a hole in the plinth. There had been pieces of broken champagne slippers thick with dust under the rotting furniture.

Jell was there, in the largest room, lolling his thin limbs on the couch. On the broad sill under the long window sat Bill, whittling a bird from a piece of wood in his big hands. On the table there was a heel of bread and a chunk of cheese, apples from the safe, some bottles of beer. Jell and Bill lived here pretty much most of the time, not over at the quarters like they were supposed to. Rufina didn't know and she wouldn't like it. That was the best characteristic of the house: you could get away with anything. People kept to their own parts. Mostly it was a place he didn't want to be. He liked it better outside. There were rooms he hadn't been into yet himself, like the big one at the front downstairs, for which Rufina carried a key. The trophy room, she called it. Trophies for what?

He and Bill had drunk half the bottle of Scotch, smoked cigarettes, mucked about on the piano, had a laugh. There was a letter from banished Joe, which Irving read aloud for Jell since he couldn't.

A bird screamed from a tree by the water, startling the daylights out of him, bringing him back. He had to get used to it. A white cockatoo – he knew them. In a tree that wasn't a gum, with smaller softer leaves. A splash of colour higher up – a flock of lorikeets. He would learn them all, trees and birds, as well as he knew them at home – rimu, kauri, puriri, karaka, piwakawaka, tui; his heart lurched. He would learn the Australian names off the Aboriginal stockman, Albert, who would know the old names for them, not whatever daft, dull little English names they'd been given. Or German. Did the Germans do that too, go around renaming the world? He supposed they did. They were white, weren't they? It was a white man's occupation, to make things theirs.

The heat was increasing as the morning wore on, and it felt as if it rose from the earth rather than came from above. Even the birds were drowsier when it got to midday and his horse hung his head in thirst. He took him back down to the creek, let him drink before riding back to the house.

As soon as Jarulan came into view he felt himself observed and rode with his gaze on the distant high windows of the belvedere. There were shadows, three of them, framed in individual panes – two adults and a child – too high and too far away to see their faces and their outlines eclipsed by the shifting sun, which rose and fell with the motion of the horse. Who were they? As far as he knew there were no children in the house. Rufina must have visitors. On the drive out from Lismore he'd asked the carter, 'Are there neighbours?'

'Only the Tyrells,' came the answer, 'and there's no love lost between them and the Fenchurches. Since the war.'

He supposed he meant, since the Tyrell men went away to be killed never to return. And Rufina was a Kraut and her lot all to blame.

'There's another story,' the carter had told Bill and Joe and Irving, while they shared the cab of the truck for the journey. 'Wrong side of the blanket and all that. More than once, over the years.'

He didn't elaborate and Irving didn't press him, since he wasn't that interested then. Now he was. Gossip worse than a woman, his father had scolded when he found out Irving had talked about Eddie's drunkenness on the farms he worked on, had gossiped with the womenfolk who posted his pay cheque home from the more remote farms. He blushed now, thinking about it. He had gossiped, all right. Enjoyed the attention. The women were curious about his family, because he was half-caste. Some of them were downright nosy when they found out about Eddie and what he was. On the closer farms the old man had played at dances and people would tell him what they thought. A live wire! Sings like an angel! A real card! But there are two sides to every card, he would think.

At the belvedere window the figures had moved to stand together, the child in the woman's arms, and he felt obscurely that he was the focus of their attention. Why would he be when the view was so vast, with mountains, plains, fields, forest and river? They could be looking anywhere but at him, sweaty and hot under his felt hat, which showed how porangi the Aussies were – a felt hat in a climate like this. Too hot by bloody far. He'd get himself a straw one.

The horse didn't like this approach to the house and Irving thought he could see why. From this angle it seemed to lean away from you, vertigo induced by the walls sitting off-centre to the rise of the land, like a stone held in the bend of a slingshot. There was a tension, the threat of rebound. A piece of the belvedere roof had been rebuilt, re-slated, mended. It looked almost as if there had been a fire up there.

He got down to open the last gate and heard horse's hooves – a light cantering – and there was Rufina on her mare. Had she been watching for him too? Had it been her up there in the attic? But she wouldn't have had time to get here, down the stairs and saddle up and everything – unless the horse was ready waiting. She had recently washed her face; it was damp and streaky. Or had she been crying for some reason? He couldn't imagine it. She wasn't the sort for crying. The skin was papery and red around her eyes, as though she'd been rubbing them. She rode up, through the gate as he opened it, her battered hat pushed high on her forehead. She was a golden colour from the sun, a soft gold.

'Come with me,' she said. 'I want to show you the memorial.'

'Memorial?'

She didn't seem to be able to look at him directly, those red eyes glancing away from his as soon as they met them. She passed by, too close; the horse almost trod his feet.

'The one we can see from up there.' She pointed towards the belvedere.

'I've seen it. Rode past it.'

'I want you to see it properly.'

'I don't go much on memorials.' Some towns he'd passed through, here and at home, the memorial was the main thing, the only thing, a lump of granite in the main street, usually within falling distance of the pub doors. He'd seen fathers and brothers in varying states of inebriation at all hours, women sober, laying wreaths. Mostly silent. Too much, too quiet grief. They didn't let the tears come, didn't let them flow freely.

He and Rufina rode on, two abreast.

'This one you'll like.'

'Will I?'

'Your grandfather built it.'

'With his own hands?' He tried to keep the sarcasm out of his voice. People like her said that – she grew, he built, he made – when they meant he'd paid other people to do it. Rufina smiled gently and looked away towards the river road, and he had the uncomfortable feeling she was flirting with him, the angle of her head coquettish – but her voice, when it came, was hard.

'No, of course not. He designed it. The column and so on.'

At the lion gates he leaned down to lift the catch, feeling her eyes on him again. He could feel her drinking him in.

'You would be good at polo.' When Irving didn't respond she continued, 'A sport played on horseback with sticks and—'

'I know. I've seen it.' And he had, once, on a rich farm in the Waikato. He would like to play it himself. He'd thought that when he'd watched it. Now he wondered if he'd be rich enough one day to have a polo field, one of his own. A cap and red jacket, a shining precise mallet.

The cicadas were deafening, too loud, as if they were inside his head. At the foot of the hill the temperature surged in the unearthly way it did here, cranking up five degrees in ten minutes. Sweat ran to sting his eyes; up ahead the blurred view of a sign, 'Memorial Hill', hand-painted, pointing away from the lower road.

'This is new, where the road goes flat beside the water; they built it just before the crash – Hing Ye and his brothers, the tobacco farmers.' She gestured to the next farm, down river. 'It used to go up the hill. This road.'

'You're not friendly with him? This Hing Ye?' She'd never mentioned him before.

She shrugged. 'Not particularly.'

It was because she was German, he supposed. Her isolation. Wouldn't she feel a kindred spirit with them? At home the Chinese kept to themselves. Perhaps they did the same wherever they went.

They began the climb, letting the horses take their own pace. It was too hot to be riding out now. Midday. No cover. He wondered again what it would have been like, this land, before they cut all the bush. Sparse shade flickered further up, promising some relief – there was never enough of it here. And she was feeling it too. Wide semicircles of dampened cloth marked the sides of her shirt.

'I'm changing his name,' he said. 'I don't like it.'

'Kaiser. That's his name.'

'I'll call him Boss after his father.'

'No you won't. It buggers them up. You don't change their names.'

The curse words she used. His grandfather must have and she'd learned them off him before she knew English properly. Or was it just that she wanted to shock him, indulge in a level of intimacy he wouldn't share with any woman? He didn't like it. The flirting again. The ordering him around. He'd liked her better when they sat in the belvedere, when she was quiet and listening, asking him thoughtful questions about New Zealand, about the work he'd done there, about Eddie. Or had she been getting his measure then, sizing him up, biding her time – till now.

'Changed plenty.' And he had, horses he'd worked with, horses that had come and gone. Called them all sorts of names – Numbskull, Kaihamuti, Putoko, Lightning. They didn't mind. Answered to any bloody thing.

'Eh, Boss?' He patted the mane, leaned forward to blow gently into one ear. 'Bossy boy, old matie.'

Rufina made an exasperated little noise – he could only just hear it under the racket of the birds and insects – and rode on ahead of him. Her saddle was the same as his; she'd helped him choose it at the saddlery in Lismore. Identical. She had insisted, even though he'd liked another one better. She hadn't said why, even though the one he'd liked was cheaper. She had told him, 'Don't worry about that. I want you to enjoy yourself a little.' The saddler's boy had stared at them, lip curled, silently following them around the shop as if he was worried they were thieves. Outside on the street people ostentatiously got out of their way, crossed the street to avoid coming too close, or slowed their vehicles to get a good look, as if they thought he and Rufina wouldn't notice. He followed her lead, kept his head up, lengthened his stride. He couldn't help but be impressed by her mettle. Her bravery. There was something of the warrior about her, inviting him to rest his eyes on her whenever they were alone together.

He wouldn't look at how sweetly her slender hips rose above the cantle, how lightly and easily she sat the horse. Boss flicked his ears – the horse didn't like riding behind the females. Neither did he. It was against the natural order. He let the stallion push past and take the lead.

There was the view of Jarulan now, the angled roofs and white frames of the belvedere, the outbuildings, the gardens. He was reminded again of what he'd seen at the windows.

'Have we got visitors?'

Rufina was silent, or perhaps she had answered him and once again he hadn't heard her. Was he going deaf? This was a country to go deaf in. He glanced back – she had let her horse stop to crop the grass at the side of the road and was digging in her pocket for her cigarettes.

'Rufina, I asked you if—'

'No we haven't. And don't tell me why you asked. I don't want to know.'

He stared at her.

'You go on. It's just up there.'

He rode on ahead, a sick feeling in his guts. The heat, the screaming of every living thing, her odd behaviour.

The memorial stood in a shallow bay at the crest. It was more ornate than he had imagined it would be, how he'd seen it from the belvedere and upper windows of the house. There was a little fence; he looped the reins over it and lifted his eyes to the first face of the column.

Don't tell me why you're asking. Is that what she'd said?

Pidcock, Pidcock, Williams, Smith, Smith, Smith, Smith, Brae. Four Robinsons. All with rank and battalion, mostly the 41st. Brothers and cousins. He'd seen the same at home, names repeated over and over, from big families.

He read the list to the bottom, the stiff, cold words – but his grandfather would have thought it was dignified, eternal, the names chiselled into the stone. All that loss. There could never be another war like it. He turned away.

Rufina was only just now coming to the top of the hill, on foot, smoking, leading the horse. She'd taken her time.

'All right?' he asked.

She went to put her horse in the shade and came back, not meeting his eye, to take Kaiser's reins. *Boss's* reins. He'd done something to offend her. Was it disrespectful to tether Boss to the fence? Was the fence part of the memorial, not just to protect it? It was beginning to rust, black flakes peeling from the waist-high cast-iron rail. One stuck to his hand, like a fish scale. He had the sense of standing on a precipice, with everything he knew to be true and moral sliding violently away from him into a cavernous void, brimming with burning air. He'd ignore her, look at the memorial. That's what they'd come here to do.

Pushing his hat down more firmly on his head, he went around to the other side. Uncle Llew. According to his father, the old man's favourite.

Pte Llewellyn Mungo Dominic Fenchurch.
41st Battalion of 11th Infantry Brigade
Died of wounds. Aged 20
Fell December 25th 1916
Western Front, Armentieres, France

Christmas Day. He read the uncle's name over and over again, slowly, and felt the tears come, felt them run down his face. At home there were thousands who hadn't come back, Maori and Pakeha; many he was related to, but none called Fenchurch. He didn't wonder what had moved him; all he knew was that it felt good to weep. Homesickness, grief, an anxiety centred around this relative by marriage, who was behind him now – directly behind him – and he would turn to face her but she had put her arms around his waist and leaned her cheek against his back. He could feel the brim of her hat between his shoulder blades and dampness. His sweat and hers, mingled. Or tears.

Was she crying because it was her lot that started it? Because they lost?

'Let me go,' he said gently, though he had a violent urge to throw her off. She released him but stayed where she was. A moment passed where he was drained of the will to walk away, when the heat of her kept him facing the dead uncle's stony name and rank. Nearby, a cicada that he knew without looking would be the size of a frog kept up a steady rifle fire into his head. The faces that rose to surround him were not from that, not from the war that everyone tried to forget, but those of his sisters and brothers at home, of the girl who would not marry him, the vicar he'd disappointed by not answering the call, his lost Joe, his poor mother.

She was touching him again, a fingertip caress to his forearm, and it was enough to move him away towards Boss, who had seen his intention and came towards him amiable as a dog.

I would have your mood, thought Irving, instead of this tumult.

'I want to talk to you,' Rufina said. 'Don't go.'

'I have to.' But he stopped, reins in hand and staring at his new boots. Dusty and scraped already. He would go back to the house and take them off, relieve Bill of whatever duties he had and sit together barefoot on the verandah on the south side of Eddie's wing. In the cool. The relative cool. They could go for a swim in the river.

The crunch of her boots on dirt and stone, the slip of her hand into his. 'Look at me.'

He did, though it cost him. She was hatless, the hot wind stirring her hair, lifting it from her smooth face. He quelled an impulse to push past her and pick her hat up from where it lay in the dirt, put it back on her head. Her face. The golden colour of it. She was summoning courage to back whatever decision she had made. He could see it in her eyes. Resolute, but lacking the nerve.

'Jarulan will be yours. I will make it legal. In your name. You can have Joe, your brothers, whomsoever you like, I think perhaps in a year hence.'

Hence. She talked an odd mixture of blasphemy and Bible. He nodded. That's what Eddie wanted. What he wanted.

'But in the meantime, between now and then, you will be my lover.'

Lover? A laugh broke out of him, startling them both. What did she mean? She wanted him to love her? How? She was his grandfather's widow. She must mean lover in the European way, lover when no love was certain. Adultery. He shook his head.

'You won't?' Her voice had risen and she was blushing, as if she hadn't expected him to refuse her. 'In that case you can leave. Go and find your no-good friends.'

Fury burst in him to match hers. Her appalling proposal and the insult to his friends. No-good. She had no idea. They were *too* good, too trusting. He had worried about them every day since they had left. In this country there were dangerous blinkered men, all over this country, men who would hate them on sight. Men who thought killing a coloured man was nothing.

He climbed onto his horse and rode away, not back to the house but down the other side of the hill to where the path rejoined the river road, breathed deeply of the clean air and put himself together. Tried to.

After a canter for most of the downhill ride, Boss was happy to walk and they made their way slowly. The great gums along the banks were alive with raucous birds, a rising hot wind stirring the branches. Yellow dirt road. Not red. Didn't they say the heart of Australia was red? He would like to see it. Up ahead a glistening brown snake lay on a curve in the road, sliding away into the grass as the horse drew closer. It was one of the small surprises of the place, how snakes generally didn't want to stand and fight. In Sydney he'd watched some wharfies goad one with a stick, a big black bastard that had crawled out of a banana crate. It had done its best to get away from them.

Empty pasture opened up on his left, rabbits teemed on the side of a hill, a hawk circled against the hot sky. More eagle than hawk. Black and wedge-tailed. Big joker, a bit like the one hanging in Jarulan's hall. The first time he saw the stuffed one circling him he'd jumped out of his skin and Joe and the others had teased him about it, off and on for days, imitating him and falling about laughing.

The living giant wheeled away, a small rabbit in its claws. *Cwaark cwaark* went the birds in the trees. At home there were places where the birds had disappeared completely. Whole species extinct. Here, even though the land had been given the same treatment of clearing and draining and division, it seemed the birds had stayed around. There was a toughness in everything, a kind of resilience that New Zealand didn't have. Aotearoa was kinder. Much. No snakes. Gentle climate. But the odd thing was that because this place was tougher, you rose to meet it. Didn't you? He had. He had to work this one out. Toughen up. Or disappear.

When they reached the place the snake had lain he looked into the grass from the safety of the saddle. No sign of it at all. He felt disappointed, like a kid. Seeing snakes was a pleasure. As wonderful as seeing wallabies and wombats and echidnas and all the creatures. It was the animals here. The wildlife. There was so much of it.

On the next bend a camp came into view, a piece of canvas stretched between two trees. Two men and a woman sat on wooden chairs unloaded from a cart, which stood piled with a mattress, boxes, a rifle. A baby carriage sat on a wonk on the very top, empty. An old horse had on his nosebag and from a blackened billy on the fire came the smell of rabbit.

By way of greeting, Irving called out, 'There's plenty more of that back there – help yourselves,' and they stared at him, the woman barely able to lift her head. Perhaps it was weighted by the hat she wore, brimless, close, the kind of hats women wore in the years after the war. It was feathered and flowered, out of keeping with the rest of her shabby clothes. A glimpse of her face showed her thin and badly burned by the sun. Sick, was she? He should ask them to come with him, lead them back to the house and give them food and beds until she got better. The house must be full of beds; there were rooms that he still hadn't seen. One room that Rufina kept locked at all times, the key in her pocket and no numbered hook for it on the board by the kitchen door.

'Rabbits,' he said, since the swaggies were looking at him as if he'd spoken in a language they didn't understand. He pointed back along the road. 'Not far.'

The men's faces were shaded by their hats. One of them nodded and set his chair rocking on the uneven ground.

'Goodbye, then.' Irving rode on. He wasn't going to get involved in their suffering, the sick woman, the paltry comforts, the empty baby carriage. Besides, he knew that Rufina didn't like the swaggies coming in close.

Dash it. He'd do what he wanted. Jarulan was as good as his. He'd see a way.

He turned back. The family, or man and wife and friend or brother or whatever they were, were doling out their rabbit stew onto tin plates, eating, but just as desultory as before. Behind them the river ran, sparkling and pooling near the bank, the dense bush on the other side hung with vines. Some washing had been done – a woman's dress and some smalls spread over the flat rocks at the river's edge. An attempt at comfort and cleanliness he hadn't noticed before.

'Gidday again,' he said. 'Do you need a bed for the night?'

The men looked at one another, still chewing. The woman was as unresponsive as she'd been earlier. It occurred to Irving that whatever she had could be catching. Some of the shanty towns were full of sickness. Where had these people come from? There was a camp at Glen Innes, others on the coast. There had been riots, Albert had told him.

He tried again. 'It's not far. Give you a hand with your gear.'

They still hadn't replied. Maybe they were deaf. Or ghosts, not real. Another trick of light. The woman looked up, avid suddenly, and Irving could see that she'd come loose. The long road, near starvation, sunburn, whatever tragedy the empty pram signified. Of course she had. She had the look on her face that crazy women get before men fight. Loving it. Wanting it. A strand of dyed red hair came loose from her hat and stuck to her sweaty cheek.

One of the men, the younger one, put down his quart-pot of tea and got to his feet.

'What sort of bed? Hole in the ground? You're an Abo, aint ya?' His face was grizzled, belligerent, less florid than the woman's. 'You're having us on.' He drew closer.

'No.'

'No you're not an Abo? Half-caste?'

'Forget it.' Irving turned Boss's head to leave.

'Fine nag you've got there.' He made a grab for the bridle but Boss had taken a dislike to him and reared his head away, stamping. Irving felt the man's eyes on him, take in the saddle, the boots, rise to the hat. The other man had left his seat and behind him the woman was watchful, smiling, her pale lips twisted into an insane looking smirk.

'Ask him where the house is,' said the second man.

'Forget it,' muttered Irving, turning his horse to ride off just as an upraised hand at the corner of his vision delivered a sharp slap to Boss's rump, hard, stinging him into bolting like an agitated colt, his legs all awry, kicking and squirming. Irving held on, just, and heard the laughter behind him. One of them could be retrieving the gun from the cart to fire after him. The woman's laughter was a bird's, like the murdered-baby cry of the Australian crow.

On his third co-ordinated stride the horse leapt into a gallop and headed away from the hill and the river camp, taking the long road around the Fenchurch flats towards the distant Tyrells' road. For half an hour Irving's back prickled, wondering if they'd come after him, the pale Abo in stolen clothes on the stolen horse.

No. This place wasn't home, never would be. How much did he want the damned farm, or any of it, anyway? He could go back. He could leave tomorrow. This afternoon. Sell the clothes off his back, further down the road sell his lovely Boss. No cash to call his own since she hadn't put him on the payroll. 'You're family,' she'd said.

A couple of miles along the level road the horse slowed to a trot, lifting his feet smartly, sweaty and breathing hard. Up ahead was the hairpin bend, narrowed and hummocked with the roots of a giant gum. This was where Aunt Louisa was thrown from a horse and ten years later come to grief with her car, dying slowly six months later. The same tree. A ghost gum, gleaming white, heavy trunk and high boughs.

High up, a lofty mass of leaves took on the shape of a beseeching child, hands clasped. It gave him a start. He stared; he could make out her wild thick hair, which as he drew closer he could see was represented by a plant that had taken root in the crook of a limb. Her bent legs trailed vines like bandages, heavy with white flowers that gave off a strong smell of sugary rot. She was all shifting patterns of wind and leaves and branches, the breeze blowing in again from the coast, melting the illusion away the closer he drew. Stupid. The hairs rose at the back of his neck. Think of something else, of the wind. How he'd never get used to it, how it mostly came from the north here. At home it was the west. That smell from the vines was putrid, made less offensive for the clean sting of the eucalypt. The girl had looked so real he'd thought she was about to call out to him.

He was light-headed with hunger, that's what was causing it. Nothing since the doorstep he'd taken with him out to the fence-line. He paused under the tree, dreaming of the kitchen, thinking of how as soon as he got in, he'd go into the kitchen and knock up a batch of scones. They wouldn't be able to stop him. In fact, they'd be glad, that old auntie and the old man's by-blow girl, who seemed struck dumb every time he went anywhere near her. He'd get her to give him a hand. Cook the tea, even. Give the old girl a proper rest. Why not?

Boss didn't like the corner either, resenting being reined in there, mumbling the bit while Irving gazed up at the tree, so they moved on. Something bad must have happened at that place, or enough people believed that it had, which was the same thing, mostly, he was coming to realise. The tree was more mournful than the memorial, more inhabited – but he had turned his back on all that, years ago, by practising his faith, which had saved him from primitive superstition. That's what the vicar had told him, the modern Anglican. Forget all that Maori stuff. One Holy Spirit and no other. All you need.

He had hardly prayed since he'd arrived at Jarulan, though there were times on the journey from New Zealand that he'd prayed more fervently than he'd ever done in his life, every night before sleeping and again on waking, and not for himself, or rarely. More for the strugglers he'd met, the angry men and broken women. The hungry children. The trio at the river had gone bad. Who could blame them?

He prayed all the way back, asking God to help him with the bigger problem. It was wrong, what she'd asked him to do. So wrong. Sinful.

Half a mile up the Tyrells' road he felt God answer him, tell him everything would be all right. Not to worry, it was in His hands. He relaxed a little, tried to enjoy the ride. This afternoon the men were taking him around the herds before the drafting, teaching him some ropes. Scones first.

Before the Jarulan gate on the southern boundary he turned off, taking the fences all the way to the stables, where he was very glad there was no sign of Rufina or her horse.

11.

'THE PARTIES WE HAD WHEN MIN WAS ALIVE!' AN HOUR later, as she rounded the corner of the house Rufina heard Nance's voice carry clear in the still, thundery air.

Too hot. If only there was a breeze. But then if there was it could blow searing, unwelcome, making her even more uncomfortable. She longed for a bath, felt herself festering, sweaty and hateful. What had she done? Why didn't it rain? If only the clouds would break.

'Everyone in the district here for Christmas and Easter. Those were the days. Never minded the work for it, not then, not me.'

It wasn't until she climbed the low steps of the verandah that she saw at the far end Nance and Ma Tyrell, clearly recovered from her illness. They sat in the shade cast by the washing, side by side on the battered wooden bench seat below the kitchen window, faded hems lifted above their misshapen knees.

'No one comes here now,' Ma Tyrell was saying, 'not since the German came. And now the blimmin' Maoris!'

Rufina let her boots ring louder on the hollow boards, driving in her heel. A party! Would she dare to throw one? You're on then, you old cow! We'll do it. The first entertaining since Matt died. Show themselves off. No more hiding away. This is how we live.

'Good afternoon, *ladies*.'

They were sitting there, doing bloody nothing at all as if it was their birthright. Rufina put her hands on her hips and glared at the state of the place. Rubbish around, a pile of broken plates, a bucket of rank water steaming with new-hatched mosquitoes, the forty-gallon drum incinerator burning with what smelt like old boots, tainting the washing. Dog dirt, a rusted pan.

'Mrs Fenchurch!' The Tyrell woman was all smiles, as if she thought Rufina would stop to yack, when she wouldn't, because the notion of a party had taken hold. How would it be to clean the place up and invite everyone, the Chinese tobacco farmers further down river, who somehow managed to hold on to their land in the face of all the fervent clamour about Australia for the White Man, the snobby Bracewells from the farm to the north, and the distant Davies from the west? The Tyrells. There could be beer and food for the hands, for all of them, all shades of the rainbow. Show them all how this is the new order, how things were going to be, everyone getting along and playing nicely, like good children.

'Don't be so arrogant,' came Matthew's voice, a whisper in her ear.

When the screen door banged shut behind her she stood for a moment in the cool of the hall, taking off her hat, lifting her hair up from her damp neck, pulling her blouse away from her sticky chest. The action gave her Irving's face when she made her proposal, how he had lifted one hand to his heart and stared at her.

With horror. Disgust, even.

There. It was named. What she thought she saw.

A mirror. She needed to look at herself, really look at herself. Was she so ugly? She needed a bath, a frock, cologne. There were dresses, many, some hanging so long unattended that they were half-eaten away by insects. She would find one still whole, or near enough, and make herself beautiful. She could be beautiful, people told her so often, when she was younger. She could do this. She could make him see her as a woman, still young, not a widow approaching middle age.

Not his grandfather's widow. Not related to him at all.

Back out to the verandah. 'Where's Lena? I want her to boil some water for my bath.'

The two old women were bending to feed a fat waddling cockatoo crusts of stale bread. Grey scaly feet clipped the peeling boards, the bright yellow crest bobbed and waved, the old women cooed.

Further evidence of Nance's decline then, since it would likely poop on the sheets. She used always to chase them away.

'Nance? Where's Lena?'

'Haven't a clue.'

Fury rose again. A day of it, one passion after another, leaving her dull and headachy. The nearest sheet offered itself for a vicious yank, streaking its fine patina of mildew. How long had they hung there, anyway? A week? More?

In the kitchen she hefted pots to the stove and stuffed the firebox with enough coal to set it roaring. No point in asking Nance for help, to lug the steaming buckets up to the bathroom as servants had done countless times in the hundred years since the house was built. Electricity had been promised for years from Lismore, but still even the town itself was poorly supplied. Bloody Australians! You could guarantee that even after the devastation of the war German houses of this ilk had hot running water. Couldn't you guarantee that?

On her third trip up the first flight of stairs she heard laughter beyond the screen door. Irving returned, jovial, teasing Nance and Ma. Too happy. Had he even thought about her proposal in the hour or two that has passed since she made it? She would know his laugh from the other side of any closed door. Recognisable for its open joy. As if it had never been used to signify spite or assume superiority.

But he's no saint, she thought. No man is. And she didn't want him to see her lugging her buckets all hot and sweaty. She hurried up into the shadow of the stairwell, Ma Tyrell's raspy squawk following as far as the landing, explosive on a word that sounded very like 'scones!'

The bath was perfect, tepid, all she needed in this heat, in the modern bathroom she had put in ten years ago, with a copper bath almost long enough to be able to stretch her legs in. The single tap with cold water filtered along pipes from the river. Luxury. Black and white tiles, red and blue ornamental glass in the window; the only unpleasant note struck by the often-problematical flush toilet that stank even with the lid closed. And the frequent unwanted guests.

There were several now: a stationary long brown stick insect glued to the wall beside the brass cistern, a spider web in the links of the chain, flies circling and a mantis praying in a dusty corner, yellow and green, about two inches long, its little paws rubbing together, the red-eyed head swivelling. As long as it stayed there she didn't mind, because it was beautiful in a horrifying way, a line of glittery dots on its wings lit up by a shaft of thundery light. Wings meant it could fly, which meant it could dive for the bath and struggle against her skin, which was crawling now at the thought.

The open window offered more solace; a sliver of bright rainbow ribboned a black cloud, swollen and sagging.

Rain, any minute. Since Irving came it had been unseasonably dry, as if the summer rains were holding themselves off to let him go out and about and get his bearings. Matthew used to say that if the summer rains were late then there would be flooding; that it was inevitable that the river would rise. The third year of their marriage the water came so high that it lapped at the chin of the

Virgin Mary at the top of the river stairs, much as the bathwater did at her own, and completely swamped Aphrodite, Hera, Hebe, Athena, Venus and Fortuna.

The praying mantis scurried up the pipe, legs clattering on the lead, before going more slowly along the wooden sill and making a seeming arbitrary decision to stop and wave its antennae at the rain, which was blowing in now. At long last. Weighty as birds' feet drops plunked on the second floor verandah roof. The dusty balustrade speckled. If more people lived in the house then the bathroom window would have to be curtained for decency, but no one ever came up here to stroll the periphery. The second floor was private, vast, hers alone.

It's mine in which to do what I like with whom I like.

The soap, French, a long-ago gift from Matthew. Think of Matthew. No, think of the soap. Lavender. A pale mauve. Slippery. How very odd it was that until she verbalised her plan to Irving she had not given a thought to how she would with any decency continue with the comfort of her imaginary conversations. The prospect of the real one had cancelled consideration of the fantasy. What if she had said, 'I am going to seduce your grandson. It's my last chance, do you see? I am not too old to have a child. And he will be like you. You can't begrudge me that.'

There was his frown and wide-eyed look of horror before the light in them changed to narrow judgement of her.

'Go away, Matthew.' She said it aloud, lifting her streaming foot to lie against the chill of the cold tap.

A peacock screamed from the garden – they were multiplying again; she would set Irving the job of dispatching some of them, with his new rifle. She'd popped off half a dozen when she went to get the lame peahen and could have shot more. Why had Min introduced birds that make such a noise when she was already surrounded by native species dinning in her head? A flock of lorikeets came to shelter from the rain, screeching and muttering, and the mantis remained at his post, looking out, unconcerned for his safety. A bird could so easily poke its head in and eat him.

But weren't lorikeets nectar eaters? Seeds and flowers, no diet of small life? The mantis could know that too, the instinct planted deep in his rotating head. The crowd of bright birds that fluttered below his vantage point could be benign, without the smell of predators, whatever that would be. A chemical hint in the air dimly perceived by the dumb creature that tells of a diet of his own kind? The insect was male, she supposed, since the females were bigger, swelling after the rains with huge egg cases affixed to their segmented abdomens. Repulsive. She preferred the dried-out-seeming stick insects, like the one sliding now on the damp wall, its grip loosened.

It hadn't been horror on Irving's face. It had been fear. The realisation hit harder than the earlier idea, clenching deep in her stomach and setting her legs tingling. He was frightened of her, when she never meant to frighten anyone ever, especially not him.

No. Be honest. You frighten Lena on purpose, you've trained her to obey you from the time she was a child, as antidote to Matthew's excesses. That is, if they were excesses, the clothes and holidays, not what any man of means would do for a child he acknowledged as his own.

Rufina defended herself to her conscience – if Lena had been different, more attractive, cleverer, likeable, then I might have treated her less cruelly. It was never my fault. Her foot returned to the bath and her attention to the mantis. He'd gone. Did he take his chances and fly out into the realm of likely predators? She could only think about the insect for a second before her mind returned to Lena and how there would come a time, probably soon, when she would have to make it up to her, to compensate for past wrongs. She could see that now. Irving would work it out, see who she really was.

She'd seen him looking at Lena, his blood calling out to hers. The same blood. He'd probably figured it out already. Perhaps he even made a habit of it, looking for connections, being part of a new world where that new way of thinking was taking hold since the war. No man was better than any other, regardless of race or creed or class. Or legitimacy. Had that changed too? Even though Evie had tricked Matthew, lured him. He was never that kind of man, the sort that went running after peasants.

You never heard that word here, peasants, although that surely is what the Tyrells were. Irish peasants, transplanted.

Footsteps clipped along the corridor, stopping outside the bathroom, or were they closer to her bedroom directly across the hall? Her pretty, restful, anticipatory bedroom, with a fresh white mosquito net over the new bedspread; slipper chair and two-seater couch by the fireplace re-upholstered in pale green leather. Was it Lena looking for her? She had exclaimed over the improvements, much as she had over the new bathroom when she was a child, installed in the small room once used to corral Min during her fits of insanity.

Rufina waited for Lena's voice, whispery, unsure, to call out. Or for a knock on the door. She pictureed the pimply sad face in its agony of indecision and took pity.

'I'm in here. You're too late to help. Go away. It's all right.'

Silence. The footsteps crossed the hall to the bathroom door.

'Hello?'

The doorknob shifted a quarter and returned to its previous position.

'Lena?'

'No, it's me.'

Rufina didn't recognise the voice. Quiet, female, emphatic. Not Lena, or Nance. The bathwater was cold. 'Hello?' The door opened a little. 'No. Don't come in. I'm in the bath.'

Silence again, but after a moment the footsteps led away, only this time, Rufina could swear, there were two sets continuing along the corridor towards the belvedere steps. An adult and a child, was it, two light steps sounding between each heavier one?

Shedding water, she scrambled out, grabbing a towel for modesty – though with regard to whom, exactly? – and flung the door open, slipping on wet feet onto the polished floor of the hall.

'Hello?' She tucked the towel more firmly around her chest. 'Hello?' Ma Tyrell was it, putting on a voice, taking liberties of the kind she might take when she thought Rufina was out of the way, bringing one of her many grandchildren to see the grand house, to see the shining belvedere?

'Ma? Is that you?'

No one overhead on the hollow floor of the belvedere: she would be able to hear them from here. And how would the poor old nag have made it up the open stairs by now? She would be in plain view.

Just as she was about to turn back into the bathroom there were footsteps in her room across the hall and a shadow rose and fell across her feet.

'Rufe?'

So Lena was here all the time, playing tricks. She had a feather duster.

'How long have you been in there?'

'Not long. You told me to do the dusting, remember? Before you went up to the memorial.'

Irving must have told her that's where they went. What else had he told her?

'Did you try the bathroom door?'

'No, Rufe, I didn't.'

Rufe. That was Matthew's name for her. Rufe, who now put a roof over his by-blow's head. 'Don't call me Rufe.'

Waving the feather duster, Lena grinned, showing her bad teeth, and looked Rufina up and down, 'Will you be wanting your clothes, Ma'am?' She turned back into the bedroom.

Rufina found herself following, as if she had thought for a moment that the girl was going to lay them out for her on the bed, as she herself had done for Louisa and her employer before that.

But Lena strode to the far end of the room, opened the screen on the window and held out her duster to shake it vigorously onto the verandah. A small cloud of dust puffed against the rain, falling steadily beyond the balustrade, streaming silver against the murky green of the river hill. Multitudes of shrieking lorikeets took to the air, alarmed by the headless shivering feathered thing.

'Silly birdies,' Lena chided. 'I won't hurt you.'

There was something different about her. Rufina, inspecting underwear in her duchesse drawer, repositioned her towel and straightened to examine Lena more closely just as the girl knocked a modesty lamp flying, one of the set sent as a gift by Rufina's mother. It landed on its side, seeping kerosene onto the floorboards.

'Darn it.' Lena picked it up and stared first at the small oily puddle and then at her duster, as if she could somehow clean it up with that. A smudge of white dust frosted her nose. Dusting powder from the worn pink puff that sat on top of a ceramic jar beside Rufina's hairbrush? But that had been empty for years, since before Matthew died. She'd only kept the pretty pot to fill a gap on her dressing table.

'What have you got on your face?'

Surprised, Lena wiped at herself and examined the results.

'Flour. Irving is making scones.'

'Scones?'

'Yes. He came back hungry from his ride and wanted to do some baking. Nance doesn't mind.'

Rufina pulled on her combinations, soft cotton striped with rayon, a miraculous absence of buttons and domes. They would be the best thing to wear under a silk dress, even though they added another full layer, which could be unbearable in this temperature. She wouldn't bother with a bodice.

Scones. Is that what Lena said? What on earth …?

'You misheard him, obviously. Irving would not make scones.'

The wardrobe gave up three dresses, one after another. Pink, green and yellow, the palest of shades, fashionable a decade ago. Low waisted, sleeveless. Against Rufina's tanned forearm the yellow silk was creamy, perfect – but sickly against her white shoulders. Closer to the mirror, she scrutinised her appearance. The sun had marked her throat, a V that dipped below her collarbone. And she'd lost weight since she last wore it. Perhaps the dress wouldn't gape so if she was to do it up properly – the first button came away in her hand.

A squeaking noise – Lena was on her hands and knees scrubbing at the oil, spreading it with a questionable rag produced from her pocket which could have been her handkerchief.

'Don't worry about that. The floor is stained anyway. Off you go.' She was distracting her from her own task. Off with the yellow dress, on with the pink, which was nibbled here and there, a hole in the seed-pearly shoulder. She should have given it a firm shake; could she feel something crawling across her back? She tore it off, hearing the fabric give.

Lena got to her feet, ungainly. 'Scones won't be ready for a while yet. He couldn't put them straight in because you'd left the fire roaring.' She took a step closer. What are you dressing up for?'

'No reason. Just seeing if they still …' She didn't bother finishing her sentence.

'What?'

'I'm thinking we – I should say, I – will hold a party.' The girl had made her blush, damn her.

'A party?' Scathing. 'Who would come?' Lena had caught herself in the mirror and moved closer, though she surely had no cause to. She giggled, 'Look! There's more flour up here!' and rubbed at her greasy hairline. A falling shower veiled her face. 'He's so funny! He sprinkled flour all over me for a joke – just kidding around, you know.'

'That's enough, Lena.'

'*Helena*,' the girl said under her breath.

'Irving is not in the kitchen. He is your employer, or very soon will be. That is, if you don't go away to Sydney. And surely you will very soon. Go on your way. Join your mother.'

Lena adopted the stricken expression she assumed whenever Rufina mentioned Evie.

Rufina was breathless suddenly, overheated, and the low slipper chair scooped her up again. If she were alone she would also remove the combinations. The legs that stretched before her were patched by the sun, the lower shins brown, her thighs and knees luminous white, like Ma's and Nance's. The unwilling comparison came to mind while Lena was asking, 'What's wrong with you? Are you sick?'

She supposed she could say that she was. If Irving really was in the kitchen then she could ask Lena to send him up.

And then what? Spring her trap?

She understood suddenly what she had to do. Send Lena away with no instructions at all. Dress as simply as she always did and go downstairs. If Irving really had taken it into his head to make scones, those dull, lifeless, stodgy cakes of which the English-speaking world was bafflingly fond, then she would join in the fun. Five o'clock. Hours until sundown, until their drink in the belvedere when she would have him all to herself.

12.

After dusting the bedroom Helena hurried downstairs to set the table in the cool of the eastern verandah ready for Irving's scones. Nan told her what a good girl she was, arriving on that side of the house all giggly with Ma, while Bill and Jellicoe fetched the spindly chairs from the morning room and set them round. When Irving brought the scones out, piled high on a plate with lots of butter and jam, he smiled at her too, and Helena didn't think she'd ever been as happy as she was then, the six of them sitting around with the rain falling loud and warm on the roof. The men had beer with their scones, which were very good, high and fluffy and the same golden brown as the beer, and she and Nan and Ma sipped hot tea. When Irving gave her a sip from his glass she put her lips exactly where his had been, like a kiss, and the thought made her blush.

Jell brought Irving's guitar out from Eddie's wing and the men sang songs she'd never heard before, with gentle harmonies twisting in and out from under the tune. With every song, as soon as she thought she had the hang of it, Ma would join in, and Helena wished she wouldn't, because the music really was much nicer to listen to with just the men and not Ma's old quavery voice singing high in Irish, which she said sounded a bit like Maori, not that anyone else agreed with her.

The enclosing rain seemed to go with the singing, slinging heavy and deep into the parched soil of the garden, while Irving's honeyed voice filled her from the toes up, until her whole body felt as though it had become part of him, and she let her head rest against his shoulder, which was actually quite difficult to do since it was his strumming arm. When he shifted her off with a gentle nudge, just the merest shift of a muscle under her ear, she didn't mind. It was enough to sit so close as to sense a vibration in her chest when he sang the deepest notes, and to see the delight in Ma's trilling eyes as she sang her yowling soprano. Bill knew more songs than any of them, even Irving, who had not only the ones he'd learned from Eddie but the Maori songs as well. Bill had the Maori songs, but also Aussie ballads about convicts and deserts and lost love, sad and lonely, his old face furrowed when he sang them. He had few teeth and a broken nose; Irving would surely never look like that, even when he was Bill's age.

'How old are you, Bill?' she asked in a gap, after he'd taken the guitar from Irving and was twisting the pegs to retune, and Nan looked at her in alarm as if she'd said something wrong, but she hadn't – it was the way she'd said it, slow and sleepy – so she sat up straight and said in her normal voice, 'Bill?'

He didn't answer, played a few chords and Irving sang a line of something and stopped, because it can't have been the song Bill was thinking of. Ma had taken up Bill's tobacco pouch left on the table and was rolling herself a fag.

'Bill?' Helena said again. 'Don't you know? Our Blacks never know how old they are either.'

'I'm forty-two, Carp Eye.'

He thought she had fish eyes. He looked cross.

'Put some jam on a scone for me.' Irving didn't want her to worry about being ugly, but Bill was talking over the top of him, 'What do you mean, "our Blacks"?'

Helena couldn't think of why he was asking the question. Ma interceded for her. 'Well. You must be their Blacks in New Zealand even though you're more a brown colour, aren't you, and our Blacks here are—'

The doors of the morning room flew open and Rufina appeared, and Helena wondered if she was not the only one who accepted, just in that instant, that Rufina had been there for some time listening, hidden by the curtain, since the music stopped.

'Hello, everyone.'

Her hair was still damp from the bath and her lips were smeared with rouge that Helena hadn't known she possessed; at least she had never worn it when the old man was alive. Instead of one of the fine dresses she'd been trying on upstairs she wore an old house dress in faded blue cotton with lilac flowers. It fitted her closely, showing off her arms and small breasts. There was a freedom in having small ones, thought Helena. If I was to wear a dress like that I'd look ... like a cow in full milk – that's what Nan had said, when they'd gone to Lismore to buy her a chemisette. And Helena had stared glumly at herself in the mirror and thought how, if the Roof was her real mother, then she could have been built like her, not a bosomy Fenchurch.

Evie's body she had no recollection of, but that Ma had told her she looked a bit like Bridgie without the burns, all thin and birdie. Instead of that Helena had to be a cow in full milk, with carp eyes.

The men were all staring at Rufina, even Jellicoe. She smelt flowery, fresh and clean, with an underlying cloying smell, like pollen. Scent gone dark with age from the old bottle on the dressing table. Cut glass with a little puffer to spray it on your throat. *Worth.* Helena took another sniff.

'That perfume you've got is on the turn, I reckon.' She knew she shouldn't have said it but it was true. A bit like kero, that perfume. Irving was wrinkling his nose.

'Another cup from the sideboard, Lena,' Rufina snapped and took Helena's chair the moment she rose.

The golden time of songs and scones was over then. Helena went through the morning room and down the long corridors to the kitchen, fetched a thick white cup and was halfway back along the hall, almost under the wedge-tailed eagle which had listed sideways over the winter and still hadn't been straightened, when she realised she had the wrong sort. From the sideboard, Rufina had said, because she would be Lady Muck even today. Curse her.

From out on the verandah came the thin sound of Rufina singing, in German, and either Irving or Bill on the guitar was doing his best to keep up.

The joy that had fizzed in Helena's heart ebbed away completely, draining into her stomach and leaving a closed, sad feeling, as though her ribs were drawing closer together. Her head felt heavy on her neck and she wanted more than anything to run as fast as she could out to the table and kick Rufina hard in the ankles or slap her cheek, but instead she turned and went back to the dining room at the eastern end of the corridor and knelt before the sideboard where the bone china was kept.

It was always hard making a choice, each cup different from the other, perched on its matching saucer and side plate. The interior of the dark cupboard was a blazing garden, with gold rims, rings of sunlight suspended above brilliant blossoms. She stretched out her hand and made a selection: lilacs on blue, the same colour as the flowers on Rufina's dress, wanting now to please her – and why was that? As she stood with the setting carefully balanced in her hand she realised that if she were to go to the window and lift aside the nets over the narrow side pane, she would be able to look along the verandah to where they all sat and watch them for a moment without being observed herself.

There they were, much as she'd left them, except the guitar sat motionless in Irving's lap, silent as a lump of wood. Ma and Nance were gazing at Rufina attentively, and it took Helena a moment to realise, because the sound did not carry this far, that she was still singing to them in her thin high voice. Her mouth formed around the words in a peculiar strenuous way, and her hand extended in an encompassing gesture. A day came back to Helena from when she was small, maybe seven or eight, and the three of them – she and her father and Rufina – had taken the launch up the river to Lismore. Rufina had sat in the stern singing at the top of her voice, the wind whipping her hair and hauling the words from her mouth, and then suddenly she and Dad were having one of their rare arguments. Sing in English, he'd said through gritted teeth, shaking her arm, and Helena had been frightened.

Irving had begun to strum the guitar again and Jell was standing to sing with better effect, so Helena left the window and hurried back to them with the cup and saucer, only to be sent to the kitchen for more hot water for the teapot, and only after she'd done that did she notice that there were not enough chairs for her to return to the group properly so she stood behind Irving, letting her hands rest lightly on his shoulders and laughing at all his jokes, without letting her gaze settle for an instant on Rufina's face. She knew without looking that it would be a blue fury and all because he liked her better than he liked Rufina, and this was because they were blood and Rufina was not, and because they were the workers of this world and the same things drove them to anger or laughter. Rufina was the nob on the outside.

From the folds of her skirt Ma produced the old corked linctus bottle which she always kept filled with brandy, and dashed some out into Nance's cup and then her own. The old ladies were loving every minute; it was so new and different to be there on the verandah all together, eating scones cooked by a man – by Irving! They sang songs from the war – 'Wish Me Luck as You Wave Me Goodbye!' and 'Pack Up Your Troubles' – and from before the war – 'Won't you come home, Bill Bailey, won't you come home?' and 'Paper Doll' – and Helena sang as loudly as she ever had and the parts the men sang all different from the other were so heavenly it made her want to weep with joy. Once or twice she caught Jell staring at her in delight and saw that her high feeling was infectious, returned. He came in quick with his remarks and rejoinders.

'You've got the same mouth as Irving,' he told her. 'The same shape of chin. Look at that, Bill, what do you reckon?' and Bill had lifted his eyebrows, smiled a bit but shook his head as if he was embarrassed, and started straight in on another song, a Maori one with a chorus she could learn quickly – 'Hi-nay eh hi-nay eh.'

When the light left the pearly grey sky it flung a high brilliant rainbow across the west, a farewell streamer like a ship leaving port. A fitting close for the end of the best day in her life, she considered. Everything would be different now. She could feel it.

'How beautiful,' said Irving, pointing, because he wasn't as used to rainbows as she was.

'They're everywhere here, all summer, when the rains come,' Rufina told him. 'And lightning and thunder.' She took it as her cue to go indoors, slapping her arms at the rise of mosquitoes. 'We won't be needing supper, Nance – all those scones!' and she made a gesture low down, as if to say the scones were weighing heavily on her stomach.

Had she eaten even one? Helena couldn't recall.

Close to Irving, the Roof bent and said very quietly, so that her words only just rose above the sound of the rain, 'And I'll see you in the belvedere in a little while,' and then tousled his hair. Irving reared back. Perhaps he was vain about his hair. It always had a perfect curl, a wave, rising above his high brow.

Rufina dropped her hand. He looked as if he might be angry with her. When she reached for him again, to smooth it down, he wouldn't allow it. 'Don't!'

An ugly red blush spread over Rufina's face and neck, and she hurried off towards the morning room, muttering at Helena as she passed, 'Time to close the house up now.'

How wonderful it was that they all ignored her, fetching more beer from the stores and a bottle of Dad's wine from the cellar, and singing and talking until midnight. Before she went to bed Jell gave her a kiss on the cheek and she thought she might have blushed too, but not with shame as Rufina had done. As she slipped past Ma and Nance snoring on the morning room sofa she giggled to herself and was still beaming as she climbed into her bed in the room under the stairs. Even more precious than Jell's shy kiss was Irving's 'Goodnight, cous'. She had only nodded in reply; there had still been no explanation of their relationship but it was in the open now that they were family. She was allowed to love him. They were blood. She was more connected to him than Rufina would ever be.

13.

He came to her. She heard his footsteps, a little drunk and unsteady, pass her bedroom and go up the stairs to the belvedere. She heard his ascent halt as soon as his head would have reached floor level, when he would have been able to tell the high room was in darkness, that the little lamp that sat on the sea chest between the chairs was not lit. Rufina pictured him looking along the floorboards and turning to come back down. At the bedroom door the footsteps paused – she saw the glow of the candle he carried – and she called his name softly. After a moment his shadow moved away, his nerve failing him.

His nerve! She remembered a dinner party conversation in Sydney, a German collector one of the guests. He had a story about Napoleon's 'nerve', how it had been removed from his corpse on Saint Helena, sprinkled with sulphate and put in a box, and at varying stages of desiccation had passed from owner to owner. Frau Schneider and the other women had tittered behind their hands and Herr Schneider had looked outraged that such a topic would be discussed. Rufina recalled feeling nauseous. And she was filthy-minded to recall it now; perhaps the beer she'd shared with Irving had had a greater effect than she'd thought.

A bitter taste filled her mouth. Her heart thumped. A mosquito had bitten her on the palm of one hand. It pulsed and flared; she rubbed it on the linen sheet, made it worse. It was appalling, what she had suggested. What kind of monster had she grown into?

Still, once something was begun it must be finished. It could never be the same between them again. He knew she wanted him and could only ever be either disgusted or afraid, unless she helped him. The way he had looked at her up at the memorial – the shock and sadness in his beautiful eyes, brown but flecked with green. The Fenchurch showing through. Until that moment he had liked her. What was she to do?

The answer seemed to rise up from the earth, seep into her own bones from the lost bones of all the women who forever had, for reasons of marriage or birth, had to take similar action. It would be no different here from in Europe or anywhere – dynastic families would preserve themselves, do what they had to do, no matter how immoral.

If she had him to herself it would be easier. She should have stayed firm on sending Bill and Jellicoe away, the old beetle-brow and his prematurely work-worn sharp-faced boy, whom she had observed was growing sweet on Lena. And that wouldn't be bad, would it? It could dovetail nicely, a youthful love affair to draw any prying eyes away from her own arrangement. Begin as you mean to go on. *Gleich beim Ziel anfangen.* She would.

A nightjar called dolefully from the garden while the rain kept up its steady beat. The river would be rising. For a moment or two thoughts drifted to the stock on the low fields, and whether the hands had moved them higher.

Oh, but she wanted him. She pictured herself flying along the dark corridor and through the old nursery wing, down the back stairs above Lena's room to Eddie's apartments. Irving's now, but too often shared with Bill and Jellicoe, who would doubtless be there asleep on the bed or cast on various ottomans and sofas in the bigger room. The gentlemen's club. That is how it must have appeared in Eddie's day, with the naked statues, the potted ferns and palms, some as high as the vaulted ceiling, the heavy wall hangings and drapes, the pukkah fans. Now it was spartan, by comparison. She could swoop down, as quietly as a moth, peep in and see if there were other bodies around him, as she had the first night when they all slept on the front verandah. And if the others were not there, if they were sleeping elsewhere, then what? She would go to him, draw him to her, let him discover what she really was.

She would never have the nerve. The impulse left her feeling hopeless, lost – but only for a minute, until the same deep certainty welled as before. Her course was right. She would have him but not tonight. It would happen. It was fated but not yet. The mere fact that he had climbed the stairs to the belvedere, that he had stood for a moment breathing into the dark of her room, meant that he was thinking about her. He was concerned enough for her happiness after her distressing exit from the party, such as it was, to come in search of her. And he would again. All she had to do was wait.

14.

He woke in the morning to raised voices, Rufina and a man's, and went out the French doors of his sitting room and around to the front of the house. It was the swaggie he'd met on the road yesterday. One of the men from the river, the one who had insulted him. Rufina had dressed hurriedly, her old trousers and a shirt buttoned wrong, her hair unbrushed, as if she'd seen them from the window of her bedroom and hurried down.

As Irving drew level the swaggie said, 'You keep late hours, mate.' His jacket was soaked, the rest of him rumpled and dirty. An uncomfortable night, then. Irving resolved to pretend not to recognise him. 'It was that cove who invited me.' The man nodded towards Irving. 'Said we could have a bed.'

'Not me. You've got me mixed up with someone else. Another Abo.'

Sarcasm and anger. Rufina picked it up and looked sideways at him and he saw the blue rings of exhaustion under her eyes. Old Mary at home would say 'peaky'. Pale under the light burnish from the sun. A sleepless night examining her conscience. He hoped so.

'It was you, all right,' said the man.

The rain fell steadily, walling off the house from the river and hills. The swaggies must have had some shelter – the man wasn't as wet as he could be.

Further along the verandah the woman hunched on the edge of the boards, her feet in the rain, the other man's arm around her. She still wore her battered cloche hat tugged down hard over her head, a ragged cardigan thin enough to show the bony lumps of her spine.

'Where's your cart?' Irving asked, and the man's eyes glimmered with stupid triumph: Irving had forgotten his earlier pretence. He pointed out into the rain, beyond the rose garden.

'You can't stay,' said Rufina. 'I've told you. Off you go. Off my land.'

'You see,' the man persisted, 'after your stockman invited us we all sat down and wondered if it could be true, that he could have – what do you call it? The *authority*.' He looked searchingly at Rufina, who was colouring up. Irving had never known a woman like her for the blushes. He'd noticed it first in Rotorua. It made her seem uncertain, or ashamed, or angry. A woman of turmoil. Unstable, was she? He wouldn't have thought so. Not until yesterday.

Now he wondered, as she stood with her hands on her hips glaring at the intruder, whether she was actually insane. That would explain her loss of decorum. Back home there had been talk of a woman on a farm sent away for behaving like a bitch on heat. That's how it was explained – a farmer's daughter mad for anyone with the right equipment. Sent north, up to Kingseat.

'Mr Fenchurch was mistaken,' Rufina said. 'None of the farms around here will take you in. We have an agreement.'

The woman in the cloche hat began to cry, sniffling and mewling like a cat, and there was a dull knock of wood on wood as the companion shifted to comfort her – the butt of the rifle striking the boards. It had been concealed from their view by the angle of their bodies and the verandah post.

'Where are Bill and Jellicoe?' Rufina asked in a low voice.

'In the quarters.'

'All night?' She seemed disappointed. 'The whole night?' She gave him a look he couldn't decipher and began to turn away, but the man stopped her.

'Just a minute.'

'Some bread, Missus?' The woman was struggling to her feet, one cracked old shoe coming loose and listing in a muddy puddle like a broken boat. 'Some bread we could take away with us?'

Rufina wouldn't look directly at the woman, who had her hands clasped towards them like a supplicant, her sleeves fallen away from her wrists to show bands of bruising as if they at some stage had been gripped or tied together. The men let her beg, the one closest brazenly watching Irving for his response.

'There are still some scones,' Irving said. 'I'll fetch them.' They were his to give. Nothing else was, not really. Not yet.

'No,' said Rufina quickly. 'I'll get them. You stay here.'

She continued on her way, not into the house as Irving expected – the scones were folded into a cloth in the kitchen – but through the rose garden and around the southern side of the house, towards the accommodation. After she passed from view he folded his arms, squared his feet. What was he supposed to do now?

He went back to his sitting room, carried out a wooden chair. On his return they had all come to stand on the verandah, watching after him. The same unease that had filled him at the river did so again but he put the chair down for the woman.

'Here. Rest yourself. Mrs Fenchurch won't be long.'

She did as he said, stiff and shivering, though the morning was warm. Balls of midges had come to spin at face level. He swatted. The Australians barely seemed to notice them.

'What's your name?' It was the man who had said nothing so far, the one who had been sitting with the woman.

'Irving.'

'Fenchurch? Mr and Mrs, eh?'

He wouldn't explain their relationship. There wasn't a name for it anyway, not now. He offered his hand.

'Irving Fenchurch. You are?'

'Eric Campbell,' the swaggie said, 'and this is my mate, John Lang.'

The other man laughed and even the woman managed a twisted smile, showing her rotten teeth. They were joking, the names weren't real, a response to his name, which they didn't believe. John Lang was a name he'd heard before, hadn't he? He never looked at the newspapers here, nothing in them interested him, but John Lang was someone, he was sure, high up. And the other name rang a distant bell. From his time in Sydney, from the speakers in the Domain. Eric Campbell. But then New Zealand was full of Campbells. All those Scots, thousands of them, all called names like Eric Campbell.

'Look at him,' sneered the woman, 'hasn't got a clue. Thinks you're dinkum.'

'I'm not from here.' Irving wondered if it was wise to tell them anything at all about himself.

There was another silence before the woman let her head fall against the back of the chair and said drowsily, 'I could sleep for a thousand years.'

The rain was lightening a little, chinks forming and filling again, and the insect racket was picking up. From far away, faintly, rang a church bell, carrying in the still air. Matins. It was Sunday of course. Another Sunday he'd let slip, like a Godless sinner. He wasn't though, was he? Not yet. Perhaps not ever. He felt tarnished by Rufina's demands.

A bird screamed from the camphor laurels that invaded the hillside behind the creamery and the abandoned rabbito's hut. It was hard to imagine what the place had been like before they came, his Fenchurch ancestors, who'd made their money off cutting down the forest. Red gold. The cedar. Would have been beautiful.

'Dreamy sort of a bloke, aren't you?' The woman was peering up at him. In a gentler wondering sort of voice she said, 'Lost in your thoughts.'

'You worked on a farm before?' Irving asked the man closest to him. The one who said his name was Eric.

'I have,' said John Lang. 'Jack's a city slicker.'

So the other one was Jack.

'Good at shooting rabbits?' Irving indicated the gun, though he already knew from the contents of their pot.

'I should say so. And possums.'

'Rabbits are the problem round here. And dogs.'

'Need a dogger?'

They did. Wild dogs made up of dingo and heeler and shepherd and who knows what else would come out of the bush and kill calves. There was a story of a lame dingo cross hanging around down the river last winter and coming up to get into the rubbish heap.

'Come on.' He helped the woman up – she smelt of sweat and something else chemical – and led them through the softening rain towards the old rabbito's hut. On the way they passed the horse and cart, left behind the rose hedge. The old horse drooped in his tackle, though the swaggies hadn't come that far, had they? Unless they'd missed the gate and gone on miles along the empty road towards Clunes and turned back. Irving went to unclip the straps; the horse walked out from between the shafts and immediately dropped his head to crop.

A look passed between the two men but they said nothing and went on, following him between the first of the trees that lined the carriageway.

The rabbito's hut had weeds through the floor, which had been laid directly on the dirt so hadn't lasted. A warped slab of wormy wood hammocked under his foot as he stepped in. One of the men put his hand out to stop him going any further.

'Could be snakes.'

There was only the sound of the rain on the dripping roof but perhaps – he bent his ear – there was a rustling? Australians worried too much. Hadn't he just walked through the long grass past the creamery in bare feet? Not a snake in sight. He whistled for his dogs to have a look – and remembered they would still be chained up in their little street of stone kennels, unless Jellicoe had let them free. Sunday. Day of rest.

Out of the interior gloom loomed a box bed and three-legged table on a tilt. He felt ashamed of what he was offering them. If he was truly the boss it would be a couple of rooms in the house.

Jack had had the same thought. 'Can't you do better than this?'

Footsteps sounded behind them and a sharp 'Hey!' A woman's voice. It gave Irving a fright; he barked his head hard on the low transom as they all turned – Rufina carrying a rifle, flanked by Bill and Jell with a startled Albert bringing up the rear. None of the whites with her, not the hands or the head stockman or cook. Did she think they wouldn't turn on their own kind? She used the rifle to prod Jack in the shoulder.

'Go on. Get.'

She looked ridiculous, like a mad woman. She must be having a joke – he laughed, felt more laughter bubble up after the first bark.

'None of that, Ruwhenua. Where are the scones?' A blink at the nickname, of which she would have no idea of the meaning. He saw rage quickly follow, the same flush filling her neck and face.

'If you don't go, we'll take you out to the road.'

Bill was armed too, with a rifle older and dustier than hers. And Jellicoe, drooping, still half-asleep, was holding Irving's own rifle, new, used once and only to shoot a tin can off a post. He held it low, pointing at the ground.

Still bent uncomfortably in the doorway, Irving put his hands on the swaggie woman's shoulders. He stepped out, pushing her gently ahead of him, and realised the others could think he was using her as some kind of shield. He wasn't. Rufina wasn't about to shoot anyone. She was being stupid, unkind.

'Rufina Fenchurch, this is . . .' He waited for the woman to supply her name.

'Evie.'

His grandfather's widow stared, those turbulent icy eyes fixed on the woman's face. 'Evie?'

The woman gave a sharp laugh, lifting her hand to her ruined mouth. 'What my mother called me and it's stuck all me life.' Standing this close to her he could see the deep crow's-feet, the smile lines in her cheeks. Before whatever disaster or slow impoverishment that preceded taking to the road, she had led a happy life, or happy enough. White faces wrinkled up so early that you could read their natures by the time they were thirty. She was perhaps about that age. A smudgy skirt of some kind of serge hung to her knees, too hot for this climate. The yellow dress he'd seen spread on the rocks acted as a kind of blouse, bunching where it was tucked in.

With a quick, fluid movement, Rufina lowered her gun and tugged the hat from Evie's head. Hair half-dyed red but mostly mouse and streaked with silver clung to the bony head. 'It is you!'

Evie looked surprised. 'What? I don't know you, lady.'

'Stop it, Evie.'

Evie snatched back the hat and jammed it on her head.

'She's Evie Falkirk,' supplied the nameless man, Eric Campbell.

Rufina drew closer, scrutinising Evie's face. 'You could be. So easily could be. What is it, nineteen, twenty years? A long time.'

'We're from Gosford. Just out of there. You know it? North of Sydney,' said Eric. Maybe he was her brother. The same beaky nose.

'I said they could have the hut but it's no good.' Irving took the rifle from Rufina. She was still staring suspiciously at Evie. 'The roof's gone and—'

'Don't think you can appeal to my sympathies. You must have planned this all along, to come back.'

'You've got a slate loose, lady.'

The women glared at one another and the dogs arrived, the youngest a crossbreed Irving wasn't sure about yet, bounding roughly around his legs. The shepherd and the bluey stood back, awaiting instruction.

'Day of rest,' Irving told their eager faces. 'Sunday.'

Beside him there was a sharp crack, flesh on flesh, and an eruption of flailing arms and legs. Although he hadn't seen who made that first blow, he had a fair idea. Their hands were locked in one another's hair, Rufina kicking with her dusty boots at Evie's skinny shanks and grunting, like an animal.

'Ladies!' said Bill, a twitch at the corner of his mouth as if he was in some way amused by them. Irving hated seeing women fighting; he'd seen it in the village at home, in Sydney, on the road – women of all colours and creeds.

Together, they pulled the women apart without much effort and he was aware as they did so of Albert and Jell melting away towards the accommodation, disappearing as fast as they could. As soon as she was separated Rufina broke into a run too, overtaking the men and rounding the house with the young dog barking maniacally. Nipping at her heels, Irving noticed, though Rufina paid it no heed, disappearing along the verandah and through the front door, slamming it after her. A moment later he heard her feet drumming along the hall.

Next to him, Jack had his arm around Evie and they were whispering – but he couldn't hear them. It was true. He was going deaf; he wasn't just imagining it.

'You oughta get her locked up,' Evie said clearly, when she saw him looking at her. She had a long scratch on her face.

'Sorry, Evie,' he said. What else could he say?

'Who does she think our Evie is?' asked Eric.

'Don't know.' He would find out.

It was like a disease here, the unrest, something Rufina had caught. It was trying to get him too, he could feel it. His people – the outsiders – had brought it with them, and he felt it keenly, how the unsettling immanence didn't spring from some alien long dead past, from the lost, original inhabitants, but rose around him in the present. More a warning than a haunting.

He took the tramps around to the kitchen, sat them at the table, fed them the scones, made tea. He introduced them to Nan, who bathed Evie's face and dabbed it with cochineal, and Helena, who explained to them who the other Evie was – her mother. He took a chance to ask Nan, quietly, 'So it's not her then, you're certain?'

'Not in a million years. Nothing like her. She's got brown eyes. Evie's eyes were blue.' She followed him to the porch. 'Don't leave me with them.'

'You'll be right.'

He went out to the water butt to splash his face before going upstairs to see her. If he didn't go up she could come down again, and in her current state of mind could embarrass him further. At the kitchen door he paused, thinking he would ask Nan to come with him, or Helena, for protection, but the impulse was born of cowardice. He started up the stairs, each footfall a betrayal of himself, of the man he'd been until now. Would he find her in the bedroom or belvedere? The belvedere would be preferable, less dangerous.

Her bedroom door stood ajar, the soft dark beyond, as if the curtains were still drawn. A chink of morning light striped the floor, picking out petals in the worn carpet, travelling over discarded garments. For a one-time maid she was disorderly, but she could be, couldn't she, since Helena did for her.

A soft weeping reached his ears, not so soft that he couldn't hear it. Did she know he was there and so had lifted the volume?

The same reluctance paralysed him at the breach as it had last night. If he didn't go in to comfort her then what kind of man was he? Until yesterday she'd shown him nothing but kindness. And the demand she had made of him, what was it but an urge to draw him closer. Further kindness, though wrong-headed.

He went in – there was the musky scent of the perfume she had doused herself in before she'd joined them for the party, the old worn frock tossed over a chair.

Another step so that he drew level with her dressing table. She was in the bed, an inert mound opaque through the mosquito net.

No. She was behind him. The weeping had stopped and there was a word, two syllables, the consonants lost to him but the vowels the same as his name – and she was rising from one of the chairs near the fireplace, her arms open, coming quickly towards him as if she knew he would give no resistance, that he was hers.

'I came to see if you were all right,' he said, as if he was defending himself, but he found himself responding to her as he would do if she was his wife, or as if he was one of the shearers from home out on a Saturday night with a goodtime girl, or as if he was embracing his fiancée, with whom, because of their faith, he had never done this, or that, or carried her to a bed. At first it was that distant girl he longed for, until the memory of her tearful refusal to accompany him to Australia intruded and he opened his eyes to Rufina.

Her white face, her encircling arms, the press of her body against his.

Pleasure. Nothing more or less. She had made herself anonymous. A woman, a body. She had rewritten the rules to suit herself. It would cost him nothing.

15.

THE NEXT NIGHT HE STAYED AWAY, AND THE NEXT, AND Rufina knew better than to complain. A third night went by, a fourth. To catch a man you have to think like a man, and a man wanting another's fealty does not exert pressure. He makes himself plain and then waits for the other man to respond. She told herself she was better to sleep alone, to conserve her strength, to survive the too-hot late-summer nights. It was as if the heat pulsed up from under the very ground, as if the earth had stored enough of the day's relentless sun to fight fire with fire through the sweaty dark hours.

On the fifth night she ran a bath, setting the water dribbling at its full force, tepid from the single tap, before she went back to her room, undressed and put on her wrap, a scarlet silk kimono that proved stifling. Back to the bathroom for her towel and then a chair on the verandah outside her bedroom to catch whatever breeze there might be. She left the French windows open so that Irving would know where she was, should he come looking for her, and occupied herself making a list for the party.

It would be in a few months, in the autumn, at Easter, and extravagant – roasted meats and cakes and brandy, beer, sherry and music. Wine and singing. Irving and his friends could practise up some dance songs. She would say to the neighbours – bring your men and their families! She would get alongside Albert and tell him he could invite his friends and family, if there were any remaining since the police had come from Lismore on the new native policy and broken up the camp, rounded them up and taken them away to see if any had white blood in them. There was a theory you could tell by the moons in their fingernails, absent in full bloods. Was it true? Assimilation! Did anybody know what it even meant?

She'd do some of her own assimilation, but make it happy. She would invite the vicar who married her to Matt and the Catholic priest from Bangalow; she would invite the carter who had brought Irving and his friends to Jarulan, all her own staff, the cook, the new rabbito and doggo and their woman, Evie, who was sister to one and wife of the other, and who had lost her only child. She would even invite the ghosts.

A shape fell across the paper. The military cap, the outstretched arm. She wouldn't look. She wouldn't let it know she could see it. Who are you? she wanted to ask. Leave me alone!

'There you are.'

It was Irving, so light on his feet he may as well have made no contact with the ground, his face in shadow. At last he'd come. She glanced up at him, at his red cotton shirt and canvas trousers. He'd come in from working, only washed his face and hands.

'What are you doing?' He gestured towards the paper, the wafer-thin stationery she used normally to write to her mother.

'A list. People to invite for a party. You and Bill and Jell can make up a band.'

'A band, eh?'

A wicker chair had migrated south along the verandah in the last storms. Irving went to pick it up and a huntsman the size of a dinner plate scuttled away from under, vanishing behind a downpipe. He put the chair close beside her, closer than he needed to, so after a moment she took his hand and drew it up to lie in her lap, their fingers interlaced brown and white. She felt his eyes travel up her cocooned body to her face – she could feel his gaze resting there – but she wouldn't meet his eye, not yet. She was frightened of what he might see there, what he might not want to see but register anyway. She would give him no hint of how she'd longed for him these past nights.

'You sure about that?' asked Irving. 'About the band?'

She nodded.

'Too hot, eh?'

'Catching a breeze, if there is one.'

He blew gently on her shoulder. 'There's one.' Blew again. 'Another.'

She could so easily melt into his arms, kiss him, let herself believe he was falling in love with her. Of course he would not. Could not.

'I'm going to have a bath.'

He leaned away, back into his chair.

'The water will be coolish and brackish,' she went on, 'but it's all right.' She stood up, keeping hold of his hand while he looked up at her and read her intent. She led him to the bathroom.

The bath was three-quarters full and their bodies brought the murky water lapping to the brim. They lay with her head on his chest, he with his eyes closed, exploring her slippery submerged body gently, his even breath skipping when hers did, the thud of his heart under her ear. They didn't talk – what was there to talk about?

The glass at the window blackened, the night insects took over from the day, the bath cooled and soothed, and when they finally left the water he was wanting her again, properly, so he carried her still wet to the bedroom. It was her turn then to see him, to know him as well as she could by the light of a modesty lamp brought to glow beside the bed. Immodesty lamp! She nearly laughed, and Irving, looking down into her face, saw the impulse in her eyes. A query rose in his, a guardedness, and she felt herself return to the reality of what they were doing. She would never know him properly; he had resisted her and would resist her still. The bathtime caressing had been that of a man starved of women, a man the church had got to. He was shielded from her because of that – his religion – and also, yes, by his Maori-ness, his mother's blood wrapping him around and drawing him away from her. Who was he? Would she ever know? She drew his face closer, kissed him, tried to make it true that he thought only of her in that instant and in that moment, that she was everything for him. The pleasure she gave him made him hers.

*

In the morning he woke before she did, dressed quietly and went downstairs to the library. At the desk he opened the curtains and lit the lamp to help the dawn and started going through the papers. There were heavy files with green or deep red mottled covers, bound with cloth. The ones dating from his grandfather's day were neat and tidy; the more recent, less so. Pages were left blank, as if during the months and dates that headed them the tracking of money was suddenly not important. At the back of the second ledger was a column topped with his own name – a list of all the things she'd given him since his arrival, what she'd paid.

He closed the back cover, opened it again, re-read. What did she mean by it? Did she anticipate a time when he would have to make it up to her? The words were neat, as chiselled and terrifying as the names on the memorial up the hill. The hat and clobber, the saddle, the dogs, the gun. The new guitar. The Bible, a gift that surprised him, since they'd never talked about God. A list of the new furniture, the price paid for paint and new drapes bought for the wing, all itemised in a neat hand.

Eddie's wing. He'd go there now. The book-lined room was oppressive with its gloom and stale smell, crumbling paper, the cruel account, the greedy ancestor in oils on the wall. It wasn't until he was blundering along the dawn verandah that he remembered what he'd gone to the library to do. The title deeds. The list had pushed him away from his goal. The title deeds. That was what they were called, the documents that went along with owning land. Title deeds and signatories and clauses and subclauses – causes of anguished consternation among some of the older men on the shearing gangs back home. Land unwillingly sold, contracted by villains to thieves. If you were going to claim ownership, you had to have the papers. You had to have the proof. Eddie had said, 'Make sure it's yours on paper.'

If Eddie was here Irving would tell him, 'But I don't want it, Pa.'

He didn't. For a while maybe, then somewhere else, or home. After breakfast he would go back to the library and find Rufina's list and strike out the total at the bottom – hundreds of pounds. He'd turn it into a nought. He'd write 'Aroha' and she could wonder what it meant.

Outside the door to his wing he paused and stared at the ground, hands on hips, examined his big toe on the boards and suddenly couldn't breathe. What had he done? Done again? Try to breathe. Forgive me, Father. But the breath wouldn't come that way either so he tipped his head back, mouth pulling in air, and knew that not only the Holy Ghost but his grandfather judged him as well; two stern figures who hovered above him, judging him.

He opened his eyes, wanting the eternity of the sky and the promise of redemption, but what he saw was the underside of the verandah roof, peeling corrugated iron and wormy wooden beams, crawling with ants and beetles, and a bat. A tiny bat hanging upside down from the rafters, ugly little snout waffling, beady eyes cloudy. When he reached up and took hold, it bared its pointed teeth but didn't struggle. Under his hand the folded wings felt silky, the wildly beating heart frightened. A white ruff around the ratty piggy face and over-sized ears, whorled and glistening as shells. It could be very old or very young. And sick, to be out all on its own, stirring after daybreak. He tucked it inside his shirt, facing outward, in case it decided to have a chew on him. What kind of food did it live off?

Bill was on the bed, snoring, with his boots on. Irving half-thought he'd wake him to ask him if he knew. The bat would be hungry. Maybe it had flown around all night with its mates and found nothing. Poor little pekapeka.

A cage was what was needed, to keep it safe. He'd seen one recently, outside a door. Which door? There were so many doors. It was the other morning, when Helena had the front door cranked open and was energetically running the carpet-sweeper up and down the runner. There had been a cage there, sitting on the floor. He'd go and get it.

On the wide windowsill near the bed was an insect graveyard, formed since Jell was forever opening the screens and forgetting to close them again. A green and red bug showed signs of life, so Irving picked it up by one leg and held it close to the bat's snout. The pink mouth opened wide though the eyes remained half closed. He put the beetle in and watched with interest as the jaw worked and flakes and legs and bits floated down and settled on Bill's sleeping arm.

When the bat was finished, he went back out around the verandah to the front door, which wasn't locked. Never was, as far as he knew. It was heavy and stiff and made a racket as he pushed it open, catching up the edge of the carpet inexpertly replaced by Helena. The little bat shifted in his hand, the deeper gloom of the vestibule making it more alert. The cage had been shifted to lie just inside a room, the room Rufina usually kept locked. Helena must have cleaned in here too and forgotten to lock the door afterwards.

He shunted the door wider, bending to put the bat inside the birdcage. It was old-fashioned, with bars close enough together to contain his new friend – and caught a gleam of glass all around him, myriad staring eyes. As he straightened he felt a shiver run the length of his spine. What was this place? Window after window of stiff dead animals pretending life. A pelican with black waxen paddles and plaster pouch; a family of koalas with the mother carrying a tiny baby; a bug-eyed possum; a balding echidna with spikes fallen to the case floor like a handful of kindling; a forlorn squinting dingo pup set pigeon-toed; wombats with doleful expressions. There were birds of types he'd never seen living, one long-legged and spindle-toed positioned on green paper lily pads with a mirror to imitate a pond. 'Christbird' read the label. It was an animal that could walk on water! His interest quickened. He'd seen this kind of thing before, of course, stuffed animals – a mongoose and a snake in a pub in Sydney, a tiny fawn in the hall of a Waikato farmhouse, hunting trophies of stag and boar heads – but never so many, so bizarre, all at once.

In the far corner there was a partition and behind it he found a sink with a tap, a bench, knives and tools, a bag of clay. Lying in a cleared space was the skin of a tree frog, wrinkled and green, like an empty purse. A clay head lay beside it, crumbling, unsuccessful, and a tiny body fashioned with sticks and kapok. Water beaded the blades of a pair of scissors. She had been in here recently, then. Rufina. When he asked her about the room one night in the belvedere, she had told him it was special to Matthew, that she was keeping it that way. Not a word about this hobby of hers. He supposed that's what it was. A hobby, how she occupied herself while the work of the farm went on around her. When she wasn't making a show of feeding the pigs or collecting eggs or mixing the poison for the tick gate she was in here, defying death.

A footfall sounded on the other side of the partition, then another, and the sound of cloth brushing against glass.

'Hello?'

No answer, so he went out to see Rufina holding the cage, the bat huddled at the bottom. She was dressed for work, in her trousers and shirt, with the addition of an oilskin apron.

'What a fright you gave me, Irving,' she said, her voice sounding false, high-pitched. She put the cage down on top of a vitrine, none too gently. Sprawled on the cage floor the bat stretched its arms for balance, the thin bones sewn into the membranous wings. The silver shell ears flickered and stilled. One of them had a tiny tear at the top. A sign of age, maybe.

One glance at her flushed face was enough. He had intruded without her permission. 'The door was open.'

She gave him a little disbelieving smile and gestured at the bat. 'You want me to mount this?'

Stallions mounted mares, dogs mounted bitches. What was she talking about? He realised one side of his mouth had lifted into a leery grin. She meant stuff it. Stand it up. She stepped past him, behind the partition. The clunk of a glass bottle, the smell of ether that rose from a square of cotton she carried back. Fumbling, he rushed to open the cage door and gather the creature into one hand.

'I'm going to fix it up and let it go.'

She was close to him, the stink of ether stronger. He felt her breast brush against his arm; she was holding the wad towards the tiny head protruding from his gentle fist.

'It's dying anyway. You can see that,' she said. 'Anyway, you shouldn't be handling it.'

He'd let it go now, get it away from her. Out of the room he went, through the vestibule, across the verandah and out into the garden. Where did bats live when they were at home? He would return it to his mates, to its family; he'd find it another snack. On a flowering bush sat a brown and yellow butterfly, not so beautiful that he felt guilty crushing it and holding it to the hungry mouth. This time the bat's appetite wore off quickly, leaving the butterfly half-finished. Irving brought the yellow wing to his nose, sniffed it – it smelt of nothing. Pollen, maybe. He flicked it away, the sticky black body adhering to his fingers.

At home, pekapeka lived in caves in the bush. He'd find a cave, though he'd not noticed any. Maybe along by the river.

'This is ridiculous. Come back.' She had followed him. 'I'll show you how it's done.'

The fountain. The nearest approximation to a cave, where the little fella would be safe and where, if Irving remembered, he could bring it another snack later. Where it could have a drink of water. From where, when the night came, it could fly out and head for home.

Rufina followed him all the way and stood watching as he clambered over the low wall, splashed through the inches of brown water mellowing from the season's rain and reached into a deep niche between a woman clothed only in her long stone hair, a lamb at her feet, and a man with a scrubbing brush of dead grass on top of his head. The central column behind them was like a tree trunk, whorled as the trunk on the family crest on the landing window. The axe, the bull, the bird, the cedar. Family pride set into the glass and the fountain. He turned to face her, the bat still in his hand, its ears drooping. Perhaps it *was* going to die, and soon.

'You've got this sort already, then?'

She nodded. 'Matthew made a display. It's a business to catch them. Nets and so forth.'

He reached into the niche again and felt for a ledge, lay the bat down. In farewell he patted it gently and felt in return a little prick, just one, from one of the tiny teeth. He withdrew his hand, examined his thumb.

'Did it bite you?' Rufina asked sharply.

'No. Not really.'

'Matthew never touched them.'

'How did he make the display, then?' She was trying to unnerve him.

'After he'd washed the skins. Treated them with carbolic and so forth. They carry disease.'

Only hours ago he was making passionate love to this woman, holding her in his arms in the bath. In the early morning light her skin looked fragile, as thin and pale as the paper she'd been writing on when he'd come to find her last night. It wouldn't happen again. She'd said he had to be her lover and he had been. He'd fulfilled his part of the bargain. He would ask her about the title deeds but not now while she was staring at him in that peculiar, strained way. He'd have to pick his moment.

His feet left wet prints all the way along the verandah back towards Eddie's wing, where he roused Bill and Jell and went to the kitchen. Nan and Helena were cooking breakfast, Helena in high spirits. While they were eating, the swaggie woman came in and had some too. She told them a little of her adventures and travels, and although Irving could see it was hard going, he envied her her freedom. The open road. The long stretches of coast. When Evie laughed at some jibe of Bill's, throwing her head back, Irving saw she had teeth like the pekapeka, pointed and sparse.

'Where are Eric and Jack?' he asked her.

'Out shootin'. This place is overrun.'

He nodded. It was, but not as bad as some of the farms he'd seen in his own country. Whole hillsides coming alive, a wheat field seething with them. He longed for it suddenly, home, rabbits and all. The cool air in the evenings, faces of people he loved, the long dry days of summer, not this endless rain. It was starting again, streaking the kitchen window above the wooden bench.

What was he to do once he got the deeds, once he owned the farm on paper? Then what? He didn't want to stay here. Did any of them?

'Jell?'

The boy looked up from his eggs.

'What are your plans?'

The question made the kid uneasy. He glanced at Bill and then at Helena, who reddened as she handed him another piece of toast from the conical grill at the stove. Wrong person to ask, since Jell wouldn't be making his own plans. Not yet. He was seventeen last birthday. Less than three years was all the difference between them, Irving and Jell, yet Irving had had all the experience he needed to call himself a man.

'You remind me of your grandfather,' Nan said, watching him across the table. 'Even though you're dark. You're very like him.'

'Shame he's gone,' said Irving, and meant it. If Matthew hadn't died, then Rufina would never have come to New Zealand looking for Eddie. He remembered years ago, when he was a little boy, asking his father where he was from and if he would go back there. I never can, his father had said. I never would. He explained to him what a remittance man was, a man paid to go away and stay away. A solution to save his own skin as well as the hides of his family.

Is that what I am now, Irving wondered. Remittance man gone the other way and with only the promise of money. Make sure it's yours on paper, Eddie had said. Sell it as soon as you can, before the vultures gather.

Bring the money home.

Of course. That's what Eddie had meant all along. Why hadn't the old man explained that bit? What this money could do at home, the houses it could build, the farms to keep and grow and prosper! The plans he could make. A doctor nearby with a proper clinic, improvements to the school.

He wasn't one of the remittance men, then, because they never went home. He would, one day. He calmed down, felt himself settle away from the shameful idea of being in exile and finished eating his breakfast. Perhaps remittance men didn't exist anymore. It seemed an old-fashioned thing, from the days of coaches and gaiters and musket wars.

Into the day and on with the work. There was the ride down to the river to see how much she'd shifted in the rain, cattle to move to dry land depending, the pigs to see to, a tiny bat to check on. He stood and went out, Bill and Jell coming along with him.

16.

Just before noon on Easter Saturday, Nance, Irving, Bill and Bridgie were setting up trestle tables under the trees near the fountain and Helena had been despatched to the river to collect stones to weigh the corners of the cloths. Nance had no clue that the idea for the party, and therefore all this extra work, had come from her very own gob the day Rufina overheard her and Ma on the kitchen porch. She didn't remember the conversation but then, these days, she didn't remember much at all, being dog-tired most of the time without a thought in her head. And the bells – how had they confused in her mind, the large bronze dinner bell and the smaller breakfast dingdong with the Chinese pattern, as well as the rows of bells on the kitchen wall to summon a non-existent maid. The other day the nursery bell was going off as if a kid was swinging on the pull with its bum on fire, and it wasn't until she had struggled up as far as the first landing that she remembered there were no children in the house. None at all. So she must have either imagined it or the house was playing up again, as it did. As it would always do. Rufina was the only one still bothered by it – the soldier who came to see her, and the whistling, whirring noise that rose from out on the carriageway. Not a bird anyone knew – but then some were mimics. Lyrebirds would pick things up and sing them back to you, even the noise of a tractor. Nance thought maybe it was a beautiful lyrebird singing; she hadn't seen one for years and it had only started to call after Irving arrived.

Irving, busy spreading a trestle on the uneven ground, had the look of a man who had seen a ghost. In the past few weeks he'd grown more serious, hollow-eyed, spending most of his time working. The A Model Ford had had its mouth open for days, the tractor had had an overhaul, as had the muck spreader and the chaff-cutter, and lately he'd been coming in from the barn with bruised and oily hands wanting to help with the cooking. What a love he was. Nance considered that Eddie must love the bones of him and couldn't for the life of her see how he could have borne it for him to go so far away. So very far away.

Helena returned with her apron bulging with stones just as Rufina came from the house with a canteen of the third-best cutlery. This was to be the party for the staff and hands. The toffs, as far as the German had worked out who they were, would be gathered inside.

'Ophelia are you, then?' Rufina stopped to look at her. 'With your pockets full of rocks.'

'Who?' Helena, glowered.

'There is a willow grows aslant a brook,' Rufina began, like a poem. 'Something, something … her clothes spread wide and mermaid-like, awhile they bore her up … Till that her garments, heavy with their drink, pulled the poor wretch from her melodious lay to muddy death.'

Helena turned her back on them, offended, and who wouldn't be, thought Nance. Show off.

As she moved around the tables Helena slapped her cargo down one to each corner. Clouds of fine silt puffed on impact.

'Didn't you wash them first?' Nance demanded, sounding more snippy than she felt, and Rufina giggled in that new girlish way she had, taking one end of an old door to lie on the trestle for the last table.

Irving hadn't listened to the poem, or couldn't. A breeze blew strong enough to take Rufina's words away from him – but he sent the girl a sympathetic glance. Anyone could see Helena was out of sorts.

'You look pretty,' he told her. 'You've got …' and he tapped his own mouth.

And she did. Lots, like a movie star. Deep red. She must have put it on when she was down at the river. Two whole hours till the guests were due but the lass must have thought she wouldn't get another chance. Now she was pulling the metal tube from the pocket of her dress and holding it out to demonstrate the little button on the side that you pushed up to make the lipstick protrude. Like a dog's thing, thought Nance.

'It's the fashion,' Helena said.

'Where did you get it from?' Rufina's hands were on her hips, which Nance had learned to recognise as a bad sign.

'Jell got it for me. When he went into town with Irving to get the ice.'

'Suits you.' Irving grinned at Jellicoe, who was blushing.

'It looks cheap!' Rufina was almost shouting. 'Take it off before everybody gets here.'

'I won't.'

'Leave her alone.' Irving laid a hand on Rufina's arm. She glared at it for a moment, as if it was an unwelcome spider, then spun on her heel and stamped inside, leaving the others to continue preparations without her.

With the bang of the screen door behind her, Rufina dismissed from her mind irksome Lena and her stupid lipstick and the misplaced tenderness from Irving that would have been better directed at herself. He was only being careful, which was their arrangement. It had all been secret until now, but not for much longer. How could it be?

She set off towards Eddie's wing, where weeks ago she had decided the main party would be held; it was the natural setting because that's what it was before: the site of many gatherings at Jarulan. Since Irving had made it his he hadn't cluttered it up with belongings, so it was easy to make it welcoming. How lucky I am, she thought, that he isn't naturally acquisitive, though I could have made him so with all my gifts.

Down the main corridor and through the door under the staircase and down the long south wing to the reception room, where two long tables were set beneath the tall leadlight windows. Food had already been laid out underneath organdie cloths. Too early. It could spoil, the sponge cakes and bacon-and-egg pie, the sliced ham and tomatoes, the curried eggs and jellies. There were slices and biscuits, Swiss rolls, tarts and meringues, and, slumped on a platter, the alarming dish Nance called a beef shape, made of mince and onions and steamed for hours with generous amounts of red food colouring. It looked like clotted blood.

Rufina wanted to lift it away, slip out the side door and feed it to the dogs before the guests got here – but the trick today was to keep Nance happy. She and the girls had been labouring in the kitchen for days and Irving too, who had a talent, it transpired, for baking. She would far rather he had spent the time here, in this room with Bill and Jell, practising up dance songs. Piano and guitars waited for them on one side of the dance floor, which had been polished for the occasion, rugs pulled away. Chairs were set around to invite conversation. Against the far wall the cut-crystal punch bowl glittered, still empty, to be filled later with a mixture of rum, ginger beer and pineapple juice. Irving had made a special visit to Lismore to collect the ice. And lipstick, it turned out.

Club sandwiches hid under a damp cloth. Two could be extracted without destroying the pattern and after that a cream puff found its way to her hungry mouth. She sat for a moment on the settee to enjoy it, to imagine how it would be with everyone here. Irving said even the ice merchant knew about the party, that his daughter was coming along with her beau, who was a stockman for the Bracewells, and that he'd met up with Hing Ye, the closest of the tobacco farmers, who was looking forward to it. It was only the day before yesterday that the Davies, who farmed to the west, had sent word they would attend with their entire household. What a lark! She licked her fingers.

But the cream seemed to be on the turn already, though the day was cool and the puff was on a shaded part of the table. Or was it just that cream disagreed with her now? Nausea gripped her so violently that her head shot through with pain, a stabbing throb to the temples – and she stood, unsteadily, sure she was going to lose the pastry and the cream and the milky coffee she drank for breakfast. If anyone should walk in now it would be obvious that not only had she pilfered the party food – though she paid for it all, it was hers anyway, really – but that she was going to have a child. She remembered Louisa doing this, and various friends of Frau Schneider's, being taken suddenly ill in just this way and having to lie down. So far, in her experience, lying down made it worse. Better to remain upright.

The sickness ebbed a little, allowing her to take the corridor through the south wing past the scruffy little room that was now Helena's and once was Evie's hideaway. The door was standing a little ajar, the tatty curtain billowing; the window had been left open. She went in to close it, noting how tidy the room was, how carefully Matthew's daughter kept her few things. Pinned to the wall beside the bed was a tiny sepia photograph, a corner lifting in the breeze. Rufina pulled it away to peer closely – Evie, looking like a flapper in beads and waistless frock, with a woman in a leopard-skin costume. 'Dulcie D and me' on the back in pencil. So she fell into bad company in Sydney, then, as suspected.

Rufina would put the photo back where it was, only the drawing pin had dropped under the bed and it would make her feel sick again to bend over and look for it.

On the dresser there was a silver hairbrush engraved with the initials *H.T.* and nicely polished, except for a gouged bar against the second letter, as if someone had tried to turn the *T* into an *F*. How pathetic. Rufina would not allow it, had never even entertained the idea. Lena Tyrell, beginning and end. She picked up the brush and turned it in her hand, seeing her own soft reflection slip along the surface – and the face of a man standing behind her holding a sheaf of music.

The pain in her head again and her own heartbeat so loud that she could hear it as she swivelled to face him. To face no one. The man had gone, a man shorter than her, a man with black hair and sad eyes. Not the soldier, who was tall – but a short man, a glimpse of him, a fantasy, caused by a patch of oily polish on the brush back not properly rubbed away. There was no one there. Close the window.

But it was closed already, firmly latched, the curtains hanging slack, framing the view of the gardener's shed.

She hadn't imagined it. The window had been open. It must have slid shut very quietly, of its own accord. As she stood there, her skin prickling, a flash of colour in the shed caught her eye and after a moment the swaggies' woman appeared with an open tin of shellac, stick protruding as if she had been stirring it. Oblivious to Rufina standing at the window she passed by and out towards the rabbito's hut. Home improvements then. Yesterday one of the men had been fixing the floor.

Once, a few weeks ago even, Rufina would have thrown the window open and demanded to know what she thought she was doing, helping herself to Jarulan's stores. The impulse was there but slower, less commanding, only rising to the surface of her mind after the woman had disappeared. Was this pregnancy too?

The hunger and sickness, the weakened wrath? And she, who had always been a vigilant observer of every shift and change around her, was so much less so that it could only be another symptom. The swaggie woman must have closed the window while Rufina gazed at the hairbrush. A trick of light, a refraction in the curved silver had picked up her face at the window and Rufina had only imagined it as a man's.

Her heart was racing again. As she went towards the door she put her hand on her chest – steadying, loud, banging away in her ears.

'What are you doing to me, my darling?' she asked the unborn child. 'And what am I doing wasting time in here?'

Another interesting development lent by the condition – fleeting bouts of vitality; she took the stairs two at a time and ran lightly along to the bedroom to dress. Her muscles and sinews felt liquid, youthful, as if she could run clear out across the farm and be carried by her own fuel for miles.

In the wardrobe hung the dress she had bought from the drapers in Lismore, not as well cut or fashionable as she would have liked but lovely enough, in rose-coloured watered silk with a sweetheart neckline, generously ruched at the waist and falling to midcalf. The draper had assured her it was the only one of its kind, understanding her concern that a guest could arrive identically dressed. Not many in the district would be able to afford it, Rufina knew, and besides, she had spent so much on Irving it was time for a treat for herself.

To fill the intervening hour or so before she had to get ready, she lay on the bed with an impenetrable book that once belonged to the first Mrs Fenchurch. *The Europeans* by an American called Henry James. Concentration eluded her. Only intermittently was she drawn into the lives of the European cousins visiting America, their nineteenth-century manners and concerns. She found herself thinking again and again that a German in Australia would be far more interesting and that he should have written about that, and each time the thought occurred it was immediately overwhelmed by the reality of her predicament, of Irving and the baby. It was all she should be thinking about, really, of what to do, of what plans to make. Should she go away for the necessary time and return babe in arms and announce to everyone that he was adopted, that she took him from a foundling home? If the child's pale antecedents – herself and Irving's Fenchurch line – overwhelmed the coloured then they would believe her. 'I have no child of my own,' she could remind them all. 'I needed one.'

Or the other extreme course of action: she and Irving could marry. Be open about it all. Show themselves as modern and liberal, as trail blazers. To marry one's late husband's grandson should be no more shocking than marrying his brother or son, and that was not without precedent. Hamlet, so recently in her mind in the garden, had a mother who married his uncle. I am closer in age to Irving than I was to Matthew, she told herself. We share no common ancestor. We are not related. We share no blood. We have done no wrong.

On what she was beginning to think of as Irving's side of the bed lay a Bible. Another gift, but she didn't like it lying beside the bed and she would tell him so. He had gone to fetch it the other night, after she had told him how she had never read it herself and he was astonished by this, could not think why that would be, and it was easier to pretend to atheism than to admit to Catholicism. Her family had not possessed a Bible; the only two at her English boarding school belonged to the visiting priest and Mother Superior. Protestants were profligate with them, the reading of them in their own language, the quoting from them, the making of their own interpretations.

Irving had hurried down to Eddie's wing, returning with his copy to lie beside her again, holding the book in his beautiful hands and reading from what he said was the Song of Solomon.

She had never heard of it, and now all she could remember was 'Let him kiss me with the kisses of his mouth: for thy love is better than wine,' though he had read more than that, a few verses, until she deflected him from it with her own kisses.

She reached across to pick it up and leafed through, finding the story of the bride dreaming of searching for her groom, of how she would lie with his left hand under her head and embraced by his right. 'I am sick of love,' she says, meaning sick *with* love, surely, and Rufina envied her. There were passages she didn't understand, or suspected were obscene – 'My beloved put his hand by the hole of the door, and my bowels were moved for him.' She laughed aloud, read further on: 'I am my beloved's, and my beloved is mine: he feedeth among the lilies.' Irving fed among the lilies, that was for certain, here at Jarulan, she thought. She wouldn't have it any other way. She would shower him with lilies.

The books of the New Testament, Matthew, Mark, Luke and John, rapidly flicked through, offered nothing of interest until she let her eyes rest for a moment at the name of the first apostle. Matthew. It didn't move her, staring at the name there in black and white. Her own Matthew was as far away from her as he could be, gathered into Heaven or whirling through space or disappeared into a non-existent afterlife, whatever was true. A scrap of paper protruded at Saint Paul's first epistle to the Corinthians. Irving had used a pencil to score a deep line beside the first verse of a chapter. She read with a sinking heart, the overwhelming nausea returning: 'It is commonly reported that there is fornication among you, and such fornication as is not so much as named among the Gentiles, that one should have his father's wife. And ye are puffed up, and have not rather mourned, that he hath done this deed might be taken away from you.'

The words 'his father's wife' were underlined so heavily they almost obscured the words below. 'Ye are puffed up.' What did that mean? Angry or arrogant? And he 'might be taken away from you'.

And so he could be. Taken away by his own conscience. Blown away in a puff of sudden mourning for his innocence. She often thought, when she saw him riding out, he could ride away and not come back.

She put the Bible back, rolled off the bed and went out of the French windows to the balcony. Innocence be damned. He'd told her last year in Rotorua that he had a woman, a girl he wanted to marry. As a boy he'd gone out working at only twelve or thirteen, out into the shearing gangs and grubbing gangs and farms and hills to fend for himself. And how innocent could any young man be with all that male company, let alone with a father like Eddie?

A towel draped over the railing. She picked it up and gave it a sharp crack to dislodge any insect travellers. The years here had taught her not to assume anything left lying about wasn't newly inhabited. A cloud of tiny moths flew giddily into the early afternoon sun, blundering about before careering downwards. As she folded the towel, a soft crepuscular weight dropped to her bare foot and scuttled away before she had time to properly see what it was. A cockroach maybe, black and glossy. Or a redback or a funnel web. But she wasn't bitten, and she let herself feel as lucky and grateful as Irving should feel himself. His God wasn't watching him, no one was judging them, not even Nance, who was spared the stripping of their bed and soaking of the evidential sheets by Rufina herself, who had made it into a kindness extended to the old servant to save her the effort.

Inside again she dressed slowly, choosing a string of jet beads to lie against her breast bone and pearls for her ears. Afterwards she sat at the dressing table and brushed her hair until it shone.

17.

AT FIRST THEY HADN'T KNOWN WHERE TO PUT THEMSELVES — outside with the stockmen and staff, or inside with Rufina's guests. Irving wanted to be with Bill and Jell, and Jell wanted to be near Helena, who was needed to help, so that was why they ended up in Eddie's wing, rather than from any desire to mix with the disparate bunch inside. The gawping faces reminded Irving of the tourists at home, intent on the boiling mud pools and geysers and carvings and small boys diving for coins from the bridge. The fascination here was the grand lonely house, the rooms with their rich furnishings and curtains, carved ceilings, the painting of the Fenchurch ancestor borrowed from the library, the artfully arranged seats. It was the sight of one another togged up for the party; it was staring at Fenchurch's Maori grandson and at Bill and Jellicoe. Irving was ill at ease.

As soon as they came in, Nance, who was also decorated with Helena's lipstick though not as thickly, shoved a tray of sandwiches at him. 'Here, hand these round.'

There was the smell of Bay Rum and 4711, of sweat and Flit, which had been sprayed around earlier that morning to dissuade mosquitoes. A sun-boiled red-and-white farmer with his hat still on inside thoughtfully looked Irving up and down, took a sandwich, and chewed, still staring. Beside him stood the nearest tobacco farmers, the Hing Yes. They'd arrived in an old truck, the men standing in the back and three women crowded in with the driver in the cab. Only one of the women was inside, together with the oldest man, who contemplated the sandwiches before declining. Irving ate one himself, cucumber, tasteless. Out of the corner of his eye he saw Bill drifting towards the guitars.

'Irving, aren't you?' asked the woman, smiling with small brown teeth, oblivious to her companion's tempering glance. The few Chinese women he'd met never said boo but this one had a sparkle. Much younger than her husband, if that's who he was, and head to foot in dark blue satin, flowers and birds edge to edge. A high collar stood around a little neck slender enough to snap in a high wind. 'We have heard of you. Mr Fenchurch's grandson.'

'That's me, all right,' said Irving. He shook the old man's hand, since he couldn't shake the pretty woman's, and suddenly Rufina was at his elbow taking the tray, acting all gay and strange, urging him to join Bill on stage.

'Give us some Bing,' said a man as he passed.

Bing – bigger than Cole Porter or his namesake Berlin – but Irving didn't know any and felt his confidence ebb. Bing Crosby. Very vaguely some lines lifted in his mind about the dark of the night and the yellow day, and the usual longing of love songs. There wasn't enough of it to even begin figuring it out.

Bill sat at the piano and played the opening lines of 'Isa Lei', a Fijian song he'd picked up along the way, and Irving came to lean beside him, harmonising a sliding third above, 'Isa Isa, you are my only treasure.' Bill had his eyes closed and his fingers spreading over the shiny keys. They sang quietly, and conversations continued around them, the occasional exchange leaping to Irving's buzzing ears – weather, the economy, the last stock sale, rumblings of war in Europe. A man with a booming laugh drowned out the closing chords of each verse as if he'd planned it.

As the punch flowed, the party got rowdier, hardly bending an individual ear to 'Pack Up Your Troubles', or 'Mockingbird' straight after, so they picked up their guitars and sang a waiata aroha that everyone knew at home. 'Me he manu rere ahua e', the lover wishing he was a bird so that he could fly swiftly to her arms. 'Kua rere ki to moenga, Ki te awhi to tainana', hold you and caress you. 'E te tau, tahuri mai.' Despite or because of the soppy words, they lifted the tempo, played with a strong downward strum and Jell joined them to swell their voices. They sang it right through three times, enough for Helena and her Aunty Bridgie standing close to start swaying and singing along *la la la*. The tobacco farmer and his wife were attentive and most of the others slowly shut up and listened. At the French windows the resident swaggies appeared with Albert and some of the others from the outside table, and Irving beckoned them in, catching Rufina's disapproving stare in the crowd but letting his gaze travel past her.

They sang the 'Tennessee Waltz' and then someone called for 'Don't Fence Me In', and in a flash everyone was singing along, some harmonies lifting here and there. Only a few voices knew all the words, everyone joining in on the lines about open land and starry skies and riding to the west. The song could have come from here but it didn't, it was American.

The carter's wife from Lismore came up to sit at the piano for the next few numbers, songs from the war mostly, and she wasn't too bad, though Irving thought that it might have been better if she didn't sing along in her high flutey voice. True, he could hardly hear her above the guitars and Bill and Jellicoe, and then she called up her lad, who began 'O for the wings for the wings of a dove' while the other musicians stood idle. By the third squeaky verse the guests grew restless and talkative so Bill and Irving took the chance to melt away outside again, to where the keg stood and the stockmen were dancing. A stag dance, almost, since there were not enough women to go around.

Flasks of fiery Scotch were passed hand to hand, and Irving took his turn from each, glad to be outside and away from the attention of the other room. Time sped, slowed, sped again, and drunker than he'd ever been he conceived of the notion to go and release his dogs, which had been tied up before the guests arrived. Across the kitchen yard and past the servants' quarters he went, through the gate and past the old creamery where there were vehicles – the motors and carts of the visitors. The sawing and buzzing of the night insects was quieter, and he thought at first it could be the changing season but knew in his heart it wasn't; it was because of the change in his hearing, less and less of it all the time.

He let the dogs off, let them run around in the cool evening air and stood looking up at the house, the myriad windows of the belvedere flaring with the last of the light, the shadowy gables and eaves. The longer he stayed at Jarulan, the more Rufina took him into her bedroom, the more he willingly returned, the more normal life seemed and the more trapped he became. It couldn't go on. Some part of him wanted Rufina to be the one to end it; she had started it, she had forced his hand, and so she should show her wisdom and seniority in bringing it to a close.

The shadow of a man passed across the landing window, the red shield in the crest obscuring it for an instant before the silhouette regained its shape in the clear panel at the side. Not a man. Evie Falkirk, the swaggie lady, the outline of the hat she wore to hide her sparse hair. It crossed his mind that it was odd for her to be upstairs, since she had no cause to be, not since Rufina had ordered them out of the nursery wing, where they had stayed for a few days after they first arrived. Perhaps she had left some of her belongings up there and was suddenly in need of them. She hadn't had much to begin with. Another couple of shadows loomed and shrank – Eric and the other man. If he wasn't so drunk he'd go and find out what was going on.

He lay down in the grass, though he knew he shouldn't because of snakes. The dogs bounded and the young one pounced on him, puppy-like. He calmed it enough to let it lie on his chest and gazed up at the stars, emerging now through the high, deep blue-black. Were they different from the stars at home? He hadn't ever known the map, had no cause to. Tawera, the Evening Star, Venus – one and the same – had risen in the east. He searched for Matariki, the Pleiades, still too dim to pick out – or was it that in this country he was shifted sideways, northwest of his own sky? Rehua, the brightest star of all, the one called Sirius in English, shone to the south. The Dog Star.

Sirius. That's what he'd call this pup, which had no name yet. Sirius, asleep on his chest, keeping him safe until morning.

So dead to the world was he that the noisy protracted departure of the guests did not disturb him. Neither was he woken by the chill of the coldest hours before dawn. The dogs slept close around him and the grog robbed him of cohesive dreams, leaving him with only shards and fragments – a ravening mouth searching for his, a prize bull cast and bloated in a ditch, the thin white arms of a woman held beseechingly towards him, or was it a child? Yes, a child with its feet bound in strips of cloth and the rigging of an old sailing ship whistling around them, the child tugging at him, pleading with him to take her home, and he couldn't find the words to tell her he couldn't, that he was lost himself and very cold, and the furious child shook him with the strength of a man – it was Albert shaking him awake, none too gently.

'You're wanted in the house. Big trouble.'

'What's happened?'

But Albert wouldn't tell him. 'Go and see Missus,' he said, his eyes sad.

He went first to the bedroom since that was where she most often wanted him but it was empty of her. Back down the stairs he went, his dull ears pricked for any human movement in the vast house. He was reluctant to listen too closely, to open himself to the unseen forces the women talked about – the soldier, the woman in white, the rolling wheels … There – from the corridor that ran past the library on the northern side of the house, the way to the trophy room – the slide and slam of a drawer. The library door was open and Rufina was bent over the desk, wrapped in an embroidered silk robe that reminded him of Mrs Hing Ye's gown. She had only just arisen it seemed, her hair unbrushed, her face creased with sleep.

'Go after them,' she said, as soon as he entered.

'Who?'

'Those people you brought to the house. They've stolen from us.'

He first thought she was talking about guests from the night before, but he had invited no one. She ran on, firing questions at him about his whereabouts and why hadn't he and Bill played for longer and did he realise how distressed she was when she couldn't find him?

'Where were you?' she asked again, as if the first astonishing thing she had told him was secondary to his neglect. His tongue refused to respond, lolling like a broken bale in the bilge water of his mouth. He needed a drink of water, or some tea, and he wondered if Nance and Helena were up yet. He looked for the polished wooden clock on the mantelpiece – it was gone. So was the emu egg that had stood beside it, mounted on a domed base with leaves of wheat and lizards and frogs wrought in silver. He had thought it was beautiful. Rufina was drawing close and studying his face.

'What do you know about it?'

Nothing. He knew nothing and would have told her so – but then he remembered how he had seen Evie and the men on the upstairs landing. Rufina must have seen the flicker of recollection cross his face because now she was tugging at him like the little girl in his dream, pulling him out of the room and down the corridor, out of the house towards the stables.

'We'll take the Ford. We'll go and see where they are.'

It was her first utterance without an accusatory tone and he felt himself find a bit of balance. 'What else did they take?'

'Jewellery – my pearls and some paste. Silver from the dining room. The Tasmanian tiger.'

Irving hadn't been aware that there had been a tiger, Tasmanian or otherwise.

'We kept it in the nursery room since Louisa lived there,' she told him. 'She loved it.' Rufina hesitated, as if she was reluctant to go on. 'And Boss. They took Boss.' Her voice broke on his name, the name Irving had given him.

They were almost at the garage, built as a lean-to at the end of the stables. Irving stopped short and returned to the stable door at a run. Albert was in there, hanging over Boss's door, the only horse they had taken.

'Knew a good horse when they saw one, they did,' Albert said, without turning to look at him. Irving went to stand beside him, slipping a comforting arm across his shoulders. Together they stared into the empty stall, weeping. Albert had loved him as much as Irving did.

Rufina had the engine running by the time he had gathered himself again, the effects of the night's drinking knocked away by the loss.

'Here,' she slipped across the bench seat, 'you drive. We can't waste another moment. Where was it that you found them? They could have returned there.'

Down the driveway and along the river road she kept her hands clenched in her embroidered lap. He took the old road up the hill, the one that led past the memorial, even though he knew the swaggies would not have gone back to their camp. The last place.

'How?' he managed, as the car laboured up the gradient. 'How did they do it?'

'I suppose the number of people in the house provided cover,' she said, and something else in addition, which he didn't hear above the rattle and bang of the engine.

'We don't know for certain that it was them, then,' he said. 'Could have been anyone.'

She squeezed his knee, clamping the other hand over her mouth, and it took a second or two for him to understand that she wanted him to stop the car. He pulled on the brake, skidded to a halt in the dirt. They were almost at the crest, the memorial rising above the trees.

Rufina heaved into the long grass at the side of the road while Irving stayed in the car, gripping the steering wheel and staring blankly ahead. He was not going to look at her in case it made her ashamed and embarrassed. Dry retching from the sounds of it; nothing in her stomach to get rid of. A flock of cockatoos came to rest in the mango tree above her; he let them take his attention, the bobbing sulphur crests and quick eyes. He wondered if they knew one another, if they could distinguish one from the other and remembered their sister or father, and so knew not to fall in love, if birds did fall in love – and was so occupied when Rufina climbed back in and slammed the door after her.

'All right?' he asked.

She nodded. 'On.'

For a moment the memorial stood in the window, dust willies lifting at the rusty fence, then the gums and she-oaks resumed down the hill to meet the new river road, where the swaggies' old campsite was deserted, as Irving knew it would be. He slowed to show her, pointing out where he had met them, and Rufina gave a little moan as if she would be sick again, pale as he'd ever seen her, deathly pale. A dead lamb. He stopped completely and leaned across her to open her door.

'I'm all right.'

'Too much to drink last night, eh,' he said, as a statement. That's what was causing it. He'd feel sick himself if he wasn't so sad.

'Turn it around and we'll go through Bangalow and down to the coast road.'

'We could keep going this way up to Lismore. Inland.' That's the way he'd go if he were them. Head to the centre and get lost in the desert.

'No – they'll be going the coast road.'

He did as he was asked even though one or two of them could easily have gone the other way: they could have split up, two taking the cart and the other Boss to sell as soon as he was far enough away for the buyer not to make any connections. Splitting up would be the wise thing to do, if they wanted to succeed. Fury flickered and rose. Damn them to hell! On the day he'd met them they had thought Boss wasn't his. He was. As much as anything was. The Ford, the farm, the house, the woman beside him.

None of it was his, actually. That was the truth of it. Not yet. Perhaps never. The adventure could be over today, right now, with the loss of the horse – a sign that he should leave.

They passed the lion gates of Jarulan and skirted the lower fields until the road swung away from the river to wind its upland way to Clunes. The air rushing in the open window felt dry and cool; lush grass silvering in the scudding wind. There were sweet scents rising from the earth and a clean sky threaded with wisps of cloud – the kind of day for hopes and dreams, if it were an ordinary day.

'Your grandfather fell in love with me here, on this road,' Rufina said. 'I remember the moment it happened – we were riding for the doctor after Louisa's fall.'

Irving felt his guts clench, low down. He didn't want to know about that, how that tree and this road and that view of the mountains bore witness. He didn't want to know – but he heard himself ask, 'And the same for you?'

Some of the colour had returned to her cheek. She flashed him a look that seemed guilty, even remorseful.

'Not right away. Later I grew to love him. At first I was flattered, I suppose. Grateful. And curious. I had never before known a man like him – and he was part of all this, part of Australia.'

Irving gave the steering wheel one short, sharp punch and felt the better for it. He would not look at her but he could tell she was smiling, and he realised she had told him all that not for the pleasure of recall but to see his response. She was testing him.

There was no sign of the swaggies all the way to Clunes, where St Peter's doors stood open. Of course, it was Sunday. He wanted suddenly, desperately, to worship, playing it through silently of how it would be if he parked among the other motors and horse-drawn wagons and took his place, the only brown face among the congregation. He would take Rufina with him. She had shocked him with her ignorance of the Bible. Perhaps if she had more knowledge of it then she might learn to regret her actions.

'You don't seriously think the thieves would have gone to church?'

That scornful tone. He wished she wouldn't. Shaking his head, he drove on past the general store and a row of little wooden houses that reminded him of New Zealand, and up the last steep hill to where the road turned a sharp corner at the top, the highest point for miles around. He stopped again to search along the valleys and lower roads for a glimpse of the cart and old horse, for Boss, for the red cloche hat. A sign read 'To Dunoon', the smaller road leading to their left. Thick green forest enclosed it for as far as he could see. They could be hiding in there.

'We'll go on,' Rufina instructed, 'to Bangalow.'

'If I were them I'd go that way.' He pointed into the green tunnel. 'Hide away until it was safe to come out.'

She stared at him, then smiled, leaning across to ruffle his hair. 'Such a lad. It'll never be safe, not while I'm around. There's a policeman in Bangalow – we'll call in.'

It was another hour through green fields and stands of palms and camphor and mango trees, under a railway bridge and across a stream to the little town, which was really just a deserted sloping main street with a couple of pubs and a line of shops behind a verandah. At the bottom of the hill, on Rufina's instructions, he turned into a side street where the policeman's little wooden house stood beside the courthouse. He waited while she went onto the porch to knock at the door.

Easter Sunday and the policeman was not at home. Rufina banged and knocked and rang the bell. Irving admiring her determination – and then the aplomb with which she returned to the car, still in her dressing gown, her feet shoved into work boots.

'Well. What now?' he asked her.

She didn't answer him.

'Ruwhenua?'

'What does it mean, that name?'

He shrugged. Likely she'd be offended if he told her. He wanted a wash, food, a sleep, but he wanted Boss more. The motor was still turning over and the petrol gauge was low. Rummaging in the glovebox, Rufina came up with a pencil stub and a scrap of paper. She wrote a note for the bobby, asking him to call at Jarulan as soon as was convenient since there had been a robbery, and went to put it in the slot in the station door.

It was when she turned to come back that he saw it, how a gust of wind blew the embroidered satin of her robe close to her body. The sickness, the sudden changes in mood – it made sense now. When she slipped in beside him he laid a hand on her belly, cupping the child.

His child.

She met his eye and he saw a wildness there before she frowned and tried to remove his hand, caressing now up and over where he imagined the baby's head to lie, its tiny hands and feet.

She pushed him away. 'What if someone saw?'

'I'm not ashamed.'

'Irving – it can't be like that.'

'Like what?'

'I will have to go away.'

'I could take you back to New Zealand.' He could, he saw suddenly that he could. He could make sure that his child was born among his own people, that Rufina would be properly looked after. No one would judge them, or if they did, it would be short-lived. He imagined his sisters and aunts cradling the baby, a fine-boned and fair-haired girl. He'd call her Grace after his favourite sister.

'Don't be silly.' She had her head turned towards the police station. 'How strange that we should have this conversation here.'

She was doing it on purpose, making statements that he found perplexing. He was tired of it. 'What do you mean?'

'It'll be illegitimate, won't it? Have you got a cigarette?'

He patted his pockets. 'Must've smoked them all last night.' He remembered handing them round, seeing the tin disappear.

'I haven't been smoking much lately,' Rufina said. 'They don't seem to agree with me these days. Cigarettes and cream and . . .'

She ran on with a list, her mouth moving, but a flat bed truck went rattling by and drowned out her words. He nodded, hoping it was the right response. His mind was still on the other thing she'd said. Illegitimate.

'There, you see? I knew you'd be horrified.'

What was she talking about now?

'Are you?'

'I'd like to go back to Jarulan now. We're not going to find them, Rufina.' He had a vision of himself returning to where he'd lain in the grass, how he could wake up all over again to an ordinary day working on the farm with Boss, having his dogs around.

'No, we have to go on. They will be travelling slowly – we could easily find them.'

'You're not dressed.' He was grasping at straws.

'I couldn't care less. I am a woman wronged. By thieves, I mean, not by you.'

She had no idea how deeply she'd wounded him by putting the thieves and him in one breath. He felt himself retreat from her, a simmering unease. All through the long fruitless afternoon he was quiet, but not so much that she could pounce on him and ask him what was wrong. At one point he reached for her hand, overwhelmed by it all – the coming child, the theft – but she contrived not to let him take it. 'It won't be like that, Irving,' she said. He puzzled over her meaning. Did she mean that it would not be close and loving, that he would not be able to be a proper father? His own father had had no clue of how to provide for the growing number of hungry mouths that came after Irving, but was always there for a pat on the head or a song or a joke, and he made peg dolls for the girls. He remembered his friend the vicar and his cheerful wife, and their theological discussions. It would be apparent now and then that she knew more than her husband and that the vicar admired her for it. He thought of the uncles and aunts, of Hohepa and Auntie Tui, of his cousin Mack and loving wife, Ngaire, all the couples he knew. Not all of them were happy, not all the time, but at least they had solid ground to stand on and air to breathe.

It was long after nightfall by the time they returned to Jarulan and his heart was leaden and feet aching, due to a ten-mile walk he'd done near Byron Bay with the jerry can after the engine spluttered and died. 'Told you it was low,' he'd said, the surf roaring in his ears, and they'd come close to an argument, Rufina denying he'd said any such thing.

Nan had left them a plate each of meat and salad under a cloth on a tray and he took his down to Eddie's wing, which Bill and Jellicoe had returned to its pre-party arrangement. When he came in they looked up drowsily from their beds.

'No luck?'

'None at all,' he said, and he meant it.

18.

The belvedere was best in the winter. In summer it could be too hot, airless, but for the past few months it had been a perfect place to spend sunny afternoons. The pregnancy made her serene, bovine, unconcerned with the general business of the farm. Irving and the head stockman could worry about that now, not her. Until her size forbade it, she rode out most mornings for the exercise and also to supervise her own project, the building of a second barn for the piggery, big enough to hold a hundred breeding sows. On her return she was as careful as she could be going up the steep belvedere steps – the climb was exercise as well.

In the autumn she had had Bill carry up the sewing machine – the belvedere had the clearest light in the whole of Jarulan – so that she could make herself various tent-shaped dresses in muted colours as well as clothes for the baby. When she tired of that she would write to her mother, whose letters had increased in frequency and anxiety. There was to be another war, there was talk of expansion to the east, everything was outlandishly expensive and she and her sister were struggling. Rufina sent money but it wasn't enough. Her mother made repeated demands to see her again, just once more, before she died. 'If there is to be another war you must come as soon as you can.'

Rufina rested her return letter on top of her stomach. On the near horizon rose the memorial, surrounded by trees so whipped by the wind they looked as though they were dancing the Charleston, and the memorial itself a tall, stern chaperone watching and observing. Taking up the pen again she described the scene to her mother – light-hearted, jokey, almost a children's story. 'You write a lot about the natural world,' her mother had observed a couple of years ago, 'but since your husband died I worry that you are not seeing enough of other people. You must guard against becoming isolated.'

'Isolation here has a different meaning to one that you would understand,' Rufina wrote in reply. Since then she had been able to fill pages with the party, the burglary, how some of their belongings had been recovered, and how delighted Matthew's grandson was to have his horse back. More ink was expended on the burglary than the party; how Irving had been right all along because the thieves had gone inland, to Casino, to the Happy Valley there, on the way trying to flog the loot before the law caught up with them. It had been a good lesson for young Irving, she told her mother, who would detect nothing other than a maternal attitude: until the theft, Matthew's grandson was altogether too trusting.

Heavily, she got up and went to the bellpull, newly installed in the northwestern corner of the room, a cable threaded down walls and through floors three storeys down to the kitchen. Two sharp tugs meant tea, three meant coffee and four meant come up and see what it was that Rufina required. A single pull signified nothing because of the risk it might not be heard, let alone heeded. There was never any sense in growing impatient but she had got into the habit of ringing, waiting a few seconds, then ringing again in case Helena or Nance hadn't counted correctly.

Helena was the usual respondent and here she was, her eyes as usual straying to Rufina's stomach rather than her face. Rufina turned the letter she had been writing upside down.

'Where is Irving?'

Helena shrugged, panting from her hurried climb. She had lipstick on again, had worn it most days since the party.

'Have you seen him today?'

A nod. 'Early. Him and Bill are out on the southern boundary.'

'Send him up as soon as he comes in. And could you bring me a jug of water and some fruit, an apple or something. No. A banana.'

Another nod and a pause, still staring. 'Not long now. Has it gone quiet? Ma says they go quiet for a few days before, building up a head of steam.'

'Does she, indeed?' Rufina didn't like to think of it, the agonies she would have to endure. Louisa's caterwauling still rang in her memory. She preferred to think about Evie, who did it alone and apparently easily when scarcely more than a child.

'Shall I ask Ma to come for you when the time comes?' the girl asked. 'Nan thinks you should. Your age and everything. Since you won't go to the hospital.'

'Really? And what else does Nance say?'

There was a pause and Rufina watched the broad slow face, the brain behind it calculating the worth of an honest reply. Eventually she shrugged. Again.

'Off you go. Don't forget. Irving, as soon as he comes in.'

After the last of Helena's footsteps sounded on the belvedere stairs Rufina turned the letter to her mother face up and read her last sentence.

'I will come to you as soon as I can, I promise.'

Should she scratch it out or make a fair copy and omit it? This was a new and unpleasant sensation, to be pulled in different directions at once. In order to keep the child secret he would have to remain here while she went to Berlin for the shortest time possible. Or she could take him with her and leave him with a nanny at a hotel or safe place close enough to be able to slip away to visit him without her mother noticing.

The child would be a secret in Germany but not here. Too many people knew of her condition – the hands, the Tyrells, the staff. And who knew who else. There had been no return invitations since the party. Which suits me, she thought. Why would I parade myself? The child will be accepted eventually by everyone; it will take time, but with influence and determination it would happen. There was room in this country for tolerance, a respect for the idea of acceptance. The willing blind-eye of the colonies bled of old-world moral definition.

It occurred to her that her mother may have a secret too, with all this talk of death and last meetings. From her dress pocket she pulled the tiny green diary she had bought on a trip to Lismore early in the year: Collins King's Own 1938, barely two inches long, small enough to always carry with her. Irving had been going through the papers in the library, she knew. This tiny ledger she did not let out of her sight, even though she had employed a kind of code that Irving might not be able to decipher. The nights he spent with her were marked with a tiny star, the day the baby quickened with a B, there were lists of possible names and the calculated date of arrival. All going well, the baby would come in November. Logically, then, she could travel the following March or April when he was around six months old. Strong enough to travel, or to leave behind.

She picked up her pen and resumed, 'I will come in the spring.' The more she wrote it down, the more it was likely to come true.

*

Irving came in late, very late, long after she had rung the bell for her evening meal, dined, bathed and gone to bed. He appeared barefoot at the door, his arms crossed over his chest, and even though his face was in shadow she could see that he was unhappy. She was the cause of it, what she had done. A small part of her wished she could return them to the early days, when she could believe she made him glad, made him forget his conscience, when they were simply a man and a woman together.

'Irving?'

Barely above a whisper and he didn't hear her. His hearing was worse. Early the other morning when she had come to sit with him on the low fountain wall before he went out to work, Sirius had kept up an irritating low moaning grizzle for the entire time it took her to smoke two cigarettes. If a dog behaved like that around Matthew it got a bloody kick in the arse. Irving, she realised, had not been able to hear it. But then, even if he had been able to, he most likely would not have punished the animal. And he was in a particularly good mood, it being the first day that the new milking machine was to arrive, a development that he was more fascinated by than she was. They'd had to let the women go, two generations that had hand milked the cows for more years than Rufina could count. She'd felt sorry for them as she watched them trail away with their belongings loaded onto carts and vans. All the dairy farms had machines now, since the electricity had come in.

'Irving?' Louder. She wouldn't say no to a cigarette now, having found this late in pregnancy that her relish of them had returned. The packet was downstairs. She lifted a hand towards him, formulating a plea to go and fetch them for her – but Irving seemed to see it as a dismissal and turned to go.

'Irving?' Nearly shouting. The baby startled, shooting out an arm or a leg. 'Irving?' Shrieking now, sitting up, but his footsteps led away down the corridor. She could go after him, just as she did the day of their very first time together. There was a familiarity in the pattern, almost a dreary comfort, but she would not. She would not run after him this time, like a beetle scurrying down the long passage, a beetle weighed off-centre by a giant egg case. A beetle of the kind where the female is voracious and preys upon the male. For a second or two she was amused by the idea, and then just as dismayed and chilled by the memory of that first time, how she tricked Irving into taking her to bed. If he had stayed with her tonight, then perhaps she could have found the strength to confess to him that it was on one level a charade, because she had known, once the wave of terror had receded, that the swaggie woman wasn't really Evie, whom she hadn't seen for many years.

But once she had taken that course, once she had behaved as if she was really quite delusionary, a terrible plan had formed in her mind. She could pretend to be so; she could make it very necessary for Irving to fulfil her expectations. No need to go so far as to scream and run about naked and tear her hair, but to make sure they could be alone very soon, so that she could caress him, bill and coo, allow him to believe that the momentary madness had altered her character. It was a great mistake ordering him to be hers the way that she had. Demanding him. From the beginning, she thought, I should have been kinder, sweeter – the girlish self that I never was.

The night was cold. She should have asked Jellicoe or Helena to set the fire in the fireplace. The bellpull beckoned, and she would have used it but the clock told her it was ten o'clock. Too late. They would be in bed. More than a fire, she wanted Irving's warm arms around her. She would ask him, during their embrace – if we had met as strangers, if I had never been married to your grandfather, would you still have liked me?

The bigger question was whether he liked her at all. A boy, a country lad, and this was all her own doing.

Go to sleep. She had always been good at willing herself to sleep to escape from any distress or guilty conscience or concern, able to close her eyes and summon the dark tide to sweep her out. But tonight the baby was wriggling and kicking, witness to his mother's solitude and his father's affront, and took hours to settle. His movements were fluid and rhythmic, almost as if he was dancing. Eventually she gave up willing him to be still and paid close attention to each leap and stretch, imagining she was watching him from a darkened theatre, a tiny, beloved figure spinning in the light.

19.

On the night his son was born Irving dreamed he was asleep in Rufina's room. In the dream he was in bed alone, just as he was in reality in Eddie's wing, since Bill and Jellicoe were away over-nighting on the northern reaches of the farm. He dreamed he woke to the strongest sense that his little sister Gracie was in the house and calling to him from across the corridor, the modern bathroom with the flushing toilet. But when he got there it wasn't that room, it was another with a cracked old leather chair, an old blind at the window and a medicine cabinet on the wall. There was a woman in an old-fashioned white gown standing with her back to him reading, and when he came in she spun so quickly and ran into his arms that he had no chance to see her face. She smelt of river water, and she was soft and old, and he thought she could have been the woman he'd seen in the painting he had found turned to the wall on the day they started clearing out Eddie's wing before he moved in. His grandmother, filling him with her love.

When he woke he was comforted by the dream, and hungry. Since Helena was moonstruck over Jellicoe and Nan was upstairs with Rufina, there had been no tea for him when he came in ravenous from tending to the springer cows, brought closer to the house to have their calves, and some of them already with milk fever. The stockmen knew how to treat it with tinctures of aconite and belladonna; some of them blamed the new machine. He wasn't going to get involved in all of that but took their advice on the treatment, the washing down, the medicine. There were hundreds of them and it took most of the day. All he'd been able to find was a scrap of ham, a sausage on the turn and a chunk of hard cheese.

Celebration now. Food. If she was the ghost the women talked about then they had nothing to worry about. It was only a flash of a dream, inconsequential, but enough to tell him that everything was going to be all right. He lit a lamp to go along the corridors to the kitchen, anticipating porridge, or eggs, a cup of tea.

In the kitchen he switched on the light, electricity run out from Lismore at long last but only on this side of the house and in the milking shed. The range lit, he set the kettle on the hotplate. No electric stove yet, but he was planning on getting one. The eggs cracked into a blue-and-white bowl – one, two, three – and then one of the bells – one, two, three – faint from the board. He cocked his head to listen for the second set, as was Rufina's custom.

Nothing.

The moment the eggs were cooked he ate them from the pot, blowing so enthusiastically that some of it flew off the spoon. He was scraping up the last of it when the bell rang again, this time many times, so that he could watch it swinging on the frayed cord and read the faded little label 'Master Bedroom' while it rang and rang with no break in between.

Nan. He was out of the room and up the stairs so fast he was still swallowing a mouthful on the second landing, running the full length of the hall and hearing finally, because he hadn't before, a low moaning that reminded him of the beasts he'd attended through the long day before. A woman's scream exploded horribly and suddenly from the lower sound, tearing and clawing at his ears, almost enough to turn him back. Rufina might not want him there in any case; she might send him away as she had lately, more often than drawing him close. But he went on, almost against his will.

At the door he paused, as was his habit, like a servant. Come right in properly, Rufina would say impatiently, as if they hadn't a moment to lose. This time, with the room lit only by a shaded lamp and Irving stepping in as lightly as a bird – the bird that could walk on water – she was not aware of his presence until the next pain took hold. Her eyes flashed and widened at the sight of him as if she were silently asking what he was doing there, and he wondered if she was keeping up the ridiculous and hurtful charade that he was not the father of the child. If not him, then who? That's what the district gossips said, Helena had told him.

'You shouldn't be here, dear,' said Nan.

'Yes I should be,' he replied, simply. At home fathers sometimes attended births. Tradition had it the father was the only man allowed among the women. These days the Pakeha doctor would keep them away. There was no doctor here.

'I've been with her all day and night,' Nan told him.

Rufina rolled in the bed and took hold of him, pushing her hot face against the fabric of his trousers. He stroked her hair, helped her to lie back against the bank of pillows Nan had arranged on the bed. She wanted him to lie beside her so he did, holding her in his arms.

'I'm going to die,' she said quietly.

'We'll be having none of that,' said Nan. 'It's harder because of your age and the first one.'

'She keeps saying that,' said Rufina. There was a long pause then and Irving thought another pain was coming, a pain she might try to make herself ready for.

'Try not to call out so much,' he told her. He had a memory of Gracie's birth, his mother labouring silently in the house next door, surrounded by her sisters and friends. When Rufina spoke again it was in a calm ordinary voice.

'If I die—'

'You're not going to die!' snapped Nan.

'—the papers you've been looking for are tucked inside a book on the bottom shelf of the bookcase.'

She knew, then. One step ahead, as usual. She misread his surprise for concern.

'Don't worry. It's all in order. Yours, and a little for Lena.'

He was pleased she'd thought of Helena. A look of terror crossed her face again, tears welling and falling through the sheen on her skin, like rain on a cold window.

'You shouldn't be here,' Nan said again.

'I answered the bell,' Irving said.

'I didn't ring the damned bell,' said Nan. 'Why would I?'

Irving shrugged and Nan went on to say something else but he couldn't hear it through Rufina's yells, so she bent and said it directly into his better ear, 'The pains are getting weaker and further apart. It's a bad sign.'

After the contraction had passed they waited again, Rufina's eyes half-closed. She was breathing deeply, as if she was asleep.

'Not a good sign. Run and get Ma Tyrell.'

An idea took hold of him. It couldn't be that different to what he'd been doing all day.

'Have you looked?'

'Won't let me,' Nan said.

Irving slipped his hand under the sheet, between her slippery thighs to her centre, impossibly hot. She tried to push him away but he murmured to her soothingly, 'Ka pai, it's all right. Keep calm, my darling,' and he felt for the head, found it just beginning to crown. Nan had turned away as if she could not bear to witness this proof of their intimacy.

'Sit her up more, Nan.' He did it himself, lifting her to sit more at an angle. 'Push now,' he said, and Rufina did as she was told, the same low groan he'd heard as he came along the corridor.

'She's been pushing for hours,' said Nan. 'It's her age. And the first one.'

He had to do more than just sit her up. He turned the sheet back properly and Rufina struggled against him.

'Hold her for me, Nan?' If she refused he'd consider tying her hands. He fought rising panic – what if the child was damaged, left for too long? He knew he was hurting her, his broad hand inside her, but he could feel the baby turning, the cord caught around its neck.

Nan was holding Rufina's shoulders. 'That's enough now. We have to try.'

He got a grip on the cord, lifted it over the tiny head. 'I'm sorry,' he was whispering, 'I'm sorry, Rufina.'

She was screaming again, words this time. 'Get it out of me. Get it out of me, Irving.'

'Push then,' he said and he could see by the way her eyes met his that at this moment and perhaps never again she would trust him implicitly.

It took only one brave effort from Rufina and his little boy slid into his hands. He bent to suck away the mucus from his mouth and nose, and Nan took the corner of the sheet to gently wipe the baby's face. Irving held him close to his chest, moving away from the bed while Nan helped Rufina with the whenua. He would make sure it was kept, buried safely, with a prayer.

In the new daylight at the window he could examine the baby properly. He was warm, pink, perfect. He took his time, ignoring Rufina's demands to return him. Across the tiny face flitted those of his family on the distant islands – his own mother's, Eddie's, his sisters', even Uncle Hohepa, and to see them all even if it was only fleeting, made him laugh out loud. The baby's eyes seemed to focus on him for a second and Irving just as quickly felt his own fill with happy tears. He brought the baby back to the bed, where Nan wrapped him in a soft shawl and handed him to his mother.

'Matthias,' said Rufina, taking him and unwrapping the shawl immediately to see all of him. 'Yes. Definitely a Fenchurch. Matthias, but we will call him Mattie.'

Irving would have liked to have been consulted, but he didn't really care. Mattie was as good a name as any.

'Mattie Hohepa Fenchurch.' He gave him his middle name, since it was Hohepa and his friends who had brought the connection between the two families. For a moment he thought Rufina was going to object but she was silent, holding the little hands and then the feet, caressing the miniature ears.

'He has your nose,' she said.

'Ae.' Irving was pleased to see it.

'And the shape of your hands and feet.'

'That too.'

'He looks more like you than me,' she concluded.

'So he should,' Nan said. 'The first-born always looks like the father.'

She put particular emphasis on the last word and Irving realised it was the first time it had been openly stated in his presence. He knew what people would think – that the child was illegitimate, that the association between mother and father sinful – and he knew that it would be difficult to bear. His own conscience still plagued him. But just now he felt nothing but pride and delight.

*

Through the first days of Mattie's life, Irving came to see him as much as he could, though Rufina did not want him sleeping with her at night.

'I can control myself, you know,' he told her.

'I know.' She was sitting with the baby on the verandah outside her room, holding him in the crook of her arm. Shadows scooped in the silvery skin under her eyes, her hair was lank in the heat. Why was she unhappy? The force of it made him turn away to look towards the memorial; the sun was still high above it, soft surrounding clouds blazing orange and red. It would sink soon and fast, faster than it did at home. He missed the twilight, but these long, lit evenings were iridescent, bright and warm for hours until the sudden dark. They were evenings that made you glad to be alive.

'I think that part of our life together is over.'

Is that what she'd said? He wasn't sure he'd heard her correctly. A gang of rosellas came to sit on the railing an arm's length away, putting their heads on one side, keeping an eye on him. He clicked his fingers gently at the nearest one, which chittered in return, its beak dry and tongue pebble blue.

What part of their life did she mean?

She was going on, 'Nan says I shouldn't do this, hold him while he's asleep. He'll come to expect it.'

'You're doing right,' Irving said shortly. 'Give him here.'

She kept hold. 'I hear you and Bill wet the baby's head. Isn't that the tradition?'

'Eh?'

'You had a celebration, with Helena and Nan and Ma and Bridgie and Bill and Jell and Albert and God knows who else, in Eddie's wing.'

He nodded. He had. Why not?

'It can't be like that, Irving.'

'Did you hear us singing from here?'

'Helena told me. Why didn't you ask me if I wanted ...' She trailed off, poured a drink of water from the jug beside her. It was capped with a lacy bonnet, small red beads rattling on the glass.

After she'd drained the cup he took it from her, refilled it and drank himself, parched, waiting for her to finish the sentence. She didn't, so he leaned down and took the baby into his own arms. He would have kissed her cheek as he bent to her, but knew she didn't want him to.

As he straightened, Mattie's eyes met his and the little face broke into a delighted grin, eyes and mouth both shining with a true, ecstatic smile. The first? Irving felt his heart blow up like a sail, press against his ribs hard enough to hurt. His own son, whose eyes were changing already, from the newborn slate to a deep amber, almost orange at the edges of the iris. Tiger eyes. He was miraculous.

'Irving?' Rufina was gesturing for him to take the wicker chair, the one from which the giant spider had run out the night they had the bath. Was that the night they made him?

'Sorry. I didn't think you'd want to be there. Too soon for you after—'

'It's the tradition for the mother not to be part of it. Don't worry. But I don't want you talking about him to anyone anymore. Let's just let things settle. Sit down, could you?'

He hadn't taken his eyes off Mattie since he picked him up, the sparse tendrils of glossy black hair, the plump little fists waving. The baby plonked himself on the nose, frowned at the impact but didn't cry – a wee fella of contentment and good spirits. Irving nibbled at the sprat chin, breathed him in, milky and clean.

'Have you just fed him?'

'Yes.'

He did as she had asked then, taking the chair and settling the baby against his shirt, which smelt a little of the new improved piggery. He and Bill had spent the day killing and butchering, starting on making the ham. Bill's idea – to do it all here. Rufina thought the pigs had gone on the boat to Lismore as always, but they were trying something new: 'Jarulan Ham: The Best of the

North'. He'd washed and changed – must be coming out of his skin. Would Rufina notice? It could be the time to tell her about the venture.

But would you look at this pepe, this little tane called Mattie.

'Look at this baby of ours, Rufina!'

She said nothing, so he glanced up at her and saw that she was crying; he hadn't heard her or realised she was so very sad. Gently he said, 'Kaua e tangi, my darling.'

'Don't!'

He flinched, not ready for her anger, or whatever it was that was going on now. He remembered the night Bill asked him straight what was going on, where he disappeared to most nights, and when Irving told him Bill had said, 'Rather you than me, mate,' and laughed in a way that had an edge to it. 'Won't end well,' he'd said.

Had she gone from him so soon? He felt nothing but coolness, empty air, no reach of love between them.

'Don't speak to me in Maori.'

Is that what was bothering her? He could relax again. Nan had told him, after half a bottle of sherry, 'You've given her what she wanted. She always wanted a baby.'

'You can speak to me in German, I don't mind.'

'I want you to listen to me, Irving.'

Helena had said, 'It'll be her baby, not yours. Don't think you'll have anything to do with him,' and Irving had told Jellicoe to ask her to shut up. He would make sure his name was on the birth certificate. He would have him christened at St Peter's in Clunes as quickly as possible.

'I am so much older than you are and I was married to your ... well, you know. You must be able to see why we can't pretend this situation is in any way acceptable.'

'Thirty ...?' He gave her a poke with his finger. 'Go on. How old are you? I should know by now.'

'No. It's not like that, what went on between us. You don't need to know anything about me. You don't. I've told you nothing.'

She'd lost him. He returned his gaze to the baby. He would take him downstairs in the next few days and show him the house, show him Eddie's wing, take him to see the horses.

'Cheer up,' he said, not looking at her. 'I'll go and see what Nan's doing in the kitchen. Are you hungry?'

As he handed her the baby he wondered when their evenings in the belvedere would begin again. This time he did kiss her, quickly, on the lips, and gave her a cheeky wink as he withdrew. When he reached the French doors he heard her say, loudly enough for him to discern her words, 'Send Helena up with my meal,' but he pretended he hadn't. He would bring the mother of his child her kai, no one else.

PART III

1939

1.

BILL, WHO WAS IN CHARGE OF THE MONEY, TALKED A BLOKE into renting them a sailing dinghy to take out on the wide flat Hawkesbury, four hundred and fifty miles south of Lismore. On either side, gum forest lifted away into the horizon forever, hill after low hill after rise after range, until the individual trees merged and the hills were like the bellies of waves. To the east lay the heads; if you kept sailing out between the low islands to the mouth of the river and across the bay until you reached the Tasman, and kept sailing, sailing, sailing, for days, you'd reach New Zealand. Home. Imagine that.

But this was pretty good, sailing an outgoing tide with Jellicoe on the tiller while Irving took the sheets, riding this heavy squat clinkerbuilt, who liked to take her time to get up, like an old horse – though she was young enough. Maybe the bloke had built it himself. Irving could see the bloke's little jerrybuilt house on the first low rise above the beach, surrounded by too-near bush for the fires, but. They were sailing too far out to catch sight of the bloke himself. Bill was beaming a mile wide and Jellicoe whistled the way he did when he was happy, holding hands with his new wife squeezed in beside him in the stern. Helena was still flushed with her victory.

None of them had liked it, her speaking up for them, but the bloke wouldn't look directly at any of them, for the usual reason with these Aussies. He had a touch himself, the bloke, could have – or had just been in the sun so much he'd turned darker than Jell, the palest of them – and only met Bill's eye when he took their money and jammed it in his pocket.

Irving swapped places with Jellicoe and bore the boat against the wind into the choppy easterly; they'd have to tack back and forth but he wanted to head that way, towards the open sea. He wouldn't go far – it was just for the feel of it. Just to see the bay open up at the mouth, where if you kept sailing on and on and on you could see on the horizon the long white cloud. Or would he rather turn them towards the north, all the way back to Lennox Head, overland to Jarulan? Back to Rufina?

No, it was good to be away. On the long drive south with Bill and Jellicoe and Helena he'd thought about Rufina a lot, almost wished she could be with them. But she wanted to be home with the little fella, and who could blame her? No, he wasn't going to miss Mattie today either, even though the child's loving, curious face broke in on him and panged a little. He reminded himself – I am twenty-two years old, I am about to take over Jarulan, I am on holiday, and Rufina wants me to have the best of it before she goes to see her mother. From Grafton had come a Chevrolet coupe utility, shining red, the chassis built in America and the cab by Holden. His own motor, useful for the farm as well as for touring. Almost as much of a miracle as Mattie.

In a wooden box in the quarterdeck they found some handlines, and in the excitement about doing some fishing Bill talked him into going ashore on one of the islands to pick oysters – some of them to eat now and some for bait. Dress tucked into her bloomers, Helena had lessons from Bill on how to flick the shellfish from their beds with one flash of the blade – though, as there was only one knife between them and Bill had her laughing so much at his jibing, he got possession of it again pretty quickly. They were too hungry to wait for her to get it right.

After a few hours out on the water and four snapper on board to cook over a fire, they headed for shore. On the beach the bloke was a bit hacked off, shouting about how he hadn't expected them to stay out for so long. There was a thin dark-haired woman with him, they'd seen her walk down from the house on the sail in, and while she quietened him down – 'For Pete's sake, Reg, they brought the bloody boat back, didn't they?' – Helena was staring at her. It was a hot afternoon and the boys needed some kai; Irving was keen to get back to the car and make a camp there, cook the fish, have a sleep.

'Thanks again,' he told the bloke, who'd taken a whole fiver off them for the privilege, so what was his problem?

'Evie?' said Helena.

Irving had a sinking feeling, as soon as he heard the name. Was Helena about to come loose like Rufina had? The woman's feet were shoved into a dirty old holey pair of sandshoes, her bare white legs with long black hairs. A scarecrow in her old frock she was, with her short cropped curly hair and too-wide eyes.

Then there were tears and embraces and Reg was inviting them all up to the little house, the women ahead of them walking two abreast. Irving could hear Helena running on with how she knew who Evie was from all the hours she'd spent, from the time she was a little girl, staring at a little snapshot of her mother stuck to her bedroom wall. She gave a report on Ma's health, and Nan, and the rest of the family, and how Rufina was about to go back to Germany, and who Irving was – 'Eddie's son!' marvelled Evie, turning to look at him. 'Look at that! Of course, you are!'

By the time they reached the lowest ridge and the dirt path to the house, Helena was panting from talking so much, and it seemed the first flush of their reunion was fading already. She fired questions – where were you, why did you never write, why didn't you let us know where you were? Evie rolled a cigarette and looked like she was about to turn on the taps any minute so the men walked away, following Reg around the house, while he told them how he had built the place from flotsam and jetsam in the river washed down from the Nepean, and how the water tank came off a ship that went aground further up the coast. Inside slumped a black coal range, a lopsided wooden sink plumbed to the sump, a sagging divan, a table and chairs, the woman's clothes lying around, bread rising in a bowl. The windows looked out over the river.

It was bliss, and Irving thought of how he'd rather have this than all the faded grandeur of his grandfather's house. It would be simpler. How did Reg get hold of the land? There was so much of it in this country. Did he take it off the Aborigines or had they already been shot and destroyed? Their fate weighed heavily on him again, as it had done so many times since he arrived in Sydney. Or was this a part of Australia they hadn't lived in? Maybe land like this, uncleared, remote – maybe the government just let you have it. What it would be like to have some, further along the river towards the coast! Or a whole tiny island. To live off fish, plant a few potatoes.

While he dreamed, Bill started up, telling Reg about the journeys he'd made around Australia, the places he'd worked and characters he'd met, and Irving didn't try to listen because he'd heard most of the stories before. Instead, he gazed out the window above the sink, which faced south towards Sydney, their planned destination, not that you could see it from here. In another fortnight they were due back at Jarulan. How Mattie would have grown. Six months old when they left and already nearly crawling.

The wind had swung around to the south and a bank of rain clouds lifted behind the opposite range. The biggest thunderhead, the shape of it, was Tarawera with his flat top, the way a child would draw it. It was as if the ghost of his childhood mountain rose behind these ancient, foreign maunga, the cloud imitating a crest less than a hundred years old since the lava last rose and caught fire, since the volcano covered and changed the land around it. The land here had been the same forever, it felt like, the forest and timeless hills.

Behind him, Bill and the bloke who only hours ago could hardly look at them were encouraging Jell to hightail it back to the beach to fetch beer bottles kept cooling in the shallows, tied to a rock. Irving watched the lad, hovering at the door anxious about his young wife, who was still with her mother, though the screeching and wailing had stopped. Had it? He cocked his head to catch the sound – the men close by and the eternal surrounding racket of insect and bird. And here Helena, saying something emphatic. Like Nan said, she'd come into herself since their marriage. Plumper and more confident as Rufina has grown less so, thin and anxious and hiding away with the baby. He wished she wasn't taking Mattie with her to Germany, he wished she wouldn't keep shutting him out. He was back in her bed again of course; she couldn't resist. And in the mornings he got Mattie from his cot and brought him into their bed and it was perfect.

In the end they all went down to the beach, the women as well, who held hands all the way down the track. When they got to the muddy shore, Jell took Helena's other hand and the three of them stood there, linked, looking out across the water. Bill and Reg clambered out onto the low flat rock and brought up the dripping bottles, their yellow labels peeling off, and opened them one from the other, handing them around. The boat needed tidying up, the fish cleaning, and there wouldn't be much time to get it all done before rain came; Tarawera had melted away, re-formed, vast across the darkening sky. They worked quickly, standing the bottles in the gritty mud between drinks.

Evie and Helena didn't help much, except for rewinding a handline each while they perched on the edge of the boat. Irving heard the words hat shop and the Cross and how, after

Reg came into the picture, there was lots of shifting around up and down the coast, getting work where they could. Hard times before they found this place. No more children, though she would have been young enough. She was about Rufina's age, roundabout.

Up at the house again they played cards, by the light of a kerosene lamp lit for the rainy gloom, and by the time he and Evie cooked the fish and potatoes that filled everyone's bellies the plans had changed. They were to make their way back up north again tomorrow, with Evie. Go home early. Give Ma the surprise of her life.

'And you?' Bill asked Reg.

'Not me. Busy here.'

'Not that busy,' Evie retorted. There was a house cow, a handful of chooks, his boat. A still. The drink was a fiery spirit made out of rhubarb. 'How will I get back again?'

'Rufina,' Helena gathered dirty plates. 'Rufina will pay for the train or a boat.'

Evie caught Helena's eye and cackled. 'Pay me to go away again, more like!'

Helena shrugged and murmured something Irving didn't catch.

'A baby?' Evie. She looked delighted. Malicious. 'Who's the father?'

Helena avoided his eye. Why would she respond, since she's off the wrong side of the blanket herself? Some misguided loyalty to Rufina.

'I am.' The words came to his mouth but he couldn't voice them because of Reg. If he knew Irving had fathered a child with a white woman, his employer, of their convoluted relationship, then who knew what he'd do? His acceptance of them was skin deep. The gin had made him garrulous. He was in Casino when they closed the railway in '32 after the riot. He skited about getting away, making this enviable life for himself and Evie on the river.

But wouldn't it be lonely here? With nightfall there was the soft glimmer of a light a mile or two off, a couple across the body of water. Neighbours, then. Distant ones.

No, Irving wouldn't want this life. If it wasn't for Mattie he'd sell Jarulan, now that he owned it on paper, and go home. He'd buy a farm in the Bay of Plenty with the money, grow sheep and sweetcorn, peaches and strawberries, run Jersey and Friesian cattle, pigs that live outside, what he understood. Sure, he was young enough to learn how to farm polar bears in Alaska if he had to. But he didn't have to, did he?

Out of her poor reserves Evie tried to find them blankets and something to cushion their heads on the floor. He'd sleep in the Chevy, Irving decided. It was not too cold a night, just wet. By the time he got to the car his head was streaming, his shoulders damp, his mood dark.

Bugger it all. What was wrong with him? He was not usually this out of sorts. He was drunk. That's what it was. He opened the cab, climbed in. Some nights on this trip they'd slept in the open back, where they would all have turns travelling during the day and choking in the dust. Once, as they rattled and shook on a rough mountain road, a kangaroo jumped clean over the top of them. That was a story to remember for Mattie. And how one night they were woken by a little tribe of hopping rats clustered around the remains of a bird they'd cooked the night before, squeaking and barking. Helena said they were bandicoots and that Rufina had a display of them in the front parlour – had he seen it? He had, the morning he rescued the bat, the bat that flew away back to his friends after a night camping out in the fountain.

Lying across the bench seat, he tried to make himself comfortable. Rain drummed on the roof, a sound he normally found comforting, but he was racked with guilt – that all too familiar buffer against sleep unless, ironically, he was lying beside the cause of it. When Rufina and he were up and dressed and going around their daily business on the farm or the house or dealing with sales agents or crops or stock or the men or whatever, she knew to keep her distance; she didn't lay claim to him. It was almost as if she ignored him. But at night, in their bed – her bed it was, really, even after all this time – it was a different story. Too different. All out of balance. All wrong. She hardly had a kind word for him in the daylight hours.

How she laughed when he told her, since she'd asked, about other women and there were none except a girl in Sydney, a loose girl, and he'd felt sick afterwards. He hadn't explained how close he'd come to taking orders, that he still tried to live the life of a good Christian, even though these days he never went to church. Couldn't stand the way they sang here.

Alone in the truck, the wind howling, his body was betraying him, tempting him to sin. He tried to think of something else, anything else, but his exhausted mind gave him Rufina again, standing with a letter in her hand a week before he left for his holiday. She had translated it, read aloud how much the old lady was looking forward to her arrival in Berlin. She'd fetched the atlas from the library to show him where the city was, watching him closely for his reaction, for the moment he understood just how far away she would be.

In the letter, Rufina's mother made no mention of Mattie and that was because, as Rufina explained to him, she had no notion of his existence. She would tell her, but face to face, and carefully.

'Why is that?' he'd asked. 'He is her grandson.'

Rufina had pressed her pretty lips together, not answered. He knew why.

'I will have to pick my moment to tell her, to explain how he came about.'

'Where will he stay, then? Where will he sleep?'

'I will have to find someone to care for him, close enough for me to pay him visits.'

'A stranger? Leave him here with me and Helena and Nan.'

'Don't be ridiculous. It's nothing to do with you.'

He had flung off, out onto the land, worked past nightfall and kept away from her for the next three days or so – or was it that long? He always went back, didn't he, stealing up the stairs long after the lamps were extinguished, all the lamps except the ones she set burning in her window. Modesty lamps, she called them, which could only be a joke.

Bill woke him after sun-up, banging on the roof of the truck and telling him to come up for breakfast. Achy from his long uncomfortable night and weighed with some of its gloom, his spirits lightened only slowly. First there was the rejuvenating freshly washed sky and then the lapping full tide that he and Bill dunked themselves in. And then the good breakfast of eggs and bacon and Helena's infectious excitement about making the long journey north in the company of her mother, restored to her at last, to say nothing of his own delight at the prospect of seeing his son again, very soon.

2.

I T TURNED OUT THAT THE FIRST M RS F ENCHURCH HAD COME from a family of grave robbers and antiquarians – wealthy Americans who had bought great chunks of ancient Europe and lugged them back to California to decorate their gardens, or sent them to Australia for Min to decorate hers. Aphrodite and Hera were thousands of years old and fetched a very good price. A man from the Sydney museum had made the long journey north to inspect them. He examined the others closely and paid good money for Diana and the Virgin too. At first Rufina had worried if he was giving them their true value but in the end didn't let it overly concern her. The main issue was to raise enough money for her journey and sojourn in Europe. It would be very expensive, even after the passage was paid for. There were shipboard costs and train fares and everything that one needed travelling with a baby, quite apart from a nanny. She had placed an advertisement in a Berlin newspaper months ago now and had had no replies.

A week before Irving's return from his tour, a dealer from Brisbane was due. Rufina had been sorting and cleaning since Irving left, sitting Mattie on a rug nearby with his favourite toy, the little red tractor that Matthew's grandsons had quarrelled over all those years ago. Furniture, paintings, specimens from the trophy room – anything of value that she didn't want to keep, she hauled into the hall. The rolltop desk from the morning room, the ugly Victorian settee, the portrait of the original Fenchurch rich from cedar and beef. Albert helped her shift some of it, the heavier pieces, but Nance was useless. She didn't understand what Rufina was doing, even though she'd had it explained to her a hundred times, usually over the top of Mattie's wailing. The baby had been out of sorts since Irving left.

'I have been thinking of building a new house for Mattie and me, further towards the mountains away from the river.'

Nance stood at the far end of the hall, a patch of hot sun dancing with dust around her legs. The library door was open, two parallel scrapes on the floorboards showing where the heavy teak desk chair had been dragged out.

'When I come back from Germany I will look into it. We don't need this big house. It's falling down around our ears.'

'There's going to be another war.' Sullen. 'Everybody says so.'

'Not one that will touch us down here. Do you really think the colonies will go through that all over again? Let England fight her own wars.'

Nance said nothing, though Rufina could read her mind: it's your lot that are causing it. Again.

'Whatever happens, it will be over quickly, faster than the last one. They won't let it drag on and on like before. Box up that Royal Albert tea set from the dining room, will you? The bloke can take it away no matter what he'll give me for it.' It had been Min's. 'And the silver candlesticks. The ones the swaggies left behind.'

It still rankled. Nance hadn't moved.

'We don't need these things anymore, don't you see? After I'm gone, close off the top floors. You won't need to go up there at all.'

'When are you coming back?'

'In September, four months. I've already told you.' If she hadn't let Lena go with the others she could have got her to look after Mattie while she finished in the trophy room. There were animals extinct and possibly of great value, including a paradise parrot she shot herself in 1926. She should have shown them to the museum curator a fortnight ago but she wasn't ready to part with them then. How quickly she was moving on.

'Shall we go to look at the koalas, Mattie?' She picked him up and carried him down the hall and into the front room. Dust furred the vitrines and the curtains had been left open through the summer enough to fade the carpet. She had hardly been in here for months. Since Mattie was born she had lost interest in it for reasons she found curious. Birth and renewal, was it? Enough of the old, the dead, the preserved beyond the natural span.

'See the koalas?'

The baby pointed towards the display, as if he had understood what she'd said and already recognised them. When she drew closer he gurgled and smiled, singing to himself as he often did when he was happy, a little three-note tune.

'And see the bat?' she asked him. 'Your father gave me that.'

It was a distortion of the truth. She had gone to the fountain soon after he put it there and found it newly dead, as she knew it would be, and knew also that if Irving had known it had died he would be saddened. He would believe he had failed the little bat, which he had tried to save; so very carefully she had picked it up with gloves and treated it the way Matthew had taught her, and hidden it among the koala family. It hung upside down among the paper eucalypt leaves at the back of the display, wings folded and eyes closed.

While Mattie sat on the floor banging and rolling his tractor, she went around the room with a list. Since the war, tastes had changed, she knew, but she would do her best to interest the dealer. The less rare animals, the wallabies and kangaroos, crows and cockatoos, might have a worth attached to them just for the skill in preservation. A large vitrine set against the partition held a collection of birds, including the cuckoo she shot soon after she and Matthew were married. At least it didn't leave any starving young, she thought, surprising herself. On the day she shot it she didn't worry about that, as far as she could remember. She opened the case to stroke the small feathered head with its yellow-ringed eye.

A solution to her problem occurred to her, as if it had risen from the bird itself. She would not take Mattie with her at all, not expose him to any possible peril at sea or on land. Storms, rampant shipboard diseases spreading faster than bushfire, just as the Spanish flu had after the last war – none of that for Mattie. And yes, she would protect him also from this new predicted war, not that she believed it could ever happen.

Dear cuckoo, you have the right idea. She lifted it out, remembering Matthew's lesson in how to set the wings as if there was life in them, not too close to the body and a tension in them, as if the bird at any minute could take flight. And I will. I will leave and take Mattie with me as far as Sydney, where I will place him with a kind woman and go to Europe alone. Safer there than with Irving at Jarulan, because she could not trust him. She'd seen the hungry, adoring way he looked at Mattie, how his youth – and yes, his race – made him love the boy more than could be good for either of them. Certainly his devotion alarmed her. He could get it into his head to take the baby back to New Zealand, to the bosom of his peculiar family. The thought of Mattie in the slab and tin hut made her shiver.

Mattie had his arms stretched out for the cuckoo, the tractor discarded for this more interesting toy. She knelt with it, let him grip the head and pull the beak.

'Bird,' she tried. 'B … bird.' It was the best idea. She would collect him on her return, healthy and happy, not dragged from pillar to post.

'Burr,' said Mattie, showing his two teeth. It was almost his first word – but no point in pretending a milestone had been reached when it had not. She let him have the cuckoo. Already the beak was awry and one wing yanked sideways to a jaunty angle.

Out of the silence came the sound of an approaching motor, between the avenue of trees towards the house. The dealer, any minute. Rufina stood again and considered the big vitrine. It could go out into the hall, since it was on castors. She shifted Mattie to one side, folded back a corner of the carpet and gave the case a preparatory shove. The castors squealed, as she expected – the thing hadn't shifted for decades. Mattie gave a little wail, startled away from his investigation of the bird. A feather stuck to his wet chin.

'It's all right,' she told him, huffing at the case. It stood as high as her shoulder and was a good three foot long. No – too big and too heavy. Instead, she would carry out a smaller one, the Christbird with his mirror pond and raffia reeds, and get a sense from the dealer if he would like to see any of the others. It was becoming fashionable now to castigate and lecture on the waste of life, the cruelty, the morbid fascination.

The case was the size of two kerosene tins perhaps, easily managed and not too heavy. As she lifted it from its stand she heard footfalls on the front steps and voices – the dealer must have brought advisors with him. Through the window above Mattie's head was a clear blue May sky, not a cloud; they would have had a pretty drive up from the coast, which with luck will have put them in a buying frame of mind. Hurrying now, in order to be able to greet the dealer when he came in – Mr Simmons, that was his name – she caught her foot in the folded-over carpet. Over she went, the case flying from her grasp. As she went down she saw it fall towards Mattie and the remains of the cuckoo – the feathers, he could choke on the feathers! – and smash to pieces, her hands spread among the shards. When she lifted her head, blood from a gash in her brow obscured her vision of four sets of legs with a pair of elastic sided boots the closest.

Above Mattie's wailing she heard Irving's voice, 'Are you all right?' and then quickly afterwards from Lena, 'No, Mattie!' and a woman, not Lena, raced forward in ancient plimsolls to gather up the baby, who had been crawling towards his father through the glass. Woozily, Rufina struggled to her feet; she must have bumped her head on the edge of the door – her hands were cut as well – but the arrivals were gathered around Mattie, who was really screaming now. 'It's in his knees,' from Jellicoe and they were leaving, running towards the kitchen with the baby to find tweezers and Condy's Crystals and whatever, leaving Rufina clinging to the door jamb with blood dripping from her hands like stigmata.

The woman with them. It was Evie. Or was she losing her mind again? Rufina had looked up from the glittering floor and seen for a moment Evie's girlhood face before the older worn one slipped into its place. Evie hadn't been smiling – but then why would she, walking in on shattered glass and a screaming baby? She had looked astonished. And curious. Yes, there was curiosity and astonishment. And also compassion. Compassion! After all this time.

Rufina picked her way out to the front verandah and sat woozily on the top step, leaning against a post. She would not be able to think of anything to say to her. Where would they start? Would Evie expect a scene of forgiveness or of mutual recrimination?

And why didn't someone come to see if she was all right?

In the end it was Evie who came, bringing a washcloth and a basin of water. She set to, picking her flesh clean and bathing the cut in her head. For the first while they did nothing but concentrate on the task – there's a bit, there's another – but stole glances at one another's faces.

'Where is Mattie?'

'With Irving. Having a cuddle.'

'Is he all right?'

'Yes, he was lucky. Only a couple of scratches, not deep.'

'Good.'

'A mouth full of feathers, though. How did he do that?'

A water dragon had come out of the garden and sat staring at them, motionless as stone. It was warm today. Soon, as the weather grew cooler, the dragons would hide away.

'Hello, little fella,' said Evie.

'Hardly little,' said Rufina. It was about two and a half feet long, with spines as big as teeth.

'We have lots of them where we live,' said Evie, and she told Rufina about her place on the Hawkesbury, and her husband Reg, and how they'd been able to weather the hard times with their garden and fishing, and how Reg sometimes took day-trippers out on his boat for money. It seemed there had been no more children. Rufina wanted to ask her about how she had missed Helena, if at all, how it had been for her when she first went away. She could see in Evie's careworn face that her life had not been easy, even though the picture she painted was idyllic. Her ministrations were gentle, patient, though by the way she squinted and brought her eyes close to Rufina's open palm she could do with a pair of spectacles.

'There,' Rufina pointed, 'and there. Missed a bit.'

Irving came out onto the verandah behind them, Mattie in his arms, and at the sudden movement the water dragon scarpered.

'You see the dragon, Mattie?' Irving said, and Rufina wondered if he'd glanced in her direction at all. 'What's going on?' he asked now in a harder tone, and she knew the question was directed at her.

'I'm sorting out a few things.' She was evasive. She'd tell him her plans but not now.

'Nan says you're talking about building a new house.' The cat was out of the bag already.

'Whether I do or not it's just an idea. I want to modernise.'

'Modernise,' he echoed softly. From inside came the sound of glass being swept up, and Helena and Nance's voices.

'We don't need all this stuff. I feel sometimes as if I'm suffocating in it all. And besides, it's not to my taste.' It was an outburst she hadn't intended to have in front of Evie, or anyone for that matter, Evie now dabbing at her cuts with a solution of Condy's and wincing in sympathy as she did so. Rufina felt a rush of affection for her, unbidden and odd. Despite Evie's long absence, or because of it, she was one of her longest standing associates in Australia. The Schneiders had gone back to Germany, the last letter full of anxiety about the possible new war. 'What if we are rounded up again and imprisoned?' Frau Schneider had worried. They were approaching their sixties now and wouldn't be able to bear it.

Rufina wouldn't be able to bear it either, if it happened. But it wouldn't!

She stood up, Evie with her and offering a steadying arm.

'I'm all right.'

Mattie gazed at her, as did Irving, their expressions of casual concern identical. It would be difficult to stick to her plan. The more she saw them together the harder it would be to separate them. She held her arms out for the baby but Irving shook his head.

'Bill and Jell have gone down to the river for a spot of fishing. Making the most of their last day off. I'm taking Matiu down to take his mind off his wounds.'

Rufina's eye fell on the bandage carefully wound around the baby's right hand and found that all she could do was nod.

'Does he need changing?'

Gamely, Irving lifted the baby and sniffed at him. 'No,' and he was gone, bounding down the river steps where fat Bacchus, removed a year ago from Eddie's wing, stood as a lonely sentinel.

He was a poor copy from the nineteenth century and not worth anything.

'Handsome lad,' observed Evie. Rufina said nothing, wondering where the dealer had got to.

'Twenty-two,' he told me.

'That's right.'

'You must be forty.'

Was Evie judging her? She wouldn't dare.

'He loves him, doesn't he? The baby. Talked of nothing else on the trip north.'

'Did he ...' Rufina turned back from the end of the verandah, where her feet had led her to watch her baby go down to the fishermen. She would observe Evie closely for any hint of falsehood. 'Did he ever talk about going back to New Zealand?'

As far as she could tell, Evie showed genuine surprise. 'No. Why would he? In clover here. All in his name now, isn't it?'

'Upon my death, yes. Until then I hold it in trust for him.'

'Well. You don't look like you're going to die any minute, so it isn't his.'

'Yes it is.'

It was Evie's turn to look suspicious. 'He thinks it's in his name now.'

'It's our own private business, Evie. Nothing to do with you.' Irving should never have discussed it with her.

'What about Helena?'

'What about me? What are you saying?' Helena had appeared at the front door with a pan and brush, the pan full of glass and balanced on top of it the remains of the cuckoo.

'Provision will be made.' Rufina had made a little, but Irving would inevitably give her more. Helena stood, looking from Evie to Rufina, waiting to be enlightened. When neither woman would meet her eye she said, 'What do you want me to do with this?'

'The rubbish heap. Where else?'

A glance passed between mother and daughter and Rufina realised she would have to modify her tone while Evie was here.

'You must have got a surprise, Rufe, to see Evie again. I told her the story of the swaggies and how you thought one of them was her.'

'Won't you call me Ma?' asked Evie plaintively. 'You said you would.'

'No. I've thought about it and I won't. Nan says if anyone is my ma it's her, since she raised me.'

Rufina sighed. She wasn't interested in any of this. She lifted her hand to make the dismissive gesture she had so many times to send Lena away and thought the better of it.

'You're my girl, Helena,' said Evie. 'Nothing will change that.' She went to her and kissed her on the cheek. Helena's eyes welled.

'You'll take her back with you, then,' asked Rufina, 'to the Hawkesbury?'

'If she wants. Not much for a young woman there, or for Jell.'

That's right, thought Rufina. She'd forgotten that they'd got married quickly, just before they went away with Irving. She hadn't attended either the service or the breakfast, hosted by Irving in Eddie's wing.

'And besides,' Helena burst out, 'I'm going to have a baby!'

Then it was Evie's turn to get teary and Nance came out to see what the fuss was all about. The remains of the mess in the trophy room were abandoned and the women disappeared to the kitchen for cups of tea and cake to celebrate.

Alone on the verandah again, Rufina wondered bleakly why it was that she was so often left to her own company when she enjoyed it less and less. She leaned over the railing and looked into the shrubs for the water dragon but it wasn't in evidence. After a while she followed the others down to the kitchen and drank her tea at the table with only half an ear on their chatter. Nance was exercising her claim on Helena, giving her all kinds of old wives' tales on what to eat and how much rest she should take, even though she had never had a child herself. Evie petted and cooed and encouraged her to eat more cake, though the girl's dress was bursting at the seams.

Rufina found herself thinking about love, about forgiveness, how Lena had somehow excused her mother for abandoning her for all these years. She saw Evie's joy at the prospect of a grandchild. She wished she could confide in them about her plan to leave Mattie in Sydney, to keep him safe, and even as she wished it she knew, suddenly, that she wouldn't be able to carry it through.

Helena caught her eye and gave her a tentative smile. 'They'll be able to play together,' she said, patting her stomach, 'Mattie and this little one.'

Rufina nodded. 'I've got some dresses you can have. The ones I made when Mattie was on the way.'

'Ta!' Helena beamed a real smile across the table then, Matthew's even broad smile, and launched into a plan to take Evie to see Ma as soon as possible, since she was once again poorly and confined to her bed.

Someone was knocking at the screen door – the dealer, whom Rufina had completely forgotten about.

'No answer round the front,' he said, a sweaty little man in a brown suit and felt hat.

'I'll be with you in a minute,' she told him. He was staring at the cut in her forehead. 'We had a little accident.'

*

Mr Simmons, as suspected, was not at all interested in the specimens, extinct or otherwise. Neither did he want the heavier pieces of furniture, but a price was agreed on the gloomy oil paintings, silver candlesticks and bone china tea set. Rufina helped him pack them into the back of his Ford truck. 'Simmons Second Hand and Antique Dealers' in gothic lettering along the sides and 'A Fair Price For Your Curiosities' on the back.

Not so fair, thought Rufina, watching him go down the driveway, a rising plume of dust and smoke lit golden in the afternoon sun.

Irving and Mattie were making their way back from the river and she went to join them at the top of the steps. Her spirits were lighter, floating. It wasn't just the casting off of the belongings of the dead, it was the change of plan made for the wellbeing of the living, a change made not so much in her head but her heart, while she sat with Nance and Helena and Evie. There would be no kindly stranger in Sydney to care for Mattie, someone she could not possibly trust entirely because the woman would be just that, a stranger. She would go alone to Germany and leave Mattie here, among the people who loved him, and return to him just as soon as ever she could – even if, God forbid, only in spirit.

PART IV

2013

1.

Matti Fenchurch

WAITANGI DAY AND THE FAMILY HAVE GATHERED AT MY son's place at Coogee above the sea. We've had roast lamb, beer and wine, and the guitars out, and now it's mid-afternoon, thirty-six in the shade, and there's a fair bit of dozing going on among us oldies. The women are in the kitchen doing the dishes, God bless them. I can hear my Aussie daughter-in-law's shrieking laugh. The teenagers have gone down to the beach, so it's just the koros and the tamariki in the bright afternoon yard, the oldies and the bubbas dozing and waking.

Each time my eyes open it's to the Sydney sun slicing off the ocean, blinding as the blade of a butcher's knife, so I have to close them again straight away. It's enough to make you long for home, for the grey-green light, for a slow walk in the bush dripping cool with recent rain. Straw hat repositioned, I breathe in the mingled distant salt of the sea and the closer car fumes from Coogee Bay Road and the spice of hot gum from the trees in the garden and the frangipani in flower.

Lovely. The smell of home. This home. There have been so many, on both sides of the Tasman. Close my eyes, remember Evie's story of the first home, the story she told on that rainy 1961 night in a Kings Cross pub. It was the days of the Kiwiroos, when bands like mine were in high demand in Sydney. I remember she started around midnight and didn't shut up until the sun was high. At first she was just another drunk old lady with too much makeup, ogling me and the boys while we sang, but she reckoned I looked just like a brown Matthew Fenchurch, and that she'd noticed that even before she'd seen my name under the picture on the playbill outside, and she'd had to come in. It was Calypso night. We were all in bright shirts and too-small straw hats, singing Harry Belafonte and the like. In a break I sat with her at the bar and she said, 'You must go to Jarulan. You must go back and see it.'

Sitting here in the sun with my little granddaughter asleep on my lap, fifty years after I heard the story, I can still recall her cracked, smoky voice reeling on and on, telling me more than she thought she was.

*

She had waited for me after the show, fending off the barman who wanted to throw her out, since she wasn't their usual club clientele – the young South Sea Poms and Maori and Aussies that flocked to hear us at the Taboo in the Cross. From the stage I'd noticed her, a skinny old lady joining a Congo around the dance floor and between the tables, everyone singing along loudly 'In the New Zealand isles where everybody smiles', all the young Kiwi misses shaking their nonos like they never do at home. 'They don't mind a little earthquake, to them it's just an earthquake, shake shake shake shaking in the Shaky Isles, shake the blues away'. When they did 'Nobody But Me' the old lady had her arm around one of my cousins, who was over on a trip. 'Nobody but me!' they all roared. More and more New Zealanders were coming every month to Sydney and I loved it. There were times when it seemed that nearly everybody I loved was all together in one place, in whichever club we were singing in, five nights a week. Party time.

At the end of a number she reached up from the dance floor to tug on my trouser leg. 'Who's your father?'

I thought she was having me on.

'Go on, love, tell me his name. Was it Irving Fenchurch?'

The band was playing the intro to the next song. I remember I had an ominous feeling, as though I was about to learn something about my father that would change my life. She looked like a little wizened witch, smiling up at me.

'I'll wait for you,' she said.

Much later we were on stools at the high polished bar, me in my Calypso rig, silly too-small hat and lei and Hawaiian shirt that wasn't true Calypso but at this distance from the Caribbean people neither knew nor cared. Evie lit another fag with her little monkey hands.

'Like a lamb to the slaughter. That's what the German told me it was like, their first time. Poor bastard. When she seduced him he wasn't even twenty years old.' Evie turned her empty sherry glass round and round, the flickering tiny stem in her brown nicotine-stained fingers. Sunseeker and heavy smoker she was, with a glint in her wrinkly old Irish eye. She had a gentleman friend with a boat and for years they'd sailed the Pacific. They were naturists – nude tannings – and liked a drink.

'Greeted me like a long-lost friend, like she'd forgotten what a bitch she was before I went away. She was full of talk about the swaggies that had moved in and stolen from them, how she'd gone a bit mad and thought one of them was me.' She lit a ciggie off the one she'd nearly finished and struck a pose, presenting me with her profile. 'Don't s'pose you remember me, do you, boy?'

I was hardly a boy that night in the bar, a year off thirty. There was a nasty stink in the way she called me that. I shook my head, not that she noticed, since she was fascinated more by our horn player Api, handsome in those days, who was packing up, bedding down the trumpet and the sax in their velvet-lined boxes. The barman came out from behind and wiped down the front of the bar, a waitress went round with a bucket and a damp cloth and emptied ashtrays, another one came out of the kitchen with a tray of sandwiches for the band and my puku rumbled – I was a skinny wee fella then. Not that I'm any taller now, just rounder.

'Of course you don't remember. You were what? Just a bubba.'

'1939?'

'Thereabouts. Just before she went back to Germany. We knew then, you see, that there would be another war and she was a Kraut to her toenails. She wasn't going to go through all that again, being an alien. She was frightened that they'd take the farm, lock her up in a camp like they did to the Germans the first time round.'

'But how long had she been here, this Rufina?'

'Long time. Twenty years. She'd come out as a lady companion before the first war. A paid friend. And not to say she didn't love Australia, or the little bit that was hers. Jarulan. She did, almost as much as she loved you, sport. You slept in her room until the very last night.'

Api joined us, bringing more sandwiches – one for Evie as well – and asking the barman for a drink.

'I want you lot to bugger off,' the barman said. 'Closing time.'

Evie waggled her empty glass at him. Together she and Api joked and teased and barracked until he broke the law and poured two more beers, while I sat there imagining my small sleeping self in the German woman's room. My great-grandfather's widow. Did she get up to me if I cried in the night? Did she feed me? Two children of my own by this stage, one back in New Zealand and one here, and bugger all to do with either of them – not a good dad for my first kids. All I knew about babies then was that they cried in the night and someone has to get up to them.

'You're wondering why she didn't take you with her, aren't ya?' Evie's attention had swum through the bottom of her glass back to me.

'Who?'

'When she went back to Germany. It was my daughter Lena who looked after you until your dad took you home. A couple of years. You were nearly three when he took you back.'

A face, suddenly. A broad, flat smile and loving blue eyes. A long high room with bright hot windows and her hand leaving mine as I ran towards a man standing at the distant end, his arms out to catch me. My father. And nothing else, except a memory of an aching heart, that she was gone, and that my father carried me to a waiting car.

Evie leaned forward and took my hands, cigarette still burning between her fingers.

'Shit, love. You didn't know. I'm sorry.'

She was, too, in that moment, sorry for me, so sorry she kissed me with her thin, hard smoky mouth, and I feel a little sorry for myself now as I look down at seven-year-old Rena asleep in my arms, hot and sticky, her hair slicked around her face. Lucky Rena, youngest daughter of my youngest son Brad and his beloved ditzy Sue. Her mother would never abandon her, not for quids. Rena will always know who she is. The little one is the reason I'm remembering all this. Earlier she was asking me where I lived when I was a baby.

'Jarulan,' I told her, 'The grandest house in the north.'

'In Aotearoa?' she asked, and was surprised when I told her New South Wales.

'Can we go there? Where you were borned?'

'Maybe. One day.'

I never have gone back. I'm frightened of what I might remember.

That long-ago night in the club, as the chairs were stacked on the tables around us and the floor swept and the stage lights dimmed, Evie told me, 'She did the right thing, leaving you behind. Likely you would have been with her in Berlin and killed like she was. Blasted sky high by the bombers. And besides, look at the colour of you – Hitler wouldn't've liked you one tiny bit!' And her wheezy old laugh ricocheted around the brown varnished walls of the empty club.

I needed to be alone for a moment. I couldn't breathe. She was rattling on, wanting to know if Irving had gone away to fight, nodding when I told her he hadn't.

'Yeah, too gentle, I reckon. One of the gentlest men I ever did meet.'

I had heard other women say this kind of thing before about my father and if I hadn't been so pole-axed I would've told her that he'd tried to sign up but he was too deaf and they didn't want him. He was a good father to me, found himself a proper Maori wife, gave me siblings, worked hard to make a successful farm that he bought with the sale of Jarulan, money that he only ever said came from the Australian side of the family.

Evie was going on, 'I saw the way he cared for you, the way he carried you around with him. And half in love with the German, I reckon. Didn't want to be, but he was.'

I sat on my stool, longing to get away to clear my head, to walk through the cool streets and think about all this, to try to make sense of it. My father loved my great-grandfather's widow. He had loved her. And then I wanted more of the story, as much as she could give me, so I invited Evie to my digs, and later, as the sun came up, for breakfast at the always-open-for-business greasy famous Hasty Tasty on Darlinghurst Road. She didn't stop talking until we'd eaten our fill and emptied three pots of tea.

By the time she'd finished I knew who I was. And I knew that even though I was only a baby when I left, I have carried that house with me all my life. On my back. In my bones.

2.

Jarulan

WE ARE JAMMED INTO THE CAR, MY YOUNGEST SON, HIS WIFE, the two gangly teenagers, Rena, the itchy, scratchy dog, and me, on the long trip north. Halfway, we stay the night at Coffs Harbour with a friend of my son's who is a successful businessman, in his big new house in Solitary Way with a view of the moana. His tall winsome daughter is a dancer, with an MA in Maori Culture from a local university. She is called Mackenzie like the famous South Island sheep rustler, and has never once set foot in her ancestral home. She makes a fuss of me; I am famous again, in a small way, or so it seems – the show bands I played in, the songs I sang. She tells me she saw me interviewed on Maori TV, a spot I did a fair few years ago for a doco on the showband era.

Marvellous, it all is. A big new modern house, all white walls and glass, wide dusky windows giving out over the ocean, the horizon growing closer as the sun slips away across the wide land behind us. The dancer finds Rena and me in the vast living room on a black leather sofa the size of a waka, staying out of the way of the dinner preparations in the shiny kitchen and avoiding the giant-screen footy in the adjoining room.

'This house you're all going to,' says Mackenzie. 'Where is it?'

'It's not there anymore,' I tell her. 'It burned down.'

'How?' asks Mackenzie. 'By accident or on purpose?'

'Well, my great-grandfather had built a memorial on the hill above the house. Rena and I found a news story from the seventies all about how there was a bit of glass on the very top that shifted in a hail storm and turned around a little so that the sun shone through it on a particular angle. One summer day it was so hot that the forest caught fire and then the grass and then the house.'

'Cool,' says Mackenzie. 'Spooky. It means fire, you know, Jarulan. I looked it up. It's an Aboriginal word for a fire started by birds.'

'The fire wasn't started by birds,' says Rena firmly.

Early the next afternoon we're on the road again, all the way up the coast to Ballina, where the wide flat river is brown and mottled as a working dog's belly. Across the bridge we go, inland towards Lismore, through the flatland sugar until the hills rise and climb, the trees change – less palms, more figs and gums, coffee plantations, macadamia. We are even more jammed in, the two youngest under a single seatbelt in the six-seater four-wheel-drive, because we are joined by Mackenzie who is filming us on her phone.

'I'm putting it up live on my blog,' she tells me. 'I've got two thousand followers.'

'I wish you wouldn't,' I tell her.

'Do you wonder sometimes what it would have been like to have grown up here? To have had a mother identifying as German after the Second World War and being Maori in New South Wales?'

'It would have been untenable,' comes Rena's serious voice. She has the tail end of a green jelly snake hanging from her mouth to below her chin. 'Australians are *very* racist, you know.'

Mackenzie turns her camera on the jelly snake. 'How do you know that, Rena? Have you heard people say racist things?'

'Koro said it would be *untenable*.'

Mackenzie is back online and reading aloud the story of Jarulan since the Fenchurch family left, how the house fell into disrepair for many years and was believed to be haunted. How in the 1960s a commune was established there for a peppercorn rent, and how it was gutted by the fire some time after the hippies left. The original farm had been broken up, sold off to lifestylers and nut farmers, coffee growers, a boutique hotel, an organic garden, and a transcendental sexual healing centre, whatever the hell that is.

'How much further, Dad?' from one of the teenagers.

My son taps the GPS – fifty-seven kilometres. Not far. The screen gives away nothing of the actual country, just a white expanse and a red teardrop marking our destination on a wavering line, which I'm not sure is the river or the road.

'Any of this look familiar, Mattie?' asks Susie, sitting up front with my son. A very quiet, steady boy, always was. None of the Fenchurch madness. They're holding hands. On the black console their wrists glitter with gold chains and watches; a diamond in Susie's bracelet catches the light and beams it into one of my eyes, sharp as a laser. I suppose Brad is as successful as his friend in Coffs Harbour. He's in that world. Corporate, cut-throat. Held on to his house in Coogee, now worth millions. I have no idea which way he votes.

'Are you remembering anything at all?' he asks.

There are jacarandas in flowerless winter mode, rolling green hills, horses wearing blankets, narrow white gauges on the roadsides to measure floodwater.

'None of it,' I tell them.

'Well, I suppose you wouldn't've travelled through here so quick,' Susie says. 'Like, you would have had a horse and cart, wouldn't you?'

'We had a truck.' A red Chevy, which my father so loved that it came on the ship with us. The Chevy and a mob of barking blue heelers. The voyage, source of my earliest memories from 1941. I remember the fiddles on the tables to stop the plates slipping in high seas, the striped cream blanket on my berth, and a flash of my father turning his head to try to catch the words of a fellow passenger on the windy deck while he exercised his excitable dogs. He had kept his word and stayed on the farm until we had news of Rufina's death. He wept, Evie had told me, wept buckets. Then started on his plans to go back to New Zealand.

On the river road we stop at a memorial at the crest of a hill, a grey stone column topped with a twisted finial that once held the glass. We all pile out and the kids read the names, excited to find an ancestor.

Pte Llewellyn Mungo Dominic Fenchurch.
41st Battalion of 11th Infantry Brigade
Died of wounds. Aged 20
Fell December 25th 1916
Western Front, Armentieres, France

'Christmas Day,' says my son.

'He has a whole face to himself,' observes Mackenzie.

'Face?' asks Rena.

'A side. See?' She puts her hand up to the name. 'He's all on his own.'

'It was built for him,' I tell her, 'for my great-uncle who died in the First World War.'

We walk around the memorial in the winter sun. There are lists of Robinsons, Pidcocks, Braes. The stone is peppered with bullet holes, as if larrikins have used it for target practice. Might have been a bullet that twisted the finial.

Hands in his pockets, my son is moving away from us to look between the trees down the bush-covered hill to where the land rolls away towards the east. I follow him, and together we take in the lofty view, the lifestyle blocks and regimented rows of coffee and nuts. It's more densely populated than I would have thought. There are scatterings of cattle, small white gleams of sheep. The house site must be down there somewhere, in a direct line, because it had a clear view of the memorial. At the foot of the hill a winding indentation leads away from the river road. It's a driveway, grassed over, and the shape of it brings something to mind. Two stone lions. They stood on either side of the gate.

'Come on,' I say to the family. 'Let's go down.'

They do as I ask, finding their places in the crowded car, stealing glances at me. Rena holds my hand. If I am remembering the stone lions, will I remember her, my mother, and the house that once filled the empty land at the termination of the spectral road?

We park the car at a broken gate devoid of lions. 'Private Land' reads a lopsided sign. 'Trespassers Will Be Prosecuted'. It has a couple of bullet holes through it, a patina of rust. There's a grassed-over path between an avenue of mango trees and old gums, their high spreading boughs above our heads. The winter sun is low in the sky behind the western hills at our backs, casting long shadows. The nearest neighbour is perhaps a mile away across the flats, a roof distant enough to give the old place a sense of remoteness – but not as remote as it must have been when my mother came here. The children run with the dog ahead of my son and his wife.

Mackenzie keeps pace with me at the rear. She has her phone trained on me as I make my way back to my past. I know the house has gone, it's not as if I expect to find it still standing as we round the old carriageway, but I can feel its presence as if it is, as if someone is watching from a high room as we proceed towards it, the smaller children arriving before the rest of us.

A cool breeze springs up, ruffling the avenue of gums, lifting our hair, and the girl from Coffs Harbour executes a half-pirouette, almost dropping her phone.

'I thought—' she starts and I know what she was about to say – that she felt someone run past us. A young man, hell for leather, as if he was running for his life. If I was to turn around I might see the backs of his heels as he rounds the corner. Mackenzie draws closer to me, eyes wide.

The gardens have gone, and the peacocks, but the wide verandah stairs still stand, weathered stone leading nowhere but a vast, shallow depression. The house site. Rena is standing on the top step, pretending she is the lady of the house and opening an imaginary door.

'Do come in,' she's saying. 'Do make yourselves at home.'

I pass by, see how the river at the bottom of a flight of broken steps is running high and brown with unseasonable rain. With surefooted strides, my teenage grandson heads down to the water, disappearing under a canopy of camphors. Mackenzie pauses to film his descent.

Susie is at my side, leaning her blonde head against my shoulder. 'Tell us what it was like here when you were little, Mattie. Can you remember now?'

But my eyes are on Rena, who is walking tiptoe down the vanished corridor, pretending to open doors into unseen rooms at either side.

'This is where the staircase was,' the child says, laying her hand as if on a vanished banister and looking up towards a long-gone landing.

'Where did all the stone go?' wonders Susie. 'It wasn't a wooden house to burn away to nothing.'

'It was taken away and used to build other places around the district,' Mackenzie says, as she passes through an invisible wall to film Rena's game.

'Come down to the river, darling,' says my son, leading his wife away by the hand. 'Let's pretend it's still ours.'

I walk alone towards an odd circular grove near the perimeter of the vanished house – ti-tree saplings, trees I don't recognise, with weaving vines. Closer, I see one long stem is not a vine at all but a green python. He is watching my approach, rippling his long muscles as I walk around his house. What is this – why has the vegetation formed this distinctive shape? I'm not game to push through to see what lies inside, given that the python might share his home with several of his mates, as well as his wife and kids, but very carefully I push apart the closest, finest branches and advance one step. Two. In the gloom pose figures in various stages of undress, some headless, as entwined with one another as the python on his branch, others rampant like the long-ago lions. There is the sound of water, a trickle, unseen.

The memory comes with a rush, enough to make me feel nauseous. I am playing here, standing inside the dry pool, a fair-headed woman watching me, another woman coming to join her, and the weight of something cool and heavy in my hand. A toy tractor. Grey with yellow wheels, the red paint chipped off.

Raised voices. Were there? Who was the other woman? A servant, perhaps, the old retainer Evie told me about. Nan, or Nance, was it?

The fair woman … I remember her lifting me out of the empty pool, I remember she had running tears. I remember I tried to wipe them away and left a smear on one pale cheek.

My mother. It must have been. I am near weeping myself, coming away from the overgrown fountain and knowing now the shape of the house, how it rises above me while I walk to where the kitchen was, which is where I would find the old lady who fussed and petted, a reliable source of food and treats. This is where the yard was, where my pups played and the wash was hung, where my stout childish legs would carry me past the servants' quarters to the stable, where I would find my father and another man. Albert. His name breaks in, pushes down through the years. His dark, kind face, much darker than my father's, his thin arms lifting me to sit astride whichever horse I chose. Why have these memories lain dormant for so long? It's as if my father purposely rid me of them by never talking to me about this place, by making me part of another family and letting our New Zealand lives overwhelm our Australian past. There are so many questions I would like to ask him.

'Here.' It's the girl with the phone, which she's holding out to me. 'Could you do me a favour?'

She has to teach me – I have no idea – but I manage well enough, once she tells me to start filming, which isn't until after she's retrieved from her capacious bag a carved gourd with a long loop of string attached to holes drilled in either side. It's a poi awhiowhio, she tells me, a traditional instrument I have never seen before, once used to call birds. In the centre of the grassy space, I think almost exactly underneath the spot where the wedge-tailed eagle once hung, she begins to spin the gourd, allowing the motion to follow through into her whole body, spinning and whirling while a high whistling chattering music fills the air around us, a choir of ghosts. Rena watches and listens, fascinated. I pan over her to my son and his wife coming back from the river, to the back view of my other grandson slouched on the wide verandah steps, to the itchy, scratchy dog attending to his fleas in the grassed-over yard, where generations of farm dogs did the same.

'Koro!' says Rena. 'You're supposed to be filming Mackenzie!'

Obediently I return the single eye to our new friend, spinning and leaping, the summoning satellite above her head, and Rena running to join her. The poi calls in a party on the breeze – a distant guitar, deep voices, singing, my father and his friends sitting for one last time on the wide verandah. The gourd's high fluting notes are my mother's German song, the same one that the tui copied at the window of the Rotorua bathhouse, the very same she sang to them all on the night of their little party.

Evie's cracked old voice is the creaking of the flax string, the telling of the tale in the rising wind around us.

Rena follows the dance, mirroring Mackenzie's squared lunging stance as she balances the pull of the flying poi and the weaving of her arms as she swaps the tether from hand to hand. They are the gatherers of my past, these dancers in the dusk, this clever young woman and my little girl. Leaping and laughing down long-vanished corridors, they show the once-restless ghosts of Jarulan who we are these days, we Fenchurches and our friends, and how the world has come to embrace us.

Lily Woodhouse is the pseudonym of an award-winning author who has now written a sweeping family saga. She divides her time between Australia and New Zealand.